The Family Curse
Magdalene Breaux

The Family Curse

Copyright 2000 by Breaux Books, LLC
Library of Congress Card Number: 00-104957
ISBN: 0-9701709-0-4

Cover design by Merewyn Heath
E-mail: Merewyn@merewyn.com

Breaux Books, LLC
P. O. Box 67
Fairburn, GA 30213
770-842-4792
E-mail: magbreaux@mindspring.com
Web: http://magbreaux.netfirms.com
          www.familycurse.address.com

The Family Curse
Magdalene Breaux

To:

Marguree

May each word bring you much Enjoyment pleasure.

Magdalene Breaux 3-23-0?

Acknowledgments

Throughout the process of writing this book, I received invaluable encouragement and support from the myriad of angels who constantly surround me. I would like to express my gratitude to them all.

From the beginning of this journey, my two sons, Larryn and Obinna, helped me to stay focused and ensured that I kept the plot on track. Debbie Harris and Shilpa Patel gave me the courage to see this project to completion. Glenn Murray helped to fine-tune the final manuscript. Merewyn Heath took time out of her hectic schedule to create the perfect cover design. Most of all, I appreciate feedback received from test readers: Oscar Battles, Alvin Doss, Carol Haynes, Calvin Miller, Willie Stokes, and Corbett Wright.

Table of Contents

Part I.
A Prelude to Karma

Honey, before you start to hate somebody, you need to learn the whole story. You don't know what they did to get what they have, or what they do to keep it.

Chapter 1.
The Beginning of the End

Don't act surprised to see me. Five minutes till the new millennium, and you would have been free. You didn't think I was coming, did you? You know why I'm here. Don't think that you can look away from me, close your eyes, and I'll all go away. I'm not a dream! I'm for real!

I've warned you, but you chose not to listen. Nobody and no one can save you now. Not even God! You can't get off! It's way too late!

You feel the breeze blowing in her face. You smell the grass. You feel her pain, don't you? It doesn't feel too good, does it? It's more intense than anything you've ever experienced before. In this precious moment in time, you are her and she is you.

***

It was midnight on that hot New Orleans summer night. The full moon and scattered twinkling stars appeared as specks of fire in the deep blue sky, casting light on the dark, murky waters of the mighty Mississippi below. Occasional sounds of ship horns bellowed in the distance. The river's waves rustled endlessly into the stillness of night.

Thick blades of Bermuda provided a blanket of comfort for Michelle as she sat at the bottom of the levee near Teche Street, watching the ferry carry its passengers back and forth across the river. Knees tightly tucked into her delicate chest, her frail arms hugged her knees.

"God. Oh, God," Michelle cried. "What am I gone do? I'm 18, pregnant, have three other chil'ren to care for, no job, and momma just passed on. I always said I wished she would die, but I didn't mean it, Lord! I didn't mean it!

"What am I gone do? Dirk would know what to do, but he's in jail for killin' Sammy and ain't never gettin' out. Sammy deserved to die. He had no business messin' with Dirk noway. That's good fo' him.

"I thought Roderick would marry me. He don't care nothin' 'bout me. He gone 'bout his business.

"It's just not fair. Why me, oh Lord? Why me?" Michelle cried. "What kind o' life I been cursed with? Don't nobody care 'bout me but you, Lord." She swayed back and forth and cried through the night, hoping that God would hear her prayers and ease the pain.

***

No, no! That's not it. Let's go back two months farther when you started it all. To June of 1974.

***

Everything was going Michelle's way. She graduated from L. B. Landry High School. Her mother, Delores, threw her a party in the backyard shed late on graduation night.

You remember, don't you? That was a small, white, wooden house with the black gable roof that stood 50 feet behind the main house. Just ahead through the door you could see the bathroom. To the right, relatives and friends wearing Afros and bell-bottoms sat around the kitchen–chatting, eating, drinking. The wide-open area in the middle was Michelle's childhood playhouse and where her grandpa, Raymond Marshall, earned a living upholstering antiques and furniture. But that night it was filled with music, food, beer, liquor, and the merriment of partygoers. The crowd danced to the beat of the Jackson Five's hit song, "Dancing Machine." Michelle's brother, Byron, was the D.J.

Two pairs of bright flood lamps, attached to each corner of the shed, provided the light for the occasion. Mosquito sticks were placed all around the yard. They sure did keep the bugs away. Kelvin and Cyril, Fred's two youngest boys, were stirring giant smokey kettles of seafood. The aroma of fresh, boiled crayfish and blue crabs filled the air, enticing passersby to partake in the feast.

Near the front door was a long table piled high with mounds of food–from golden fried chicken, creamy white mashed potatoes and gravy, and corn on the cob to Louisiana-style gumbo, red beans and rice, and jambalaya. A gentle breeze blew the red-and-white-checked tablecloth that signaled guests to partake of the feast at hand.

"Delores!" Fred barked, as he ate ravenously. "This here is some good chicken. Ain't nobody could beat yo' cookin' in all Luz' ana."

"Hush up, Fred," Delores teased as she added a large bowl of punch to the crowded food pile. "Don't let Shirley hear you say that." Her smooth, chocolate complexion; that long, thick hair; and those well-manicured nails made her appear much younger than her 48 years. People always said that Michelle looked like her mother with a short Afro.

"Come and dance wit' yo' ol' Uncle Fred, Shelly," he said as he grabbed Michelle and started to dance the Robot.

As far as Delores was concerned, Fred was her only living brother. At the time, he was 50 years old. His pearly white teeth gleamed against his deep ebony skin. He and his wife, Shirley, had six big, strapping boys. He was over six-four of solid, rippling muscle from working the shipyards. His entire body was covered with coarse strains of cottony gray hair–his hands, feet, back–all over.

In the distance, Michelle saw you put something around Kelvin's neck.

Must be a graduation present. He did just graduate from Southern and got a good job at the phone company, Michelle thought.

You began to walk toward her.

Why is this girl here? Michelle thought to herself.

She knew that there was always something unusual about you, but couldn't quite place her finger on it.

***

Do you remember? Back then you were a tall, skinny thing. You had what they called good hair. It was real pretty. Thick, wavy, coal-black, and halfway down your back. You had dark, almond-shaped eyes that brought out your cute, oval-shaped face and smooth, fair skin. You don't look like that now, do you?

Just look at you. Don't turn away from me, you pathetic little creature! Look in the mirror, I said! You're afraid to look, aren't you? You're afraid to see that large hump in your back and grossly deformed legs. You're afraid to see that large, diagonal keloid striking down your crocked face. You wanted no man to ever be interested in Michelle, didn't you? You wanted her to become a lonely woman desperate for affection, right? I bet men just beat down your door when they see that endless stream of drool that seeps from the corners of your mouth, and that thick, green fluid oozing from your right eye. Very attractive, isn't it?

People don't like to get too close to you, do they? They cringe when they see your sparse hair with all of those hundreds of fleas

just crawling about your mangy scalp, as big, blistery sores randomly erupt on your shrivelled arms.

Do you remember what you were wearing at the party that night? You wore a white sun dress with spaghetti straps. Your white platforms and bulky white silk bag seemed awkward for the occasion. You never had good taste, did you?

***

You said, "Congratulations. I hear that you're going to Southern University in Baton Rouge. Is that true?"

"Yeah," Michelle answered.

You said, "Well, why do you want to go there? The stench of the factories is unbearable. I'm not sure if you'll like it there, Shelly. You may want to go to a school here in town."

***

At the time, you were in your second year at S.U.N.O studying accounting. That never worked out for you, did it?

***

Michelle protested, "I was up there the other week, and I liked it."

***

You reached into your purse and pulled out a white pouch and handed it to her.

***

You said, "This is for you."

You waited anxiously for her to open it.

You said, "Good luck with your future and everything."

You began to walk away and whispered under your breath, "You'll need it."

"What?" Michelle asked.

"Oh, nothing."

You just giggled and walked away.

Oh, you made it tempting! The pouch was silky and soft to touch. Inside was the stone that Michelle thought was a salt crystal. She walked toward the far-left side of the shed, away from the crowd, to get a better look under the flood lamp near the driveway. Gentle gold and delicate blue hues were reflected from the surface as she held it to the light. *What a beautiful stone*, Michelle thought as she continued to gaze into the stone, captivated by its beauty.

"Let's dance." Michelle was startled. It was Roderick, her off-and-on boyfriend since tenth grade. That Roderick Harrington was something else. He was tall and muscular from playing four years of high school football. His freckled, cinnamon-colored skin, low-cut, red Afro, and full, pale lips gave him an air of innocence. Michelle turned to face him and stared deep into his eyes. You could just feel the electrical pulses his strong, athletic hands sent through her body each time he held her teeny, tiny waist. The sensuous sounds of Sylvia's "Pillow Talk" filled the air, as couples began to slow dance.

The lights were shining into Roderick's eyes. "Wow. What big green eyes you have," Michelle purred as she gazed almost hypnotically into Roderick's eyes, and noticed golden tones of brown, green, and specks of gray. Almost like the stone.

"The better to see you with, my dear," he teased. Michelle felt the bulge in his pants rub against her bellybutton as they danced the two-step. "Let's go to my place," he whispered in her ear.

"What?" Michelle was shocked and pulled away from him.

"Let's go to my place. Since everybody is here, no one will know we gone."

"I don't know, Roderick."

"What? So it's like that, huh?" Roderick pulled away in anger.

"I need mo' time. I'm not ready."

"Girl, how much time do you need?" He pointed around the party. "See? You know what they all gone be doin' when they get home?" he demanded of Michelle.

"What's that, Roderick?"

"You know. Doin' it, that's what. That's what couples do, you know." He pointed to Uncle Fred dancing with a young woman whom they did not recognize. "Even that old man is gone be gettin' some."

"Shelly," he said as he stroked her face with his fingers. "I'm a man. Now if you can't give me some, then, well. Hey, I'm just a man, baby."

Michelle and Roderick noticed Delores get into a blue Cadillac with some strange man. "Better yet," started Roderick, "let's just wait for everyone to leave and we can go to your room."

***

"Ain't nobody gone be messin' wit' my moth' fuckin' husband. Where the fuck that bitch at? I'll kill her fuckin' ass, fuckin' wit' my fuckin' husband! Who the fuck she thank she fuckin' wit' any fuckin' way? She needs to gets her own moth' fuckin' man! Fuckin' bitch!"

The strange young woman caught everyone's attention. She wore a short, pale-blue dress with matching platform sandals. Her large Afro puff was accented by a matching scarf tied at the nape.

The music stopped as the men tried in vain to calm her. Two other women managed to get her into a red El Dorado; she kicked and cussed all the way. Some guests started to leave. Byron played "Get Down" by Kool and the Gang, but the party had already lost its luster.

She must be drunk, Michelle thought.

"Y'all seen Delores?" asked Fred.

"She just left in a blue Cadillac," Michelle answered.

"Oh, Lord," Fred moaned and shook his head in disbelief.

"What's wrong, Uncle Fred?"

"Oh, nothin'. Nothin'." Fred began to walk away with a worried look on his face. "We better start cleanin' up. Y'all go on now."

"We'll help," Roderick insisted.

"No, y'all go on like I done tol' y'all!"

Michelle noticed her cousins and some of the neighborhood women talking, almost like they were concealing something from her.

"What's going on?" Michelle asked Roderick.

"It's nothin'. Just ol' folks talking ol' folks business." Roderick reassured.

"You prob'ly right."

***

You know, that was the best-looking house in the neighborhood, wasn't it? It was big and white with a large, screened porch. Always painted. Always neat. It was the first house in the neighborhood with a driveway on the side. The grass was always green. Delores always kept rose bushes planted every year.

***

Well, anyway. They sneaked into the main house and were careful not to wake the children. It was dark. They stumbled through the living room and hallway, finally to Michelle's bedroom, which was two doors on the right. Lights from the shed shined through the drapes that allowed them to see the bed.

Roderick locked the door behind them. He grabbed Michelle's waist and engaged in a deep, hungry French kiss. His lips completely surrounded hers, his tongue down her throat. She tried to push away, but Roderick's strong arms pulled her closer. He loosened his grasp long enough to remove his shirt, shorts, and briefs.

His long, hard muscle stood at attention as he undressed Michelle. He unclasped her white knit halter at the back, then at the neck. As it tumbled to the floor, he unzipped her short, short blue jean hot pants and slowly slid them and her red silk bikini panties all the way off.

Barely audible voices were still coming from the shed. *I guess they were too busy talking ol' folks business to notice Roderick come up in here,* Michelle thought as Roderick stroked her baby-soft body with his strong, masculine hands.

Roderick gently stroked her large, firm breasts, sucking each nipple in stride. He picked Michelle up and carried her to the bed. Shadowy figures scrolled across the walls. Roderick peeked out the window.

"All yo' men folk is gettin' in Fred's car." There appeared to be a sense of urgency as the headlights of the Buick sped away. "They gone now. Prob'bly gone to another party. They gone be out all night."

Roderick returned to the bed and lay next to her. He spread her legs and tried to penetrate her virgin skin. It was too tight to enter.

"That hurts!"

"Shhh."

"That hurts!"

The warm, moist walls of Michelle's body against the tip of his head were too much for him to bear. He began to pant heavily as the sea of life gushed uncontrollably from deep within his loins.

Michelle felt something warm inside of her as Roderick collapsed on her breasts. "What's wrong, Roderick?"

"Uh. Uh. Baby, that was good," Roderick moaned. He got up, started to get dressed, then quickly darted out of the front door. Before Michelle could get dressed, Roderick was gone and completely out of sight.

Chapter 2.
Disheartening

It was seven o'clock on Sunday morning and Delores had not returned home. What's new? Michelle started breakfast and woke the children to get dressed for Sunday school. The boys always looked so handsome in their dress clothes. There was Raven, who was ten. He always gave her a hard time when it came to getting dressed.

"Awe, Aunt Shelly. Why I got to get up so early?" he always complained.

" 'Cause I said so, that's why!" Michelle would bark back.

It was a different story with Crane, who was eight. He always looked forward to Sunday school because the teacher let them play games and gave out Jolly Ranchers.

Oh, yes. Can't forget about Swan. What a beautiful little girl! She looked like a doll with her pretty, copper-tone skin; long, thick ponytails; and bright smile. She had just turned five and was eager to start kindergarten in a few weeks.

The kitchen was the last room in the main house, and it overlooked the backyard. Her brother, Byron, who rented the shed from their mother, was usually awakened by the smell of Michelle's banana pancakes and bacon. It didn't seem to budge him that morning.

She could just hear Byron's snide remarks. He would always walk through the back door while they were eating breakfast and say something like, "Kids giving you a hard time again, Shelly?"

"How I got stuck with these brats anyhow? Why don't you or momma help out with them anyway?" she always protested. He was always too busy stuffing his face to answer her.

The children sat down to eat. *Byron must be sleeping mighty hard,* Michelle thought as she looked out of the window. *Doesn't seem like he's been home all night. He must o' been out with Fred again.*

Raven and Crane began to fight. "Stop it, stop it!" Michelle yelled.

"He started," Raven insisted.

"He be always lying on me," Crane yelled.

"Just stop it. I can't turn my back for one minute without y'all gettin' into somethin'." Michelle threatened, "Go sit and eat, and I bet' not hear another peep from neither one of y'all again, or else!"

The boys obeyed and began to eat breakfast like they were told. They knew that Michelle would have taken a belt to their behinds if they didn't listen.

"Damn!" Michelle said in disgust. "I'm tired of this here shit. That bitch be always leaving me with these bad-ass kids. That's not my responsibility to raise no chil'ren! I wish that bitch would go somewhere!"

The children all cleared the table.

***

That girl, Michelle, was always clean. That's something you don't know anything about, do you? She would not only wash the dishes after each meal, but also cleaned the stove, washed the table, swept and mopped the floor. You knew she was mad when she scrubbed the pots until they looked new or she waxed the linoleum floor.

***

"What's wrong, Aunt Shelly?" Swan asked.

Michelle was noisily scrubbing pans, thinking about her forced baby-sitting duties and why Roderick hadn't called or stopped by since the party. She was beginning to worry because she was two months late. "Nothing!" she snapped back. "Go sit in the front room and watch TV 'til we ready to go to church."

A few minutes later, Michelle took off the pink cotton robe that protected her church clothes. "Y'all. Let's go to church." The children gathered their prayer books and followed Michelle out the front door. With 30 extra minutes to spare, they began their six-block trek to the nine o'clock service at St. Mark's.

***

They returned from Sunday school at about 11:30. Michelle noticed Fred's blue Buick parked in the driveway from a block away and two police cars parked in front of the house. A crowd of people stood around the entrance gate to the yard. They all looked curiously at Michelle and the children. Some shook their heads and walked away.

What did Fred do this time? Michelle asked herself. They

proceeded up the three steps that led to the porch. She began to hear loud cries coming from the living room. *That sounds like Aunt Shirley and Pearl-Elizabeth. What's Pearl-Elizabeth doing in town?* she wondered.

As they entered the porch area, three of the cops came out and walked to their cars. The last one stopped by the screen door when he noticed Michelle. "I'm sorry," he said as he joined his colleagues. Michelle was stunned as she watched them drive away.

"What's going on, Aunt Shelly?" Raven asked.

"I don't know. Let's go find out."

Fred stood up as they entered the living room. The breeze from the window blew the white lace draperies against the tawny walls and brown leather furniture. Framed pictures were neatly placed on the two marble end tables–two of her uncles in military garb and one of her grandpa and his crew mates. A single white lace centerpiece adorned the maple coffee table.

Kelvin and Cyril, who were both seated on the love seat against the back wall, stared endlessly into the blank screen of the console television diagonally across the room. Byron sat on the six-foot sofa to the right with his head held low. Shirley and Pearl-Elizabeth were to Byron's left, being consoled by Ernestine.

"Pearl-Elizabeth," Michelle started. "What you doin' in town? I ain't know you was coming."

Shirley and Pearl-Elizabeth yelled even louder than before.

"Pearl-Elizabeth flew down from Atlanta early this morning, Shelly." Fred tried to fight the tears. " I'm 'fraid we got some bad news. Yo' momma. Yo' momma been shot."

"Shot? Is she gone be all right? What hospital she in?"

Shirley and Pearl-Elizabeth bawled louder than ever.

"Listen. Now listen to me, baby," Fred continued. "They know who did it, and she been charged with first degree murder. "

"What? Wait, wait. How?"

"Shelly, baby," Fred grabbed her by the shoulders and looked her straight in the eyes. "Don't worry. I'm takin' care o' all the arrangements."

"What happened, Uncle Fred?" she demanded. "What happened?"

"Well, it's like this. Last night she was out drinking with …"

Michelle could stand to hear no more. She stormed into her room and slammed the door behind her.

"Our grandma ain't never coming back?" Raven asked Fred.

"No. No, son. She ain't."

"You mean our grandmamma dead?" Crane asked Fred.

"Yes. Yes, son. She is."

The three children began to cry and hugged Fred for comfort.

***

Delores was passed through the church, as they say. The wake and funeral were both held at the church. It's supposed to bless the soul of the departed one. The church was inundated with family and friends. Ernestine comforted Michelle, who cried into her ample bosom. Byron was too shaken to show emotion. Fred and Shirley were both dressed in black, Raven and Crane were sandwiched between them. All of Fred's boys were there too, and cried like nobody's business. Pearl-Elizabeth cradled Swan in her lap.

Fred picked a navy blue suit for Delores. He knew that it would give her the sense of dignity that she yearned for so much in life. Cries were heard throughout the church, drowning out the eulogy and sermon that followed.

You sat in the back with your mother, Rosemary, and Aunt Priscilla, wearing that gaudy orange floral-print dress. You thought you were slick, didn't you? Rosemary strutted her stuff in a bright red dress, hat, shoes, and gloves to match. Your Aunt Priscilla really outdid herself with that bright yellow sun dress. The three of you hid your wide grins with fans. No one noticed, though. They were too busy mourning.

For the last week, Rosemary started to feel light-headed. But during the service, she was so dizzy that she fainted. Everybody assumed that she was overcome by grief. They knew that she used to pay neighborly visits to Delores on occasion and thought the two of them were close. When she came to, the dizzy spells stopped for good. You know why, don't you?

Your momma worked as a maid when the two of you first moved to Algiers from the Ninth Ward in 1970. You lived down the street from Michelle in the row. Michelle's grandparents lived in that same row when they moved from Morgan City. Fred and Shirley used to live in the row, too, before they moved to the house they live in now. You didn't know that, did you?

Priscilla, her husband, Thomas, and the three children moved next door to you a few months later. Thomas worked as a janitor for the Orleans Parish Schools. He took on second and sometimes third jobs. No matter how hard that man worked, he just couldn't get by.

Your momma and Priscilla were both brown-skinned with short, nappy hair. They wondered how Delores, an unmarried, jet-black, colored woman with jet-black children could live in a house that was three times the size of their apartment. How could her children always be so neat? You always wondered how a dark-skinned girl with short, nappy hair like Michelle could make good grades and act so stuck up.

Honey, before you start to hate somebody, you need to learn the whole story. You don't know what they did to get what they have, or what they do to keep it. You just create bad Karma when you do that. Nobody on Earth is fit to judge anybody else. You need to walk a mile in somebody's footsteps first. Had you done that, you would have known that Michelle's family had been cursed for a very long time.

I need to show you a few things. Come with me.

Part II.
The Early Years

That's how crabs work. They is somebody who can get close to you and plant bad thoughts in yo' mind. Or they be somebody who you trust, so you believe what they say.

Chapter 3.
The Beginning of Karma

Michelle's grandfather, Raymond Marshall, was a big, strong country boy from Mississippi. He thought that his kinfolk acted too colored and too country. Most of them were sharecroppers and never thought about doing anything else. They were just too simple for him, especially since he served his country during World War I. He hadn't seen them since he left home in late 1918, right after he got out of the war.

Michelle's grandmother, Freda Mae Carter, was from Morgan City, Louisiana. She had two older sisters. Margaret, the oldest, was indistinguishable from her jet-black hair. Martha, the next girl, was gentle brown. They were all two years apart in age.

Freda's father was the landlord, Jack Beaseley. All the colored town folk treated her extra special because she was fair-skinned with long, light brown hair and blue eyes. When her mother, Pearl, made sweets, she always took what she wanted and left the rest to her sisters. At meals, she always got served first.

Her sisters did all the chores, including her laundry. Martha spent two extra hours each week on the washboard scrubbing her sister's clothes clean and fresh. Afterward, she soaked the damp blouses and skirts in a starch and lavender mixture. Each piece was carefully folded and wrapped in wax paper. The items were placed in the icebox overnight to keep fresh.

The next morning, Margaret heated the iron over hot coals. The garments had to remain in the wax paper or they would have dried out, which would have made it almost impossible to get the wrinkles out. She pressed each piece of clothing and hung it on a hanger. Resentment toward her mother and sister grew deeper with each stroke of the iron.

"Why can't she do her own ironing?" she often asked her mother.

" 'Cause I say so."

Freda was the teacher's pet all through school, but decided not to finish anyway. She hated to do schoolwork or homework, but the teachers usually let her by. She would just daydream in class and finally decided that it was a waste of time to be in school. "I'm gone have a man take care o' me. I don't need no schoolin'," she told her classmates.

Margaret and Martha did their classwork and homework or the teacher would have whipped them with a cat-o'-nine-tails.

When Margaret was 16, she finished school. She got a job as a domestic, like her mother, to earn her way. Martha also finished school when she turned 16. When Freda turned 16, she decided that because her sisters weren't in school, she didn't have to go either. She mostly sat around the house or chatted with the neighbors. When her mother and sisters got home from work, none of the chores had been done.

"You been home all day and ain't do nothing?" Martha asked each day.

At that point, Margaret and Martha no longer did her chores, and their mother took on the extra duties.

***

Ray first caught Freda's eye in February 1919, right after Ray and Margaret started to keep company. He worked as a cook on a cargo ship. That was a good job for a colored man back then. His ship stopped in Morgan City every few weeks to drop a load. The crew stayed in town for a few days, and some of the men went out on the town. He wrote Margaret from every town his ship docked, and was sure to buy a special gift for her.

Ray cared deeply for Margaret and really admired her. He had never met a woman who had completed high school before, or one who could cook so well. To Ray, no other woman even compared to Margaret.

Some of the other women in town had their eye on Ray because they saw him as a good provider. Most of the other colored men were sharecroppers, butlers, or janitors.

***

One time when Ray was in town, Margaret prepared a big feast in his honor. Margaret, Martha, and Pearl spent all day cooking on that hot wood stove. They were so excited that he accepted the invitation that they danced and sang all day long, not even bothered by the heat. Back then, a way to a man's heart was through his stomach. With Margaret's cooking, she was sure to hook Ray. They hoped so for Margaret's sake.

Ray would only be in town for another day, so they had to work fast. She was going to be 22 in a few months. In some circles back then, 20 was considered an old maid. Ray was just one year older than Margaret, but he was a man and it didn't matter.

Martha worked as a maid for the Barlows, one of the most prestigious families in town. She often coordinated magnificent parties for her employers. So she naturally volunteered to plan this special dinner for her sister. She made a white lace tablecloth just for the occasion. The matching napkins were folded to resemble roses and carefully placed in the water goblets. The good silver and china, the ones Mrs. Beaseley gave Pearl one Christmas, were shiny enough for them to see their reflections.

Freda was gone all day and didn't lift a finger to help, not even to set the table when she got home. She was out keeping company with Ray while Margaret, Martha, and Pearl toiled in the kitchen.

Money was tight, but they managed to scrape up enough for the food. What they couldn't buy Martha sneaked from the Barlows. You could smell the food a mile away. Gumbo, roast duck, scalloped potatoes, deep-dish peach cobbler, and other delectables were nicely arranged around the table. The feast was fit for royalty.

Freda flirted with Ray all during dinner. He completely ignored Margaret and flirted right back. He only accepted the invitation because he knew that Margaret and Freda were sisters. That way, he would have an excuse to be near Freda.

"Margaret spent all day cookin' this here meal," Pearl bragged. "She is quite a fine cook. Quite a fine cook, indeed."

"Freda don't know how to cook," Martha added. "She can't even boil water."

"That's all right," Ray began, "I was a cook in the Navy and on that there ship I work on. I can whip up a meal myself."

Martha caught Ray's attention and showed him one of the napkins. "Look at how pretty Margaret folded the napkins. And she's real good at throwing fancy parties, too."

"Awe, that ain't nothin'," Ray started. "We do that all the time fo' the officers on the ship. Anybody could do that. Ain't nothin' to it."

Margaret, Martha, and Pearl saw no point in trying to impress Ray. Except for Ray and Freda, everyone else was quiet through dinner.

Ray and Freda were engaged six months later. Margaret and Martha refused to help with the wedding arrangements. It seemed that their employers suddenly kept them really busy. Other relatives also seemed busy, too. Pearl was left to take care of all the details by herself, from making the dress to preparing all of the refreshments.

"I'm tired of the South," Margaret told Martha. "I've been saving some money and plan to go to New York."

"New York?" Martha was surprised. "You don't know nobody in New York. That's the big city. How you gone make it?"

"You could come with me. We know how to read, write, and do arithmetic. We know the Lord. That's all we need to make it."

"You want me to come with you? Me?"

"Yes, you." Margaret showed her an article in the newspaper. "Look, read that."

"It says that Harlem is a good place for Negroes. That they got plenty jobs, even for women folk like us."

"There's nothing for me here in the South. I'm 22, never been married. The men folk don't want a black, black woman in the South. They want a light-skinned woman like Freda."

"Not everybody is like that though, Margaret."

"Why aren't you married then?"

Martha put her head down, tears formed in her eyes.

"We could work as domestics," Martha started. "Every town needs domestics."

"Let's pray and ask God what we got to do."

***

Margaret and Martha bought one-way train tickets to New York for two weeks away. They both planned to quit their jobs the next day.

***

"Martha," Mrs. Barlow started. "We're going to miss you. You're like one of the family." Mrs. Barlow was a slight, grey-haired woman of about 50. She handed a piece of paper to Martha. "Now, Martha, here's the name and address of my good friend, Mrs. Andrews." Martha noticed the New York City address. "She was widowed a few months ago and her girl, Nan, is getting married in a few weeks. Nan wants to find someone good to take care of Mrs. Andrews before she leaves her. You couldn't have better timing. I'm going to send a wire to her today and let her know to expect you."

"Thank you, Mrs. Barlow."

***

Everybody knew that Ray and Margaret kept company. Gossip spreads really fast in small towns, each person adding his own twist to it. Freda only wanted Betsy, Minnie, and Lula Mae in her wedding.

"They the only pretty girls in town besides me," she told her mother. The story was more scandalous than ever by the time it reached them. They refused to be in the wedding, which left Freda with no bridesmaids.

The townspeople weren't shy to let Ray and Freda know that they weren't welcomed in Morgan City. People whispered and rolled their eyes or stopped their conversations when Freda approached. Others called her Jezebel, strumpet, or issued similar insults as she walked by.

One of Ray's crewmates, Kent Simms, told him about a row apartment next door to his in Algiers, the West Bank of New Orleans. It had electricity, gas, and indoor plumbing. Some of the houses in Morgan City had electricity and gas. But most had kerosene lamps for lighting, and pot-bellied stoves for cooking and heating. Only a few houses in Morgan City had indoor plumbing. Most of the houses had outdoor wells and outhouses.

The thought of not having to pump water from a well sounded good to Ray. The location of the apartment worked out well for Ray since New Orleans was the main port city on the route. They decided to make the move the day of the wedding.

***

Ray drove up in a shiny, second-hand Ford a few days before the wedding. He was proud to show it off to his new family.

"That sho' is a mighty fine car, Ray," Pearl said.

"Thank you."

"That old thing," Martha started. "That the car that Mr. Barlow got rid of."

"You just like the other ol' colored Negroes," Ray started. "Always be jealous of what other folk got. Can't stand to see nobody with nothin'!"

"Jealous?" Martha exclaimed. "Me and Margaret goin' to..."

Margaret put her hand over Martha's mouth and pulled her outside. "You and your big mouth," she started. "Nobody is supposed to know about us going to New York."

***

Freda packed most of her belongings. Her wedding dress remained at Pearl's house. When they arrived at the dock, Ray and some of his friends took the bags to his quarters to be transported to New Orleans that day. Pearl and her sisters assumed that the bags were being taken to the motel room that Ray had rented for the week.

In June of 1920, Raymond Simon Marshall and Freda Mae Carter were set to be married. When the townspeople heard what had happened between the sisters, nobody wanted to attend the wedding. It was so quiet in that church you could hear the birds singing outside.

After the ceremony, Ray and Freda changed clothes and walked to the motel room down the street that Ray had rented for the week. That's where they put the last of their belongings into the Ford. As they made their journey to New Orleans, Freda thought of how disappointed she was that her mother didn't try to stop the rumors. She decided to punish her by failing to mention the move. She hadn't seen or heard from Pearl since that time. Ray made a point to avoid going into town when his ship docked in Morgan City.

***

The reception hall was behind the church. Pearl and Sister Joyce, the reverend's wife, helped to wrap the food.

"You might as well take some home to your family, Sister Joyce." Pearl said. "I hate to see good food go to waste."

"This sho' is some good food, Pearl. They got some fam'lies barely getting by in the country, and they would sho' 'preciate the meal!"

Pearl noticed Mother Esther, who was known as the town witch, watching her from the reception hall door and walked to her. She lived by herself in a house far into the woods, and rarely came to town.

"May I he'p you, Mother Esther?" The long, white dress and white turban she wore almost faded into the deep creases of her skin.

"I'm just seeing what's going on," Mother Esther said in that deep, hoarse voice that always scared Pearl.

"My girl, Freda, just got married."

"I know, Pearl."

"You know?" Pearl seemed puzzled.

"Yes. I know everything."

"Anything wrong, Mother Esther?"

"You better tell yo' gal to be careful." She started to the street. Pearl blinked for a second to finish wrapping a plate of finger sandwiches and Mother Esther was gone. She checked the church, the hall, and the street, but Mother Esther was nowhere in sight.

***

Pearl was on her way home from the church when she saw the girls putting their belongings into a cab. Margaret got in when she spotted her and signaled for Martha to hurry.

"Where y'all think y'all going?"

"To New York. We're grown," Martha boasted.

"Y'all don't know nobody in New York."

"Mrs. Barlow got us jobs and a place to stay," Martha informed her.

Just then, the cab drove off. Pearl was dumbfounded and thought of Mother Esther. *Did she have anything to do with this?* she asked herself.

Chapter 4.
Temptation

The Roaring '20s were good to Ray and Freda. They bought a tract of land down the street from the row apartments and built a house in 1921. The four children came right after each other. Ray, Jr., in 1922, Carter in 1923, Frederick in 1924, and Delores in 1926. The first two resembled their momma. It looked like Ray spit Fred out. He was a carbon copy of his dad. Delores looked like her father, but had that slight build of her mother.

The '30s were rough, but they made it through. Ray continued to work for the same ship line all through the Depression. Other ship lines folded and people lost their jobs. Ray didn't work as much, only six months out of the year, but they got by.

Ray had two very good friends, Gerald Mabry and Henry Dennis. He was ashamed to invite his crewmates over when he was on shore leave. After docking, he cleaned himself up before he left the ship and went home with either Gerald or Henry.

When he was at sea, Ray's yard was always overgrown with tall weeds and littered with garbage. The house was no better. Soiled diapers filled the wash tub, and dirty clothes were thrown about the floor. Ray cooked the family meals when he was on leave. He left recipes for Freda to follow while he was gone. That was useless. The children were always dirty and sickly, and nothing was ever cooked.

"My wife is real pretty," he bragged. "She look like she white."

"Yeah," Gerald laughed. "Why we ain't never seen her?"

"I married me a jet-black, chocolate woman to get some color in the family," Henry boasted.

"You got some mighty fine chil'ren, Henry. That chocolate sho' did the trick."

"Hush up, Ray!" Henry laughed.

"You think like a slave, Ray, always talking 'bout color," Gerald started. "I married me a smart woman. She real good at running the house. I gives her my whole paycheck and she gives me what I need out of that to get me by."

Gerald, Henry, and Ray didn't always get along so well. In fact, they almost got into a fight when they first met. It was January, 1919, Ray's second day on the job and Gerald's first.

"Who the boss?" Gerald asked Ray.

"It's that white man over there."

"Which one?"

"The big, country-looking one with the curly black hair."

Henry heard Ray's comment. He walked right over to him and got in his face.

"I'm a colored just like you. If you ever call me white again, I'll kick yo' ass."

Gerald and Henry both lived in Shrewsbury, across the river from Algiers. Their wives were best friends.

Gerald's place was a big, white, shotgun house. The yard was small, but well-maintained. His wife was tall and skinny with coppertone skin. Their three children were always neat and well-behaved. The house was always clean, and a hot meal was always waiting for him when he came home.

Damn, Ray thought each time he visited. *She pretty, smart, a good cook, and good mother.*

He especially enjoyed visiting with Henry, who was the head cook on the ship. He had a two-story, white house with black trim. All sorts of exotic plants and flowers decorated the yard. His wife, Gloria, could tell you all about each and every one of them. She even named their daughter after her favorite flower.

The inside looked better than any white folk house he'd seen before. The walls were covered with nice wallpaper. Furniture, china, and other niceties that Henry had collected from all corners of the world were seen throughout each room. A sweet, unfamiliar scent filled the air that welcomed Ray into their home.

When Henry was at sea, Gloria made extra money selling praline candy or other goodies to the neighbors. She also occupied her time by sewing draperies or making quilts–some she sold to neighbors or members of their church where she taught Sunday school.

Ray thought that Gloria was a real joy to talk to. She was well-spoken and read books on a variety of topics. Their three teenage children were looking forward to attending college. They were the smartest kids he'd ever seen.

"Glo," Ray always teased, "where you from, Mars? Ain't nobody on Earth could cook this good!" The cute shapes she folded the napkins into amused him. He picked one up and said, "I ain't never seen nothing like this befo'."

"She quite a woman, heh, Ray? See why I rush to get home all the time?"

After dinner, the children went into the den to study, while the adults sat around the parlor talking. Ray looked forward to the beignets and café au lait Gloria prepared for each visit.

"Y'all sho' is a handsome couple."

"Thank you, Ray. When are we going to meet your wife? I'm just dying to meet her." Gloria got up to remove the dishes. Her firm, shapely rear veered seductively with each step. Ray was overcome by passion each time he looked into her deep, dark eyes. With every passing moment, he yearned to stroke her smooth, chocolate skin and taste those full violet lips.

What a woman, Ray thought to himself. *I never knew a woman could be so beautiful. She must have some roots on me or somethin'. She be smelling so good. Her hair and nails always be lookin' so pretty. I ain't never seen nobody with no pretty feet befo'. But that woman even paint her toes. Just make me want to suck 'em!*

"Ray," Gloria called. He continued to stare into space, captivated by the strong feminine essence that had seized his soul. "Ray. What's wrong?"

"This last trip was hard! Boy! I'm not lookin' forward to goin' back tomorrow. That's fo' sho'!"

"Yeah. It was rough, I tell you that." Henry added.

Gloria felt his forehead. The sweet smell of her perfume and soft, delicate touch made Ray's temperature soar.

"You do feel hot. I better get you some aspirin."

"No. You got some whiskey?"

"You don't drink, Ray," Henry reminded him.

Gloria returned with some Jack Daniels on the rocks. Ray gulped the liquid down to ease his lust.

"Give me another one."

Against her better judgment, Gloria poured another.

"I better drive you to the ferry. Better yet, we go 'cross the Huey P. Long Bridge. That's the long way, but I'm worried 'bout you." On the way out of the door, Henry kissed his wife. Ray was overtaken by envy. "Bye, baby. We'll be back soon."

"Drive safely, Henry. Bye, Ray."

Hearing her voice sent chills up his spine. *I better get up out of here.* He knew that he had to take his secret to his grave. *A woman like that would never want me. And if she did, Henry would kill me.*

Henry, Jr. joined them for the drive. Ray slept on the back seat most of the way.

At 10:30, they arrived at Ray's. He was so drunk that Henry and Henry, Jr. had to almost drag him inside.

The smell of urine greeted them at the door. The children were half-clothed and ran uncontrollably about. Hundreds of cockroaches crawled on the walls. Two mice ran under the sofa when Henry and his son entered the kitchen. Henry opened the icebox only to find it nearly empty. The cupboards were bare, too. They removed Ray's shoes and put him to bed. Freda was sound asleep, completely oblivious to their presence.

***

It was the last day of Ray's six-week leave. He wouldn't be back for three months. He cooked breakfast and saw the children off to school. Freda was still sound asleep.

Images of Gloria kept popping up in his mind, so he didn't want to face his wife. Not yet, anyway. Wedding vows were important to him. But the pictures stayed frozen in his mind.

He imagined Gloria rubbing her big, firm breasts in his face. Freda's sagging breasts just didn't compare. Sucking Gloria's soft, pretty toes couldn't get out of his mind. Freda's corns and blackened toenails disgusted him.

Oh, God! I can't take this! He felt Gloria's soft behind in his hands as he sucked her clit, red and swollen from the pleasure he gave her. It all seemed so real. His tongue inside her hot, throbbing cunt, as it got wetter and wetter until she reached the peak of ecstasy.

"Fuck me, Ray," she pleaded. "Fuck me *real* good."

Her breasts stood at attention as he sucked each one, and put his finger in her dripping wet cunt. "I can't wait to get my dick in yo'..."

"Ray," Freda called from behind. "When you get home?"

"Last night. Henry brought me home."

"You always talk 'bout Henry and Gerald. Why you never bring 'em by?"

Ray went into the bedroom to rest. He was due out to the docks at five o'clock. Freda sat next to him. He wanted Gloria so bad that he could feel her. He pretended that Freda was Gloria and began to stroke her breasts.

"Oh, that feel good, Ray."

Freda took off her clothes and lay next to him.

Ray sucked each of her toes and licked her soles. He had a vivid imagination. The stench of fish suddenly transformed into the sweet scent of Gloria's perfume. He licked her clit until it was swollen and red, like a ripe plum. His manhood was harder than steel. He penetrated her soaking wet walls, as they pulsed against his throbbing cock. She became moister and more aroused with each thrust. That was the best love-making Freda had ever had.

Ray moved in and out, side-to-side, deeper and deeper. Freda moaned from the gut, hard and loud. His stride got faster and faster. Goosebumps covered his quivering body as he reached the height of passion. "Gloria! Oh, Glo!" he yelled. "Gloria. Gloria," his voice faded until he fell fast asleep.

Freda was speechless. She thought that she was so beautiful that her husband would never cheat. *He's just being a man,* she thought. He slept for three hours and called Gloria's name at least ten times. Then Freda became worried.

***

Ray woke up at 2:30 to get dressed to go to the docks. He filled three big pots with water and placed them on the stove.

"Who the hell is Gloria?" Freda demanded.

"What?"

"Who the hell is Gloria? Some girlfriend you got when you go on leave somewhere?"

"And if I do? I ain't got nothin' to keep me here."

The water started to boil. Ray took the first two pots and poured them in the tub.

"What you mean by that?" Freda asked.

"The house always be nasty. Ain't never nothin' cooked. You look like shit! That's why."

"You ain't never sucked my pussy befo'. You suck her pussy?"

"Why I want suck yo' nasty pussy? It smell like fish."

"Do you suck her pussy, Ray? Do you suck her toes, too?"

Ray paused and was tempted to throw the last pot on Freda. He pushed her out of the way and poured it into the tub.

"What man want come home to a nasty house and a stank woman like you after being offshore for three months? Henry house be clean and his wife always got something cooked for him."

Ray put the pots back in the kitchen. Freda followed him, each step he took. "She be always smelling nice. Her hair and nails be looking pretty. And they chil'ren always be clean."

"Who you think you talkin' to?"

"Freda. You just lazy. You ain't nothin' but a lazy, stank 'ho'."

"I could o' had any man I wanted. Yo' black ass oughta be glad I gave you the time o' day!"

Ray closed the bathroom door behind him. They continued to argue.

"I could o' had anybody I wanted, too. Henry wife is got book smarts, too. I'm 'shamed to bring him or Gerald over here 'cause the house be a mess, you be a mess, the chil'ren be a mess. They wives is good cooks. You too sorry to boil water."

"Hey, Ray! You ready to go?" Kent yelled from the street.

Ray and Kent always stopped to get something to eat and shoot the breeze before going on board. Kent was single and couldn't understand why Ray ate out a lot when he was in town.

Ray emerged from the bathroom dressed in the ship attire. "I gotta go." He grabbed his duffel bag and joined his friend.

Chapter 5.
Humility

Ray refinished furniture when he was on leave to earn extra money for the family. One of their neighbors, Ms. Mabel, always seemed to have something for him to do. Ray and Freda were suspicious of her because she always acquired new pieces of furniture. She always had a lot of money, too. They assumed that she was stealing from the Millers. Freda and Ray both changed their tune when they saw the Millers' youngest boy deliver an old chest to her.

One of Ms. Mabel's children sent her money every week. Her two daughters attended Spelman in Atlanta and decided to remain in Georgia after graduating school. They both moved to Palmetto, a small town 25 miles southwest of Atlanta, and became schoolteachers. Her son graduated from Meharry and had his own medical practice in Chicago.

Ms. Mabel was a short woman about 60 years old, but her smooth, olive complexion and well-kept appearance took at least 20 years off her age. When she wore it down, her wavy, salt-and-pepper hair reached down to her knees. Her father was Choctaw and her mother was a former slave. She had been living the solitary life of a widow since 1919, the year before Ray and Freda moved to Algiers. Since that time, she had been working three days a week as a domestic for the Millers. Ms. Mabel also delivered just about every baby in Algiers, including all four of the Marshall children, and didn't accept a penny for her services. If someone offered she would say something like, "I'm just doing the Lord's work."

Ray did work for other neighbors, too. He knew that times were tough, so he usually gave discounts. But Ms. Mabel wouldn't hear of it.

"You charge me the regular price!   You think I ain't got no money?" She would always make a big fuss of it.

Each time Ray visited Ms. Mabel, he noticed how nicely her home was decorated. It even looked better than Henry and Gloria's home.

Mahogany, brass, porcelain. Everything was polished and squeaky clean. It didn't look like anyone lived there. You could have gone through her whole house wearing white gloves and they would have been clean when you left. She had the greenest, plushest grass and prettiest flowers in all of Algiers. Not just in spring, but all year long.

Ms. Mabel went over looking for Ray. The front door was opened and she walked in. She was afraid to sit down for fear of being contaminated in some way.

"Hello!" Ms. Mabel called. "Anybody home?"

"Ray not here." Freda emerged from the bedroom and looked like she had just awaken from a deep sleep.

"How long he been gone?"

"You just missed him. He left right befo' the chil'ren got home from school."

The children were playing in the house. Fred almost knocked her to the floor.

"You ought not let them chil'ren tear up yo' house, chil'," she told Freda. "I had a husband and three o' my own, and always kept a clean house!" She noticed the autumn breeze through the house and looked toward the kitchen. There were no signs that a meal had been cooked. The three large, black pots that Ray used to heat his bath water were the only pots visible. "Ray be working hard to provide for his family. You should have somethin' cooked fo' that man when he be home. You come over to my house tomorrow, Tuesday. I'm off on Tuesdays and Thursdays. I'll show you how to run a house!"

After the fight with Ray, she was willing to do anything or listen to anyone to save her marriage.

***

For the next three months, Ms. Mabel invited Freda over as she went through the motions. She got up at dawn each Tuesday to do chores. Freda came over by 10:30. She was amazed by how much energy that old lady had. Laundry, cooking, cleaning.

The children went to Ms. Mabel's after school. She always made cookies, candy, or some treat for them. Freda told Ray, Jr. and Carter to get treats first.

"What you doing, Freda?" she was huffed. "I made them for all the chil'ren."

"In my house, Ray, Jr. and Carter gets sweets first."

Ms. Mabel was appalled. "In my house, everybody gets they fair share." She baked two dozen cookies and gave each child two. "We'll save the rest for tomorrow."

Since that time, whenever the children were visiting with Ms. Mabel, Freda made sure that they all got equal shares.

At the end of the day, they went to Freda's house where Ms. Mabel helped her with recipes, housekeeping, and gardening tips. Somehow, Ms. Mabel ended up doing most of the chores while Freda sat back and watched. After helping Freda do her chores, she sat on her porch and read the Bible until sunset. Freda was always too tired to join her and usually fell fast asleep.

***

When Ray came home after three months at sea, he was amazed to see the house clean. Freda cooked a meal of fried pork chops and rice. He had tasted a lot better, but it was edible. The children were clean and had put on a little weight. Delores's hair was neat and looked several inches longer.

"What happened?"

"I been taking house lessons from Ms. Mabel."

"Well it sho' worked."

"Look, daddy," Delores was excited. "Ms. Mabel pressed my hair."

"It needed something," Ray started. "It was short and nappy befo'."

***

Ray was outside mowing grass one Saturday when he noticed Ms. Mabel rushing toward him. "I don't feel like doing nothing today, Ms. Mabel," he said to himself. He looked up again and saw old Mr. Miller with her. *Must be trouble,* he thought.

"Ray. Ray. This here is Mr. Miller."

"So you're the one who finished that chest?" Mr. Miller asked. Mr. Miller was a tall, sinewy fellow, with shifty brown eyes and thinning white hair. He wore a blue linen suit and black wing-tip shoes all year long.

"Yes, sir. I did," Ray bragged.

"Good job. We started to throw that thing away. Then good old Mabel here told us that she knows somebody who could fix it up."

Ray listened on. Freda watched from the window.

"Well, Ray. A friend of mine, Mr. Wilson, has some old furniture that I would like for you to look at. They've been in his family for years, and he's willing to pay whatever it takes to make them look good again. Think you can do it?"

"Yes, sir. I can. Just tell me where and when, I'll be there."

"I'll bring it over tomorrow." Mr. Miller looked around as if to see who may be listening. He whispered, "I know a lot of people who need the type of service you offer. Now, things being as they are, these good people won't come directly to you. But see, Ray, I can give these people's business anyway." He looked around again. "This'll be between just you and me," and winked. "I'll have my boys bring the furniture over. You deal with them like you were dealing with me. Let me know if they give you any trouble and I'll handle them." Mr. Miller turned to Ms. Mabel. "I'll be seeing you, Mabel."

After Mr. Miller left, Ray asked Ms. Mabel, "Is this legal? I mean, I can't go to jail?"

"Naw," she started. "Let Mr. Miller worry 'bout that."

"What if people find out?"

"Don't tell nobody. I mean nobody. Not even yo' wife." Ms. Mabel warned. "Peoples gots to do what they gots to do."

"But, Ms. Mabel, it's just 'bout 'gainst the law for whites and coloreds to do business. How 'bout if Mr. Miller delivery boys tell? What if they try to mess somethin' up or lie on me or somethin'?"

"They won't tell. They won't mess with you, either."

"How you know that, Ms. Mabel?"

" 'Cause Ray, they 'fraid of what Mr. Miller would do to 'em."

"I don't want no trouble, Ms. Mabel."

"You 'member this, Ray Marshall. It's 'gainst man's law, not God's law. It's 'gainst God's law to let yo' family starve if you can he'p it. It's 'gainst God's law not to share yo' talent he done gave you with the world, whether the people be colored, or white, or polka-dot, or green.

"It's not that the Millers love Negroes or Indians or Chinese. They just smart people. They see a way to make money and go for it. They don't care so much 'bout the color of somebody's skin. The only color they care 'bout is green. That's how they so rich."

Ray understood. Back then, it was okay for coloreds to patronize certain white businesses, but white folk didn't spend their money with coloreds. It was as simple as that.

"How you think me and my husband got that there house?"

"He was a longshoreman, right, Ms. Mabel?"

"Yes, he was. But we made moonshine. While he was workin', I was sellin'. We made the best stuff around, mainly hard cider. We did that from 'bout 1910 up until he passed away in 1919."

"That was 'gainst the law, wasn't it?"

"Who you think we sold to? The law peoples and other white folk. We ain't do nothin' wrong. Ain't nobody made them folk buy no liquor. I stopped in '21 right after they came out hard and heavy with that Prohibition. I was alone and didn't want no trouble, so I stopped.

"We was tired of not having nothin'. Who said white folk gots to have ever'thing? They ain't got no right to tell me what I can or can't have. God wants all his chil'ren to have, not just some of 'em. How ya think we sent our chil'ren to college?"

***

Ray did such an excellent job that Mr. Miller brought by even more furniture for him to finish. Over the next two years, it got to the point that Ray couldn't handle working offshore and the sideline business, too.

Mr. Miller's family owned one of the local banks. Because he was so impressed with Ray's work, he offered to extend him a loan to start a restoration business. He finally convinced Ray to quit his job the next year, in September 1937.

Ray went all the way. He built the shed in the backyard and paved the driveway leading to it. Next, he bought a used pickup truck and the finest tools money could buy. He spared no expense. He thought the Negroes would try to rob him blind, so he put up a chain-link fence to secure the yard.

Business was booming from the day he opened the shop in 1938. His customers liked him and the fine work he did. Nobody could refinish wood or upholster furniture like Ray Marshall. I mean nobody. His good named traveled fast. People came from miles around to his shop. He was one of the few colored folks to have so many white customers. Well, secret customers, anyway. He refused to do business with some of the coloreds because he thought they always wanted something for nothing.

Ray Marshall was a smart man. He took out a life insurance policy a few months later. He wanted his family to be well taken care of if something happened to him. He couldn't bear the thought of Freda struggling to make ends meet. Colored folks didn't think like him back then.

One of his customers was a life insurance agent. He looked like an insurance man, too, with his slicked-back hair, nice suit, and wing-tip shoes. He had just inherited an old chest from his grandmother and brought it in to be redone. He was just starting out and had a new family of his own. So he was desperate to make a sale. He told Ray all about the policy. Ray bought it because he was colored and wanted to help him out. He arranged it so that the insurance money would pay to bury him and leave Freda with some extra money to manage the household.

Ray was proud of Ray, Jr. and Carter and made sure that they were in the shop when his customers came around. They looked like a mixture of their mother and father. Both were strong and masculine with wavy, black hair, very fair skin, and dark eyes. He had it in his mind that his sons would learn the trade and join him in the business when they got older. Ray, Jr. showed little interest. Carter and Fred were eager to get involved in their father's trade.

Carter worked a lot with his father. When it came time for Fred to learn about the business, Ray made him mow the lawn, trim the hedges, or help his mother and Delores with house chores. If a really important client were around, Ray sent Fred to Ms. Mabel's to see if she needed anything done, while Ray, Jr. and Carter assisted him in the workshop.

After school, Ray, Jr. and Carter helped their father in the business. Ray needed the help, too, since he had so much work piling up. Carter was an able-bodied assistant. He cut and sewed the meanest fabric, and sanded the toughest of woods.

Ray, Jr., on the other hand, was always breaking things, or spilling something, or just knocking things over. Ray finally assigned him the tasks of arranging the tools each morning and cleaning the shop in the evening. But he managed to break or lose his father's tools, and swept sawdust all over the shop, ruining quite a few refinishing jobs. Ray thought that it was important for Ray, Jr. to be seen by customers. As a result, he just let him sit around the shop while he and Carter worked.

Chapter 6.
A New Girl in Town

In late 1939, Ms. Mabel started pressing the neighbors' hair on Saturday mornings to make extra money. She had a pressing iron and curling iron for each length of hair. Each one was kept hot on separate burners of the stove. Ms. Mabel didn't use the store-bought hair pomade. She made her own from mineral oil and lavender. Freda hung around to keep Ms. Mabel company and gossip with the patrons. Ethel Lewis was always her last customer.

"You sho' is lucky," Ethel told Freda. "You got good hair. Don't need no pressin'." Ethel was tall and slim. Her black, shoulder-length hair complemented her smooth, pecan skin. Since that time, she and Freda spent some of their afternoons together.

Ms. Mabel hated when people went on about Freda's hair. "Y'all stop it. That go straight to Freda head. All hair is good." She picked up the iron from the stove and combed it through her hair. "Be still, Ethel," she warned. "You don't wanna get burned, do you?"

"You got good hair, too, Ms. Mabel," Freda reminded her.

"After you get through with my hair it be good," Ethel laughed. "Irving like to play with it."

"Who Irving?" Freda asked.

"That's my husband."

"Y'all got married right befo' y'all moved into that house down the street, heh?" Ms. Mabel asked.

"Yes, ma'am."

"Where y'all from?" Freda asked.

"I'm from Morgan City. My husband from Plaquemine. We met when my husband used to work on a ship that come through town."

"I'm from Morgan City, too!" Freda was excited. "Who yo' peoples?"

"Reverend William Lowell is my daddy, and Joyce Lowell is my momma. I got three big sisters. I'm the baby."

"Sister Joyce yo' momma?"

"Yes, ma'am."

"She good peoples," Freda said.

Freda looked at her and thought that she and her husband looked really young. "How old you is?"

"I just turned 20."

"How y'all can afford to buy that house?" Freda asked further.

"We saving up fo' a house. Right now, we renting from Mr. Miller."

Freda recalled how she and Ray rented that one-bedroom row apartment before they saved up for the house. *They living 'bove they means.* She rolled her eyes at Ethel. *Why can't they live in the row 'partments like we did? Why they got to live in that house?* She couldn't resist asking questions. "You sho' is skinny. You got any chil'ren?"

"No ma'am. We just got married two months ago on my birthday."

"When you start having chil'ren you gone put some meat on yo' bones." Freda noticed the large, round diamond ring and golden wedding band ring on Ethel's left ring finger. It put the plain, slender golden bands that she and Ray exchanged to shame.

"Where you got that there ring from?" Freda asked Ethel.

"It's my engagement ring."

"Who gave it to you?" Freda inquired further. "It's real?"

"She done told you that's her engagement ring," Ms. Mabel interrupted. "You don't ask people nothing like that. It must be real. You can see it, can't you?"

"You think I can be outta here by 3:30, Ms. Mabel?" Ethel asked.

"I'm just 'bout done."

"Where you gotta go?" Freda asked.

"You sho' is nosy, Freda," Ms. Mabel told Freda angrily. "That ain't yo' bid'ness."

***

Early one Tuesday morning, Ms. Mabel was getting groceries at the neighborhood store. She saw Freda coming out of my house across the street. People used to say that I was very old because I stole other folk's life force. Rumor had it that I was over 100 years old.

***

"What you doin' talkin' to Mother Ruby fo'?" Ms. Mabel demanded of Freda.

Freda didn't answer.

"I done asked you a question, gal!" Ms. Mabel demanded again. "What bid'ness you got with Mother Ruby?"

"Nothing, Ms. Mabel. I was just talking to her."

Ms. Mabel got really close to Freda. She pointed her finger in her face and looked her straight in the eyes. "Don't go messin' with no Mother Ruby. They is things you don't understand. You hear me, gal?"

Later that day, Freda paid a visit to Ethel. *Why she got to be home by 3:30 every day? No matter where she be, she got to be home fo' 3:30,* Freda wondered. *She ain't got no chil'ren.*

Ethel lived in a small, white shotgun house with dark green trim a few blocks down the street. The yard was small with plush green grass and trimmed hedges in the front. The front door was open and Freda took the liberty to walk right in. She was greeted by the smell of freshly baked bread and cinnamon.

Freda took herself on a grand tour. The off-white walls were freshly painted and the hardwood floors shined like new. In the rear corner of the living room sat a sewing machine and a wad of white lace fabric. Mellow sounds of the Glenn Miller Band spewed from the big, wooden radio next to the sofa. Blue-and-white floral-striped wallpaper covered the bathroom walls and brought out the shine of the porcelain fixtures.

They ain't even got no furniture in this here room, Freda thought as she looked around the empty second bedroom. Just then, a squeak in the floor startled Ethel as she noticed Freda from the kitchen.

"Freda," she was surprised. "I ain't know you was coming. Can I get you something to drink?"

"I was coming from the corner store next door. I just stopped by to yell at you." Freda noticed that Ethel's hair was still fresh from Saturday's pressing. She wore a hint of red lipstick and a crisp, khaki dress that complemented her slim, shapely figure.

"Irving gone be here in a minute. I'm trying to finish dinner."

"So, that's why you always go home at 3:30."

"Yes, ma'am. I needs to get dinner fixed for Irving by the time he get home from work."

Freda noticed the corn muffins and deep-dish peach cobbler cooling on the countertop, as four large black pots simmered on the stove.

"What you cooking there?"

"Collard greens with ham hocks, rice, and smothered pork chops."

"How you learn to cook like that?"

"My momma."

"Chil', you done cooked too much stuff!" Freda rolled her eyes at Ethel. "That man can't eat all that!"

"Ethel!" Irving called. "Something sho' smell good!"

Irving looked like a giant as he walked through the door. The small, black lunch pail he carried seemed awkward for such a big man to take to work. He was covered with dirt from head to toe. The odor of pure testosterone permeated the air as he entered the house. His T-shirt outlined his large biceps and pectoral muscles.

"Who you?" he asked Freda.

"I'm Freda. I live up the street. My husband do upholstery."

"You Ray Marshall wife?" He seemed amazed. Freda's hair, which she pinned into a bun, was almost completely gray. Masses of flesh showed through the oversized pink housecoat she wore. Large, dark circles and crow's feet had begun to form under her eyes. A slimy, green film covered her teeth. Irving quickly glanced at her feet and thought to himself, *Damn. That woman's feet look like white Brazil nuts dusted with flour. She shouldn't be wearing no open-toe sandals.*

Ethel began to set the table.

"Ray used to work with my friend, Kent Simms," Irving told Freda.

"I know Kent." Freda started. "He used to live in the row up the street there."

"Kent the one who told us 'bout this house. He moved up North around that time," he told Freda.

"I heard. Where he done move to anyhow?" Freda asked.

"To New York. He got a job on another ship line," Irving continued. "Them was some good times. I used to work on the ship back then. Befo' we left for sea each time, Kent, Ray, myself, and some other fellas from the dock used to meet at the diner on Canal Street befo' we started work. That was 'round '35, way befo' I got married. I ain't know Ray got married. How long y'all been married?"

Freda was surprised. "We been married since 1920!"

Irving and Ethel looked at each other in amazement, as if to say, *Damn, Ray been married that long and ain't nobody knew it?*

"I better go," Freda said as she started for the door.

Irving washed up for dinner while Ethel put the food on the table.

"Ouch!" Irving yelled and jumped from his seat. He noticed a small, white stone on the chair. He picked it up and examined it closely. "What this is?" He asked Ethel.

"I don't know."

They held it to the light and noticed shades of the rainbow reflect from it. "It sho' is pretty. You think it came from the docks, Irving?"

"I don't know. You think that woman who was here dropped it?"

"Naw. She ain't had no purse or no bag."

"I'll take it to the docks tomorrow. Maybe somebody is missin' it. If not, it may be worth somethin'."

***

That's a shame, Freda thought as she walked home. *Women folk be rushing home to cook fo' they husbands. They act like they kings or somethin'. Why can't they let them cook for theyselves?*

***

In the summer of 1940, on his 23rd birthday, Irving received a letter of conscription. All men between the ages of 21 and 35 were required to register for military service.

"They told me it's only for a year, Ethel."

"I know, Irving," Ethel said as tears streamed down her face. "But they is a war going on overseas."

"But we ain't involved in that war." Irving wiped the tears with his fingers and gently stroked her cheek. "I'll write all the time, Ethel." He held her close as her slender arms struggled up his chest and around his neck. "I love you, Ethel," he said as he stared deep into her watery eyes. They engaged in a long, passionate kiss.

A white military bus drove up to the house. Two men in uniforms got out and walked to the door. Irving slowly backed out of Ethel's arms, their eyes locked in a loving glare.

She stood there, frozen in the moment, unable to comprehend the harsh reality that had just shattered her world. Her eyes followed Irving onto the bus until he blended into the crowd of men who had boarded before him. She walked to the street in a stupor as the bus drove off and faded into the distance.

Freda watched from her porch as the bus passed by. She went inside and lit an orange candle for the occasion.

Ms. Mabel was tending to her garden when the bus passed by. She noticed Ethel standing in the street and ran to her aid. Ms. Mabel ushered Ethel into the yard and up the porch steps, hugging her all the way. "Let's go, sugar," Ms. Mabel said as she held Ethel in her arms. "Ev'thing gone be all right. Put yo' trust in the Lord."

Chapter 7.
Separation

In late 1941, Ray, Jr. and Carter were required to register with the Selective Service.

"We ain't goin' to war," Ray, Jr. told his parents. "We just got to register. That's all!"

"Besides," Carter added, "they gone pick the names by somethin' called a lottery. Everybody won't get to go no way."

Ray, Jr. and Carter were both called off to war in early 1942. A few months later, Fred registered with the Selective Service. He wasn't considered because all the boys in one family couldn't be at war at the same time.

***

"You need some he'p, daddy?"

Ray stopped what he was doing and gave him a mean look. Fred didn't see the two customers standing behind the door who stepped around when he spoke.

"I didn't know you had another boy, Ray," Mr. Canton said.

"This here my boy Fred, Mr. Canton."

"I'm Dr. Pickens. I always thought you were the yard boy. I've been coming here for years. Each time I'm here, you're cutting grass, or trimming hedges, or something. Good to meet you."

"He the youngest, so he do all the busy work."

"Your daddy could sure use the help," Mr. Canton said. He turned to Ray. "It'll be good to have your son helping out 'round the shop, 'specially since the other two gone to war. Our three children have been helping us in the restaurant since they were 12."

"When my boy finishes Meharry, he's going to help me in my practice. Well, Ray, I just came to drop off this here chest. When do you think you'll have it ready?"

"In two days, Dr. Pickens. In two days." Ray knew that with the other work, even working all day, every day, he wouldn't get to it until next week.

"Bye, Ray." The two men waved as they walked to their cars.

"Pleasure meeting you, young fella," started Dr. Pickens. "Hope to see you next time."

Even with his other two sons away and the backlog of work, Ray was still reluctant to have Fred help in the shop. He wanted to believe that business was slacking because of the war, and not because he couldn't complete the work in a timely manner.

Ray waited for the men to leave. "Boy, I told you to never come in here when customers around."

"You said I could help out long time ago. With Junior and Carter at war, I could really help out."

"You don't know nothin' 'bout the business."

"I could learn. I can't do no worse 'n Junior."

"Boy hush up. You don't know what you talkin' 'bout." He slammed the door in Fred's face.

***

Jobs were plentiful because of the war effort, but it was hard to get on at the shipyards. Most folks got hired because they knew somebody. The anger he stored up from the argument with Ray gave him the guts to apply for a job anyway. The screeching sounds of equipment reminded him of his father's shop. It was a busy place. Men carried equipment to and fro, while others were busy welding or blasting. Fred walked around in awe. He immediately felt like that was where he belonged.

"You need something, son?" a deep voice behind him asked, almost out of nowhere, startling him.

"I'm here to apply fo' a job."

"I'm Mr. Preston, the foreman. Anybody wantin' a job here gots to go through me." His coarse, jet-black hair and dark eyes contrasted sharply with his pale skin. He was at least six-four and 300 pounds, enough to intimidate some folk. But Fred was bold, looked him straight in the eye, and didn't back down from his questions. He was relieved to see a colored foreman, though.

"Yes, sir."

"You got any skills, son?"

Fred was stumped for words. A voice came in his head and told him to pretend that he was talking to his father. "Well, sir. I ain't never worked the shipyards befo'. But I'm strong and sho' do learn fast. No job is too tough or too small fo' me, sir. I'll do whatever you want me to, and whatever need to be done."

"Ummm."

"What's yo' name, boy?"

"Frederick Marshall."

"Ain't he Ray Marshall boy?" someone shouted and joined Mr. Preston. Both gawked at Fred.

"This here Mr. Anderson, Fred."

"How you do, sir?"

"Why you not he'ping yo' daddy? Don't he need he'p?" Mr. Anderson inquired.

Fred wasn't sure if he should tell the truth, that his father never taught him the business, which they wouldn't believe. Or, think of a clever, more believable lie.

"Well, sir. It's like this," Fred began. "My two older brothers worked in the business with my paw. I never got to learn too much 'bout it 'cause I was always doing the yard work. In our house, we all had chores to do. Mine was to do yard work. Besides, I'm 18 and it's time fo' me to be on my own."

The two men looked leery. "Give the boy a chance," Mr. Anderson whispered in Mr. Preston's ear, then returned to work. Fred heard what he said and became hopeful.

"You finish school?"

"Yes, sir. I just graduated from L. B. Landry."

"Okay, Fred. Can you be back here at 4:30 sharp tomorrow?" Mr. Preston asked.

"Yes, sir, I can!"

"Okay. I tell you what. Come see me when you get here tomorrow. We go and fill out yo' papers. I start you off as the porter. Most porters didn't finish high school. But, if you prove yo'self, being that you finish school and all, I see 'bout moving you somewhere else."

"Thank you, Mr. Preston. I'll be the best worker you ever had!"

Chapter 8.
The Outing

It was the last Sunday afternoon in the month. After church, Ms. Mabel and Ethel caught the ferry across the river to the Gallo Theater or one of the other colored movie houses. "We needs to treat ourselves," Ms. Mabel would always say. "We worked hard all month taking care of other people. Now it's time for us to be good to us."

They didn't like it as much when Freda forced herself on them. She was always rolling her eyes at or saying something flip about strangers they encountered. Ethel and Ms. Mabel often wondered if the people overheard her comments. *I hope she don't get us killed one of these days*, Ms. Mabel often wondered.

Freda never attended church, but just wanted to be in good company. She needed comforting since her boys went off to war. Ray was rarely at home. He worked until close to midnight in the shop. On weekends, he left late on Friday evening and wouldn't return until late Sunday evening. Fred was working at the shipyards. Delores, who was 16, quit school and started working at the tool factory. She was always busy and away from home. If she weren't at work, she would either be out with friends or aiding Ms. Mabel with something or the other. Other neighbors, who were housewives before the war, got jobs at the factories. So, Ethel and Ms. Mabel let Freda tag along because they felt badly that she had no one else to keep her company.

Ethel looked forward to their outings. Her husband, Irving, was one of the first drafted to serve in World War II. Even though she received an allowance from the military, it wasn't enough to run the house. Irving worked as a longshoreman and often worked many overtime hours. Ms. Mabel got her a job as a domestic working for the Millers to make ends meet. That still wasn't enough. So when the tool factory starting hiring Negro women, she and Ms. Mabel quit their jobs at the Millers.

Irving wrote almost every week, but she often worried endlessly about him. "I don't have a good feeling 'bout this," she said.

"He gone be all right," Ms. Mabel reassured.

"He write you every week, don't he? That must mean he fine." Freda added.

"I wrote him almost three weeks ago and ain't got no mo' letters from him."

I hope he dead, Freda thought to herself.

"You ever get letters from yo' boys, Ms. Freda?" Ethel asked.

Freda held her head down. "Ray get the mail."

"What that got to do with anything, Freda?" Ms. Mabel asked. "Don't you read yo' own mail?"

"No, Ray read the mail and don't always read it to me."

"Why you got to wait fo' him to read it to you?" Ms. Mabel asked. "Can't you read fo' yo' ... ." She stopped her words and realized that over the years Freda had always avoided reading anything. Labels, recipes, anything. She recalled several times when she was pressing hair and some of the women brought in magazines or books to gossip about. Freda always appeared to be uninterested when it was her turn to comment.

"Ain't you goin' to Chicago in a few weeks, Ms. Mabel?" Ethel asked.

"Yes. Yes!" Ms. Mabel was excited. "I ain't seen my grandchil'ren since befo' the war. It be good to get away."

"Ain't yo' son a big-time doctor?" Ethel asked.

"Yes! He and his wife, Margaret, have three beautiful chil'ren. They promised me pictures on this visit. I can't wait to show y'all."

"You got any more grandchil'ren?" Ethel asked.

"No," Ms. Mabel said sorrowfully. "My two girls who live in Atlanta think that they too educated to get married and have chil'ren. They too choosy is what they is."

"Back in my day, all the pretty girls like me didn't have to worry 'bout no ed'cation. We knew we was pretty enough to get a husband to take care o' us," Freda told them.

"Back in the day I was real pretty, but I got a ed'cation," Ms. Mabel interjected. "I know how to read, write, and do 'rithmatic. My momma told us girls to always know how to take care o' ourselves because you never know what gone happen. I'm glad she did. Look at Ethel here. If her momma didn't teach her to take care o' herself, she wouldn't know what to do now that Irving is gone to war. It's 'portant to know how to run a house and take care of yo'self!" Ms. Mabel stared straight into Freda's eyes. "No matter how pretty you is ain't no man gone want a woman who don't know how to tend to the house!" She looked Freda up and down, "and tend to herself!"

Ethel noticed the heat between Freda and Ms. Mabel and started, "I bet you got some beautiful chil'ren and grandchil'ren."

"Yes. My son is tall and good-looking like my late husband. People used to call my chil'ren red-boned. They all had dark, wavy hair and dark eyes like me, and reddish-brown skin like they daddy."

"Tell me 'bout yo' grandchil'ren."

"I got three. Arthur, III and Richard, who red-boned like they daddy. And Pearl-Elizabeth, who got her daddy's hair, but look like her mother. She a sassy li'l thing, too! Margaret is a good mother."

Freda thought of her sister, Margaret, and mother, Pearl. She thought, *What a big coincidence.*

***

Ethel really enjoyed the ferry ride back home. Freda and Ms. Mabel let her be as she stared into the mighty Mississippi River. They knew it provided her with a level of peace. "The colored section the best. You could see the water better." She told her friends, "Look how the moon shine on the waves."

"Yeah," Ms. Mabel started, "you can't see as much down below. Besides, they right 'bove the car section. I don't see how they can stand smelling the fumes from the cars."

"We better get home befo' it get too dark," Ms. Mabel told them.

"Yeah," Freda started, "y'all got to get up early to go clean Mr. Miller's house."

"What you talkin' 'bout, Freda?" Ethel asked. "We got jobs at the factory. They got so much work, they even hiring colored women."

"When y'all started working there?"

"For 'bout a month now," Ethel answered. "Why don't you come down and get a job? They hiring like crazy 'cause of the war."

"That's right," started Ms. Mabel. "A lot of the other women in the neighborhood got jobs, too."

"Them women's husbands at war. I got a husband to take care o' me! I don't gotta work!"

"Not all they husbands at war," Ms. Mabel started. "They doin' it while they can so they can get 'head."

"Yo' girl Delores work there too," Ethel told her.

"That's 'cause ain't nobody gone marry her ugly black behind." Freda's loud tone of voice attracted the attention of passersby. "She gots to work to take care o' herself."

Chapter 9.
Restless Nights

Ethel and Ms. Mabel savored their one-mile walk to work each day. They watched the sunrise in awe and thanked the creator for making each day more beautiful than the one before. The deep orange light that peeked through the darkness of night brought with it a sense of peace and tranquillity. Ms. Mabel felt most connected to her spirit at dawn. She always sensed the divine love and protection of God the strongest during that time.

The walk home at night allowed them to watch the sunset and catch up on the happenings of the day. Even if they would have had a car, they couldn't use it because of the gas rations.

For the past week, Ms. Mabel noticed that Ethel had not been herself. She had to bang on Ethel's door for her to wake up. "What's wrong, sugar?" she asked. "You don't look so good."

"I feel real tired today," Ethel complained. "So tired that I could hardly stay 'wake at work today."

"You been getting enough rest?"

"Yes, ma'am. But I been having a strange dream."

"What you mean, sugar?"

"Well, it's like I try to wake up but can't. Like something on my chest and I can't breathe too good."

She caught Ms. Mabel's attention. "When this started?"

" 'Bout last week." She noticed the look of concern on Ms. Mabel's face. "What's wrong, Ms. Mabel?"

Ms. Mabel stopped in her tracks and looked as though she had seen a ghost. "Do you find yo'self on yo' back when you wake up in the morning?"

"Yes, ma'am. That's strange 'cause I don't sleep on my back," she said. "How you know, Ms. Mabel?"

"If you ever find yo'self 'gain when you can't move, try to wiggle a finger, a toe, anything and it'll go away." She was concerned for Ethel and didn't want to scare her. "Try to open yo' eyes."

"What's wrong, Ms. Mabel? I got some disease?"

"No, you ain't got no disease. Just do what I done told you and you gone be all right." She started to walk again. "You told anybody else 'bout this?"

"No, ma'am."

"You sho'?"

"I'm sho'."

"Well, don't tell nobody what you just done told me. I mean nobody!"

***

Ethel had just finished cleaning the kitchen when she heard Freda knocking on the back door.

"Freda, it's almost blackout time. What you doing here so late?"

"Well, I know you go to work early and I wanted to catch you."

"Come in, Freda."

"You gone be needing yo' sugar ration coupons?"

Ethel thought that it was strange for her to come so late at night for ration coupons.

"Since yo' husband off to war I thought that you don't cook no sweets too much."

There appeared a sense of urgency in Freda's expressions, so Ethel opened the cabinet drawer and handed the coupons to her. "I don't even like sweets. You can have my sugar rations."

Ethel thought that it was odd. Freda's husband and two children were working and she needed more ration coupons, especially since Freda didn't cook much. *Why she want my coupons?* Ethel thought. *She know I'm just scraping by. Maybe things ain't going too well for Ray.*

"Thank you, Ethel," Freda said as she left through the back door.

Ethel kept thinking about what Ms. Mabel told her earlier and had already forgotten what had just occurred. Her words didn't make any sense. She read several Bible verses for comfort and turned in for the evening.

Ethel had trouble falling asleep. She usually fell fast asleep when her head hit the pillow. A large French window faced opposite the bed. *Maybe it's the moonlight shining through the curtains*, she thought.

She heard a cat's meow and a series of thumps against the window pane. *I ain't know it was raining*, she thought. The noise stopped. A few minutes later, a loud squeak came from the direction of the window.

She noticed the curtain move. It seemed as if something had fallen to the floor, but she assumed that it was a draft.

The bed squeaked as the sheets crept along her legs. She felt a small, cold hand touch her shoulder from behind that sent a paralyzing chill through her body. Its powerful grasp was strong enough to turn her over on her back.

She couldn't move or scream. Her eyes felt as though they had been glued shut. The tiny limbs slowly crawled onto her chest. Its skin felt like a frog rubbing against her bare arms, inching its way to her shoulders. The dull sensation of its claws caressed her neck, sending an eerie sense of terror to every cell of her body.

The stench of rotting meat became stronger and stronger. One hand moved across her lips and opened her mouth, while the other pinched her nose, forcing the very breath of life out of her mouth.

The creature took one deep breath in. Ethel felt the air leave her lungs. The creature tried to inhale once more, but the words of Ms. Mabel came to mind. Ethel tried to move a toe, but her legs were frozen. It took all the strength she had, but she strained to move a finger as the creature inhaled another breath. She began to cough and opened her eyes. A small creature the size of a raccoon stood on her chest. The moonlight shined into the large, menacing black eyes. Its gray skin was deeply wrinkled and scaly, like nothing she had ever seen before.

Ethel's Bible lay next to her, and she used it to whack it off the bed. One of the long claws scratched her arm as it struggled to grasp the sheets. The creature slid across the floor and rapidly squeezed through the tiny crack in the window whence it came.

It all happened so quickly, in a matter of seconds. As she got out of bed, it was nowhere in sight. She got a broom from the kitchen, then turned on the bedroom lights. All was still. She looked around outside, but no creature. *I must have been dreaming again*, she thought. *I hope I don't get in trouble fo' turning on the lights when it's blackout time.*

Her mouth was dry and had a strange musty taste. She went back into the bedroom and started for the lights. A large diagonal rip appeared across the blanket, and her Bible was on the floor. She felt something dripping down her legs. Blood oozed out of three deep scratches of her left wrist.

***

At the crack of dawn, Ms. Mabel heard a loud knock on her front door.

"Ms. Mabel, Ms. Mabel!" Ethel shouted, "It's me, Ethel!"

Ms. Mabel had just finished getting dressed for work, and let her in. "You up awful early, chil'. I was on my way to get you," Ms. Mabel said as they started their mile trek to work.

"Something real strange happened last night," Ethel started.

"What's that?"

"I couldn't sleep so I just laid in bed."

"Go on, chil'."

"Then this animal jumped on me and tried to attack me. It was strange, Ms. Mabel. You gone think I'm crazy."

"No I won't!"

"It disappeared." Ms. Mabel gasped for breath when Ethel showed her the large white bandages on her arm. "See? It scratched me. I put some peroxide on it. It took me five minutes to stop the bleeding."

"Was it small with a lot of wrinkles and big black eyes? Like a troll?"

"Yes." Ethel was puzzled. "How you know that, Ms. Mabel?"

"Did it move real quick?"

"Yes, ma'am."

"I know what it was," Ms. Mabel said.

"What was it?"

Ms. Mabel put her head down and was hesitant about telling her.

"Tell me, Ms. Mabel."

"It's like this. They is what you call witches. They people who get out they body and steal other people's breath. One tried to ride my husband befo' we moved to Algiers. He took his belt and knocked it 'cross the room. I got a good look at it. It looked like this old lady down the street, Ms. Millie. The next day, she was walking with a limp where my husband done hit her the night befo'. 'Cause we seen her, she ain't never bothered us again."

"Now, Ms. Mabel," Ethel said with disbelief.

"Listen, chil'," she continued. "They can squeeze between the littlest crack, and they real fast and strong, too. They come out after midnight and got to be back befo' the sun come up. Light yourself a white candle befo' you go to bed, and put a broom next to yo' bed. That's 'sposed to keep 'em away."

Ethel thought about the curtain moving and how a creature that small could roll her over.

"I don't know 'bout that, Ms. Mabel."

"Why would a animal get in yo' bed and be on yo' chest? A witch was trying to ride you. That's why you been feeling so tired."

"But why or who would do this? I never did nothing to nobody."

"You don't have to, chil'. They is some evil people in the world."

Chapter 10.
The Untangled Web

Fred worked harder than every other porter at the shipyard. He swept, mopped, polished, and even helped with duties outside of his own. When one of the other porters couldn't make his shift, he volunteered to fill in.

He worked so much overtime that he saved enough to move into a row apartment down the street from his parents–**the same ones where you moved with your momma some years ago.**

Fred had just moved into his new apartment, but needed to get the rest of his things from his parents' house. That particular Sunday afternoon, he joined his father for homemade root beer and shrimp and oyster po' boys from the sandwich shop down the street.

They chatted for a bit before gathering the rest of Fred's belongings. After lunch, he and Ray searched the house and workshop for boxes and suitcases to pack his belongings. Fred remembered seeing his mother go into the attic a few days before. "Daddy," Fred called to Ray. "They may be some boxes in the attic."

"Naw," he started. "We ain't never used it. It's too small. Putting something up in there might break the ceiling."

"I saw momma put something up in there the other day."

"How she get up there? She don't know how to use no ladder."

"She used the step stool in the kitchen. It looked like a black suitcase."

Ray remembered Freda carrying a black suitcase when they first got married. He tried to carry it for her but she snapped, "Ray Marshall, I got my personal things in here that a man's eyes just ain't meant to see," she told him. He thought that she threw it away because he hadn't seen it in so many years.

The hatch door leading to the attic was near the kitchen. They were overcome by the gush of hot air as they entered. The air vent toward the front provided adequate lighting for them to navigate around. The attic sat over the living room and hallway. It provided extra storage space, but was only four feet tall, barely enough for them to crawl around.

They looked around and saw nothing but cobwebs. "I told you, Fred," Ray started. "Ain't nothing up in here."

They started to leave when Fred noticed something in the far corner behind the hatch door. They crawled toward it, careful not to go outside of the joists. It was a large, black trunk lined with gold studs that seemed immune from the surrounding dust and cobwebs.

"I don't 'member nothing like this," Ray said. "I guess you can have it."

They pulled the trunk and noticed its weight.

"This can't be fo' yo' momma," Ray started. "She ain't strong enough to lift it."

"How it get up in here then, daddy?"

"I don't know. Go ask yo' momma."

"She ain't here. She went to the show with Ms. Ethel and Ms. Mabel."

"Well, boy. Let's go clean it up. I don't see why you can't use it. It's been up in here all this time and nobody ain't missed it."

They finally managed to get it out of the attic and struggled to carry the thing into the shed out back.

"What's in here?" Fred asked. "This thing must weigh over 200 pounds."

It was a bright, sunny afternoon, but a large cloud passed over the shed. The air thickened, making the hair stand up on Ray's and Fred's arms. As they cracked the lid, a fine mist of dust whizzed in their faces. A pungent, musty odor filled the air once the trunk was finally opened.

"What the world?" Fred started, amazed by the contents. "This stuff can't be that heavy."

A stack of Ray's dirty underwear, with the crouches cut out, were piled to one side. The bottom was covered with wax. It appeared that numerous pink and white candles had been left to burn completely. An old sailor's cap and black comb were wrapped in twine. An old World War I picture of Ray in his uniform was pinned to the left side. Several white crystals of varying sizes were scattered about.

"What those drawers doing up in there, daddy?"

"I guess yo' momma ruined them doing the laundry and tried to hide 'em."

"What's some o' the other stuff?"

"I thought I lost that cap before yo' momma and me got married." Ray unpinned his picture. "I wondered what happened to this. I might as well throw it away."

"No!" Fred exclaimed. "Let me have it. I'll frame it."

They carried the trunk to a work table and noticed that it was much lighter. They started to put the remaining contents into the tin garbage bin below. An intermittent, low-pitched, growling sound emanated from the pile of underwear. Ray and Fred froze.

"You think it's a snake, daddy?"

"Stand back!" Ray told Fred. He took a long poker that lay next to the trunk and slowly moved the garments toward the front of the trunk. Nothing was there. Ray then put the pile into the garbage bin below.

"Ain't nothing there," Ray told Fred.

"One of them drawers fell back into the trunk, daddy."

Ray and Fred jumped back several feet by what they saw. Several large, hairy, black tarantulas with small, yellow spots appeared. They looked like large, hairy fingers that slowly crept out of the chest and down the side of the table, one by one, like soldiers in formation. Ray and Fred tried to smash them with a wooden paddle, but each vanished as it hit the floor.

A gigantic, light-brown, eight-inch-long spider emerged from the last underwear. It slowly crawled up the side of the trunk, then down onto the table. The hair was blond and wavy, like that of a human. A sunbeam peaked through the window behind and gleamed into the creature's eight beady, blue eyes. It turned to face Ray and Fred and gestured by raising one of its legs. It let out three long hisses, then one final growl before it dithered into nothingness. They stood there, mouths opened wide, in disbelief of what they had witnessed. Goose bumps covered both their bodies.

"I must be going crazy," Fred started. "I swear I heard that spider say something."

"You and me both," Ray agreed.

The trunk fell to the floor and smashed into several tiny pieces. The air began to thin, and the dark cloud lifted.

"We put that thing in the middle of the table," Ray started. "How it fall down?"

"I don't know."

"Let's burn this thing," Ray said.

They arranged the broken trunk pieces and debris from the garbage pail into a wheelbarrow so that Ray could dump it all in the yard to burn.

***

"Go get the stuff you want to save and put it in the house. Give the other stuff to me," I said.

Ray and Fred were startled because they didn't see me standing behind them. Their skin began to crawl as they looked deep into my eyes and reached the depth of my very existence. In that moment in time, I had seized their souls.

Fred took Ray's old war picture and they put the other stuff in the pile to be burned. I walked them into the kitchen of the main house. "Go and close the attic door," I instructed Ray. He obeyed. "You never saw anything. You don't know anything about a trunk or anything else in that attic. You never took anything into the shed. You never saw anything in the shed. None of this ever happened."

"Yes, Mother Ruby," they answered in unison.

"Ray, you found that old war picture in the bottom of some old clothes. Fred, you decided to take it because you want to save it for your children."

"Yes, Mother Ruby," they again answered in unison.

I fixed a fresh pitcher of root beer and served it to them. They sat there for a while entranced as I erased all evidence of that afternoon. I cleared the shed and carted the wheelbarrow away. Before they came to, the wheelbarrow and everything else was back to normal.

***

Ray and Fred were sipping root beer and chatting the afternoon away. Fred suddenly noticed the clock on the kitchen stove.

"Five-thirty!" he shouted. "Boy! Time sho' do go by fast! I gots to get home and finish unpacking!"

They were both overcome with a strong feeling of déjà vu, as though they had done the same thing before. Neither of them mentioned it to the other, though, and assumed it was just nerves.

***

Freda, Ethel, and Ms. Mabel were sipping vanilla-malted shakes at Joes's. That was their favorite diner because it was so quiet and clean. It had diagonal, black-and-white checked floors and flawless, antique white walls. All tables were booths, except for the red stools at the countertop near the soda-pop machines. They liked to get one of the window seats so that they could watch people walk down the street.

Back then, Dryades Street was the colored business district. You know it's not like that now. It really went down. Folks could have fun and be themselves without fear of being harassed or having to sit in the colored section. Heck, every section was the colored section.

Freda was in a better mood than usual, not one ugly remark about a stranger all day. The crow's feet and dark circle were fading. The pale green dress she wore brought out the blue-green hue in her eyes. She wore a hint of pink lipstick and rouge that made her look like a starlet.

"You sho' looking good, Ms. Freda," Ethel said. "You did something different to yo' hair?"

"Yeah, I curled it." She ran her fingers through her hair. "Y'all used to seeing me wear it in a bun."

"It look a li'l darker," Ms. Mabel noticed. "You been coloring it?"

Freda started to blink her eyes. "I don't feel so good."

"What's wrong?" Ethel asked.

"I'm a bit light-headed."

"We better get you home," Ms. Mabel insisted.

As they started for the door, Freda fainted. A crowd started to form. Someone in the kitchen brought out some smelling salt. Two men carried her to a back employee's lounge when she came to. They brought her a cold glass of water to drink.

"I'll be fine," Freda insisted. "I ain't had nothing to eat all day, that's all."

"I'll drive y'all ladies home," Joe Mason, the owner, said. "I won't feel right if y'all got to catch the bus home."

"Thank you, Mr. Mason," Ms. Mabel said. "We sho' 'preciate it." Ms. Mabel had been going there for years and felt safe with Mr. Mason. *Besides, he a old man anyhow, what can he do?*

***

Mr. Mason dropped them off at Freda's house. Ethel and Ms. Mabel made sure that she got inside and stayed with her a few minutes. They noticed Ray in the kitchen and were surprised that he was home.

"What's wrong with her?" Ray asked.

As soon as his wife entered the front door, a dark cloud of hatred suddenly engulfed Ray. He felt a deep sense of anger toward her as he watched Ms. Mabel and Ethel help her into bed. *All that fuckin' bitch fuckin' do is fuckin' sleep all fuckin' day long. I don't know what the fuck I ever saw in that moth'fuckin' 'ho' no fuckin' way!*

Ethel glanced back at Ray and was intimidated by the intense look he gave them. *He must think she drunk. He must think we had her out drinking.*

"She got a li'l light-headed earlier at Joe's," Ms. Mabel started.

"She'll be fine. Just let her rest up."

"You think she may be pregnant?" Ethel asked Ms. Mabel when they left Freda's yard.

"Naw. She would be acting real, real ugly if she was. Lately, she been looking and acting too good."

"You don't think somebody been riding her, too, do you?" Ethel asked.

"I hope not, sugar. I sho' hope not."

Chapter 11.
Reunited

It was 4:30 that Saturday afternoon when Freda was coming from the corner store. She noticed a yellow cab pulling in front of Ms. Mabel's door. Five people dressed in fancy clothes emerged, and there were plenty of suitcases. *Must be Ms. Mabel's son and his family. I thought Ms. Mabel was going to Chicago. I guess not.*

She looked again and saw Fred helping them carry their bags inside. At that point she decided to go inside to arrange her hair and wash up, then started for Ms. Mabel's. She heard so much about this big-time doctor, until she just couldn't wait to see what rich, colored folk looked like.

"Where you think you going?" Ray demanded as Freda headed out the yard. "Shouldn't you be starting supper?"

"Ms. Mabel's son, the big-time doctor, is here. I'm goin' see him."

"You nosy, Freda. You needs to mind yo' damn own business," Ray started. "You prob'bly going over there to try to fuck him, ain't you?"

Freda was shocked by Ray's comment. The look in his eyes sent a cold chill down her spine that pierced the very depth of her being. She was relieved to see Ethel and Delores coming from Ms. Mabel's and headed toward her. Both wore white aprons trimmed in pink, the ones that Ms. Mabel made anyone wear who was working in her kitchen, over their Sunday's best. Their hair was neatly coifed in the Page Boy 'do that Ms. Mabel was famous for.

"Momma, momma!" Delores was so excited that she was panting for air. "Guess what? Guess what? Ms. Mabel son here!"

"We was trying to wake you early this morning," Ethel said.

"She was sleeping," Ray said sarcastically.

"We been cooking all morning and 'bout to sit down to supper. Ms. Mabel want you and Ray to come to supper," Ethel said.

"Yeah, momma," Delores started. "We got roast turkey and gumbo and succotash and apple cobbler and sweet potato pie and…"

"All right, all right," Ray laughed. "Sho' sound good to me. When you be at work, Delores, I don't get no home cookin'. And I needs me a good home-cooked meal! You cooked any of it?"

"Yeah, daddy. I helped with everything."

"Where they got the food from?" Freda asked. "Everybody on rations."

"Ms. Mabel say she got connections," Delores proudly answered.

"Well, what we waitin' fo'? Let me get washed up," Ray said as he dashed into the house. "Y'all tell Ms. Mabel I'll be there in 15 minutes."

"Yes, sir, daddy!"

Freda saw how nicely Ethel and Delores looked and decided to put on some makeup and change into that navy blue outfit she never got to wear much. It was a two-piece suit that was full at the hips and reached right below the knee, and made her look several pounds lighter. She adorned her slicked-back hair with a matching pillbox hat, and put on those pencil-point-heel navy pumps that she bought when she went shopping with Ethel and Ms. Mabel a few months before. "You need to fix yo' self up," Ms. Mabel always prodded. Freda never shopped much, but was glad she took Ms. Mabel's advice on that particular day. She went into the living room to wait for Ray.

"What you still doin' here, Freda?" Ray asked.

"I thought we go together."

Ray looked sharp in that blue, pin-striped zoot suit. The black, wing tip shoes he wore were so shiny that you could see your reflection in them. He put that felt hat on his head, cocked to the side. "Let's go, Freda."

During their walk up the street, Ray was somber the whole way. Freda tried in vain to strike up a conversation, but Ray just growled at her every word. Each time she tried to hold his arm or cuddle next to him, he jerked away in disgust. She thought that Ray was going to hit her right there in the street, and was relieved to see Delores waiting for them at the front door of Ms. Mabel's house. When Freda smelled the herbs and spices coming from the kitchen, she knew that home-cooked food would perk Ray's senses and cool his temper. So she thought.

The dining room was exquisite. The mahogany chairs and china cabinet were perfectly polished. A long, white, lace tablecloth dressed the oblong table. Sparkling water goblets sat next to brilliant sterling-silver place settings and fine china. In the center of each plate was a single white lace napkin, folded to resemble a rose. The dinner party–Ray, Freda, Fred, Delores, Ethel, and Ms. Mabel–eagerly awaited the guests of honor, as the feast teased their sense of smell and taste buds.

Ms. Mabel always visited her son, Arthur, and his family because she wanted to travel, especially to the North. They insisted on coming down that time, which was unusual. Arthur and his wife, Margaret, both vowed never to touch foot on Southern soil again. They wanted their children to be shielded from the harsh reality of the South and what it stood for.

Everybody was startled by the sudden rhythmic thumps that came from the stairs. Arthur, III, who had just turned 19, came down first, followed by his brother, Richard, who was almost 18. Both were tall and slim with dark, beady eyes, thick eyebrows, and wavy, black hair. The heavily starched khaki pants they wore blended with their olive skin.

"They must be twins!" Freda commented.

"They sho' look like it," Ms. Mabel started. "Arthur, Richard, come say hello to Ms. Marshall."

"Hello, Mrs. Marshall," Arthur said as he sat two seats down from his grandmother.

"Pleased to meet you," Richard said as he kissed his grandmother on the cheek and sat to her right.

"Arthur, III go to Howard in Washington, D.C. Richard gone go there, too, come Fall. They want to be doctors like they daddy."

"They sho' is some fine boys, Ms. Mabel," Freda commented.

Pearl-Elizabeth made her entrance down the stairs. Her long, thick, black, silky hair was gently curled and flowed to her hips. It bounced with each step she took. She walked as though she balanced a book on her head, which brought attention to her voluptuous bosom and full motion of her hips. A pleasant trail of jasmines followed her to the table. Freda gawked at her when she noticed how Ray's and Fred's eyes followed her every move and brought big smiles to their faces.

"Hello, Grandma," she said as she hugged and kissed Ms. Mabel.

"Hello yo'self, baby." Ms. Mabel gave her a big embrace and long kiss to the cheek. "This here the baby, Pearl-Elizabeth. She 16 and real smart, too. She skipped through school and just graduated from high school with her brother, Richard."

Pearl-Elizabeth sat between Fred and Arthur, III.

She sho' is pretty, Fred thought. *I sho' hope she stay fo' the summer. Maybe we could keep company.*

"Hello, everybody," she said.

"Pearl-Elizabeth, next to you is Fred Marshall. Next to him is his momma, Ms. Freda Marshall. At the end is his daddy, Mr. Ray

Marshall. Across from you is Ms. Ethel Lewis, and next to her is Delores Marshall, who I believe is the same age as you."

"I'm 18, Ms. Mabel," Delores informed her.

Freda kept rolling her eyes at Pearl-Elizabeth, her hair in particular. *That girl look like Ms. Mabel must o' looked when she was young, but look like somebody done throwed some black paint on her. Ain't nobody black like that could have no good, long hair like that. That must be a wig. And look at them titties. They just too big. Who she thank she is?*

"What you looking at, Freda?" Ms. Mabel asked as she noticed her staring at Pearl-Elizabeth. Freda didn't answer, but stopped rolling her eyes for awhile.

Arthur, III stood up and Richard did, too, when he looked behind him. Everybody looked toward the stairs in anticipation of meeting Ms. Mabel's son. Arthur, Jr. and Margaret were almost dressed liked twins, in crisply starched khaki pants and white linen shirts. They walked to Ms. Mabel, who was seated at the head of the table, and kissed her on the cheek.

Arthur was tall and muscular with an olive complexion. He wore his wavy, salt-and-pepper hair slicked back. His thick, black eyebrows and mustache gave him an air of distinction.

When Margaret bent over to hug Ms. Mabel, Ray couldn't take his eyes off of her firm, shapely rear. *Damn! She sho' is fine!* He experienced a slight erection when he noticed her pedicured feet and French-manicured hands. As the couple walked to their seats, Margaret left a trail of roses behind. *Smell good, too!* Ray couldn't keep his eyes off of her as she sat across from him. He admired her chignon hairdo and how it highlighted her smooth, ebony skin, pretty heart-shaped face, and full plum lips.

"Everybody, this here my son, Dr. Arthur Youngblood, Jr. and his wife, Margaret," she boasted.

Freda rolled her eyes at Margaret. *What a doctor want go marry something black and ugly like that fo'? He could do better than that. I should be married to a doctor, but they wasn't none in Morgan City.*

Ms. Mabel motioned for all to bow heads to bless the food. After raising their heads from prayer, Margaret and Freda made direct eye contact.

"Freda?" Margaret was surprised.

"Margaret?" Freda was so shocked that she spilled the water that she was drinking on the floor. Delores rushed to wipe up the mess.

"Margaret?" Ray was even more shocked.

"Y'all know each other?" Ms. Mabel asked.

All the other guests were curious.

"Freda is my sister. The one I told you about," Margaret told Ms. Mabel.

I wonder what she done told Ms. Mabel 'bout me? Freda asked herself.

"I ain't knowed we had no aunties," Delores said with excitement. "We got more? We got some uncles, too?"

"Freda Mae," Margaret started. "Is this beautiful princess your daughter?"

Delores smiled when she was referred to as a princess. She stopped, though, when she noticed Freda gawking at her.

"Yeah, she mine," Freda answered. "This boy here, Fred, is mine, too. We got two more beautiful chil'ren who off to war, Ray, Jr. and Carter."

"Yes, sweetie," Margaret told Delores. "You have your Uncle Arthur here, and an Uncle Isaac. Your Aunt Martha lives in New York."

"I got any cousins?" Delores went on.

"Yes," Margaret continued. "You have four other boy cousins, Isaac, Jr., Jacob, Moses, Luke, and one other girl cousin, Corinthian."

The use of the word cousin brought a sour taste to Fred's mouth. He was disappointed and almost ashamed by his strong attraction to Pearl-Elizabeth.

"I ain't know they had colored doctors in Morgan City, Margaret. How you meet him anyhow?" Freda asked.

"We met in Harlem."

"Harlem? Where that at?" Freda asked.

"You've never heard of Harlem?" Pearl-Elizabeth inquired. "Every Negro has heard of Harlem!"

"Hush up, Pearl-Elizabeth," Ms. Mabel warned. "Don't get in grown folk business."

"That's in New York," Arthur, Jr. answered. "It's where all the progressive Negroes moved during the Renaissance."

"The what?" Freda asked, as she hungrily bit into a roasted turkey leg, which she chewed with her mouth opened and lips smacking. Freda noticed that the Youngbloods, including Ms. Mabel, were eating with knives and forks. Everyone else used their forks because the meat was so tender.

"Let the man finish, Freda," Ray interjected, hoping that Freda wouldn't embarrass him anymore with her ignorance. He didn't know what Arthur, Jr. was talking about either, but didn't want to let on.

"The Harlem Renaissance was a time of rebirth. A time of

discovery for the Negro. It began around 1910 and continued on through the '20s. Large numbers of Negroes migrated from the South to the North during that time, in search of opportunities that were not otherwise available to them."

"Oh," Freda answered sharply. "You still never told us how y'all met, and how you got to this Harlem from Morgan City anyhow."

The Youngblood family already knew the story and thought that it was quite boring. Everyone else was curious.

"Well, it's like this," Margaret started. "In 1920, Martha and I decided that the South didn't have much to offer us."

"Y'all moved after Ray and me got married, heh?" Freda asked.

"Well, yes. We did," Margaret responded.

Freda looked Arthur, Jr. straight in the eyes. "I bet you ain't knowed that Margaret wanted to marry Ray, did you? But, he wanted hisself a pretty woman, didn't you, Ray? He said that Margaret was too black fo' him."

Ray didn't answer and froze in his chair. He suddenly had an intense desire for the Earth to swallow him alive.

"Well, Ray," Arthur, Jr. started. "I'm glad that Margaret wasn't your type, because we never would have met. For that, I owe you my life. By the way, Ray, what do you do?"

"I do upholstery," Ray mumbled.

"You do what?" Athur, Jr. asked again. "I didn't hear you."

"Upholstery," Ray repeated.

"He the one I told you 'bout who did all my wood," Ms. Mabel boasted.

"Oh, you're a laborer," Arthur, Jr. said in a haughty tone.

"You remember Isaac, don't you Freda?" Margaret asked.

"No, I don't."

Freda remembered. Isaac worked as a porter for the railroad, which was a decent job for a colored man back then. She ran after him, but he was never interested in her. He thought that she was too stuck up for him.

"Anyway," Margaret continued. "Isaac, when he was in town, and a few of us used to get together some Saturday afternoons. On one of his trips to New York, he brought back two Negro newspapers. Back in Morgan City, Negroes could hardly read. So I was excited to see that Negroes had their own newspapers! The articles were exciting, too. That Harlem was the place to be.

"I told Martha about it. She was skeptical. We prayed and asked the Lord to guide us. The next week, Martha's boss, Mrs. Barlow, got us jobs with one of her friends in New York."

"Y'all cleaned them white folks' houses, heh?" Freda asked. She caught everyone's attention. If their looks could talk, they would probably have said something like, *Shut up, bitch!*

"Well, yes," Margaret started again. "That's all we knew how to do."

"Well, Freda," Arthur, Jr. started. "Margaret started as a domestic some years ago. My mother worked as a domestic. I even did odd jobs as a janitor while I was in college for extra money. But you know, now our family has three domestics to take care of us!"

"We met some other domestics who had arrived in New York maybe a few months earlier than we did," Margaret continued. "They showed us the ropes, so to say. They showed us where to shop, where to go to church, where to go out."

"Good girls not 'posed to be going out nowhere," Freda commented. "What y'all do when y'all went out anyhow?"

"Well, we talked and exchanged ideas, mostly."

"What kind of ideas?" Freda asked.

"Our dreams, our aspirations."

"You mean y'all talked 'bout what y'all dreamt 'bout at night?" Freda asked further, as the entire Youngblood family laughed heartily, Ms. Mabel almost in tears.

"No. Our goals. What we wanted to do with our lives," Margaret explained. "Martha and I were surrounded by articulate professionals. Doctors, lawyers, teachers, poets. We felt out-of-place and almost decided to go back to the South. We prayed about it and asked the Lord to guide us. Then we realized that everyone was so welcoming, so helpful, so down to earth. Negroes really stuck together and helped each other in the North.

"We met an older lady, a schoolteacher by the name of Mrs. Bailey, from church. She took us under her wing, so to say. She took time to teach us how to speak and write correctly, and encouraged us to further ourselves. Martha and I were tired of feeling bad about ourselves. So we enrolled in school."

"All the pretty girls back home didn't have to worry 'bout no ed'cation or working," Freda started. "We knowed that we would have husbands to take care o' us."

"So, where did you get educated and work?" Pearl-Elizabeth asked Freda, who just rolled her eyes.

"Girl, hush up!" Ms. Mabel told Pearl-Elizabeth, almost bursting out in laughter. "Go on, finish yo' story, Margaret."

"I went to business school at night, while I worked for Mrs. Andrews during the day. I learned to be a secretary, and it took almost two years. I finished in 1922. They taught us how to speak and write correct English, typing, shorthand, how to dress like a professional, how to answer the phone, and carry ourselves like ladies.

"Martha liked the way the more affluent Negro women looked, so she decided to study cosmetology. She learned about makeup, hair, nails, skin, and even feet. In fact, if it wasn't for Martha, I wouldn't have met Arthur.

"Martha got a job at the Cotton Gin as a makeup girl. She made sure that all of the entertainers looked their best."

"Cotton Gin," Freda asked. "What that is? Where people go to pick cotton?"

"No, no, you silly woman!" Arthur, Jr. laughed. "It was a classy nightclub where people went for entertainment. It had live entertainment. Bands like Duke Ellington and Cab Calloway performed."

"Who?" Freda asked, revealing the fact that she hardly ever listened to the radio.

"Duke Ellington and Cab Calloway. You have heard of them, haven't you?" Arthur, Jr. asked.

Freda gave a blank stare.

"I was new to town from Meharry, with my colleague, Dr. Jude Wilson and his wife, Rebecca. Margaret was sitting there, front and center. She looked beautiful in that red, shimmering dress. Her hair was done in Marcel waves."

"Her hair was what?" Freda asked.

"You have never seen Marcel waves?" Pearl-Elizabeth asked.

"It's the way Mother Ruby used to wear her hair befo' the Depression," Ms. Mabel interjected.

"Oh," Freda said.

"Margaret looked so beautiful. I wondered why she was alone. At first I thought that she was of the evening, if you know what I mean. But, I had to find out."

"Martha always got me tickets and a good table at the Cotton Gin," Margaret started. "Sometimes my friends came with me. Sometimes they didn't. Because of Martha, I knew most of the regulars anyway. I didn't care what people thought. My sister needed my support. She was the only brown-skinned girl in that job and the others gave her a hard time. Just knowing that I was there, she told me, was comforting. That's one thing I've learned. You have to always please yourself.

Pleasing other people, or trying to worry about what other people think, will drive you crazy!

"Besides, I worked as a secretary for this colored insurance company. They worked me really hard, too. I wanted to be entertained, so I went to please myself. The music, the acts, and the food were all really, really good. Besides, people up North were so busy having a good time that they didn't pay attention to what anybody else was doing."

"I'm glad that you didn't worry about what other people thought," Arthur, Jr. started as he looked into Margaret's eyes. "Because I never would have met you," he said as he sucked her fingers and let out a sly, playful laugh. Margaret giggled like a young, innocent school girl.

As Ray watched Arthur flirt with his wife, he briefly imagined himself licking Margaret's fingers, then working his way to every nook and cranny of her luscious body.

"When y'all got married?" Freda asked as she rolled her eyes at the frisky couple.

"Well," Margaret started, as Arthur stopped his intense teasing. "In December, 1924."

"When y'all meet?" Freda asked.

"In 1923." Margaret answered.

"Y'all kept company a long time. What took y'all so long? You was already a old maid!"

Arthur, Jr. laughed, as the other dinner guests looked at Freda in disgust. Ms. Mabel especially was very annoyed.

"She played hard to get," Arthur, Jr. laughed. "I liked having a challenge. There were so many women following me around with shovels and just threw themselves on me." He glanced at Pearl-Elizabeth for a few seconds and said, "To me, that's not dignified for a woman to chase a man. The more Margaret resisted, the more I pursued.

"Besides, Margaret had a strong sense of confidence. She moved there from the South, furthered her education, improved herself. Sure she started off as a domestic, but ended up working as a secretary for one of the most prestigious insurance companies in New York. That takes a strong woman! I admired her. And still do.

"As a doctor, I entertain a lot. I needed a mature woman who could rub elbows with the elite. One who takes pride in her appearance. One who is classy. One who could run the office of my medical practice while I tend to patients. That would be Margaret."

Ray thought that he should have married Margaret instead of

Freda. He realized that his wife was then, and had always been, an embarrassment to him.

"So, how did y'all wind up in Chicago?" Freda asked.

"You sho' is nosy, Freda," Ms. Mabel commented.

"That's perfectly all right, mother," Arthur, Jr. assured. "Right before the war, the colleague I told you about before, Dr. Jude Wilson's father passed away. You see, he helped his father in the practice, which was then his responsibility. He had no brothers who had attended medical school and needed someone to assist him. Quite naturally, he chose me."

Pearl-Elizabeth cringed.

"I had been on staff at the Negro hospital in Harlem on Lenox Avenue for some time. But the thought of having my own practice was quite appealing. So I accepted his offer and have not looked back since that time."

Arthur and Margaret looked briefly at each other, as Pearl-Elizabeth cringed once more.

"What happened to momma?" Freda asked.

"I got a grandmomma?" Delores was excited.

"Well," Margaret started as she bowed her head. "Momma passed to the other side on June 10, 1926."

"Hey, that's my birthday!" Delores informed the room.

"What happened?" Freda asked.

"She had the wasting sickness. We found out a few months before by Mr. Willie, who still worked the railroads. He told Martha and me that we should go see about our mother."

"What happened to Martha? I bet she not married, heh? I bet her husband done left her wit' a house full of chil'ren, heh?" Freda asked, as she rolled her eyes at Margaret. She hoped that something awful had happened to Martha, too, or that she had a completely miserable life.

"Well, Martha married Isaac in 1928. About a year after we moved to Harlem, Isaac decided to do the same. So he quit the railroad and worked as a janitor for one of the colored mortuaries. He was so fascinated by his job that he decided to go to school to be a mortician.

"Right before the war, Isaac and Martha opened their own mortuary. Isaac does the embalming. Martha dresses the bodies. She does their hair, fingertips, makeup, whatever the family wants."

"That's nasty!" Freda yelled. "What she want be foolin' 'round with them dead bodies fo' anyhow?"

"Did you know that Ethel's husband is in the war?" Ms. Mabel pointed out to Arthur and Margaret.

"He must be a brave man," Arthur, Jr. started. "You must be proud."

"Yes. Yes, I am." Ethel smiled with pride. "Last I heard he was in Paris, France."

"That's a beautiful city," Margaret told her.

"How you know?" Freda asked. "You ever been there?"

"Why, yes. Yes we have," Arthur, Jr. bragged. "We went there right before Pearl-Elizabeth was born and had a wonderful time."

"Yes, we sure did, Arthur," Margaret agreed. "The people were so warm and friendly. No one seemed to care that we were Negroes."

"We visited the Louvre, the Eiffel Tower, and just had a wonderful time walking down the street."

"You went to what?" Freda asked. "What's a Love or a Fifer Tower?"

"The Louvre is a classic French museum. The Eiffel Tower is a beautiful monument," Ethel informed Freda.

"How you know that, Ethel?" Freda asked.

"Irving sent postcards."

"Who's Irving?" Margaret asked.

"He my husband."

"When the last time you got one of them there postcards anyhow?" Freda demanded.

"A couple months. I don't know," Ethel answered.

"You ain't got no letters from him in a real long time. That gotta mean he been killed," Freda told Ethel. "He must be dead."

"That don't mean nothing," Ms. Mabel interjected.

"He dead! Dead! Dead, dead, dead!" Freda shouted to Ms. Mabel, as she banged her fist on the table. "Ain't nothin' mo' to talk 'bout! Irving is dead! Killed in war! Dead!"

No one knew how to respond to Freda's comments. The next 15 minutes were silent while everyone finished dinner.

***

"Mother, you outdid yourself with that meal!"

"Now, I can't take all the credit. Ethel and Delores helped, too," Ms. Mabel told him. "Now y'all go on in the parlor, while I clear up in here."

Ethel was the first to volunteer to help Ms. Mabel clear the table and wrap leftovers. Delores and Fred followed suit. The Youngbloods went into the parlor.

"We better be gettin' on home," Freda announced.

"It was nice meeting y'all," Ray told the Youngbloods, as they left through the front door.

***

It was twilight, the coolest, gentlest part of a New Orleans summer day, as Ray and Freda began their walk home. The full moon was shining brightly above, almost as if to guide them safely up the street.

"You heard how proper they tried to talk? Who they think they is?" Freda commented. In the distance she saw a dark figure walking toward them.

"Shut the fuck up, Freda!" Ray shouted at the top of his lungs, which signaled a symphony of barking neighborhood dogs. He punched Freda in the face and commenced to drag her by the collar. Ray hastened his pace as they neared the house. A long trail of tiny blood droplets was left behind.

The same dark figure that Freda saw a few seconds before briefly flashed to her right across the street, as though it was watching her. She tried to cry for help, but Ray's strong hand was secured tightly around her frail throat.

Ray dragged Freda up the porch steps and across the porch. As he opened the front door, he pushed her across the living-room and against the back wall. Ray retrieved an old cat-o'-nine-tails from the shed a few days earlier and had been keeping it under the bed. He raised it above his head.

"No, Ray! No. No!" Freda pleaded, tears streamed profusely down her cheeks.

Freda felt hatred emanating from his soul as she stared deep, deep into his dark, sinister eyes. It was hot, but an arctic chill filled the room that penetrated down to her bones. All was dark, except for the moonlight that poured through the venetian blinds. Freda caught a glimpse of the dark figure just behind Ray and to his left. It faded as quickly as it had appeared.

Ray lowered his arm and went into the bathroom and took the cat-o'-nine-tails with him. Freda sat alone on the living-room floor, huddled against the wall, and shook like a leaf in the autumn breeze, too afraid to move.

Chapter 12.
Fond Farewell

"Hello!" Margaret yelled through the front door. "Hello, anybody home?"

The door was wide open, so she decided to walk in. She went as far as the back door when she saw Ray coming out of the shed.

"You sho' looking mighty good, with yo' fine self. You sho' do take good care o' yo'self," Ray told Margaret as he walked through the back door. "Freda still sleeping," Ray said. "She never get up befo' ten in the morning."

Freda walked out of the bathroom as Ray was speaking. She was surprised and embarrassed to see her sister standing there.

"Lord, have mercy!" Margaret said to herself when she saw Freda.

Freda's left eye was blackened and almost closed. Her lips were larger than normal, like they had been busted open. The entire left side of her face was red and purple. Her neck looked as though she had been hanging from a gallows. The pink house coat she wore had tiny holes all about that exposed her bare, ashy flesh. Her bare feet were scaly, with large, hard corns on each digit. She held her head down in shame as Margaret looked at her with a deep sense of pity.

"I came to tell y'all that we're leaving this afternoon."

"Y'all leaving today?" Ray was surprised. "Y'all just got here yesterday. Y'all not gone go on Dryades Street or the French Quarters?"

Margaret handed Ray a piece of paper. "That's our address and Martha's address."

"That's right. Give it to me. Freda can't read," Ray said. "Martha look as fine as you?"

Margaret became a bit uncomfortable and ignored his question.

"I have to go now. Please be sure to write."

Freda was standing in the middle of the hallway, and partially blocked the path that led to the front door, but Margaret managed to squeeze her way through the hallway. Freda peeked up for a second, long enough to catch a remorseful backward glance from Margaret.

"Write?" Ray teased. "How 'bout if I come all the way up to Chicago to see you?"

***

Arthur, Jr. went to see Fred at his new row apartment. It was sparsely furnished, but neat. Through the tiny living room was the bedroom. Off the side of the kitchen was the bathroom, which was barely large enough to accommodate the large antique tub and commode. He was just about to sit down and have his breakfast of grits and fried liver.

"Can I get you something?" Fred asked. "I guess I can call you Uncle Arthur, right?"

Arthur, Jr. laughed. "Yes. Yes, son, you can," he assured. "You have any coffee?"

"Yes, sir. I just got through making a pot of chicory."

"Ummm. Good. Give it to me au lait style."

"Oh, the way Ms. Mabel like it?"

"Yes, son. I think I'll have some of the grits and liver, too. I haven't had that in years!"

"Yes, sir!"

Arthur, Jr. tasted a few bites. "Ummm. This is almost as good as my momma's."

"Who you think taught me how to make grits and liver?"

Fred mixed heavy cream and sugar in the chicory for both of them.

"Well, Fred. I just came to tell you that we're leaving this afternoon. It was a pleasure meeting you." He handed him a piece of paper. "Here's our address and the address of your Aunt Martha. Please feel free to write or visit. We are family and should act like one."

"Y'all leaving today? Y'all just got here yesterday!"

"Well, son…" Arthur shrugged his shoulders.

"I hope y'all not leaving 'cause o' my momma. I 'pologize fo' her. She can't he'p herself sometimes."

"No, no, son," Arthur, Jr. laughed. "She's the least of my worries."

"I ain't knowed my momma had no sisters. That was a shock to me and my sister Delores both."

"Well. That's the past, son. We need to put all that behind us and move forward as a family," Arthur, Jr. insisted. "I hear you're working at the shipyards. Is that true?"

"Yes. Yes I do. It's a good job for a colored man."

"Do you like it? I hear it's hard to get on at the shipyards. You must be something else."

"Yes. I also deliver ice two mornings a week fo' extra money. Some day I'm gone get married and have chil'ren, and I need to provide for my family. Some of them other jobs don't pay too good."

"You got a good head on your shoulders, Fred. Keep it up."

"Yes, sir!"

"It's a pity that your father can't see your talent. I bet you could run that refinishing shop better than anybody."

Ms. Mabel musta told him 'bout daddy and the shop, Fred thought to himself.

"You remind me of my father," Arthur, Jr. commented.

"I do?"

"Yes. He was what they call a go-getter. He knew what he wanted and then went and got it."

"Ms. Mabel like that, too."

"Yes. My mother is quite a woman. I feel blessed to have parents like I did."

Fred thought to himself, *I wished I was born to Ms. Mabel family.*

"My father was a full-blooded Choctaw Indian. He was bold and cocky and didn't take anything off of nobody."

"What happened to him?" Fred asked.

"He was just old. He was much, much older than my mother. By over 15 years I believe. But you never would have known it. He was tall, strong, and confident. He passed right after I finished Meharry. He was proud to see all his children graduate from college, though."

"How he meet Ms. Mabel?"

"They met down in Bayou country in southern Louisiana around 1890 and got married the next year. Momma was 18 and he was 33. He was a blacksmith before he met momma and made a real good living. Then, he became a longshoreman and had the blacksmith shop on the side.

"He was a smart man and knew ways to make money. I remember momma making hard cider and liquor from potato skins and other fruits and vegetables. They used to sell this huge grape brick in some stores. We children used to soak it in large kettles of water and let it set for over a month. Then we put it into bottles that momma sterilized and stored it in the shed out back. People used to buy that stuff like crazy! I'm telling you!

"Dad had never been married, and decided that it was time for him to settle down. And he did. We were stepladder children."

"What's that?" Fred asked.

"We were all one year apart," Arthur, Jr. explained. "I was born in 1893, my sister, Agnes, in 1894, and my baby sister, Augustine, in 1895. Neither of them is married."

"Why not? They gone be lonely old ladies. Spinsters."

"They went through a great deal to finish their education and don't want to give it up to get married. Besides, they think all men are evil and don't want to be bothered."

"That's somethin' else."

"You're a big, young man, Fred. You must be over six-four. I bet you weigh over 200 pounds."

"I'm six-fo' and 250," Fred answered proudly.

"I bet you don't take anything off of anybody, do you?"

"No, sir!" Fred answered proudly. "Don't nobody mess wit' me 'cause I'm so big."

"If you ever want to make extra money, Fred..." Arthur, Jr. said as he handed him a small bag. "...the key is to work smarter, not harder."

"Yes, sir."

"You can sell these. I can get more if you like. A colleague of mine, George Pickens, lives here in town and can help you out."

"I know him. His daddy come by the shop. He just finished medical school and started he'ping his daddy out in his practice. They doctor's office is 'cross the river in the Seventh Ward."

"Yes, that's him."

"How you know him?"

"The old alumni make a point of getting to know the new alumni."

Fred gave him a blank stare.

"Alumni are students who graduated from a school. I'm an older alumnus because I finished Meharry in 1918. George is a new alumnus because he graduated in 1944," Arthur, Jr. explained.

"Oh," Fred said as he nodded his head.

"Well, he can get you more. Just tell him who you are, and he'll take care of you. He owns that new joint in the Ninth Ward. The Pixie."

"Yeah," Fred started. "Some of the fellas at work be talking 'bout it. I ain't knowed he owned that."

"You ought to go there sometimes. He'll pay big money for a big man like you to keep trouble away, if you know what I mean."

Fred looked in the bag and saw what appeared to be pieces of tissue paper and dried grass.

"Who gone buy this stuff?"

Arthur, Jr. expertly rolled one joint and asked Fred to do the same.

Arthur, Jr. held his head back, lit the joint, and playfully exhaled three circles of smoke as he stretched his arms across his chair. "Here," he urged Fred. "Do this." He demonstrated to him how to inhale. Fred followed suit.

He then looked Fred straight in the eyes. "You sell what Pickens gives you and give him what's due. You keep the rest. It's as simple as that."

"This stuff make me feel good. What kind of cigarettes these is?"

"The funny kind, if you know what I mean. Reefer." He got really close to Fred and looked him straight in the eyes. He told him in a firm voice, "Be careful who you smoke this around and who you tell about it. Do you understand me, son?"

"Yes, sir!"

"Well, Fred. I had better be going." Arthur took one final drag to finish his joint before he started for the door.

"Remember what I told you," Arthur said from the doorstep. "Give Pickens his share and keep the rest."

"Yes, sir!"

"Don't forget to write. You got that?"

"Yes, sir!"

Chapter 13.
The Enlightening

That Saturday afternoon was nice and sunny. Ms. Mabel prepared beignets and New Orleans-style tea, as she, Margaret, and Ethel sat around the kitchen table. Fred and Delores were sitting on the back porch taking in the fresh air. They volunteered to tend to Ms. Mabel's garden out back and were finished, but pretended not to be in order to eavesdrop on their conversation.

***

Don't look at me like that. Like you don't know what New Orleans-style tea is. That's right, you don't know anything about tea since you never really cooked and ate out a lot. It's tea served with cream and sugar. Now, you got it. Well, anyway.

***

"This is a surprise," Ethel started. "Freda never mentioned having no family. She not the reason y'all leaving so soon, heh?"

"No, no," Margaret assured. "She's the least of my worries."

Ethel noticed how Ms. Mabel and Margaret glanced at each other in a curious way.

"I 'pologize for the way Freda acted yesterday, Margaret. She always act real rude to people," Ms. Mabel told her.

"That's okay, mother, she was always like that. I guess it's the way our mother and the townspeople spoiled her rotten."

"I went to say good-bye to her and Ray this morning, but look like she'd been beaten. I didn't know that Ray was that kind of a man. How long has this been going on?" Margaret asked.

Ms. Mabel and Ethel looked at each other in amazement. Fred and Delores were surprised, too.

"I don't know nothin' 'bout that," Ms. Mabel said.

"I don't either. This the first I'm hearing it," Ethel told her.

"She can vex his nerves. I guess he just tired of it," Ms. Mabel said.

"You sho'?" Ethel asked Margaret.

"Yes," Margaret informed her.

"Let's stay out o' other folks bid'ness," Ms. Mabel warned.

"You been calling Ms. Mabel mother," Ethel observed.

"Well, she is like a mother to me."

"How 'bout yo' own momma?" Ethel realized her blunder. "Oh, I'm sorry."

"That's all right," Margaret comforted.

"Didn't yo' momma visit y'all in New York?" Ms. Mabel asked.

"Yes, mother. She did. It was right after Mr. Willie told us 'bout her being sick," Margaret started.

"Mr. Willie sneaked momma on the train one day. She was sick, but couldn't wait to see us. I was worried because it was February and cold as heck. Too cold for a sickly, old woman.

"When Martha and I greeted her at the train station late that Sunday night, we hugged each other like nobody's business. We were all filled with joy until we cried all the way to our brownstone apartment. The cab driver thought that we had just returned from a funeral and didn't charge us a cent for the fare.

"The next day, momma, Martha, and I caught the subway for the fun of it. Momma was so tickled about riding the subway that we decided to ride wherever it could take us. We walked around the city. She was amazed by the big buildings and all the well-to-do colored folk.

"My boss, Mr. Willis, let me have a few days off with pay after I explained to him that my momma was coming to town. The three of us went by my job. The insurance company owned a small, four-story, red-brick building in the heart of Harlem. The inside walls were all white, almost like a hospital, and the floors were a shiny, white marble. Momma was in awe when she saw all the colored people dressed in business suits and high heels working in the office, walking about carrying briefcases.

"Momma had never seen, or even heard of, an elevator. When we got on, she was amazed by Mr. Smith, the elevator man, when he asked everybody for their floor. She felt like a queen having her every need met.

"She saw where I sat, right in front of Mr. Willis's office. Momma saw my typewriter, my nice mahogany desk, my phone, my nameplate, and other things I needed to take care of Mr. Willis. Momma was excited to know that I was a big-time secretary, as she called it. She met Mr. Willis and some of the other people in the office. He told momma, 'Your girl, Margaret, takes real, real, good care of me. I'm lost today without her.'

"Mr. Willis was one of the founders of the company. I got the job because his wife and the wife of another one of the founders were there when I applied. Mrs. Willis told her friend, 'I feel safe with her. Ralph would never, ever be interested in her in a million years. She's so black and ugly!' And she saw to it that I got the job."

"That was a real ugly thing fo' her to say!" Ethel commented. "You real pretty!"

"Thank you. But, I didn't care," Margaret continued. "I got used to it growing up in Morgan City. I just wanted to be a secretary and make a decent living because I thought that I would never get married."

"Why not?" Ethel asked.

Margaret put her head down for a moment. "Well," she started. "I was over 20. And ... well ... if you were over 20, then well ...

"Anyway. Arthur was tending to patients at the hospital and couldn't get away. But that didn't stop our fun! No, siree! We went shopping and I bought her a few new pieces of clothes. Then, we went to our apartment to rest up.

"Later that night, we went to visit Martha at work backstage. She was so excited to meet the performers, and was amazed by how Martha dolled them up. 'Chil', you sho' is somethin' else!' she told Martha.

"We went out front to our favorite table. Arthur joined us later in the evening, after he finished at the hospital. We had a nice steak dinner and champagne. When the band started playing, momma even got out on the dance floor and practically danced all night! She was like a different person. The day before, she looked sickly and weak. But that night! That night she had a special glow about her. It was like momma, Martha, and I had a special bond between us. We were never close before, but I thought that things would be different from then on. I guess the champagne, partying, and bright lights of the big city could make the worst of enemies become friends. That's why I loved Harlem so much."

"So, y'all and y'all momma wasn't close befo'?" Ethel asked. "I can't even 'magine not being close to my momma. But, I'm glad y'all got to be close, though."

Margaret put her head down after gulping some tea. "Well, we didn't."

"I thought y'all made up?" Ms. Mabel asked.

"Well, yes. Sort of," Margaret continued. "Martha, Isaac, Arthur, and I saw her off to the train station later in the week. She still had that glow. We promised to write and keep in touch.

"Just before she boarded the train she said, 'Now you take good care o' my grandbaby.' We just laughed and thought she was just being funny. Then she asked Martha and me if we'd heard from Freda. Neither one of us had. God forgive me, but we were so busy getting on with our lives in Harlem that we completely forgot about the South, including our momma. She seemed disappointed, and her glow wasn't quite as bright when she waved to us as the train left.

"Over the next few months we wrote to each other almost every week and sent money back. In December, after Arthur, III was born, we sent a picture. Then, her letters stopped. But we continued to write and send money anyway. Mr. Willie caught up to me one day and urged Martha and me to visit home. He told us that our momma was really sick and was asking for us.

"Arthur, Isaac, and Martha were all able to get off from work for a while to go to Morgan City. I was home tending to the baby and quit work, so leaving was no problem for me. So we caught the first train. Arthur, III was a baby, so we left him with Mrs. Bailey back in Harlem. I was expecting again and wasn't up for the long train ride. Mr. Willie convinced us to go by letting us ride the train to Morgan City free.

"It seemed like it took forever for that train to get to Morgan City. We got to see the countryside again, which we enjoyed for the first time since we left the South. All the trees were just so pretty.

"When we got there, everything looked pretty much the same. Mother Esther was by momma's bedside, tending to her every need. 'Yo' chil'ren here, Pearl,' Mother Esther told momma. 'Freda! Freda! Is that you, chil'?' she asked over and over again.

"Mother Esther took us to the other room and explained that she had the wasting sickness. That she was holding on to life by a thread, waiting to see her children.

"Mother Esther went on to say, 'She lonely. The town folk don't speak to her. Since y'all left, they accused her of running her chil'ren away. She be made fun of all the time. People can be cruel. Some said she was cursed and ain't been by to see her since she been sick.'

'What happened to Freda, Mother Esther?' I asked.

'She and her new husband snuck out o' town the day they got married. While yo' momma and Sister Joyce was cleaning the church, Freda and her husband was on they way out o' town. She ain't knowed it yet until a few days later when somebody told her that they packed they things and left town. Don't feel guilty or sorry for her. She brought it on herse'f.'

"Mother Esther went back into the room with momma. I heard her say, 'Margaret and Martha is here with they husbands. They came a long way.' Momma shouted at her, 'I don't want see no Margaret or no Martha. I wants my baby, Freda!' Mother Esther became angry, 'You gots to make yo' peace wit' them like I done told you! Freda can't he'p ya.' Momma still kept asking for Freda. 'Freda, my baby, Freda!'

"Mother Esther came out and asked Martha and me to come in and see momma.

'Martha? Margaret?' Momma called. We stood by her side. 'I'm sorry for the way I treated y'all. I had no bid'ness making y'all do y'all sister chores. I ain't do her no favors either by not makin' her fend fo' herse'f.

'I had no bid'ness making y'all feel like nothin'. It's my fault y'all run way to New York. If I would o' loved y'all like a real momma, y'all would still be right here wit' me. I shouldna o' whipped y'all like I did all the time. I shouldna o' call y'all names like ugly and black and taw baby. Y'all got feelings and should o' been loved by yo' momma.

'I'm proud o' y'all. Margaret, you a big-time sec'tary married to a big-time doctor. Too bad I ain't gone be 'round to see my grandbabies. And you, Martha, you hobnob with movie stars and 'bout to be married to a good man.

'I'm so sorry. It's too late. I'm paying fo' it now. Please. Please forgive! I know I been a bad momma. Be better mommas than I was. I been a bad 'xample. All three o' y'all girls gots diff'rent daddies. The only one I know fo' sho' is Freda daddy 'cause out all o' mens I been messin' wit', he was the only white one. Don't go messin' wit' a lot o' mens. Know who y'all babies daddies is. Y'all stay married and be good to y'all husbands and chil'ren. Don't be like me. Ain't never been married and ain't got nothin' or nobody. But, please forgive me!'

"She cried and cried. Mother Esther stayed by her side. Martha said, 'We been forgave you, momma.' Momma sighed with relief when she heard those words.

"We sat by her side and both took her hand. She looked us straight in the eyes and said, 'Y'all forgive Freda, 'specially you, Margaret. Tell Freda to stop. She don't know what she messin' with and...' She took her last breath before she could finish. She tried to get the words out, but couldn't. I guess she told us what she needed to free her soul. Hearing those words from our momma was like a burden was lifted. Martha and I felt so much better about momma and about ourselves.

"Mother Esther insisted on burying momma in the next few days. So we got rooms at the motel down the street. She handled all the arrangements for us. We didn't know where to find Freda for services. The reverend refused to pass momma through the church and the colored funeral home refused, too. So Mother Esther performed a ceremony right in the spot where momma passed over to the other side, in the same position, wearing the same clothes. She sprinkled some stuff on momma's body to keep it from smelling, and chanted over the body. We wanted to make her look pretty, but Mother Esther told us not to touch the body.

"No one came inside to view the body, but the nosy neighbors just looked on from the outside. The next day, the body and Mother Esther were both gone. 'Til this day, we don't know what happened to the body or Mother Esther.

"As we were leaving for the train someone shouted, 'Y'all outta be glad y'all left the South. Ain't nothin' here noway.' Someone else shouted, 'That's good Pearl dead!'

"God forgive me, but the way my momma treated Martha and me helped us to be independent and have the lives that we have today. I asked God to forgive Freda for what she did. I guess it was stealing Ray. But I thank her. If I would have married Ray or someone like him, I would probably have Freda's life. God forgive me."

"It ain't bothered y'all that she was still wanting to see Freda and not y'all?"

"No. We felt sorry for her," Margaret explained. "She had two daughters who were right there, but wanted the one who wasn't. What was strange, though, is that she knew I was pregnant before I did."

Ms. Mabel then understood more about Freda and why she never did much for herself or family. Ethel and Ms. Mabel, as well as Fred and Delores, who were listening from the back porch, lost even more respect for Freda.

"We were glad to give her pleasure the last few months of her life. At first, we felt sorry for leaving her after Freda had gone, and no one heard from her. But, like Mother Esther said, she brought it on herself."

"I remember what my momma used to always say," Ms. Mabel started. "That you gots to be careful how you treat people. What you do or say to people, whether it be good or bad, come back to you or somebody close to you, seven times over."

Chapter 14.
The Lonely Road

"Delores!" Freda yelled as she knocked on Ms. Mabel's door.

"What's wrong, Freda?" Ms. Mabel asked.

"Nothing," Freda answered. "I need Delores, that's all."

Delores was in the kitchen with Pearl-Elizabeth chatting and paring apples for the pies for Thanksgiving dinner. She spent a lot of time with her newly found cousin. They had a great deal of catching up to do.

Delores walked with her mother to the street. Freda rolled her eyes the whole way. Ms. Mabel watched from the porch.

"I done told you not to be hangin' 'round no Pearl-Elizabeth. That girl is bad news!" Freda whispered in a stern voice.

"But, ma," Delores protested. "She my cousin."

"Gal, you do what I done told you!" Freda warned. "Now go on home."

"I got to get somethin' from Ms. Mabel house," Delores said.

"All right. But get on home after you get what you left by Ms. Mabel. You be spending too much time by Ms. Mabel anyway. Ain't they things you should be doin' at home?"

Freda started back down the street. Delores returned to paring apples and conversation with Pearl-Elizabeth.

***

It was the day before Thanksgiving. The past few holiday seasons were special to Ms. Mabel. She invited what she called her "second family" over for dinner. Delores and Ethel helped to cook, and Fred took care of any heavy work, like putting up decorations. Ray and Freda came for the food. Now that Pearl-Elizabeth had been staying with her for the past five months, it would be like having a complete family again.

Freda really enjoyed that time of year because it gave her the sense of family that she never had. Even though she always gossiped and had something mean to say, they just expected her to be that way. The November air always sent a feeling of peace throughout the neighborhood. Well, except that year anyway.

Mr. Miller's youngest son, Gerald, owned the neighborhood store. He and his wife, Betsy, ran the shop downstairs and lived on the second level.

Gerald was about 35, but his thick, brown, curly mane had already begun to bald in the center. He was kind of chunky with a large, gutsy beer belly.

His wife, Betsy, looked as though a good wind could have blown her away. She was petite and couldn't have weighed more than 95 pounds. Her thick, auburn locks and green eyes made her skin appear as pale as snow. Tiny freckles covered most of her face.

The store was painted a pale orange, with Coca-Cola advertisements on the side facing Teche Street. The entire front was glass. Two cement steps led to a slab out front. Directly overhead was an orange-and-white-striped awning that shielded customers from the hot sun or rain when they stopped to gossip.

"That girl is just too fast! That's good fo' her that her maw and paw put her out. Ms. Mabel oughta put her out, too," Freda told Ethel and the ladies who were standing outside relaxing, groceries in strollers, ready to pull home. "She needs to learn to keep her legs closed!"

Pearl-Elizabeth walked right up to Freda and stood as close as her protruding belly would allow her to get. "I know you're not talking about me, Aunt Freda, you old stinking battle-ax!"

"Don't call me no Aunt Freda! You ain't my niece! You ain't got no manners! You needs to 'spect yo' elders. You hot momma!" Freda shouted.

Everyone in the store stopped what they were doing and quickly went outside. No one else said anything. Ethel and one of the onlookers went to get Ms. Mabel to the scene.

"You ain't married and have the nerve to come to New Orleans to have that bastard chil'. That's a disgrace. In my day, we would o' ..."

"You need to shut your ass up! You don't have room to talk," Pearl-Elizabeth started. "My momma, Aunt Martha, and you, Aunt Freda, all have different daddies. Neither one of you know who your daddy is."

"Gal, shut yo' mouth befo' I shut it fo' you!"

"Your daddy was a married white man, and my grandmomma was his whore. You're a bastard just like my momma and Aunt Martha!"

"You needs to shut yo' black ass up. I don't see how you got preg'nant anyhow. You black as tar. Don't no man want no woman as black as you!"

"You so nasty that your husband doesn't even come home. He stays out all weekend because he fucks everybody but you! You need to go and take a good bath with some lye soap! And you need to go brush that green stuff off of your teeth! Then, he may want to fuck you, too!"

The crowd started to laugh. Freda slapped Pearl-Elizabeth in the face. Pearl-Elizabeth rolled her fists and punched Freda in the nose with a right, followed by a quick left. She took Freda by the hair and started to throw her face into the glass panels in front of the store, but Mr. Miller grabbed Pearl-Elizabeth to calm her.

"What's going on here?" Ms. Mabel asked.

"Yo' grandchil' need to learn to 'spect her elders."

"She was messin' with yo' baby, Ms. Mabel," an older woman yelled from the crowd.

"Yep!" another woman started. "She called yo' baby a bastard and a 'ho'."

"They lying, Ms. Mabel," Freda protested.

Ms. Mabel looked Freda straight in the eyes. "What did you say to Pearl-Elizabeth?"

Freda looked at Ms. Mabel, as blood streamed from her nose.

"I ain't gone ask you no mo'!" Ms. Mabel insisted. "What did you say to Pearl-Elizabeth?"

"Nothin'," Freda said.

"She lying," the crowd yelled.

"She called yo' baby a 'ho'," an old man yelled.

"Your baby was minding her own business, getting what you sent her for," Gerald Miller started. "Then, Freda here started messing with her."

"Yeah!" the crowd yelled.

"Freda," Betsy started in that squeaky voice. "You should know better than to hit a pregnant woman! Shame on you!"

"That's right! She shouldn't be hitting nobody preg'nant no way!" someone yelled from the crowd.

"That's right!" the crowd yelled.

Ms. Mabel got really close to Freda and looked her straight in the eyes. "You better be careful what you say to people, you hear me, gal? Don't you never, ever step foot in my yard again. You not welcomed in my home no mo'! Do you understand me!"

Freda nodded as tears streamed from her eyes. The crowd looked at her with hate as she stumbled home.

"Lord, so help me Jesus! I will kill you deader than dead if I catch you, or even hear about you messin' with me or my family again!! You got that?" Ms. Mabel shouted to Freda.

***

Ms. Mabel always got an early start on the holiday season. Fred was busy putting up Christmas decorations and the tree. Delores had just completed peeling and veining the last of a huge pile of jumbo shrimp for Ms. Mabel's traditional Thanksgiving dinner gumbo the next day.

"Delores and Fred, y'all need to go on home," Ms. Mabel said as she, Pearl-Elizabeth, and Ethel walked through the kitchen door. She was very agitated. Fred and Delores had never seen her like that before.

"We ain't finished yet, Ms. Mabel," Delores told her as she added chopped celery and parsley to a large pot of crabs that rapidly boiled in a fragrant broth of cayenne pepper and bay leaves.

"I ain't gone tell y'all no mo'!" she told them. "Y'all go on home like I done told y'all! Me, Ethel, and Pearl-Elizabeth can take it from here."

"Well," Delores started, "we could finish tomorrow."

"Y'all can stay home tomorrow," Ms. Mabel told them.

"But that's Thanksgiving, Ms. Mabel," Fred informed her.

"Like I done said, y'all can stay home tomorrow."

Fred and Delores left, confused as to why Ms. Mabel ran them away.

"What's wrong with Ms. Mabel?" Delores asked Fred.

"I don't know. I hope we ain't did nothin' to 'fend her."

Ethel ran after them before they reached home.

"What's wrong with Ms. Mabel, Ms. Ethel?" Delores asked.

"She had a run-in with y'all's momma," Ethel informed them.

"What happened?" Fred asked.

"Y'all's momma was messin' with Pearl-Elizabeth and they got into a fight."

"You mean a argument, right?" Fred asked.

"No," Ethel continued. "A fight, fight. A fist fight."

"You lying!" Delores exclaimed.

"No. I wish I was lying, but it's the honest-to-goodness truth," Ethel told her.

"Why would momma want to hit somebody pregnant fo' anyway?" Fred asked.

"I don't know. I was there and saw the whole thing," Ethel informed him.

"Well, that's 'tween Ms. Mabel and momma. That don't have nothin' to do with Delores or me."

"That's right," Delores agreed.

***

Delores and Fred got some boxes from the shed. They packed all of Delores's belongings and hauled them over to Fred's apartment. Freda was locked away in her bedroom and Ray was working in the shed.

"What's all this racket?" Ray asked. He noticed that Fred and Delores were packing her things. "Where you think you goin'?"

"I'm goin' over by Fred 'til I find my own place," Delores informed Ray. "I'm workin'. I can take care o' myself. I'm tired of livin' here."

"What brought this on?" Ray asked.

"Ms. Mabel put us out her house. We can't go there no mo'. Not even fo' Thanksgiving dinner," Fred told him.

"Why not?" Ray asked. "What y'all do? Ms. Mabel is good peoples!"

"We ain't do nothin'," Delores explained.

"Well why come y'all can't go there no mo'?" Ray asked.

" 'Cause momma and Pearl-Elizabeth got into a real fist fight, that's why," Fred explained.

"What?" Ray asked in disbelief. "You lying!"

"No I ain't. I wish I was," Fred told Ray.

"Have mercy!" Ray said as he paced the floor. "Freda!" he banged on the bedroom door, almost knocking it in. "Freda get yo' ass out here right now!"

Fred and Delores were startled. They had never seen their father enraged before.

"Freda!" Ray demanded as he banged even harder. "I said get yo' ass out here, woman!"

Freda finally opened the door. Her nose was still bleeding and her left eye was blue. The red pullover sweater she wore was ripped, and her hair was tossed about.

"What's this I hear you fighting with Pearl-Elizabeth?"

"She started," Freda answered. "That girl is bad news. Delores shouldn't be hangin' 'round her."

"You mean to tell me that you hit somebody pregnant?" Ray asked.

"She hit me first," Freda insisted.

"Woman!" Ray shouted at the top of his lungs, as Delores and Fred looked on. "What the fuck you thinkin'? After all Ms. Mabel done did fo' you, and you gone repay her by gettin' into a fist fight wit' her pregnant grandbaby? Woman, what the fuck is wrong with you? You crazy?"

Ray motioned for Fred and Delores to come with him. "Come on, y'all," Ray told them. "Delores, go put yo' stuff back. You ain't goin' nowhere."

"Where we goin'?" Fred asked.

"To 'pologize to Ms. Mabel," Ray answered.

***

Thanksgiving at Ms. Mabel's wasn't as formal that year. It was much more laid-back and relaxed. The scent of fresh cinnamon and chocolate permeated the air. Everybody was laughing and drinking wine, just being themselves. Uninhibited.

After dinner, Ms. Mabel and Delores served fresh walnut brownies and eggnog spiked with brandy in the parlor. Everybody gathered around the fireplace, as the radio played softly in the background. Ms. Mabel, Pearl-Elizabeth, Ethel, Delores, Fred, and Ray. They talked for hours upon hours about everything and anything. A strong sense of family and love was present.

They played endless games of gin, spades, chess and checkers. As the night fell, Ms. Mabel turned off the lights and enjoyed the illumination that the fireplace provided. Ethel and Pearl-Elizabeth made sure that everyone had plenty of eggnog or hot, homemade apple cider. They all gathered together near the large French window in the front of the house, absorbed in each other's company, and admired the stars and moon above.

"This must be the best Thanksgiving I ever had," Ray told Ms. Mabel.

"It seem so different," Delores commented.

"Yeah," everybody agreed.

Just then, they all realized that Freda wasn't there. The negativity that she brought with her always dampened the holiday mood.

"We need to do this mo' often," Fred told them.

"Yeah," they all agreed.

Chapter 15.
The Wedding

Fred had been keeping company with a girl named Shirley Mae Payne, who worked as a waitress in the restaurant near the shipyard. Her chocolate skin was the silkiest you ever wanted to see. She stood about five-six and had long, dark, pressed hair. Her curvy figure and sassy attitude caught Fred's attention. They dated for a year when Fred asked her to marry him. When she accepted, he took her to meet his parents and sister. Delores and Shirley acted like old chums from the get-go.

"Hello, Mr. and Mrs. Marshall. I'm Shirley Payne." She extended her hand. Ray noticed her soft, silky hands and flawless manicure. "I've heard so much about you. It's a pleasure to finally meet you." Her big pearly smile lit the room.

"Why don't you take Miss Payne out on the porch, Delores."

"Yes, momma."

It was the middle of July and hot as heck outside. Freda frowned at the loud laughs coming from the porch.

She seemed so familiar to Ray, but he couldn't figure out where they've met before. That graceful walk, her sweet perfume, and flawless skin. Shirley wore open-toe shoes that showed off her polished toes. He knew only one person with feet that pretty. *That girl sho' remind me of Gloria*, Ray thought.

"That girl is ugly," started Freda, "can't you do better than that?"

"I really likes me a fine, black woman," Fred bragged.

"I know what you mean," Ray said to himself.

"Ain't nothing fine 'bout her."

"Well, momma," Fred got out of his seat, angry at his mother's insensitive comments. "She ain't like you, with your high-yella self. You got yo' pride 'cause you is high-yella. A woman like Shirley got pride 'cause she respect herself, not 'cause she yella."

"Who the hell you think you is? Don't you be talkin' to yo' momma like that, boy! You show some respect! Just 'cause you grown don't mean I can't whup yo' ass!" Ray turned to Freda. "The trouble with you is that you never give nobody a chance. She seem like a mighty fine girl to me."

Fred took a deep breath and walked to the porch, surprised that his daddy stood up for him.

"Let's go, Shirley."

"Y'all ain't even had dinner yet."

"We'll eat later, Delores."

"Baby, what's wrong? "

"We gots to go, Shirley."

They walked down the street to Ms. Mabel's. She was out front planting flowers and stopped as they walked in the yard. Pearl-Elizabeth was sitting on the porch tending to the baby.

"Ms. Mabel, Pearl-Elizabeth, this here Shirley Mae Payne. Ms. Mabel, we gettin' married."

Ms. Mabel stood up. "Well bless yo' heart," she said as she hugged Shirley. "Let me get a look at you." She spread Shirley's arms and looked her up and down. "You sho' is a pretty li'l thing. Fine, too! Look like you gone have some mighty fine babies."

They all laughed. "Why don't y'all come in and I'll fix y'all somethin' to eat."

"That's okay, Ms. Mabel. I gotta get to work soon. I just wanted to stop by and introduce you."

"Ain't you Josephine girl?"

"Yes, Ma'am," Shirley answered.

"I 'member when she married yo' daddy," Ms. Mabel turned to Fred. "You sho' is a lucky man. You better treat her right, you hear me? The Paynes is a good, Christian family."

"Yes ma'am, Ms. Mabel," Fred answered. "We gone send invitations to our Aunt Margaret in Chicago and Aunt Martha in New York. Uncle Arthur gave me they address when they was here last year and told me and Delores to keep in touch with them. You think they gone come, Ms. Mabel?"

"Yes, sir, Fred!" Ms. Mabel assured. "They wouldn't miss it!"

***

Frederick Warren Marshall and Shirley Mae Payne wed on September 1, 1945. The day before, Isaac and Martha arrived from Harlem early in the afternoon. Pearl-Elizabeth was disappointed that her cousins were not able to make it down. Ever since she moved in with Ms. Mabel the year before, none of her cousins ever wrote.

Later that night, Arthur, Jr. and Margaret came down from Chicago. Ms. Mabel had plenty of room and put them up for their brief stay in town. Pearl-Elizabeth knew that her brothers would probably not be there, so she wasn't quite as disappointed when they didn't show up.

Pearl-Elizabeth stayed in her room the whole time that her parents were in town. She only came out to go to the bathroom. Ms. Mabel tended to her new great-grandson, Solomon, during that time.

To her parents, Pearl-Elizabeth was a disappointment and a fabricator. *Why do they believe him over me?* she often wondered. *Why would I lie on him? What reason do I have to lie on him? They took his side over me! Instead of face the truth, they just threw me away! Sent me to grandma last summer like I was trash!*

"Arthur, Margaret, come in the parlor and meet somebody," Ms. Mabel urged.

When they got in the parlor, Martha was bouncing little Solomon on her knee. He was ten months old and had already started to get into things.

"Who do we have here?" Margaret asked, as she and Arthur got closer.

Little Solomon looked up when he heard them approach and started to laugh. Arthur and Margaret were shocked when they looked into the baby's aqua-blue eyes. Solomon was a truth that they could no longer hide with excuses. Deep down, they believed Pearl-Elizabeth, but it was less painful to deny her allegations.

It was a big pill for them to swallow because Solomon was a carbon-copy image of his father, Dr. Jude Wilson. They couldn't accept the fact that this man had not only lied to them, but had betrayed their trust. He was someone whom they had known for years and grew to respect and admire. Their children were good friends. Margaret and his wife, Rebecca, were good friends. He and Arthur were colleagues, for heaven's sake! Business partners! They went through thick and thin at Meharry.

When this man was having a hard time with his studies, Arthur helped him. One time he didn't study for a major exam. Arthur let him cheat at the risk of them both being caught and expelled. Arthur bailed him out again after his father passed and he didn't know how to run his medical practice. Arthur moved his family to Chicago from Harlem just for that purpose. That's what friends do for each other.

"That's yo' grandson, Solomon," Ms. Mabel said proudly. She noticed the long looks on their faces and said, "Well, ain't y'all gone hold him? He ain't gone bite. He almost ten months old. He was born the day after Thanksgiving. I delivered him myself, right upstairs there."

"It's late," Arthur, Jr. told Ms. Mabel. "We better get some rest for the wedding tomorrow."

Arthur, Jr. and Margaret turned around and went upstairs to their rooms. They ran from Solomon like he was the plague.

***

Fred and Shirley had a rainbow wedding, which was popular in the '40s. All six of the bridesmaids wore the same style dress, but in different colors. Delores's long, magenta, chiffon dress complemented her smooth chocolate complexion and trim figure. Ethel's long, black hair and creamy skin were highlighted by her violet, chiffon dress. The other bridesmaids wore pale-blue, pale-green, canary-yellow, and melon-orange.

Shirley was a beautiful bride. She looked like an angel in that long, satiny dress with little roses all around. A ring of white roses adorned her head, surrounded by long, curly locks. Ms. Mabel pressed and curled her hair all night. "Chil', I done fried, dyed, and laid yo' hair to the side!"

Gloria sang at the ceremony. Her melodious voice filled the church and touched the hearts of all who attended, especially Ray's. *I ain't know she could sing like that. Is they anything that woman can't do?* Ray wondered.

The reception was held in the church parlor next door. The place was jam-packed with people. Everybody was having a grand time, except for Freda, who stood in a corner by herself, near the huge pile of wedding presents. She criticized the food, the guests, everything. It brought back memories of her wedding and how empty the church was.

"They gone be living in the row 'partment. They ain't even got no space to put all them presents. They ain't gone put 'em in my house! That's fo' sho'!" Freda mumbled as she looked at the pile. There were boxes of all sizes and shapes. All of the wrapping was beautiful and flawless–from white with white silky ribbons, hunter green, blue and white polka dot, to tartan with red and black ribbons–each with a separate card.

On the rear wall was a long table covered with a white lace tablecloth, piled high with food–gumbo, finger sandwiches, chicken wings, barbecue ribs, tuna salad and crackers, fruit punch with fruit cocktail, and a myriad of other treats. The wedding cake was on a separate table to the right. Each of the six layers was trimmed with icing to match the colors of the bridesmaids' dresses. Ms. Mabel couldn't find a colored bride and groom for the cake at any store, so she made two gingerbread cakes to resemble a man and a woman. Then she used food coloring and icing to create the tuxedo and wedding gown. Ms. Mabel, Josephine, Delores, and Ethel got up at midnight to prepare everything.

Most of the guests were either Shirley's relatives or friends of the family. Some of Fred's friends from school and the shipyard attended. Arthur, Jr. and Margaret, and Isaac and Martha were there. Pearl-Elizabeth was home taking care of the baby. Arthur, Jr. and Isaac volunteered to tend the bar.

And of course, Ms. Mabel was there. You would have thought that Shirley was her girl. She helped make the dress, cooked some of the food, and helped out with decorating the hall.

Delores was at ease with Shirley's family and the families of her newly found aunts. She mingled with the guests, and they all complimented her on how lovely she looked. She laughed, danced, and had the best time in her life.

"Ray?" A voice called from behind. It was Gloria, who walked over and hugged Ray. She had that same sultry stride he remembered. Her soft breasts against his chest and sweet perfume sent chills through his body. The passion he felt for her so many years ago was still with him. She still had that hourglass figure. Didn't look like she had aged one day!

"Hey, Ray!" Gloria started. "What are you doing here?"

"Fred is my boy."

"What you doin' here?" Ray asked.

"Shirley is my niece. My brother Eddie's daughter."

"Shirley sho' is a beautiful bride." Ray thought that's how pretty Gloria must have looked at her wedding.

Freda walked over and rolled her eyes at them. Ray and Gloria gave her a curious look. Her hair was pulled back, which gave full view of the crow's feet and dark circles under her eyes. Several buttons were missing off of the white dress she wore that exposed thick folds of flesh. Her lips were chapped, which brought attention to the green and orange film that covered her blackened teeth. Ashy patches covered her bare, hairy legs.

"This here my wife, Freda. Freda, this here is Henry wife, Gloria."

"Henry from the ship?"

"Yeah, Freda. That's the one."

"Where he at?" Freda asked.

"He had a heart attack and passed away last year," Gloria told them.

Ray was praying that Freda wouldn't do or say anything that would upset Gloria.

"You so black, you probably spooked him to death," Freda said.

"She so funny, always telling jokes," Ray laughed.

"You talk about me," Gloria started. "Y'all look like Lou Armstrong and Raggedy Ann."

The photographer finished taking pictures of the wedding party. Ray was relieved when he called for the parents to pose for a few shots at that very moment.

"Gotta go," Ray started, "I'll talk to you befo' we leave." He grabbed Freda by the arm and almost dragged her to join the other parents and the wedding party for pictures.

"Hey, momma. Hey, daddy." Delores was excited about being in the wedding. The chiffon felt so soft and brought out her complexion. The photographer took ten shots with the parents. Taking pictures all day made Delores feel like a movie star. "How do I look?"

"You sho' look pretty, Delores," Ms. Mabel said.

"She sho' do," Josephine agreed.

"You sho' look pretty in that dress," Ray admired.

Freda looked her up and down in disgust. She rolled her eyes. "Who you think you is? Ain't nobody black as you got no business wearing no hot pink dress!"

Delores started to cry and ran to the bathroom. The other members of the party looked surprised and appeared frozen for a few seconds.

Ray took Freda near the bar. "What you want go do that fo'?" He squeezed her hands to keep from hitting her. Arthur, Jr. and Isaac wondered what was going on. "People just want to have a good time. You can't stand to see nobody having no good time!"

"Freda, Ray," Margaret started. "Here are Isaac and Martha. The children couldn't make it down. Maybe next time you'll get to see Arthur, III and Richard again."

"It's been a long time, Freda. Good seeing you again," Martha started as she gave Freda a hug. "The children couldn't make it, but if we visit again, I'll make sure that they come along."

"Good to see you, Freda. How you been doing?" Isaac asked.

Freda noticed that Martha hadn't gained a pound since she last saw her in 1920, and she smelled like fresh jasmines. Her hair was done in a Victory curl, which was popular near the end of World War II, and her nails were French-manicured. Martha's makeup was flawless. The two-piece suit and white pencil-point pumps she wore accented her strong calf muscles.

***

I used to have a pair of pencil-points back then. They called them pencil-points because the heels were as skinny as a pencil. The toes were really pointed, too. You had to buy them a size or two too big because they were so narrow at the toe! When they came back in style again in the late '70s, I used to wear them with this bad pair of straight-leg Chic jeans and this black blouse with the one arm! Honey, I was looking *good* every time I wore them, too. I'm telling you!

***

Anyway, Isaac still looked as handsome as ever. His salt-and-pepper square-top haircut and thick mustache blended well with the gray suit he wore.

"Good seeing y'all again," Ray started as he shook Isaac's hand.

It started to thunder, and the sky became dark.

"Let's go, Freda, look like it 'bout to storm." Ray went to say good-bye to some of the other guests. Freda steadily rolled her eyes at Shirley. She strolled by where a few of the ladies were talking, hoping to start gossip.

"That gal look like a tar baby."

"What the fuck did you say?" Shirley's mother, Josephine, asked Freda. All attention was focused on Josephine. Guests standing nearby quickly left the immediate area. "I'll slap the shit outta yo' yellow ass." Josephine was a short, stocky woman with a lot of sass. She didn't take anything off of anybody.

"Let's go, Ray. I don't want to be around no loud, common, ig'nant Negroes." She started for the door. Ray was still in the back of the room talking to Isaac and Arthur, Jr. When he realized what was happening, he decided to take Freda home for sure.

Josephine heard Freda's comment. "I done asked you a question. What the fuck did you say?" Josephine insisted and stood right in Freda's face.

"I ain't said nothin'," Freda answered.

"You lyin'. Sound like you called my Shirley a tar baby."

"I ain't said that," Freda answered.

"Well, what the fuck did you say then, bitch?"

"Nothin'. I ain't said nothin'," Freda insisted. She tried to go for the door, but Josephine blocked every move she took.

"You callin' me a liar?" Josephine asked Freda.

"No."

"Don't nobody call Josephine Payne no liar!"

Josephine turned her back to Freda and gestured for Shirley to come over to her. Ray saw that as an opportunity to escape. He grabbed his wife and walked toward the door. "You gots to 'pologize to my baby Shirley. Now tell Shirley you sorry."

Ray thought that Freda was right behind him as he neared the door.

"Naw. You ain't goin' nowhere." Josephine pulled Freda back toward her by the arm and gave her a powerful backhand slap in the face. "Don't you ever," followed by a right punch to the nose, "disrespect my daughter again," and a left to the jaw that knocked Freda's head against the doorframe on the way to the cement floor.

Ray tried to step in, but Fred held him back, knowing that Shirley's relatives would use any excuse to start a fight. He picked his wife off the floor, as angry, insulted guests looked on, almost daring them to say another word.

Freda was disoriented for awhile, but nobody cared. Everybody got back to the party. The music played and people started to eat and drink like nothing had happened. Blood streamed profusely from her nose. Her jaw looked blue and had already started to swell. She still had trouble standing, and balanced against Ray's big, strong chest.

There were onlookers, but no one came to her aid. Delores was being consoled by Ethel in the back of the room, but they both pretended not to notice anything. Fred looked at his mother, then walked away and joined his bride on the dance floor. Martha stood near the bar and laughed loud and hard until tears streamed from her eyes.

"That's not funny," Margaret told Martha. She turned to Arthur, Jr. "Why don't you go and help. You see that she needs help," she urged.

Isaac gave Arthur a dirty look. "I'd stay out of other people's business if I was you," he told Arthur. "I've seen things like this in Harlem. The person who tries to help usually ends up getting hurt, while the people involved in the fight go on their merry way. I know. That's how I got some of my business at the funeral home."

Arthur sipped his drink. "Besides, she brought it on herself. She should have known better than to go to a colored person's wedding and bad-mouth the bride."

"You sound like your momma, Arthur," Margaret told him.

"He's right, you know," Martha added. "You know good and well how she was when we were coming up. It's a shame that she hasn't changed. She had it coming."

Freda was relieved to see Ms. Mabel walking toward her carrying a light blue towel. Ms. Mabel led Freda to a table near the door and sat her down. She wiped the blood off of Freda's face. "Here," Ms. Mabel gave her an icepack. "Keep this on your nose."

Freda felt a strong sense of comfort in Ms. Mabel's presence and was hopeful that meant that they could rekindle their relationship. She looked Freda straight in the eyes, "Like I done told you befo'," she started. "You gots to be careful what you say to people." Ms. Mabel signaled for Ray, who was standing behind her, to sit down. "It be best if y'all go on now." She got up and walked away as Ray's and Freda's eyes followed her. Ms. Mabel looked back when she reached the bar and noticed that they were still sitting at the table. She motioned with her hands, as though she were brushing a bug away, for them to leave.

Ray got Freda up from her chair and they again started for the door. It was pouring down rain. Ray and Freda left the building and began their six-block walk home.

Chapter 16.
The Return

"It's starting again," Ethel started. "I was so tired that I forgot to light the candle and put the broom out. Besides, I thought it was over."

"What happened?"

"A loud noise woke me up. It sounded like a glass breaking. When I looked, I saw it run under the curtains. I don't know if it went back out or was waiting for me to go back to sleep.

"It was dark, so I went to the kitchen and put a fresh pot of coffee on the stove. I lit a candle for light, since it was blackout time. I heard that Ms. Jessie down the street got into trouble fo' turning on the light during blackout time.

"When I lit the candle, the house looked different. Like I was in water or somethin'. It made the hair on my arms stand up. I was too scared to go back to bed, so I read the Bible under the candle to make me feel better."

"You did the right thing, chil'," Ms. Mabel reassured. "Just hand it over to God, chil'. He'll know what to do. He'll make ever'thing all right."

They walked in silence for the last few blocks to work. Orange streaks lit the sky as they admired God's wonder.

"It just came to me," Ms. Mabel said.

"What?"

"As I was looking to the sky I just thought of what you can do," Ms. Mabel said.

"What?" Ethel asked.

"You know them posters they got hanging 'round at work?"

"The ones about night work?"

"Yeah. Them the ones. We can sign up to work nights. The factory got a bus to pick us up 'round 10:30 or so at night, and drop us home early in the morning. We get to make ten dollars extra each week."

"How 'bout Pearl-Elizabeth?"

"She'll be all right. The Lord is lookin' after her."

"That's sound real good to me, Ms. Mabel, 'cause after last night, I'm scared to be alone in that house at night."

***

Ethel went home with Ms. Mabel after work. She was too shaken to return home. She felt comfort in the fact that she would be working at night and sleeping during the day from that point on.

"You better go get some things fo' the night, Ethel."

"It's starting to get dark, and I don't have a good feeling 'bout going in that house."

"Okay," Ms. Mabel started, "I tell you what. It's 7:30 now. We could take us a catnap 'til 'bout 9:30. We get up and I'll fix us somethin' to eat. Then, I'll go with you down the street and wait with you while you get washed up for work. Remember, we got to be by Newton Street at 10:45 for the bus to get us."

"Okay, Ms. Mabel. That sounds good to me. I sho' do 'preciate that."

Ms. Mabel walked Ethel upstairs to one of the spare bedrooms and gave her a house robe to change into. The room was light and overlooked the backyard. It smelled of cherry wood and fresh jasmine. A green-and-white floral-print paper covered the walls, and long, flowing white draperies adorned the two huge French windows. The white bedspread matched the canopy that covered the bedposts.

"I 'member my momma used to tell me 'bout witches. She was a slave. Some of the slaves was straight from Africa and knew magic. You think they used what they knew to free theyselves? No. They was evil. They would get out they body and go ride another slave. Steal they breath, they life force."

"Why would they do that, Ms. Mabel?"

" 'Cause they was evil! The person they be riding would be too tired to work. So the master would whip 'em. The witch would watch them and get a big kick out of that person getting whipped. The same thing happened each day until that person would either get sick and die, or get whipped to death. The witch would get stronger as the person got weaker."

"That's stupid, Ms. Mabel," Ethel commented. "Why didn't they ride the master?"

" 'Cause, my chil', Negroes is like a big bucket of crabs."

"What you mean, Ms. Mabel?"

"If one try to get out, they all pull 'em back in with the rest o' 'em."

"How they get rid of the witches?"

"You shouldn't have no mo' problems, though. My momma used to say that if you catch 'em, you know who they is, and they don't come back. She also used to say that if they suspected who it was, they would wait by they cabin at night. When the witch got out they skin, all the folk would get some salt and put in it. When they get back, they couldn't get in they skin. They would find that person dead the next morning."

"How I find who it is and they skin?"

"That I don't know, chil'. Let's just pray and ask the Lord."

"That's a shame people be so evil."

"What a shame, Ethel, is that witches lose they soul."

"What you mean?"

"Well, it's said that in order fo' them to get them powers, they got to sell they soul. That mean that when they die, the devil take they soul."

"They burn in hell? Just to make somebody else suffer?"

"That's what they did. They evil. That's why I worship the Lord with all my soul. If you with the Lord and do His will, ain't no evil can bother you."

"I go to church."

"That ain't enough, chil'. You gotta feel the Lord in yo' heart. Anybody can go to church, but just anybody can't know the Lord."

Chapter 17.

To Catch a Witch

It was nine o'clock and Ethel was awakened by the smell of fresh bacon. The sizzling grew louder as she neared the kitchen downstairs. Through the banister she saw sliced tomatoes and toast on the countertop.

Ms. Mabel was already dressed for work. She fixed plates for both of them of tuna club sandwiches and a large pitcher of lemonade to wash it all down. As they sat down to eat, a knock at the back door startled them. Pearl-Elizabeth was sound asleep. So they thought.

Ms. Mabel peeked through the door curtains and was shocked to see me standing outside. She was reluctant to let me in, but did so anyway. Pearl-Elizabeth watched from the banister upstairs.

"You're having a problem with a certain witch," I said as I stared directly into Ethel's eyes. "You are going to be working nights from here on. She doesn't know that yet. So this is your only chance to catch her."

Ms. Mabel and Ethel looked at each other in amazement. They had just asked about working nights earlier that day, and nobody else could have known. No one else knew about the problem Ethel had been having, either.

"I'll be at the back door of your house. Right after you get dressed tonight," I told her.

How she know we was going to my house? Ethel thought. *She awfully young to be sounding like a old lady.*

***

I guess she thought that my deep, raspy voice seemed too mature for my youthful demeanor. I was not like she had imagined. I appeared to be in my 20s at the time, not much older than she was. I was looking *good*, too! My hands were done in a French manicure. That shoulder-length Page Boy hairdo brought out my high cheekbones and heart-shaped face. I wore a crisp, khaki

pantsuit that hugged my hourglass figure. Women didn't wear pants much back then. Hell, I wasn't a woman anyway, so I didn't care. To Ethel, my eyes were so dark and menacing that they appeared to be black voids into nothingness. I spooked her.

***

"You know who it is?" Ms. Mabel asked.

"Yes," I answered. "She got to be stopped. She is very powerful, but lacks the discipline and wisdom to use it wisely. The forces frown upon that."

"Who is it?" Ethel asked.

She became frightened when I looked at her again. "It's whomever you never see or hear from again." I opened the door and stopped for a moment. "Tonight when you leave for the bus, take the back way to the main street." I turned and left.

"The back way is the long way, Ms. Mabel."

"We better do what she say. She must have a reason for it."

"She give me the willies," Ethel confided in Ms. Mabel. "Did you see her eyes? They were big and round like circles. Not like almonds like most people. And her skin didn't look right."

"What you mean?" Ms. Mabel asked.

"It looked real thick. Like a alligator or somethin'."

***

They walked down the street to Ethel's house. Ms. Mabel sat in the living room as she got dressed for work. It was past blackout time, so they lit several candles around the house for light. Ethel insisted on having the kitchen light on anyway.

Ms. Mabel fixed them some tea. It was 10:15, and they had a few minutes yet to leave.

"Did Mother Ruby come while I was in the bathroom?" Ethel asked.

"Naw," Ms. Mabel answered. "But if she say she gone be here, then she gone be here."

"If she don't come soon, we gone miss the bus."

"Now, Ethel." Ms. Mabel started. "She gone be here at the right time. Don't worry."

A gust of wind blew through the kitchen window and knocked one of Ethel's loop earrings to the floor and under the stove.

"I thought I closed that window," Ethel said. She reached her hand into the tiny space under the stove. "Found it."

When she picked the object up, she noticed that it was the same stone that she and Irving found before he went off to war. She reached again and found the earring.

"Where you get that from, chil'?" Ms. Mabel asked in a worried voice. "Where you get that from?"

"Irving bought me these earrings."

"No, I mean that load stone."

"I don't know. One day when Irving came home from work, he sat on it. He thought it was from the dock. I thought he took it back. I guess he didn't. The next week, he found out he was going to war."

"You don't know where it came from?"

"No ma'am."

"Was anybody in yo' house around the time you found it?"

"Well, come to think of it, Freda was just here. Yeah. That's right. 'Cause Irving asked me if Freda dropped it."

"Anybody else?"

"Naw. Ain't nobody else been in the house 'cept the iceman and milkman."

"Umm."

"It sho' is pretty."

"Ain't nothing pretty 'bout no load stone."

"What you mean, Ms. Mabel?"

"Well, my momma and the other old folks back in my time used to say that it bring burden on people who have it."

"Burden, Ms. Mabel?"

"Yes. It 'posed to put a heavy load on anybody who touch it. Sometimes you don't have to touch it. Somebody could just work a spell on you and hide it in yo' house to make you have problems."

"Why would somebody want to make me and Irving have problems? We ain't did nobody nothing, Ms. Mabel. We ain't," Ethel said in frustration.

"Let's pray over it. It's time fo' you to test yo' faith in the Lord."

"All right, Ms. Mabel," Ethel said as she bowed her head in prayer.

Ms. Mabel held the stone in her hands, closed her eyes, then took one deep breath in. She bowed her head and began, "By the power vested in me by the Lord Jesus Christ, I bless this stone and command it to do the will of God. It is only a graven image, oh Lord. We put no other God before you, oh Lord. And we bind the power of darkness. In the name of the Father, the Son, and the Holy Spirit, I command you to get back evil! God in heaven is the Father. For thine is His kingdom, and the power and the glory. Forever. Amen."

Ms. Mabel wrapped the stone in newspaper and threw it in the garbage.

"I've got something for you to do," I said.

Ms. Mabel and Ethel were startled. They thought that I had appeared from nowhere.

"Take this." I handed a small bottle to Ethel. "It's mustard seed."

"What should I do with it, Mother Ruby?" Ethel asked.

"Come," I said as I took Ethel's hand and led her into the bedroom.

She quivered when she touched me. Ms. Mabel followed. I wore a white robe and nightcap like the one Ethel wore. I got into Ethel's bed and pulled the covers over my head.

"What is she gone do?" Ms. Mabel wondered to herself.

"Sprinkle the contents of this bottle around the bed, careful not to miss a spot. Don't step in it either," I told Ethel.

Ethel obeyed. I chanted while she sprinkled the seeds around the bed. All the seeds were gone.

"Now," I began. "Place the empty bottle at the point where you first began pouring the seeds, and put the lid at the point where you poured the last seed."

Ethel obeyed, not questioning the rationale behind what she was doing.

"When you return in the morning, the seeds will be in the bottle on the floor. Don't touch it! Don't move it out of that spot for three days. On the third day, somebody is going to ask you to let her go. At that time, I'm going to get the bottle from you."

"Let them go?" Ms. Mabel asked.

"Yes," I told her. "The witch got to get all of the seeds into the bottle before dawn or they lose their soul right then and there. As they pick each seed, a piece of their soul gets attached to it. The person who has the seeds has their soul."

"So, I will have her soul?" Ethel asked.

"No, child, I will. Since I'm in your bed and the seeds are surrounding me, that means that the witch is after my life force."

"Well, what if she spill the seeds by accident, Mother Ruby?" Ms. Mabel asked.

"Then the witch loses a part of her soul," I explained.

Ms. Mabel and Ethel noticed that it was 10:45.

We missed the bus! Ethel thought.

"Your bus is not leaving without you. He'll wait. Trust me."

***

Ms. Mabel and Ethel took the long way to the bus like I had
instructed. They were ten minutes late, but the bus was waiting.
Neither the passengers nor the driver seemed to care about having
to wait for them. When they arrived at work 15 minutes later, it
was so busy and so few people wanted to work that shift, that the
supervisors didn't notice that the bus was late. Ms. Mabel, Ethel,
and the other workers who were tardy didn't even get their pay
docked.

***

It was three o'clock in the morning when I saw the curtains
rustle. A shadow streaked across the floor. There she was, moving
really fast, but I saw her. She tried to climb in the bed at the
middle, but couldn't. She stepped into the mustard seeds and they
were attracted to her body like magnets to steel. She looked so
funny trying to get them off, but she knew what she had to do. She
scrambled around for five minutes trying to find the bottle. That
Ethel sure did hide it well.

She finally found the bottle and began to put the seeds into it,
one by one. You see, the law says that only one seed may be put
into the bottle at a time. It was 5:30, and she put 475 in the bottle.
But there are always 500 seeds. She looked pathetic scrambling
around, looking frantically for seeds. It sounded like rats were
running around the floor.

Some of the seeds had been scattered way under the bed. Ethel
did a good job. She found the rest of the seeds tucked away into the
deep folds of her skin. At last she found the lid and carefully
snapped it tightly on the bottle. She mustered up all of her strength
to do so. That was difficult because the bottle was almost as big as
she was and those long claws got in the way. She knew that if she
spilled the seeds, she would have had to start all over, and certain
doom would have been inevitable.

With only moments to spare until sunrise, she quickly ran to
the window and squeezed through the crack whence she came,
never to bother Ethel again.

***

"Could I sleep by yo' house Ms. Mabel?" Ethel asked. They were
the only two in the back of the bus and whispered so that no one could

hear them. Ten other women sat in the front, too loud and too busy gossiping to notice the two of them in the back.

"Why sho', chil'."

"Mother Ruby gave me the creeps," Ethel said as she quivered. "Oooo. . . the thought of her in my bed, ooo … . Her hands felt ice-cold and felt rubbery."

"People say she real, real old."

"You think she got rid o' the problem I been having?" Ethel asked.

"If she said she would, then she would," Ms. Mabel reassured.

"How long you known her?"

"Since me and my husband moved to Algiers back in 1910."

"Did she always look so young?"

"Yes. Yes, she did."

"What is she?" Ethel asked.

"Karma…" Ms. Mabel became still. Her skin drained of its color, as a somber looked suddenly appeared across her face. She looked as if she had seen a ghost.

"Karma, Ms. Mabel?" Ethel asked. "Like in reaping and sowing, and what goes around comes around?"

"Now they is things we don't understand," Ms. Mabel snapped. "It's just best not to go asking no questions and let some things be. You understand, chil'?"

"Yes, ma'am."

They sat in silence for the remainder of the ride home. For the first time, Ethel really admired the sky and was captivated by its beauty. Deep orange and golden streaks gradually appeared across the horizon. The sun gradually pushed away the stillness of night as the new day was born. The fading moon and stars took her problems and concerns along with them into eternity.

At that moment, she was overwhelmed by a strange energy. It began as a tingling sensation at the crown of her head, and radiated down to her toes. An orgasmic sensation flowed down her spine and engulfed her being. The feeling lingered in the center of her chest and sent tiny pulses throughout her body. It was better than any time she had ever had with Irving. She was immersed in a deep sense of peace and love–a knowingness that she was in God's presence.

"Ethel," Ms. Mabel called. "Ethel, this our stop."

Ethel was deep in thought, captivated by the heavens above, completely oblivious to the world around her. Ms. Mabel shook her to reality, though. Ethel was still in awe as they stepped off the bus.

"What's wrong?" Ms. Mabel asked.

"It's so strange," she started.

Ms. Mabel was afraid to ask, and thought that something else mysterious was happening to Ethel again. "What's strange?"

"I was looking at the sky, and it made me feel so good. Like I was in another world."

"Now you know why I like the sky so much. When I was young, me and my husband tried dope."

"You, Ms. Mabel?"

"Yes. But, when I look at the sky, 'specially right befo' dawn or dusk, it be better than any dope I ever had. Chil', I think you done finally found the Lord. That's what old folks call being born-again. Now you really know the Lord. You keep it up ever'day, and won't no evil come near you."

"Yes, ma'am, Ms. Mabel."

Chapter 18.
The Broken Spell

Ms. Mabel went with Ethel to her house to get some clothes and other essentials for the next few days. As they opened the front door, a feeling of peace filled the air. Through the living room was the bedroom. Ethel noticed a fresh set of linens on the bed. The Lord was still with Ethel, so she didn't flinch when she saw the bottle on the floor next to the nightstand, filled to the rim with the mustard seeds. She grabbed a few items from the dresser and bathroom and threw them into an empty suitcase she pulled from the closet.

They heard a noise coming from outside and were afraid to know what it was. Ms. Mabel peeked out of the front room window anyway and saw that it was Big Joe Thompson, the iceman. He was unloading a big block of ice from his truck. He was over six-four and weighed over 300 pounds. His curly, black hair blended well with his smooth brown skin.

Ethel hid the suitcase in the living room until he reached the back door. He was startled to see her standing there when he entered the kitchen.

"Good morning, Miss Lewis," he started. "I ain't knowed you was gone be home. Look like you ready fo' work."

Ethel was caught off guard, then realized that she was still wearing her work clothes. "Oh, yes. Yes I am."

While he loaded the icebox, she joined Ms. Mabel in the front room. Ethel was careful not to pack or do anything to let him know that she wouldn't be there for the next couple of days.

Back then, people could leave their homes unlocked and didn't have to worry about being robbed blind when they returned. They would come home and find everything right where they left it.

"Good day, Miss Lewis," Joe yelled from the kitchen as he carried his dolly through the back door.

They peeked through the window and watched his truck drive to the next house up the street. At that time, Ethel pulled the suitcase from behind the sofa and started to pack again. They peeked out of the window to make sure that the truck was completely out of sight, then made their way to Ms. Mabel's house.

***

On the third day, Ethel returned home after work with Ms. Mabel at her side. Ms. Mabel fixed them a breakfast of grits, eggs, and bacon and they chatted the morning away. They compared notes of how beautiful the sky was and being in touch with God.

Ethel left the bottle of mustard seeds on the bedroom floor, but stared endlessly at them from the kitchen table.

"I don't like this house no mo'," Ethel complained.

"Well, chil'," began Ms. Mabel, "it's because so much evil done happened up in here. Ain't no room fo' both God and evil. Since you done found the Lord, you just can't stand to be 'round no evil."

"How 'bout them mustard seeds? Since I found the Lord, what should I do with them?" Ethel asked.

"Just do what Mother Ruby done told you," Ms. Mabel started. "Just like the police take folk to jail who break man's law, God got people here on Earth who punish folk who break His law, too."

"Like Mother Ruby?"

"Yes, like Mother Ruby."

It was about 10:30. As Ethel cleared the table, they heard a knock on the front door.

"I'll get it," Ms. Mabel insisted.

She peeked through the front window and saw that it was Freda. "She up mighty early," Ms. Mabel said to herself.

"Is Ethel home?"

"Yeah, she right there in the kitchen."

Ms. Mabel let her in. As Freda headed for the kitchen, she froze and became jittery when she noticed the bottle of mustard seeds on the bedroom floor. Ethel went into the front room and noticed Freda's reaction to the seeds.

***

"Ms. Mabel and Ethel have been working nights for the past week," I told Freda. They were all shocked to see me standing behind Ms. Mabel. I walked over and picked up the seeds. "This belongs to me." They were all so shocked that they didn't see me leave. They thought that I had vanished into thin air.

***

Freda had a concerned look on her face. "I need to get back to the house. I just came to yell at you." She turned around and went out of the front door. Ms. Mabel and Ethel watched her wobble home. She was so shaken that she could barely put one foot in front of the other.

Chapter 19.
Homecoming

It was 9:30 on a cool December '45 morning. Space heaters warmed the house. From the kitchen window, Ethel noticed a white military bus coming down the street. She didn't get her hopes up again. Three buses had passed through the neighborhood over the past few days, and Irving was on none of them.

"You want some more coffee, Ethel?" Ms. Mabel asked, trying to keep her mind off the bus.

"No, ma'am." Ethel answered flatly.

They heard thumps on the front porch, then a loud knock.

"Oh, Lord," Ethel said. "I hope they ain't coming to tell me Irving dead. I'm sho' glad you here, Ms. Mabel."

The knock became louder.

"You better go answer it, chil'," Ms. Mabel said.

Ms. Mabel gently squeezed Ethel's hand and walked her to the door. She looked deep and long into Ms. Mabel's eyes for comfort before she opened it.

Standing at the portal was Irving, who was dressed in dungarees. He was carrying a large, green duffel bag across his left shoulder, and his dog tags were still dangling around his neck.

"Irving!" Ethel was ecstatic.

Irving entered the house, grabbed Ethel by the waist, and threw her into the air.

"Thank you, Jesus!" Ms. Mabel exclaimed as he held her arms high in the air. She looked toward the heavens. "Thank you, Lord. You done answered my prayers. Thank you, Jesus!"

"How you been, baby?" Irving asked.

"I been fine. Ms. Mabel been looking after me," Ethel told him.

"We gots to celebrate," Ms. Mabel told them. "Let's have Sunday dinner. Today is Friday, that'll give me time to prepare." Ms. Mabel left, saying, "Thank you, Jesus!" all the way home.

Irving went into the kitchen and filled four large pots with water.

"How 'bout a hot bath?" he asked Ethel.

"That sho' sound good to me."

"I miss you, baby," he said as he looked deep into Ethel's eyes. Passion flowed from his strong, masculine hands into the essence of her being as he held her waist.

He licked her lips and gently kissed her face, starting at her nose and up to her eyelids, down to her neck. He whispered in her ear soft and low, as he nibbled every niche of her lobes, "I miss holding your soft, warm body. I miss how you come when I stroke you."

They engaged in a long, deep, passionate kiss; Irving's lips completely surrounded hers, as their tongues mingled in a quiet interlude. The water started to boil on the stove and Irving pulled away from Ethel. He drew some cold water in the bathtub and mixed the hot kettles right in.

"Ethel," he called, as he summoned her to the bathroom. Irving was completely nude.

Irving's body looked like that of a hard-working man–hard, solid muscles from head to toe. That excited Ethel to the maximum extent. She remembered all too well how many hours of pleasure his long, hard cock gave her, as she succumbed to all of his manly desires. Playing with his hairy chest and legs reached the depths of her feminine soul. Each touch of his hands reached the profundity of her womanhood.

Ethel disrobed and joined him in the tub. She lathered some soap in a towel and began to bathe Irving. She washed his ears, his chest, and back. She lost control when she washed his firm behind–it felt so firm and looked so good. Irving stood up in the tub. His long, hard muscle was at attention. Ethel washed his legs and inner thighs, and playfully teased Irving.

He sat back in the tub, and she washed his feet. Ethel sucked each of his toes and licked the soles of his feet, then ran her tongue between each of his toes.

"That sho' do feel good, baby, sucking my toes like that," Irving moaned, as he stood up again. "I know something else would feel good if you suck, too."

Ethel looked up at him with a smirk on her face.

"I was waiting to wash the best part last," she teased.

Ethel got on her knees and lathered soap in her hands. She reached to his big, black balls and started to message them with her hands, careful to work her way up the shaft, to the head, where she focused the most attention. Back and forth, she caressed, slowly, as Irving moaned.

"Oh, baby," he started. "That feel too good!"

She rinsed the soap off of his hot, throbbing cock. The warm water cascaded down his legs, handful by handful.

"Oooh. Sssss," Irving groaned. "Don't stop!"

Ethel put as much of Irving's balls that could fit into her mouth. She ran her tongue up and down his shaft, back and forth several times until she reached the head. She sucked his cock so hard, back and forth, up and down, like an ice cream cone, until he almost came. He pulled away.

"What's wrong, Irving?"

He sat back in the tub and pulled her by the waist on top of him. He tried to penetrate her, but she was so tight from being celibate so many years. Irving got out of the tub, dripping wet, and sat on the commode. Ethel got some petroleum jelly out of the medicine cabinet and sensuously rubbed it on Irving's cock, up and down.

"Come and sit down, Ethel," he invited. "I'll be real easy."

Irving gently eased his cock inside of her. He kissed and fondled her nipples, which made her wetter and hotter until he was completely in, all eight inches.

He thrust hard and deep, in and out, as he squeezed and pulled her soft bottom apart, up and down. Irving made Ethel so hot as he bounced her up and down like a see-saw. "Oh shit! Shit!" he shouted, his body jerked uncontrollably, as he ran his fingers through her hair. "Shit! Shit," his voice faded as he came. Ethel pulled away, and Irving's cock looked like it had been dipped in whipped cream.

They held each other for a few minutes. Ethel sat in his lap and he put his strong arms around her. He kissed her hair and forehead several times. "I love you so much, Ethel."

"I love you so much, Irving. I missed you so much."

Ethel got up, and a long stream of come ran down her legs. Irving started to rub it on her legs, then put some into her mouth. She sucked his fingers as he became aroused.

"Let's go in the bedroom," Irving insisted.

"No. I ..." Ethel started. "Let's go in the second bedroom."

"Why?" Irving asked. "They ain't no furniture in there."

"Well, you ain't gone believe me."

"What?" Irving asked.

"Mother Ruby been sleeping in the bed, and I don't feel good 'bout sleeping in it no mo'."

"Mother Ruby? Ain't she the witch over there?" Irving asked. He completely lost his erection. "What she doing in my bed?"

Ethel spread two blankets and pillows on the second bedroom floor. They both sat down.

"A witch been riding me."

"You lying," Irving said in disbelief.

"No. I'm not. Just ask Ms. Mabel."

"I heard 'bout things like that from ol' folks. A witch was 'posed to been riding this ol' man in the neighborhood where I grew up. I heard he caught it with his belt and kilt it."

"Mother Ruby changed the bedclothes and burned the old ones, but I still don't want sleep in that bed. I been sleeping by Ms. Mabel after work. I don't like this house no mo'."

"Work?" Irving was surprised. "You working? Ain't no wife 'o mine gone be working nowhere 'cept cookin' my dinner and doin' my laundry."

"I needed to work. The money the Army sent wasn't enough to run the house."

"I knowed you wasn't cleaning no white folks house, was you?"

"Well, at first. But the factory started hiring Negro women, and me and Ms. Mabel got jobs there. We been working at night since the problem started."

"You gone have to quit, Ethel."

"Other women who husbands went to war work there too."

"I don't care, Ethel. You got to quit, and I mean today!" He pointed to the clothes in the bathroom. "So thems yo' work clothes, heh?"

"Yeah, they is."

"I'm here to protect you from that witch now."

"Mother Ruby took care of it with some mustard seeds."

"I heard 'bout mustard seeds." Irving started. "The witch is 'posed to pick 'em all up by daylight or lose they soul. They 'posed to come ask you fo' they soul back. Did they ever ask you fo' they soul back?"

"Well, three days later Freda came by," Ethel started.

"I knew it! I knew it!" Irving shouted. "I knew they was something funny 'bout that woman."

"Well, Mother Ruby came and took the seeds befo' she could say anything. Since Mother Ruby was in the bed, she was after her soul, not mine."

"Oooh," Irving started. "That's real bad."

"Why?" Ethel asked.

" 'Cause nobody 'posed to mess with Mother Ruby or anybody like her. People who mess with them get in real, real bad trouble. I heard that nothing or nobody could save them. Not even God."

"But, Irving," Ethel started. "God is the creator. He is the most powerful being. Period."

"Yes, I know," Irving started. "But if you disobey His word, then ain't nothing can be done fo' you."

"But don't God forgive us for sin?" Ethel asked.

"Yes, he do."

"So why can't he forgive them for messin' with Mother Ruby?"

"Let's say we have chil'ren and set the word for 'em, say, not to jump off the porch. Let's say that the doctors and the hospital is hell. And what if they jump off the porch anyway and break they leg? Could we forgive 'em?" Irving asked Ethel.

"Well, we told them not to jump off the porch, and they be hard-headed and did it anyway. We could forgive 'em, but ain't nothin' we could do fo' 'em if they break they leg 'cept send 'em to the hospital."

"Same thing with the Father."

"But you still ain't say why people ain't 'sposed to mess with Mother Ruby," Ethel insisted.

"I'll give you a real-life 'xample," Irving started. "When I was 'bout 15 or 16, I 'member this witch named Mother Rose back home in Plaquemine. She was young and real pretty. But people used to say that she was real, real old. She was tall with this nice brown skin and long, jet-black hair. She carried herself like a lady, so it was hard fo' people to believe that she was a witch.

"This man, Mr. Lou, made a bet with his friends that he could get into Mother Rose drawers. They warned him not to go messin' with her, but he didn't listen. 'I'm gone have me some o' that pussy,' he bragged to everybody."

"What happened?" Ethel asked.

"At first, he used to meddle with her when he saw her on the street. He would get real personal, like he knew her real, real good. Then he started going over to her house, sometimes unexpected and when she had people over there getting prayed for. One time, this lady, Ms. Mildred, was 'sposed to be cursed and went to see Mother Rose. She was just a prayin' and a chantin' over Ms. Mildred when Mr. Lou just walked right in. 'Hey, Rose,' he said, 'how you doin', gal?' Mother Rose was just 'bout finished breaking the spell, too. 'You fool!!' Mother Rose yelled at Mr. Lou. 'Get out! Get out! You scattered the spirits!' Then she started chantin' and sprinklin' some stuff all over the place. Ms. Mildred was real, real upset at Mr. Lou. She told him, 'You ain't nothin' but a no-good, triflin' Negro. What Mother Rose want wit' you anyhow? You bet' leave her alone if you know what good fo' you!'

"People used to say that you not 'posed to break no prayer circle. That it 'posed to make the spell even harder to break. 'I don't believe in that stuff no way,' he told people. He thought it was funny.

"He started spreading rumors 'bout how he been messin' wit' Mother Rose and how she was real easy. Nobody believed him. People got real, real 'fraid when he started talking like that and walked away. They was 'fraid Mother Rose would get them. People warned him not to mess with Mother Rose.

"One day I was walking down the street. Mr. Lou was showing off in front o' his friends, Mr. Ollie and Mr. Jerry, and went to Mother Rose house. He told them to wait outside while he get him some pussy. They had li'l chil'ren, ol' folks, and women folk around, but he ain't cared who heard him.

"His friends waited and waited 'gainst they better judgement.

'Boy, he musta got him some,' Mr. Ollie said.

'I sho' hope he know what he doin'. I hope his dick don't fall off or somethin',' Mr. Jerry said.

'We fools fo' waitin' here. What if Mother Rose see us or somethin'?' Mr. Ollie asked.

'Yeah. Let's go, man. I don't want her hexin' me!' Mr. Jerry said.

'Me neither,' Mr. Ollie said.

"They finally left. The next day, Mr. Lou didn't show up fo' work. His wife and chil'ren ain't know where he was."

"What happened to him?" Ethel asked.

"People said that Mother Rose fixed him real good for disrespecting her. Nobody know what happened to him 'til this day. It's like he fell off the face of the Earth or somethin'."

Irving put his arms around Ethel as she placed her head on his warm, furry chest. She felt safe and secure now that her man was finally back home. They fell fast asleep.

Chapter 20.
War Stories

Irving and Ethel walked slowly down the street, hand-in-hand, savoring each moment together, as they made their way to Ms. Mabel's after church. As they passed Freda's house, they noticed the curtains close. "She being nosy," Irving told Ethel. "Let the Lord take care o' her."

As they entered Ms. Mabel's yard, the smell of fresh spices greeted them.

"Come right on in, folks!" Ms. Mabel told them. "Everybody, y'all know Ethel. This here her husband, Irving. Irving this here, Fred Marshall, Ray Marshall boy. This here Delores Marshall, Ray Marshall girl. This here Shirley Marshall, Fred new wife. And this here my grandbaby, Pearl-Elizabeth, and my great-grandbaby, Solomon."

"Good to meet all of y'all," Irving said.

Delores wore that pink-and-white apron and was setting the table. Fred was bringing some of the food to the table. Shirley, who was five months pregnant, was folding napkins. She, too, was wearing that famous pink-and-white apron. Pearl-Elizabeth was clearing the kitchen.

There was roasted chicken, apple dumplings, and sundries of other goodies lined around the table. Ms. Mabel got the good china, silverware, and linen for the occasion. She even managed to get a bottle of champagne.

Irving and Ethel noticed Solomon in his playpen, which was set in the dining room. He was bouncing up and down, shaking his rattle, laughing like nobody's business. Ethel picked him up and sat at the table. She and Irving cradled the baby as they looked into each other's eyes. "He getting so big, Pearl-Elizabeth," Ethel said. "How old he is now?"

"He's 13 months old," Pearl-Elizabeth told Ethel.

Irving thought that it was curious for Pearl-Elizabeth to have such a fair-skinned baby. Solomon had milky skin, a full head of black, curly hair, and aqua-green eyes.

"I can't wait 'til this one come out," Fred teased Shirley.

Delores ran into the bathroom down the hall, almost in tears.

"What's wrong with her?" Shirley asked.

"I don't know," Ms. Mabel said. "I'm gone see."

The bathroom was right under the stairway. It was small with pink-and-white striped wallpaper. To the rear, high over the white porcelain antique tub, was a small window that provided extra light. The two of them barely fit in the tiny room.

"Delores," Ms. Mabel called. "What's wrong, sweetie?"

"Nothin'," she said as tears rolled down her cheeks.

"It must be somethin' 'cause you wouldn't be crying. Is it 'cause ever'body got a baby or married and you want the same?"

Delores cried even harder. "I want to be married, but don't nobody want me."

"Oh, girl. That ain't true," Ms. Mabel reassured. "You just ain't found the right one yet. You still young. You got time."

Ms. Mabel wet one of the pink towels that was folded on the sink. She held Delores in her arms and wiped her eyes and face. They headed back to the dining room where everyone was waiting for them. Little Solomon was in his highchair.

Everyone bowed heads while Ms. Mabel blessed the food. Fred went around the table and poured champagne. "Let's make a toast," Ms. Mabel said. "To Irving and his safe return."

"Here, here," they all said and raised their glasses. Little Solomon even raised his baby bottle.

"Tell us 'bout the war," Delores insisted.

"Yeah," Pearl-Elizabeth agreed.

"First, I was in Texas. Then I was in Paris, then Germany, then Japan," Irving told them.

Everyone anticipated more. But Irving became quiet.

"Well?" Ms. Mabel asked. "Then what?"

"I don't know, Ms. Mabel," Irving started.

"Don't know what?" Ms. Mabel asked.

"If y'all want to hear 'bout the war. Besides, it's somethin' ladies ought not hear 'bout," Irving said.

"We can take it," Ms. Mabel insisted, and was adamant.

"Yeah!" everyone agreed.

"Okay. If you say so," Irving continued. "I had four really, really good friends. We had a lot of good times together. We thought that we would make it through the war together. We almost did, too. I'm telling you Tommy Lee, Ernest, RayRay, and Big Joe was some good peoples.

"I went in the same time as Tommy Lee and Big Joe. We met Ernest and RayRay in Paris 'round '42.

"Tommy Lee was straight from the Alabama woods and acted real country. He was kinda short with bow legs. He looked funny when he walked 'cause he didn't swing his arms. He always had this serious look on his face.

"Ernest was tall and skinny with big poppy eyes. His lips looked like they took up his whole face. He had a li'l bitty flat nose. When he smiled, he had a big gap between his teeth. Not just the top teeth, but the bottom ones, too. He looked like a caveman, with them big calves and skinny, li'l bitty knees.

"RayRay was the youngest. I think he was from New Orleans, too. He was naïve so we had to protect him from some of the other men. They would always pick on 'im. He was tall, high-yella and big and strong as a ox, with curly, black hair. He was real clumsy and made mistakes that cost some men they lives. We was scared that he would do something to get us all killed. He wasn't too bright, but was good peoples.

"And Big Joe, he the man. He real, real black. I mean blue-black. He 'bout my height, but his arms is big as my legs. He got muscles from head to toe.

"When we was in Paris, we had a ball. The five of us would go out and drink all night long. That was befo' things got hot and heavy. One night we took RayRay to this brothel and he..."

Ethel and everyone gave Irving a strange look.

"Anyway, we had a lot of fun together. We ain't even knewed each other whole name and didn't care. That stuff don't matter until it's too late. I'm telling you, that was a beautiful city. Yes indeedy! Nobody cared that we was colored, 'cept for the white soldiers. They told the French that we was animals. That we had tails. That wasn't bad enough, when we had German POWs..."

"What's a POW?" Pearl-Elizabeth asked.

"Prisoner of War. The enemy. People we fought against and captured," Irving explained.

"Oh," Pearl-Elizabeth said.

"They told the Germans that we was animals and had tails, too. Them white boys tried to turn the POWs against the coloreds. We the people who helped them catch the Germans!

"When we went to eat, the POWs got treated better 'n the coloreds! They not only had better food, but they got served first, too! They sat in the white section."

"Ain't that somethin'," Fred started. "Coloreds was fighting 'gainst Hitler and the way he treated folk, and them white boys treating the colored soldiers the same or worser!"

"That was wrong," Irving continued. "So a lot of colored soldiers stayed in France or Italy or Germany after the war. They refused to come back to a country that treat them like dirt, 'specially during war!

"Things was pretty easy 'til '44, when we went to Germany. We had to dig these trenches, foxholes, stay in them all night without so much as moving. If we wanted to sneeze, the Sarge told us to hold it. We couldn't even relieve ourselves either. Sarge told us that the enemy would either see us move or have dogs to track the scent. We didn't think that made sense, but orders is orders. We did as we was told.

"Sometimes it got cold or rainy or hot. It was just miserable. One man had ants or something crawling up his arms, but couldn't move. So he just suffered. I knowed he was itching real bad, too.

"We made it through Germany, so we just knew we would make it through Japan. We heard that the war was just 'bout over. We went to Japan in '45. We had to dodge bullets and be careful not to step on mines.

"I 'member that day like it was yesterday. RayRay was in front of Tommy Lee. Something fell from RayRay's backpack and he stooped to get it. That was long enough for Tommy Lee to trip over 'im and onto a land mine. He was in front of me so his guts exploded all over me. Blood was everywhere. His bone fragments is still lodged in me today. They pierced my flesh like needles, but I had to keep moving."

Everybody at the table held his stomach and stopped eating.

"It's hurts real, real bad to see one of your friends die like that. 'Specially since you can't do nothin' 'bout it," Irving continued.

"We saw a missile or bomb or grenade or something coming straight for us. Hell, when you at war, they all look the same. All you need to know is that you need to get out the way. None of us wanted to wait around to see what it was, so we ran into the woods as fast as we could. I looked back and RayRay tripped over a rock or something. I started to go back for 'im but Big Joe stopped me. 'No, no, Irving. You gone get killed if you go back. Then we lose boths y'all.' Ernest went back anyway when Big Joe wasn't looking.

RayRay got up and it hit about 50 feet behind him and didn't hurt him. He just froze there and couldn't move. We saw something going straight for him. 'Come on RayRay, come on RayRay!' we yelled. But he still didn't move. We ran farther into the woods, 'cause we was being shot at and bombed at and grenaded at and everything else at. I heard moaning and crying. I looked back and it was RayRay. That thing hit a big rock a few feet behind him. A piece of that rock or something shot straight into RayRay's stomach. 'Help me! Help me!' he yelled. But they wasn't nothing nobody could do for 'im. I watched him hold his guts in his hands as the Japanese soldiers shot him full of holes. 'Come on Irving,' Big Joe said. 'We gots to get outta here.' Ernest tried to go back and save RayRay, but…"

"I don't want hear no mo'," Ethel said. "Any o' yo' friends live?"

"Ernest lost his left arm, but he still 'live. Big Joe and me the only ones to make it out 'live and whole."

"Did you ever learn yo' friends' names?" Ms. Mabel asked.

"Yes, ma'am. Ernest is Ernest Brown. He went back to Al'bama. Big Joe is Joseph Murray, he in New York. Tommy Lee was Thomas Lee Williams, III. RayRay was Raymond Marshall, Jr."

"Did you say Raymond Marshall, Jr.?" Fred asked.

"Yeah," Irving answered. Ms. Mabel and Ethel looked concerned.

"Don't you remember Ray Marshall from the docks?" Ethel asked.

"Yes, I do. He …" Irving paused. "He ain't Ray boy is he? I ain't know Ray had no chil'ren until I met Fred and Delores today. We ain't been living in Algiers too long befo' I went to war. So I never got to know the neighbors 'cause I would go to work early in the mornings and come home after six or so, then went straight to bed 'cause I was tired. I guess I never put two and two together. Besides, the Army woulda notified the family by now if it was him. Besides, this Raymond Marshall was high-yella."

"Ray, Jr. is high-yella, too," Ms. Mabel started.

"Yeah, but this boy was clumsy. He wasn't too bright. Kinda goofy," Irving continued.

"That sound like my brother. He was real clumsy. I mean real, real clumsy," Fred said.

"I'm sho' glad you home safe and sound," Ms. Mabel said. "You had Ethel here worried half to death! I sho' hope this RayRay ain't Ray, Jr."

"Besides, like I said," Irving started, "they probably woulda notified the family by now. Besides, that happened back in August."

"I sho' hope you right, Irving," Ms. Mabel said. "I sho' hope you right."

***

"That sho' was a mighty fine dinner Ms. Mabel prepared for us this evening," Irving told Ethel, as they lay between the blankets on the second bedroom floor.

"It sho' was," Ethel agreed. "I ain't gone know what to do with myse'f now that I quit the factory," Ethel told Irving. "Most o' the women work in the neighborhood."

"Besides, some of 'em husbands back from war. They might stop working, too."

"Yeah," Ethel started. "Maybe so."

"I should be able to get my old job back at the docks," Irving started. "They said that everybody should get they job back after the war, no matter how long they been gone."

"What if they don't, Irving?"

"I'll just have to find another job. Besides, they is this new thing called the GI Bill. It 'posed to promise money for ed'cation, houses, and other stuff to war vet'rans like myself. Besides, the way I figure it, we ain't got nothin' to worry 'bout."

"You said you could get money fo' a house?" Ethel asked.

"Yes. I believe so," Irving said.

"Irving," Ethel started. "I don't like this house no mo'. I wish we could move to some place else."

"Let's pray tonight," Irving told Ethel. "The Lord will guide our way."

"I ain't knowed you was a praying man, Irving," Ethel told him. "I was surprised you even went with me to church this morning."

"After being off to war, in the trenches of hell, you get to know the Lord real quick. I mean real, real quick."

Chapter 21.
Good-bye Blues

It was 10:30 on Monday morning. Ethel was sitting at the kitchen table reading the newspaper. She had just finished her chores for the day and decided to treat herself to a fresh cup of homemade cocoa. The Andrews Sisters' "Bugle Boy" bellowed from the radio in the living room, but failed to capture her complete attention. Irving walked through the front door.

Oh, oh, Ethel thought. *He ain't get his job back.*

Irving raced to the kitchen, "Ethel, Ethel," he shouted. "Guess what?"

"You got yo' job back?" she asked.

"No. Yeah. No," he stumbled. "Better 'n that. I got a new job in New York and they want us to move on out Wednesday, day after tomorrow!"

"What?" Ethel was surprised.

"Yeah! Ain't that good news?"

"Yeah, it is, Irving!" Ethel said.

"It's with the same company that Kent Simms went to work fo'. Some of the company big shots was down on the docks today and said that they was looking fo' some strong men. They lost some of they men during the war and have a lot of work coming in. The only catch is that we have to be willing to move to New York."

"That's awful fast, Irving. How we gone get to New York by Wednesday?" she asked. "I am coming with you, ain't I? Or do I gotta stay here?"

"No, no, baby," he started, "we both going. We got to leave first thing Wednesday morning, but the job don't start 'til after New Year in three weeks. They say that'll give us time to get settled in the new city."

"We being paid fo' that time, too! The company gone pay fo' us to move and fo' the hotel they gone set us up in. I ain't never heard o' nothin' like that befo', 'specially fo' no colored men. They must be real, real desperate fo' men to work."

"We prayed last night to get out this house. It must be the Lord's doin'. You know the Lord work in mysterious ways!" Ethel said.

Irving pulled a list from his pocket and gave it to Ethel. "They gave us a list of 'partments we could move to. See!"

"Yeah, I see!" Ethel jumped up and hugged Irving around the neck. "That's real good news, Irving. Oh, Irving! You such a good man. I thank God I got you fo' my husband!"

They looked deep into each other's eyes.

"I thank God ever'day that you my wife, Ethel!" he said as he kissed her lips. "I was gone from you all them years. We ain't even been married that long when I left. Just knowing that you was gone be waitin' gave me the strength to make it through the war. All I want to do is take real good care o' you and our chil'ren when we have 'em."

Ethel got up from the kitchen table and fixed Irving a big mug of hot cocoa.

"Boy," Irving started. "This here cocoa sho' taste good. It feel good too, 'specially after I been out on that chilly river since six this morning."

"Anything fo' you, Irving," Ethel teased as she poured him more cocoa. He slapped her on the behind before she sat down to the table again.

"The way I figure it, I gone see 'bout that new GI Bill I been hearing 'bout, and see 'bout gettin' us a real house! Hell. I might even get some training or even go to college, if they'll pay fo' it.

"Hell, I served this country, and did a damned good job doing it, too! I was busting my tail out there on the front line, being shot at, and bombed at, and everything else at! Them decorations and medals they done gave me ain't doin' no good! I got scrap metal and bone fragments in my body that the doctors say is too small to get out of me. I just gotta live with 'em 'til I die!

"I wasn't sho' if I would live or die each minute o' the day. We had to stay up, sometimes fo' days at a time. I was 'fraid to sleep when I got the chance 'cause I didn't know if I was gone be blown to kingdom come! I gone try to get ever'thing that they got to give! I done paid my dues and ever'body else dues too!"

***

Ms. Mabel went back to working days at the factory. Irving and Ethel went by later that night when they knew she would be home. Christmas lights trimmed the house, and lights from the tree inside flashed through the window. A single handmade reef that was decorated with a red velvet bow, holly, and pinecones hung on the entrance door.

"I hope it ain't too late, Ms. Mabel," Ethel said as she walked through the door.

"It never too late fo' you, Ethel. Y'all come on in," Ms. Mabel said as she led them down the hallway to the kitchen. "Make yo'self at home. Can I get y'all something?"

They sat in the kitchen. Pearl-Elizabeth was cleaning up from supper.

"No, thanks," Irving said. "We just ate."

"I'm gone quit the factory this Friday," Ms. Mabel informed them. "I'm getting too old to be working so much anyway. After you quit, Ethel, it ain't so much fun no mo'. Besides, Pearl-Elizabeth here is gone be starting Dillard in January and gone need me to watch the baby while she 'tend school."

"That's wonderful, Pearl-Elizabeth!" Ethel told her.

"Thank you," she answered.

"What you gone go to school to be?" Ethel asked.

"A nurse."

"That's good. You should be able to get on at Flint Goodrich after you finish. They always need nurses."

"I was thinking 'bout goin' to school myself. They have that new GI Bill that gone pay fo' ed'cation fo' vet'rans like myself. But I don't know what a colored man could go to school fo' and get a decent job when he come out."

"They is plenty o' things," Ms. Mabel said. "Just ask the Lord to guide you. He'll show you the way."

Irving and Ethel looked at each other, then Ms. Mabel.

"Well, Ms. Mabel," Ethel started. "We moving to New York."

"New York?" Ms. Mabel shouted and put her hands over her mouth. "Good God almighty! When y'all decided to move?"

"I was down at the docks this morning to see if I could get my old job back. They was these big shots from the ship line that Kent Simms got on. You remember Kent Simms, heh, Ms. Mabel?"

"Yes, I do. He that big fella that used to live up the street in the row, ain't he?" Ms. Mabel asked. "The one who look like a big hairy bear."

"Yup! That's Kent Simms. Well, I got on with the same ship line. They must need people to work real, real bad 'cause they offer to pay all our moving 'penses, our hotel, and even our train tickets up there."

Ms. Mabel and Pearl-Elizabeth looked at each other in disbelief.

"Well, I better give y'all Martha's address," she said then retrieved a black pen from the left pocket of her navy-blue uniform dress. "Where y'all gone be staying anyhow? Martha live in Harlem."

"I don't know. They gave us a list of 'partments we could see 'bout moving to."

" 'Partments?" Ms. Mabel started. "Pearl-Elizabeth, get me that there paper in the drawer there." Pearl-Elizabeth handed her the paper and she began to write Martha's address and handed it to Irving. "Here. Now Isaac and Martha have some houses they rent out to people. When y'all get there go by and say that Ms. Mabel said to give y'all one of them there houses."

"Who is Martha?" Irving asked. "What's her last name?"

"Oh," Ms. Mabel said. "I ain't put they name on it. I forget you never met them. They name is Dickerson. Isaac and Martha Dickerson."

"That's my aunt," Pearl-Elizabeth told Irving.

"Yeah, and she also Freda sister, too," Ethel told him.

"I ain't know that Freda had no kin," he appeared hesitant. "I don't know."

"It's all right, Irving," Ethel assured. "I met Martha and she real good peoples. She ain't nothin' like Freda. Besides Fred and Shirley wedding, they ain't seen each other since 'bout '20."

"I wouldn't be sending you to nobody who wasn't no good peoples, Irving!" Ms. Mabel told him. "Now. When y'all leaving?"

"Day after tomorrow," Irving told her.

"Day after tomorrow? Y'all ain't gone be here for Christmas next week?" Ms. Mabel shouted. "Why so soon? That don't give me no time to prepare dinner or no party!"

"We don't need no dinner or no party, Ms. Mabel," Ethel told her.

"I gotta do somethin'," Ms. Mabel told Ethel. "Y'all come on by tomorrow 'bout this time. I'm gone do a li'l somethin'."

"We need to sell our furniture, 'cause we can't take it wit' us. If we can't sell it, then we have to put in out on the street to be picked up by the garbage people," Irving told Ms. Mabel.

"We gone start all over," Ethel said. "We don't want no 'minders of that house."

"What did Mr. Miller say 'bout y'all moving?" Ms. Mabel asked. "He got somebody else to move in there?"

"He say it's fine. I don't know if somebody else 'posed to move in. Probably not, since we just told him today."

"You know," Ms. Mabel said as she shook her index finger, "Fred and Shirley could use a bigger place and some mo' furniture. Tell you what, I'll ask Fred if he want to buy the furniture. I usually see him before I go to work."

"All right, Ms. Mabel," Irving told her.

"We better start packing," Ethel said.

"I'm sho' gone miss you, Ethel," Ms. Mabel said.

"Me too," Pearl-Elizabeth said as she hugged Ethel.

"Ee oo!" little Solomon said as he hugged Ethel's leg and laughed.

Ethel picked him up and gave him a long kiss to the cheek. He giggled and giggled as she squeezed him tight. "I'm gone miss you, li'l Solomon," she said. "No. You a big boy now. I'm gone call you King Solomon."

Everyone laughed, and tried hard to fight the urge of tears that was hidden deep behind the laughter.

***

Irving and Ethel arrived at Ms. Mabel's around 7:30. They could smell the cinnamon from the door.

"Smell like Ms. Mabel apple cider," Ethel said. "I know her apple cider anywhere."

"Come on in," Ms. Mabel said. She was still wearing her work clothes, but had a great deal of energy.

This time, Ms. Mabel led them into the kitchen, which was much cozier and intimate than the dining room. Pearl-Elizabeth and Shirley were just straightening up. They had baked ham, black-eyed peas with ham hocks and rice, cabbage, and corn muffins.

Delores was cooling fudge brownies on the countertop. She also prepared hot apple cider spiked with rum, and eggnog spiked with brandy. Fred and Ray were setting the table.

"Since y'all ain't gone be here fo' New Year's, we thought we bring New Year's to y'all," Ms. Mabel said.

"Shirley and I may not cook like grandma, but we sure did try hard," Pearl-Elizabeth told Ethel.

"We sure did," Shirley said.

"It sho' taste good to me," Irving said.

"This is real good," Ethel agreed. "We sho' do 'preciate this. Y'all don't know how much. We gone really miss all y'all."

"You write, you hear, Ethel?" Ms. Mabel said.

"Maybe you could visit, Ms. Mabel."

"I sho' would like that," Ms. Mabel told her.

"I went to see Mr. Miller 'bout that there house," Fred told Irving between bites of ham. "He said me and Shirley can have it. I heard you selling that there furniture."

"Yeah, man," Irving said. "We can't take it wit' us. We startin' all over."

"We leaving the furniture, dishes, pots, pans, linen, ever'thing," Ethel told them.

"Why don't we 'cuss what you want fo' the furniture after dinner," Fred told him. "We got 'nough pots, pans, sheets, and you name it from wedding presents. But we could sho' use the furniture."

"I could use the pots and pans," Delores informed them. "I'm moving to my own place over the weekend."

"Better yet," Irving started. "Y'all can just have it."

"Naw," Fred said. "We don't take no handouts!"

"We pay fo' ever'thing we want!" Delores told Irving.

"It ain't no handout, y'all," Ms. Mabel said. "They just want to move on to they new life. Taking money fo' that stuff just gone remind them of the past. How Irving went to war and how they was separated. That's all it is." Ms. Mabel and Ethel exchanged glances. They both knew that she was right, but left out a vital part of the story that Fred or nobody else needed to know.

"If you put it that way," Fred said. "We'll take it."

***

Delores, Pearl-Elizabeth, and Shirley cleared the table and cleaned the kitchen, while everyone else went into the parlor. Ms. Mabel always decorated the Christmas tree with the most shimmering golden tinsel and green and red bulbs. Presents were carefully placed below. Ethel looked at it long and hard because she realized that that would be her last time spending Christmas season with Ms. Mabel.

The wood crackled in the fireplace as it gently radiated warmth throughout the room. Its flames twinkled brightly like a star in the night, sharing its brilliance with the earth below, guiding spectators safely along their journeys through life.

Delores, Pearl-Elizabeth, and Shirley brought in refreshments and served Irving, Ethel, and Ray. *This the first time I been in Ms. Mabel house and ain't had to do nothin'*, Ethel thought.

"Here, take a brownie," Delores said as she handed Ethel the porcelain serving tray.

Delores be always trying to make folk eat sweets. She need to cut back herse'f. Look like she gettin' fat, Ethel thought as she bit into the rich chocolate fudge dessert.

King Solomon saw the excitement and ran straight into Ethel's lap. "God, I'm gone miss King Solomon. He so cute and cuddly. He so full of love and energy. He so innocent. Don't know no evil," Ethel said as she cradled him in her arms.

Everybody gathered around Irving and Ethel and gave them gifts.

"What's all this?" Ethel acted surprised.

"Since y'all ain't gone be here fo' Christmas next Tuesday," Ms. Mabel started, "we decided to bring Christmas to y'all."

"We felt the same way," Ethel announced. She opened the large, red shopping bag she carried and handed out gifts to everyone there, including King Solomon.

They all sat on the floor near the fireplace. Everybody nibbled brownies and sipped eggnog or apple cider through the night. Ms. Mabel began to sing "Holy Night" and the party joined in. Even King Solomon tried to keep a tune in his baby talk.

"Y'all looking forward to the move?" Ray asked.

"Well, yes and no," Ethel said. "I look forward to being in a new city and Irving new job, but I like the people here in Algiers. I kinda want to stay here, but sometimes you gotta do what the Lord tell you."

"Y'all good peoples," Irving started. "I heard so many good things 'bout y'all from Ethel. I'm sorry I ain't get no chance to really know y'all like Ethel do."

"Ever'body move from time to time," Ms. Mabel said. "Me and my husband moved from the Bayous to Algiers. We missed the people there, too, but we had to do it 'cause my late husband had a chance to make a better life fo' his family.

"Arthur and Margaret moved from Harlem to Chicago because Arthur had a chance to run his own practice." Those words made Pearl-Elizabeth uncomfortable. "And you, Ray," Ms. Mabel started. "Even you and..." Ms. Mabel paused and realized that the name she was about to say would have been like a shrill noise to everyone's ears.

"I used to hear ol' folk say," Ms. Mabel continued. Everyone looked at her strangely when she said *ol' folk*. "They used to say that if you turn down op'tunity, it would never come yo' way 'gain. My momma used to say that's why so many people be miserable in life. 'Cause the Lord lead them to op'tunity and they missed it. It was staring them right in the face, and they didn't see it. If the person it was intended fo' don't take it, the Lord give it to somebody else who could see it and 'preciate it."

At that moment, Ray realized that Margaret was his opportunity. *I had her right in my hands*, he thought. *But I had such foolish ideas back then 'bout beauty and let her slip away. Now somebody else got her. The living proof of that is in this room, and her name is Pearl-Elizabeth. Now I'm mis'ble married to ol' lazy, stank Freda who can't cook or fuck worth a damn to save her soul!*

"Do op'tunity come 'gain, Ms. Mabel?" Fred asked.

"Sometime it do, sometime it don't," Ms. Mabel answered. "If it do, it'll be prob'ly years later. I think it's like the bus. They come by on schedule. If you ain't ready to catch it and you get there late, you miss it and got to wait fo' the next one. Depending on the day o' the week, it could be 15 minutes or a hour. But, like the bus, after a certain time, they stop coming altogether. And you just be mis'ble wondering why nothin' don't never go right fo' you."

"How you know if the op'tunity is right, Ms. Mabel?" Fred asked.

"You gotta trust the Lord to guide you. That's how." Ms. Mabel told him. "But some folk miss op'tunity 'cause they too 'fraid to take it. They come up wit' all kinds of 'cuses why they can't or shouldn't do something. Then years later, they say what they shoulda this or woulda that.

"Then they is other folk who miss op'tunity because they lack the wisdom to see it staring them right in the face. The Lord speak to us in many ways. They may see a poster, hear somebody say somethin', hear somethin' on the radio, or just get a gut feeling. That be the Lord speaking. But they be the ones who so busy worryin' 'bout other folk bid'ness, or worryin' 'bout some petty stuff somebody done did to 'em, or just busy goin' through the motions of the day. They just miss it.

"Then, they is others who miss op'tunity 'cause they let other folk discourage them. Them other folk could be either jealous or envious of them, or too 'fraid to take op'tunity they own self and don't want see nobody else make it either. And them fools fall right into the trap other folk done set fo' 'em. 'Specially colored folk. Like I done told Ethel befo', we like crabs in a bucket. When one try to make it, the others pull 'em right back down with the rest o' 'em. The devil work through them kind o' crabs."

"He do?" Fred asked.

"Yes, he do," Ms. Mabel answered.

"How?" Shirley asked.

"Them the kind o' crabs that act like the devil did when he tricked Adam and Eve in the Garden of Eden."

"What do you mean, Ms. Mabel?" Shirley inquired further, between big gulps of hot apple cider. "I thought he made Eve eat from the tree of Good and Evil."

"The Bible is written in what they call parables, in symbols. So, I don't believe that they ate off no real tree, but that tree mean something else altogether."

"Like what?" Fred asked. "I got to hear this," he said as he scooted closer to Ms. Mabel in anticipation of what was coming next.

"Me, too," Shirley agreed and scooted right next to Fred.

"Well, it's like this," Ms. Mabel started. "I think they had mo' people on Earth at that time than them two. But they was the two who brought mankind down, just like some of them crabs who bring people down today.

"If you think about it, Adam and Eve was just as happy in that garden! They ain't had no worries! They had all the food they wanted to eat, so they ain't know nothin' 'bout going hungry. They ain't had no clothes, so they ain't had to worry 'bout lookin' good or tryin' to impress nobody.

"God gave everybody they own mate that was just right for 'em, so they ain't had to worry 'bout nobody foolin' 'round on 'em. That's what it really mean by Eve was created from Adam's rib. She was the right woman made just for 'im. The reason why people have trouble with they mate today is because they wit' somebody who wasn't meant fo' 'im. If they woulda asked God, He woulda gave 'em the mate that was right fo' 'em. The devil can't bust up no union that God made!"

I wish I would o' done that, Ray thought.

"They ain't had to worry 'bout workin' or strugglin' 'cause ever'thing was provided. They was well taken care of. Then, the devil came 'long and put ideas in Eve's head that somethin' was wrong."

"Well, why did he pick Eve?" Shirley asked.

"The devil always pick the weakest person. He know ever'body weakness and use it against them. She was probably the newest person in the garden, naïve. God probably told 'em not to talk to the devil, who was really the tree of Good and Evil. But he tricked Eve by disguising hisself as something else or somebody else who she trusted. That's how crabs work. They is somebody who can get close to you and plant bad thoughts in yo' mind. Or they be somebody who you trust, so you believe what they say."

"You right about that," Fred started. "Yo' enemies can't hurt you 'cause you don't let 'em 'round."

"That's right," Shirley started. "You won't listen to anything they have to say because you know that their heart is in the wrong place."

"You don't have to believe what they say!" Ms. Mabel explained.

"You don't?" Fred asked.

"No," Ms. Mabel continued. "You just have to hear it!"

"If you don't believe what they say, how can they do you harm?" Shirley asked.

"They plant evil thoughts by they words. That's why you gotta be careful 'bout who you be 'round and what you hear. They was a lot of fruit on that tree of Good and Evil. But criticizing, putting people down, giving people bad ideas, and just plain old bad-mouthing was the main ones. And how do people criticize, put folk down, or bad-mouth?"

"With their words," Shirley answered.

"For that fact, you need to be careful what you see, too!" Ray added, as he thought of his weakness for beautiful women.

"And what you say," Irving added, as his voice almost seemed to have come from nowhere. They all looked to the back of the room where he was perched against a mahogany end table. He was quiet all evening, so his comments startled everyone. "My momma used to say that you could talk evil into yo' life by yo' own words."

"So you got to be real, real careful of what you see, speak, and hear?" Ethel asked.

"That's right," Ms. Mabel agreed. "You see, the devil was jealous of mankind and started criticizing Eve. He was feeding her bad thoughts and discouraging her. That didn't just happen one time. No siree! It probably happened over some period of time. Weeks, months, even years! She kept thinking about what the devil told her, and thinking about it, and thinking about it. That's what broke her spirit. He made her feel so bad about herself by telling her all kind o' stuff, like it was wrong to go naked. He planted other bad ideas in her head, too. I bet he musta told her that they was lazy and that they should work real hard fo' what they got."

"I know about bad ideas," Irving started. "Back home in Placquemine, this lady, Ms. Mildred, lost her husband like that. She had a nice house and ain't had to work like the other ladies in the neighborhood. Them other women kept tellin' her that her husband was foolin' 'round, how he was no-good. But he was really working hard on the railroads. People kept tellin' her the same thing over and over, until she finally left him. After that, she had to work real, real hard as a maid and moved from her big house to some li'l bitty row 'partment with her three chil'ren.

"Ms. Lula, one of the friends who was telling her them lies, ended up marrying her husband and living in that big house. People said that Ms. Lula used to go by Ms. Mildred's house a lot, especially right before her husband used to come home from work. They say Ms. Lula musta hexed Ms. Mildred. That's why she left her husband and big house to go live in that li'l bitty 'partment."

"Sound like to me that the only hex Ms. Mildred had was to have a friend like Ms. Lula," Fred said.

"Yeah," Shirley agreed, "and let Ms. Lula get in her business."

"Seems like they had it pretty good in the Garden of Eden," Ethel said. "I wish things was like that today."

"It was pretty good," Ms. Mabel started again. "They had plenty food to eat, ain't got sick, and ain't know no pain. They was meant to live forever, too! But that old devil started tellin' Eve that she gone get old, sick, and die some day. Then Eve started telling that mess to Adam and the other people. After awhile, everybody started to believe that lie. It was too late to stop it because people already started to live it! Just like when one of them crabs go spreading gossip and lies about somebody, and people believe it, it's hard fo' that person to clear they name. That's what happened with God and mankind back then when the devil told lies about God.

"Then when God came a callin' one day, they hid theyselves because they was naked. Think about it! They was already naked! God made them that way! Why would they be shamed to be naked in front of God unless somebody told 'em it was wrong? They had to leave the garden because the devil convinced them that they had to work hard fo' what they had. That was a lie, too, because God provided them with ever'thing. If He wanted them to work hard, don't you think that He woulda made it that way from the beginning?"

"So we ain't supposed to work, Ms. Mabel?" Delores asked.

"Well, yes and no," Ms. Mabel started. "Yes, God intended fo' us to work and to share our talents with the world. But he ain't want us to get all wore out working like we do today! Back in the garden," Ms. Mabel sipped some eggnog, as the fire crackled behind her, "everybody probably had a job. God put 'em in a place that they prob'bly liked to work, doing what they was good at. One person prob'bly gathered fruits and nuts for the village, while another sang and danced to entertain folk, while somebody else was a storyteller. Ever'body had a purpose. They wasn't no money back then, so ever'body worked together for the common good of the village. Ever'body did his fair share."

"I wish it was like today, boy!" Fred said as he shook his head. "At my job, don't nobody work together. When you turn yo' back, somebody be tryin' to stab you in it! And somebody always be tryin' to push they work off on somebody else. That's somethin' else, I'm tellin', boy!"

"Sometimes, I get mad with Adam and Eve for making God put them out the garden," Shirley said.

"They was so convinced by what the devil said," Ms. Mabel started as she took a few more sips of eggnog, "they was no way they coulda stayed in the garden. God didn't put 'em out, they put they ownself out by believing that they didn't deserve God's blessings.

"You know what they say, 'God can only do for you what he can do through you.' That mean that if you believe that you should have hardship and don't deserve His blessing, then God can't move in yo' life. And them crabs do a good job puttin' folk down and makin' them believe that they don't deserve God's blessings. When you stop believing the garbage that them crabs say and know in yo' heart that you deserve the best God got to offer, then He can make miracles happen in yo' life.

"My momma used to say that way, way back in time, ever'body knew how to do magic. But because man was so evil, God took they power 'way. The devil musta told people that it was wrong to use they powers and made 'em lose it. So people used they magic less and less, and didn't bother to teach they chil'ren about it either. During the Dark Ages, people was killed for using magic. So, over the years, man just lost it. God didn't take it away!

"Everybody got magic. It's like learning how to walk. It's natural. Something strange may happen to you, and it's really yo' magic working. You might think you not feeling well or might dismiss it altogether. But it's there.

"You hear people say it's wrong to use magic. You hear the preachers preaching 'gainst people using magic. They say it's the devil's work. Well, that kinda true." She pointed at the raging flames behind her and everyone looked that way. "Take that fire there. It's heating the house and that's good. But you could take that same fire and burn the house down, and that's bad. So magic is the same way.

"The devil know that if ever'body could use magic, they would be like God. And if they like God, they would 'ventually ward him off. That's why he spread the lie that magic is bad. Y'all 'member it say that only the Tree of Life could save mankind? Well, that so-called magic is the fruit of that tree. It's what put us in touch with God. The devil and his demons, and them crabs, is what keep people from eating from the Tree of Life.

"I have dreams that come true and sometime have these feelings that I can't 'plain. Sometime I just know things. It must be my woman's intuition I guess, but I believe men get it too. This is 'specially true when I get quiet and go deep, deep in thought. Some folk would say that that's from the devil, but in my heart, I know it's from God."

"I read a book about that, grandma," Pearl-Elizabeth said as she cradled a sleeping King Solomon in her arms. "The deep, deep thoughts you're talking about is what they call meditation. It's supposed to put you in touch with your higher self, in touch with God."

"You can give it some fancy name if you want to. But you see, if ever'body was to have dreams, or use they intuition, or get deep, deep in thought, then they would rec'nize who the devil, his demons, and them crabs is right away. They could then ward them off!"

"The devil don't want that to happen!" Shirley said.

"No, he don't," Ms. Mabel agreed.

"Well, how do we protect ourselves from all this evil?" Shirley asked. "What can we do?"

"Our job is to rec'nize them crabs and 'void them like the plague. It don't matter who it is. Yo' momma, daddy, sister, brother, anybody. If they a crab, they ain't no good fo' you. Don't have 'em 'round."

It seemed that everyone in the room thought of several crabs. They all shared one in common, Freda, each for a different reason.

"A crab don't have to be a person," Ms. Mabel continued.

"It don't?" Fred asked.

"No. It can be yo' job, yo' church, yo' house, or anything that's a hassle to you. Anything that cause you pain and grief. Anything that drag you down."

"Umph," Fred said. "I never thought 'bout it like that befo'."

"The Father don't want his chil'ren to be mis'ble," Ms. Mabel continued. "Not even for a second out of any day. He want all his chil'ren to enjoy they life ever'day. And that's the truth!"

"How you get rid of them crabs?" Delores asked.

"It's not easy, chil'. 'Cause sometime you don't know who or what yo' crab is 'til it's too late. We also got to make sho' that we ain't no crab to ourself or nobody else," Ms. Mabel started. " 'Cause if we is a crab, either we pay or somebody close to us pay, for bringin' somebody else down or makin' somebody else miss they op'tunity. That's why you gots to know the Lord and ask fo' his he'p ever'day."

I'm gone miss talkin' to Ms. Mabel, Ethel thought as she looked into the fire and sipped eggnog. *I learn somethin' new from her ever'day. It's like she gimme a new way to look at life.*

***

Yellow streaks appeared across the horizon, as it erased the darkness behind it. The sun peeked through, little by little, until it made its presence known. Ethel and Ms. Mabel both admired the sky as they sat in Fred's blue Ford on the ferry.

"Look how pretty the sun look 'gainst the waves," Ethel told Ms. Mabel. "I ain't know it could look so pretty from the car section."

"Ever'thing 'bout the Lord look pretty ever'where, chil'," Ms. Mabel told her.

"What time you gotta be to work, Ms. Mabel?" Fred asked.

"At seven o'clock," Ms. Mabel told him. "I told 'em I was gone be late. It ain't gone hurt if I'm late just this one day. So what if they dock my pay! I ain't never been late befo'. That job ain't goin' nowhere!"

They all sat in silence as the ferry carried them gently over the mighty Mississippi. Fred kept the engine running.

"Chestnuts roasting o'er an open fire, Jack Frost nipping at your nose. Yuletide carols … Merry Christmas. Merry Christmas …" Ethel hummed as the tune played on the radio. Ethel placed her head on Ms. Mabel's shoulders. Ms. Mabel placed her arm around Ethel and began to rock back and forth. Fred and Irving were in the front seat and softly hummed along.

The conductor blew the horn to signal drivers to start their engines. The engineer secured the ferry to the dock. Shortly thereafter, the traffic cop began to direct cars off of the ferry and safely onto Canal Street.

"We wish you a Merry Christmas … and a happy New Year … we wish you a Merry Christmas … and a happy New Year … good tidings …a Merry Christmas…" Ethel hummed along with the radio, as Fred and Irving joined in.

***

"We here, y'all," Fred informed his passengers.

Ethel reluctantly withdrew from Ms. Mabel's embrace. Fred and Irving went around the back of the car. The loud thump of the trunk closing signaled Ethel and Ms. Mabel to leave the car. They saw Irving carrying four large suitcases toward the depot and knew that it was time to go.

"It's time to go, baby," Ms. Mabel told Ethel, as she fought the avalanche of tears.

Fred and Ms. Mabel stayed with Irving and Ethel until it was time to board the train. "Chestnuts roasting on an open fire … yuletide … Merry Christmas … Merry Christmas," Ethel hummed along with the music that played over the loud speaker.

"All aboard!!" the conductor announced.

"'Bye, man," Fred said as he shook Irving's hand. "Take care o' yo'self."

"You do the same, man," Irving told him, then boarded the train.

"I'm gone miss you, Ethel," Ms. Mabel said as tears streamed from her eyes.

"I'm gone miss you, too, Ms. Mabel."

"I love you, Ethel!"

"I love you, too, Ms. Mabel."

They could stand it no more. A gush of tears flowed endlessly from their eyes as they stood there, locked in an impenetrable embrace. Their cries were heard throughout the station, and caught the attention of passersby.

"Come on, Ethel," Irving told her, as he tried to pry his wife apart from Ms. Mabel. "The train 'bout to leave."

The train conductor and workers were touched by Ms. Mabel and Ethel. A few of the passengers were so moved that they started to sob themselves.

"'Bye, Ethel," Ms. Mabel shouted as Ethel boarded the train. "I'm gone miss you, baby!"

"'Bye, Ms. Mabel," Ethel bawled. "I'm gone miss you, too!"

Ms. Mabel's eyes followed Ethel to her seat, as they looked deep into each other's eyes through the window. Their stares remained locked until Ethel was completely out of sight.

"Come on, Ms. Mabel," Fred said as he placed his arms around Ms. Mabel's shoulders and held her tightly. "Time to go."

Ms. Mabel bawled all the way to the car, catching the attention of passersby. *That Freda! God find her!* Ms. Mabel thought. *If it wasn't fo' her, Irving and Ethel wouldna had to move! That ol' evil heifer! She need to go back to Hell where she come from! God find her soul! God find her soul!*

Chapter 22.

Trouble in Hell

It was seven o'clock at night, and Fred was just getting in from work. Shirley was waiting for him at the front door, wearing her coat and gloves.

"Umm, ummm!" Fred said as he walked in front of the apartment and smelled fresh cinnamon. "I wonder what she done cooked today!" He noticed three large pots on the stove from the front steps, then Shirley stopped him before he entered the door.

"Fred," Shirley started. "Your daddy said for us to go to his house when you get home, no matter how late. It's real important."

"What so important?" Fred asked. "Can we eat first?"

"Your daddy said it's real, real important, Fred. We can eat later, baby," Shirley insisted.

"All right," Fred said as they headed out the door. He turned back once more to take a whiff of the dinner that so tempted his taste buds.

A black Ford was parked out front when they arrived at the house. A stranger was sitting inside with the windows cracked, listening to the radio.

"I wonder who that is," Fred said to Shirley as they passed by.

When they got inside, Freda was seated against the back wall. Delores was still wearing her work clothes and seemed to be in a hurry.

"We got a package from Carter, Fred!" Ray said. "I ain't want to open it without y'all here. That mean he alive, y'all! He alive!" Ray showed them the postmark. "Look, he in Paris, France!"

"I wonder what's in it?" Fred asked.

The package was flat, square, and hard. It was carefully wrapped in heavy mailing paper. "Do not bend" was stamped twice on the front and twice on the back. Ray tore the paper as everyone else looked on anxiously. It was a handwritten letter and photograph of Carter in his uniform. Ray read the letter out loud to his family—

Dear Mother and Father:

I made it through the war with not as much as a scratch. We had some rough times, and I wasn't so sure if I was going to make it out alive. But I did.

I like it here in Paris so much. I'm even starting to learn French. How about that for you?

The French don't care that I'm colored. The only people seem to care that I'm colored are the white soldiers. I've seen many colored soldiers die because of so-called friendly fire. They died at the hands of whites and other coloreds over foolishness. Sometimes it got hard to tell who the enemy really was. We had to fight the Germans and Japanese. At the same time we had to fight the whites and coloreds, too. It wasn't easy being a colored man in the war. I'm glad it's finally over.

In Paris, I don't have to face the same pressure that I do back home. It seems like a colored man has a fair chance here. Even after risking my life fighting for my country, I don't believe that I will be treated with respect if I return back to Louisiana. I will have to sit in the back of the bus. I will still be cussed at, called names, and treated like an animal. After being here, I can't stand the thought of having to face that again.

That's why I've decided to call Paris my home. I won't be returning back to Louisiana. Paris is where I belong.

I've included a picture of me in my uniform. It was taken right after training camp in 1943. I promise to write often and I hope you do the same.

Love,
Carter

***

Freda sat there stunned, at a loss for words. She took the photograph from the package and ran her fingers across the metal frame. Tears began to cascade down her cheeks.

"I gotta go," Delores said. "My ride waiting outside."

"Who that is, Delores?" Fred asked.

Ray gave Fred a curious look, while Freda continued to stare endlessly at the photograph.

"Go on," Ray told Delores. "Tell 'im."

"That's Elgin," Delores told Fred.

"Go on," Ray told Delores. "Tell 'im the rest."

"I'm pregnant and me and Elgin moving in together."

"Oh," Fred started. "When y'all got married?"

"Hell no! They ain't married!" Ray shouted.

Freda continued to rock back and forth, this time cradling the photograph in her arms.

Delores ran out of the house before anyone could say another word and quickly got into the car with Elgin. The next thing they heard was the screeching sound of tires.

***

Delores moved to the Ninth Ward off of St. Claude Avenue the afternoon after Ethel left for New York. Elgin Wilkerson convinced her to live in sin with him. He was a smooth talker, dressed to kill, and made good money working the shipyards.

"What's a piece of paper anyway, Delores? That don't mean nothing."

Delores was four months pregnant and Freda insisted that she leave the house. The only place she could have gone was to Elgin's.

"Daddy, how you gone let yo' daughter live in sin like that?" Fred asked Ray.

"Boy, that girl stubborn," Ray started. "She got a mind o' her own. Ain't nothin' I can do."

Fred turned to Freda and asked, "Momma, how you gone let Delores shack up with somebody?"

Freda ignored him, walked into her bedroom and closed the door behind.

Fred took matters into his own hands. First he contacted Dr. Pickens, who helped him to get the marriage license without Elgin's permission and without all the red tape. Dr. Pickens pulled a few strings and was able to get it the same day.

Elgin was several inches shorter than Fred was, and much skinnier. Fred caught Elgin going home from work the next day. He sneaked up on him from behind and knocked him down with a two-by-four. Three of Shirley's brothers stood over him.

"You ain't gone fuck over my sister, moth' fucker. You gone marry her."

Fred hit Elgin in the knees with the two-by-four, then one of Shirley's brothers pulled out a sawed-off shotgun.

"You gone marry my sister, moth' fucker."

"You crazy. You crazy!" he gasped. Fred pulled out a pistol and put it to his ear. "Don't shoot! Don't shoot!" he pleaded. "Don't shoot!"

"She ain't waitin' no mo'," Fred told him.

They dragged him to St. Mark's Baptist Church. Benjamin Payne, Shirley's uncle, was the pastor there. Delores was wearing a short, white dress and held a small bouquet of flowers. Shirley stood by her side. Shotgun in back, Elgin married Delores that night, Friday, December 21, 1945.

***

It was ten in the morning on Christmas Eve, 1945. Freda was just getting dressed, and Ray was in the shed working. An Army jeep drove up to the house, and two men dressed in military attire stepped out.

"That must be Junior coming home," Freda said as she frantically ran to the shed to get Ray before the men reached the front porch. "Ray! Ray!" Freda shouted. "Junior done come home! Junior done come home!"

Ray and Freda heard a loud knock on the front door. When they opened it, one of the men was facing toward the street.

"Junior!" Freda exclaimed.

When the officer turned around, they were disappointed that it wasn't Junior.

"Are you Mr. and Mrs. Raymond Simon Marshall, Sr., of Teche Street, New Orleans, Louisiana?" the first officer asked. "I'm Officer Anderson and this is Officer Smith."

"Yes," Ray answered. "That's us. Why don't you gentlemen come in."

They all sat in the living room. The officers removed their hats. Ray and Freda expected good news about Junior.

Officer Anderson was tall and muscular, with dark, curly hair and dark eyes. From a distance and from behind, he looked like Junior. He couldn't have been more than 24 years old.

Officer Smith was tall and slim with ash-blond hair and baby-blue eyes. He, too, couldn't have been more than 24 years old.

"Maybe we should go and get our other son and his wife. They probably want to hear what y'all got to say, too."

"We don't have much time," Officer Smith said. "We'll make it brief."

"He live down the street," Ray started as he motioned to Freda. "My wife, Freda, could go get him. It won't take but a few minutes."

Ray and Freda noticed the looks on the officers' faces. Officer Anderson bit his lower lip and twirled his hat about his finger. Officer Smith stared at the floor for a few seconds, then at Ray and Freda. Ray motioned to Freda to sit back down. "Maybe we could tell them later."

"Your son, Raymond Simon Marshall, Jr., was killed during active service."

Freda looked shocked. "No, no!" she cried. "That can't be! That can't be!"

"When and where did it happen?" Ray asked.

"It happened last August in Iwo Jima, Japan."

"How y'all know it was him?" Freda asked.

"He was still wearing his dog tags," Officer Anderson informed her.

"Dog tag?" Freda asked.

"Yeah," Ray told Freda. "It's those things that look like silver bracelets that they wear 'round they neck. It have they name and other information about them on it. Everybody get 'em. I had 'em when I was in World War I."

"Why it take so long fo' y'all to come and tell us?" Freda asked.

"It took us a while to find all the bodies and identify them," Officer Smith said. His voice had begun to crack and his face turned redder than beets.

"Mr. and Mrs. Marshall," Officer Anderson started. "Your son died a hero's death, in the line of duty defending his country. You should be proud."

"The Army will pay for the memorial service," Officer Smith said.

"Memorial service?" Ray asked. "How 'bout a funeral?"

The officers looked at each other. Officer Anderson twirled his hat even faster around his finger.

"The body was too badly decomposed when we found it. A memorial service is all we can do. I'm sorry."

***

Ray and Freda were not churchgoers, so the memorial service was held at the colored funeral home across Newton Street. It was small with white walls and white tile floors. Straight ahead was the casket covered with an American flag. Soldiers dressed in military garb stood at each side. A picture of Junior sat on top.

It was two days after Christmas, and many people in the community weren't in the mood to pay respects to the family at that time of year. Besides, they really didn't know the Marshall family very well. Those who did couldn't stand to be around Freda.

Besides Ray and Freda, the place was nearly empty. Delores stopped in for a few minutes while Elgin stayed outside in the car. Fred wore a black suit. He sat with his knees apart and head held low. Shirley was by his side.

"I'm sorry about your loss," Pearl-Elizabeth told Ray and Freda. "I'm just down the street if you need anything."

Pearl-Elizabeth and Freda made eye contact that seemed to spark a feeling of mutual respect and kinship.

"I'm sorry about Junior," Ms. Mabel told Ray and Freda. "If they is anything I can do, just let me know," she said as she hugged Ray. When Ms. Mabel put her arms around Freda, she began to cry loud and hard.

"Why?" Freda shouted. Her cries were heard all the way to the street. "Why? Why?" She fell to her knees as Shirley and Ms. Mabel tried in vain to console her.

Shirley got her some water from the kitchen in the back. Ms. Mabel fanned her with a paper fan.

"It's gone be all right," Ms. Mabel assured. "It's gone be all right."

The casket was taken to the hearse outside for its journey to its final resting place in the family plot that Ray purchased during the '30s. Ms. Mabel and the rest of the family rode in the limousine that followed behind. Elgin followed them to the cemetery in his car.

"I thought I would be the first to be buried in that plot," Ray said. "It sho' is sad to bury one o' yo' chil'ren."

No one said anything the rest of the trip. Freda was deep in thought. Her eyes were fixed on an imaginary object before her.

A feeling, a knowingness struck Ms. Mabel as she looked to the clouds above. *Freda wasn't the one who was ridin' Ethel*, she thought. *If she was the one who vexed Ethel, she wouldn't be sitting here next to me.*

***

The soldiers folded the flag into a triangular shape and presented it to Freda. The casket was then slowly lowered into the ground and covered with dirt. The top two feet of the plot were above ground and surrounded by white cinderblocks.

The officers presented Freda with a picture of Junior in his uniform. She hugged and caressed the frame, as though she were cradling a newborn infant. To her, Junior looked like the epitome of valor in his uniform. The military hat, with its wide brim, accented his square jaws and dimpled chin. His back was straight, with shoulders and chest held high.

All that Freda had of Junior was his picture, a two-dimensional token that bridged the gap between her world and his. Junior's brusque facial expression and deep, dark, penetrating eyes offered a profound sense of intimacy to the audience who had admired his image–even for a moment.

To her, Junior was a prisoner, a soul trapped within a universe of finite time and space, bound by the confines of the picture frame. Her son was taken hostage by one quick camera flash. She yearned for him to be a part of her world, that ominous place called life. Forever separate, Freda knew that their paths would never again cross.

Part III.
Full Speed Ahead

You open to all sorts of things when you ain't connected to the Lord. When you with Him, He protect you.

Chapter 23.
A New Day

Delores's husband, Elgin Wilkerson, decided that he no longer wanted the responsibility of a family. He was working the shipyards and put in a lot of overtime hours, but he spent all of his money on fancy clothes and a good time. There was hardly anything left for food, clothes, or the house. He finally walked out in 1950, when their daughter, Robin, was four years old. In the meantime, Delores and her little girl had to survive.

One day, Robin was playing outside with a friend. They noticed her father walking down the street carrying a bag of groceries.

"Look!" Robin was so excited. "My daddy is bringing us something!" She was heartbroken when he passed them, not even saying a word.

"No he ain't," her friend said. "He taking it to that Spanish lady he shackin' with down the street."

Elgin stopped by sometimes to bring money or toys for Robin. But he left town when Fred urged Delores to go after him for child support. Nobody heard from him since that time.

***

Delores made two friends, Aletha Watkins, who lived around the corner, and her aunt, Ms. Iris Turner, who lived next door.

Aletha was about 25 at the time. She was short and stout with smooth chocolate skin. Her black, shoulder-length hair was always pushed back into a ponytail. She had been working at the tool factory on Japanica Street since the war, and got Delores a job there after Elgin left. It paid well, and she was able to work a lot of overtime hours.

Ms. Iris was a widow whose husband was killed during World War II. She lived on a military pension, but made extra money selling cold-cups, pralines, and popcorn balls to the neighborhood children. Ms. Iris looked like an older version of Aletha. People always thought that Aletha was her daughter and not her brother's.

While Delores was at work, Ms. Iris looked after Robin.

"Robin is a good, sweet li'l girl," Ms. Iris often told Delores. "She keep me real good company."

For the next two years, Delores put in a lot of overtime. She bought a new phonograph, albums and 45s, and a new black-and-white console television. Delores replaced all of her old furniture, and even bought a white bedroom set for Robin's room.

Robin wore the prettiest little dresses, and had the prettiest bows in her hair. During the summer, Delores took Robin to Lincoln Beach, the colored amusement park on Haynes Boulevard, at least twice a month. Sometimes, she took King Solomon and Fred's boys, too.

One Sunday, Delores invited her parents and Fred and his family over for dinner. It was a cold February day. Space heaters were located in every room and gently warmed the entire house.

"Oooo," Ray said. "It sho' feel good up in here!"

"It sho' is freezing outside today, boy!" Fred said.

"Hello, sugar!" Ray shouted as he opened his arms to Robin. "Come give yo' grandpa a big hug." He hugged Robin, then reached into his pocket and gave her a crisp, new dollar bill.

"Thank you, grandpa!" Robin was excited as she looked at it.

"Ain't you got some sugar for yo' Uncle Fred and Aunt Shirley?" Fred asked Robin. Shirley, who was expecting again, reached into her purse and gave Robin a popcorn ball.

"Thank you, Uncle Fred! Thank you, Aunt Shirley!"

Robin took Fred, Jr., Stephen, Rueben, and Curtis to the back room to play. Cyril was only a year old, and too young to join the others. Robin shared her popcorn ball with her cousins.

The white lace draperies complemented the brown living-room set and mahogany coffee and end tables. The television was blasting in the background as Freda looked on in fascination.

She don't need nothin' like that, Freda thought. *We ain't had no television, and still don't! We doing just fine!*

Down the hall was Delores's room, but they didn't bother to go in. Across from that was Robin's bedroom. Pink-and-white-checked curtains brightened the room. Several colored dolls and teddy bears lined her bed. Across from the bathroom was the extra room that Delores turned into a sewing and hobby suite.

"That ol' gal don't need her own room!" Freda commented. "And what you gone do wit' that other room anyhow? You got all that there junk in it! You can't live in all this house. You got too much!"

The kitchen was huge, with a large, white refrigerator, range and double-sink. White cabinets with peek-through glass covered most of the walls. To the back was the door that led to the backyard.

"Who cut yo' grass?" Freda asked Delores.

"One of the neighborhood boys cut it in the summer," she answered.

"You got a li'l bitty yard anyway," Freda commented. "That boy just cheatin' you out yo' money."

They finally sat down to eat. Delores prepared tossed salad, roasted chicken, green beans, sweet potato pie, and lemonade.

"I like what you did with this place, Delores," Shirley commented.

"Thank you," Delores told Shirley. "I like what y'all did with y'all place."

Two years before, Fred struck a deal with Mr. Miller to buy the house he and Shirley had been renting. Since that time, Fred converted it into a camelback house. He added another room to the back behind the kitchen that he turned into a den, and an upstairs level with two more bedrooms and a bathroom. He added a spiral staircase in the den. The second level, however, only extended from the last downstairs bedroom on the back. From the street, the house looked like a camel.

"How you get the money to buy all this here stuff anyhow, Delores?" Freda asked. "You must be doin' somethin' illegal. If you is, I ain't gone bail you out no jail!"

"She ain't doin' nothing illegal," Ray told Freda. "You oughtta be glad to see her doin' good."

"I work a lot o' overtime at the factory, so I bought what I wanted," Delores informed her.

"You always be workin' all the time. Where that gal o' yours be?" Freda asked.

"Ms. Iris next door watch her."

"Ms. Iris?" Freda asked. "Who that is? You shouldn't be leaving yo' chil' with no strangers!"

"This here some good chicken, Delores," Ray commented.

"It sho' is," Fred agreed.

"Chil," Shirley started. "You must give me your recipe!"

Freda rolled her eyes at everyone at the table. The strong emotions in her eyes made the children become quiet. "It ain't that good!" Freda commented. "I done had better. Much, much better!"

***

All was dark. The space heaters in Robin's room and the bathroom provided a hint of light to the house. A soothing warmth filled the air as

Delores tucked Robin in for the night and gently kissed her forehead.

"Can I sleep with you, momma?" Robin asked.

"Sugar," Delores started. "You got yo' own room with yo' own pretty li'l bed and pretty dolls."

"I'm scared, momma," Robin said.

"Scared?" Delores asked.

"Yeah," Robin started. "Grandma scare me. She 'mind me of the evil witch we read 'bout in school. The one who eat the chil'ren!"

"Oh, baby," Delores started. "Why you say that 'bout yo' grandma?"

"She just look evil, wit' them blue and green eyes and wrinkled skin. She always be real mean, too. That's how that witch be who eat the chil'ren!"

"Oh, baby," Delores assured as she hugged and kissed Robin on the cheek.

"And grandma got that long, pointy nose, just like the evil witch who eat the chil'ren!"

"Robin, that's your grandma."

"And grandma ain't got no teeth. One time when we was by her house, I saw her take her teeth out! Just like the evil witch who eat the chil'ren!"

"All right, baby," Delores started. "How 'bout if I sleep in here with you?"

"Yeah!" Robin shouted. "Now grandma can't come and get me!"

Chapter 24.
Compromising Values

It was May of 1953. On Friday and Saturday nights Fred worked as a bouncer at the joint Dr. Pickens owned. It was down the street from Delores's house. Delores hated bars, but used to baby-sit for Shirley, when she wasn't too far along pregnant, and Pearl-Elizabeth so they have a good time. While they were out partying, she took Robin, King Solomon, and all of Fred's children out for ice cream sundaes and didn't ask their parents for one cent.

The children liked to go for ice cream at Sam's because it was so big. One side was the drugstore, with a pharmacy in the rear and aisles of toiletries, games, books, and especially candy. To the far right were double-glass doors that led to the ice cream parlor. It had white walls with white tiled floor. To the rear was the bar, behind which were soda-pop machines, soft-swirl ice cream machines, and ten flavors of traditional ice cream. Four booths lined the front. That's where the children liked to sit because they could watch the cars pass down the street. To the far right were two tables that sat near the entrance door. Beside them was the jukebox.

Each time Delores took the children to Sam's, she noticed that the same strange man always smiled at her. He was tall and slim with smooth, ebony skin. He was always looking sharp, from his head to his feet.

One day when Delores was waiting for the bus to go to work, the same strange man was waiting, too. "You have a handsome family," he told her. He was wearing a navy blue suit and carrying a black leather briefcase.

"Thank you," Delores started.

"You and your husband must be proud."

"I ain't married."

"Those aren't your children?" he asked.

"Only the girl is mine. The others is my nephews."

"My name is Clarence. Clarence Darrensburg. I'm kinda new in town. I've been living with my sister down the street. I'm going to apply for a job at the colored insurance company on Dryades Street. I'm an insurance man, you know. Wish me luck!"

"Good luck, Mr. Darrensburg," Delores smiled. "Good luck."

That Sunday after church, Delores and Robin were getting ice cream at the corner drugstore. Clarence Darrensburg walked up to them.

"That ice cream sure looks good, little girl," he told Robin, then paid for Delores's and Robin's ice cream cones.

"You don't have to," Delores told him.

"It's no big deal. I'm just being neighborly," he started. "Where I'm from, people do things like this all the time and no one questions it. But, here in New Orleans, people are suspicious of everything you do!"

"Thank you, Mr. Darrensburg," Delores told him.

"Thank you, Mr. Darrensburg," Robin repeated.

"Are you ladies going somewhere?" he asked. "Why don't we have a seat and grab a hamburger." He looked at Robin and asked, "Do you like hamburgers, little girl?"

"Yeah!" she screamed.

"Her name is Robin," Delores informed him. "Where you from?"

"From up North. Cincinnati, Ohio."

***

Over the next few weeks, Delores and Clarence went out on several dates to the movies. Each time, they took Robin with them. He bought them all the popcorn and soft drinks they wanted. They usually went for burgers afterward. Three weeks later, he moved in with Delores and Robin.

***

Delores and Aletha were walking home from the bus stop on St. Claude Avenue. It was seven o'clock and was already starting to get dark. Children were playing stickball on the neighborhood street. Neighbors were sitting on their front porches chatting with other neighbors, enjoying the gentle late August air.

"Chil'," Aletha said. "Why you let that man move in with you like that? You don't know nothin' 'bout him. You don't even know who his peoples is."

"His sister and her two boys live up the street," Delores told her.

"Who? Albertha?" Aletha asked. "Chil', Albertha ain't his sister. They was shackin' and she put his ass out 'cause he ain't had no job!"

"Besides, chil'ren need a man to he'p raise 'em."

"Well, why don't y'all get married then?" Aletha asked.

" 'Cause, Aletha," Delores started. "We can't find Elgin fo' him to sign the divorce papers. Clarence said I would be a poly, polygistmas something if we get married. I could go to jail."

"Ain't they some way you could get divorced anyway?" Aletha pushed. "If I was you, chil', I go see me a lawyer to see what I can do."

"Clarence said that them lawyers cost too much. He said they just take yo' money and don't nothin' fo' you."

"Chil'," Aletha started. "If he really wanted to marry you, he would push heaven and earth to find a way. He wouldn't care how much it cost or who he had to pay! And that's the God-honest truth!"

"We makin' the best of it."

"He found a job yet?" Aletha asked. "He been living in yo' house for damn nearly three months and ain't got no job?"

"He sell insurance. He trying to get sales."

"That's what he told Albertha. She met him one day when she was comin' home from work. She was waitin' on the bus when Clarence started talking to her. He was wearing a blue, pin-striped suit and carrying a briefcase, trying to look important. He told her that he was a big-time insurance agent and was waitin' to get sales. After 'bout three months, she caught on to his game and was 'bout to throw his ass out on the street. Then you took 'im in."

"He is a insurance man. He gotta make a sale to get paid," Delores said. "He don't punch no time clock like we do. They get paid different than we do."

"Chil'," Aletha started. "Aunt Iris said that he be home all day. He don't get up 'til 'bout 11 or 12 o'clock. Then he go down to the bar and be hanging on the street corner 'til befo' you come home."

"He be tryin' to make a sale," Delores insisted. "The people Ms. Iris see him talkin' to, he be trying to sell to."

"Chil'," Aletha said as she rolled her eyes. "Them folk who be hangin' out on the street corner ain't got no money! They pimps just like Clarence!"

"Clarence ain't no pimp!" Delores insisted. "He just need to get a sale, that's all."

***

Over the winter months, Delores's utility bills doubled. It seemed like the more groceries she bought, the less she and Robin had to eat. The more overtime she worked, the less money she had to spend.

Robin, who used to get new clothes almost every month, didn't anymore.

"That girl don't need no new clothes," Clarence told Delores in his at-home, not-so-articulate manner. The suave, ambitious, well-spoken man she met so many months ago had become a slovenly, indolent, slang-pouring sycophant. "You spoilin' that girl rotten! She can get some mo' wear out the ones she got!"

Clarence, on the other hand, bought a new outfit almost every week. "Delores," he would say. "I'm a insurance man. You want me to be lookin' good so I could make a sale, don't you?"

The furniture was worn and torn. The sofa and love seat were ripped at the seams and the stuffing showed through. Not only had the varnish begun to fade off of the coffee and end tables, but large scratches were also noticeable. The knobs were broken off of the television, which didn't matter because the thing barely worked.

***

"What happened up in here?" Fred asked one night when we dropped the children off. "Look like a hurricane done ripped through."

For the past year, Fred had been working two jobs. So when he stopped by to drop the children off, he was usually in a rush to get to the bar on time. When it was time to pick the children up, he blew the horn and they all ran to the car. He, Shirley, or Pearl-Elizabeth never really came in to visit for long.

Delores took Robin and her cousins to the back room to play.

Pearl-Elizabeth noticed a pair of men's shoes under the coffee table, but didn't say a word. She quickly walked to Delores's room and peeked in. Men's trousers littered the floor.

"Fred and Shirley, let me use the bathroom before we leave," Pearl-Elizabeth shouted.

"All right, Lizzy," they answered.

"I'm gone wait in here and watch some TV," Fred said.

The toilet seat was up. Men's razors and cologne populated the medicine cabinet, and slippers were on the floor. Pure evidence that a man was living there.

Fred tried to turn the television on, but the knobs were broken. When he finally got it on, he turned through the stations. Just about all of them were fuzzy.

Shirley walked to the kitchen to get a drink. When she opened the refrigerator, it was almost empty. All of the cabinets were also bare.

Pearl-Elizabeth emerged from the bathroom as Delores came from the back room. "You got a Negro living in here, don't you Delores?" Pearl-Elizabeth asked.

"I kinda figured that," Fred said from the living room. Stephen and King Solomon always be talking 'bout this man they play catch with."

They walked to the living room. The sofa squeaked as they sat down.

"You bought this stuff about two years ago. It should still look new. You let that Negro tear yo' stuff up? He worser than chil'ren. We got six, from seven years old down to a year old. Our house not tore up like this," Fred said.

"Or eat up all of your food!" Shirley commented.

"After Elgin, you should know better," Pearl-Elizabeth told her.

"You was glad to get rid o' 'im, and look like you got somebody even worser," Fred said. "That Negro working anywhere?"

"He sell insurance. He trying to make sales."

"Does he bring home any money?" Pearl-Elizabeth asked.

"Like I said. He trying to make sales."

"That mean he ain't got no job, Lizzy." Fred got up in disgust. "Delores," he said as he paced the floor, "I don't believe this. How you gone let some lazy, triflin' Negro live up in here with you and Robin?"

"You need to be setting an example for Robin. How can you expect her to have good, strong moral values if you don't teach them to her? For that fact, you shouldn't be living in sin and have our children seeing it either!" Pearl-Elizabeth said.

"Oh, honey," Delores told her. "You ain't even got no room to talk! You go out drinking, smoking, and stay out 'til wee hours o' the morning, and have the nerve to tell me 'bout morals? That's why Ms. Mabel don't wanta watch King Solomon 'cause she don't condone yo' partying all the time! And you supposed to be a educated nurse, too!"

"Let me tell you something, Delores." She looked straight into Delores's eyes. "I'm really careful about who I have around King Solomon. I don't bring strange men around him. And no man. I mean, no man is going to get pussy from Pearl-Elizabeth Youngblood unless he marries me first."

"Well, how you got King Solomon then?" Delores asked.

"I was young and was taken advantage of by somebody I trusted. But at least I learned my lesson. Have you learned from your mistake, Delores? No, you have not! Because if you would have learned from your first mistake, you wouldn't be living like this!

"Yeah. Sure, I like to go out, drink, have a good time. So what?

I'm not hurting anybody. Not myself or King Solomon. Nobody. And that has nothing to do with me being educated or a nurse. What law says that educated people are not supposed to have fun?"

"Everybody should have fun," Shirley said.

"What's the Negro name anyhow?" Fred asked.

"Clarence Darrensburg."

"Well, Delores," Fred said as he clinched his fists together. "Is you gone tell Mr. Darrensburg to leave or am I?"

"Leave?" Delores asked. "He ain't goin' nowhere. I need somebody to he'p me raise Robin."

"Well, why don't you get married? Either to this Clarence or find somebody else?" Shirley asked.

"Clarence said that he want to marry me, but can't."

"Why not?" Fred asked.

"Because I can't find Elgin to get a divorce."

"Delores, I'm a man. Take it from me," Fred started. "If he want to really marry you bad enough, he will find a way. That's all they is to it."

"That's right," Pearl-Elizabeth agreed.

"We better be going," Fred said. "We gotta be at the joint in 15 minutes."

They all started for the door.

"You need to stop by the joint to visit with Fred, Delores, while we watch the kids," Shirley said.

"What you do there anyway, Fred?" Delores asked.

"I'm what they call a bouncer. I make sure that people don't get outta line, don't cause no trouble. We don't have too much trouble, though. So they just pay me to stand 'round all night."

"I go to keep Fred company," Shirley said. *I go to make sure that Fred is not messing around*, is what she really thought.

"It's really nice. They have live bands, good food, and really nice people!" Pearl-Elizabeth said.

"Naw," Delores said. "Thanks, but no thanks. I don't like no barrooms."

"It's not a barroom, it's a really nice club. Besides, how do you know if you've never been in one before?" Pearl-Elizabeth asked.

"Some things I just know," Delores said as Clarence walked through the door. Fred gave him a really mean, intimidating look.

"Clarence, this my brother Fred, his wife Shirley, and Pearl-Elizabeth," Delores said.

"Oh, so you're King Solomon's mother!" Clarence said in his

charming, articulate manner that seemed to surface only in the presence of beautiful women. "He's really a good boy."

"Thank you," Pearl-Elizabeth said.

"I'm sorry. Where are my manners?" Clarence said. "Would any of you like something to drink?"

"No," Shirley said. "We were on our way out."

"So, you're a nurse at Flint Goodrich, right?" Clarence asked Pearl-Elizabeth.

"Yes, I am."

"How long have you been a nurse?" Clarence got really close to Pearl-Elizabeth, almost at the point of smothering her.

"For about four years. Five, if you include my internship at the hospital."

"So. You graduated from Dillard, right?"

"Yes," Pearl-Elizabeth said. "You sure do have a lot of questions. Delores must have told you a lot about me."

"We really have to be going," Shirley said as everyone headed for the door.

"Who new black Chevy that is?" Delores asked. "I know the blue Ford is yours, Fred."

"That's my new car," Pearl-Elizabeth said. "I got it last week. You like it?"

"Yeah," Delores said. "It's real nice. One of these here days, I'm gone learn to drive and get a car."

***

It was three in the morning and Clarence hadn't been in that long. The children were all fast asleep. Delores kept folding cots stored in the back room for their visits.

Headlights flashed, then a car door closed. Clarence heard thumps up the stairs followed by a loud knock at the door. He peeked through the drapes and saw that it was Pearl-Elizabeth.

"I wonder what she want?" he asked himself as he opened the door.

"Delores home?" she asked. Her speech was a bit slurred and she had trouble standing.

"She sleeping! What you doin' waking people up this time o' morning?" Clarence asked.

"I don't feel too good. Just let me rest up on the sofa and I'll leave in the morning," Pearl-Elizabeth insisted. "Please!"

"I don't know," Clarence said. "You seem like you drunk."

"Get the fuck out my way, moth' fucker!" she shouted and pushed him out of the doorway. She had more strength than he realized.

"Shhh. Shhh," he whispered. "You gone wake everybody up. All right. All right, Lizzy," he said.

Pearl-Elizabeth removed her shoes and collapsed on the sofa. She fell fast asleep.

Clarence went into the bedroom to get an extra pillow and blanket. Pearl-Elizabeth was on her back and Clarence noticed her large, shapely breasts.

"She got some big titties. I bet I can play with 'em. She so drunk she won't even know it."

He began to slowly unbutton her blouse and exposed the black lace bra she wore. "Mercy, mercy," he said as he ran his hands over her breasts and caressed the nipples. "Lordy, Lordy, Lordy." He slid his hand under her skirt. He playfully pinched her crouch and tried to remove her silky, soft panties.

"Get yo' moth' fuckin' hands off my moth' fuckin' pussy, moth' fucker!" Pearl-Elizabeth reacted with lightning speed and struck Clarence in the head with the revolver that she tucked neatly in the back of her skirt, knocking him to the floor. "Who the fuck you think you fuckin' with, moth' fucker?

"Don't you ever," she slapped him in the face as she stood up, "ever," followed by a punch to the nose, "put yo' hands on me again, moth' fucker!" Then a left to his chin that knocked him against the coffee table. Pearl-Elizabeth lurched over him and watched the blood stream down his face.

Delores ran into the living room as she tied the belt of her pink terrycloth robe. The lights suddenly came on.

"What's going on up in here?" Delores asked.

"Yo' cousin here came here trying to come on to me, that's what. When I turned her down, she hit me with that there gun."

"He lying, Delores."

"Well, what is you doin' here this time o' morning fo' then?" Delores asked, then noticed that Pearl-Elizabeth's blouse was unbuttoned.

"I wasn't feeling well enough to drive home, so I thought I could sleep on the sofa until the morning. When I was trying to sleep, Clarence started fondling me. That's when I hit him."

"Delores, don't believe her. She lying. She just mad 'cause you got a man and she don't."

"What would I do with a no-good, low-down, trifling Negro like you? What can you do for me anyway? You have nothing I would want! Nothing. Not even that sorry dick between your legs!"

"Pearl-Elizabeth," Delores started. "I think it's best you be leaving. King Solomon can stay. Fred'll have to drop him off when he get his chil'ren."

"Oh, I'll leave," Pearl-Elizabeth told Delores, then went to get King Solomon, who rubbed his eyes all the way to the front door. "I don't believe you're going to let garbage come between family. Blood is thicker than water. I would never do you wrong, Delores. Some day you'll find out. I hope it's not too late. Good-bye, Delores," she said as she left.

Chapter 25.
Problems, Problems

Delores came home early one Friday night when she was supposed to be working overtime. The house was cold, like nobody had been there all day. Clarence didn't get in until two in the morning.

At work that Saturday, one of the other women told Delores that he was out with other women, spending her money. She confronted him later that day when she got home.

"Baby, I ain't gone lie," he started. "I was out spending money on women."

Delores was shocked.

"But I was out makin' sales," he continued. "You got to wine and dine yo' cust'mas to make 'em want to buy some insur'nce. People be at bars. So I go to where the people be at to sell insur'nce."

"Well, did you get some sales?" Delores asked.

"I got some pretty good leads. I should have some pol'cies by next week."

Over the next few months, Clarence still didn't get any sales. Delores was worried because she was pregnant. She continued to work, though.

"Maybe you should consider another line o' work," Delores told Clarence. "We need some real money comin' in. We gone have 'nother mouth to feed."

"What?" Clarence was excited. "Insur'nce is alls I know how to do."

"Well, you ain't doin' it too good!" Delores told him. "You need a real job."

"Woman!" he yelled. "Stop nagging me!" He picked up his coat and stormed out of the door.

***

Delores was tired a lot, especially as she neared term. But she continued to work, while Clarence continued to try to make sales.

Except for Aletha, no one else at work knew that Delores was pregnant. They thought that she was putting on a few pounds, that's all. She was about five-eight with wide hips. A combination of her build and wearing loose-fitting clothes hid her condition.

Delores worked the night shift and got home too late to see Robin off to school. She decided to stop by to see Ms. Iris one morning.

"Come on in, chil'," she told Delores. "Come on in the kitchen. I just sent Robin off, but still have some grits and bacon left."

Delores liked to visit with Ms. Iris. She lived in a large, white, Victorian-style home trimmed in hunter green. The front and back yards were small, but well-manicured. There was a large concrete porch in front with a hanging swing.

Through the front door was the living room, which was done in beige antique furnishings, including a mahogany grandfather clock in the corner. The hardwood floors were always perfectly polished. Four bedrooms and the bathroom lined the long hallway that led to the kitchen.

Ms. Iris made some scrambled eggs, which she served with toast, grits, and bacon to herself and Delores.

"Thank you, Ms. Iris," Delores said as Ms. Iris poured her some fresh coffee. "I 'preciate you lookin' after Robin when I work nights."

"Like I done said befo', she a real sweet li'l girl." Ms. Iris started. "That's why you gots to learn to look out fo' number one!"

"What you mean?" Delores asked.

"You need to do what's best fo' you and Robin," Ms. Iris started. "You was doing real good by yo'self. Then, you let that no-good Negro move in who done dragged you down. You was already struggling with one child. What you want go have 'nother fo' anyhow? 'Specially fo' Clarence. All that Negro do all day long is sleep, eat, and run the streets."

"Clarence gone make some sales. I know he is," Delores assured Ms. Iris. "He care fo' me, Robin, and this here baby in my belly."

"If he care so much, he would be providin' fo' his family!" Ms. Iris told her.

"But he trying to make sales. He said all he know is insur'nce. He don't know nothin' else!"

"Chil', don't let me get started up in here!" Ms. Iris began. "One time during the Depression things got real bad fo' me and my late husband, Frank. We had three chil'ren to feed. We had them blackberries you see out back growing wild. Hun'reds of 'em, thousands of 'em. We picked as many blackberries as we could.

Sometimes them thorns got us real good, but we was just a pickin'.

"We put them berries in these li'l brown bags. Frank went on Canal Street and sold 'em on the street corner. Ever' last bag of them blackberries. Ever' last one!

"A man'll do what he can to provide fo' his family. Whether it be pickin' berries, or scrubbing floors fo' white folks, or shovelin' cow manure. Ain't no 'cuse."

"Besides. He must care 'bout me 'cause when we met, I had a bunch o' chil'ren wit' me. What man want a woman wit' a bunch o' chil'ren unless he really care 'bout her?"

"Some men look for women with chil'ren 'cause they figure they gone always be food in the house," Ms. Iris explained. "He know that a momma ain't gone let her babies starve. And don't let times get bad. Oooo, chil'! That Negro gone take the last morsel of food right outta yo' chil'ren mouth. You bet' believe that he'll let you and yo' chil'ren go hungry and take what he can fo' hisself! That's right! Chil', when another fool come 'long who gone take 'im in, he gone leave you so fast, you won't know what hit you! He be gone 'bout his bid'ness!

"Delores, baby. You need somebody who gone love you and yo' chil'ren. Somebody who gone take care o' you and yo' chil'ren. You need a man who really is a man and know how to provide fo' his family. You need somebody who gone be he'ping you out, not the other way 'round.

"Here you is, seven months pregnant and still working. It's March and be freezing cold sometimes. You be out there waitin' fo' the bus to go to work, rain, sleet, or snow. That'll be fine if it was just you and Robin, or yo' husband died or was sick. But it's not right fo' you to be busting yo' tail like that.

"What man gone want his woman working? What decent, able-bodied man gone want his woman working, 'specially when she pregnant and he just be sitting on his ass all day long?

"I be scared if I was you. Scared that I'm gone drop that baby at work. You ever thought 'bout that?"

"No, Ms. Iris, I ain't."

"You ever thought 'bout what you gone do when the baby get here? How that gone affect you workin'?"

"What you mean?" Delores asked.

" 'Bout what you gone do when you have that baby. If you don't work, do yo' pay get docked?"

"I don't think my pay get docked," Delores told her.

"Will you still have a job when you get back?"

"I think I'm gone still have a job."

"Think?" Ms. Iris asked. "Chil', you need to find out fo' sho!" She took a long gulp of coffee. "How 'bout the name on the birth 'tificate?"

"What 'bout the name?" Delores asked. "If it's a boy, we gone name 'im Byron. If it's a girl, we gone name her Michelle."

"What I mean is who name gone be on the line that say 'Father'? It ain't gone say 'Unknown,' is it? Or is Clarence gone give the baby his name?"

"Clarence said that Elgin name gone have to go on that line since we still married. He said his name can't go on that line 'cause we ain't married."

"Lord, have mercy Jesus!" Ms. Iris shouted. "He could get his name on that 'tificate if he wanted to!"

"Yeah," Delores started. "But Clarence said that we would need a lawyer and it would cost too much money."

Ms. Iris gave her a blank stare. "Clarence, Clarence, Clarence! It's always what Clarence said! Clarence say this! Clarence say that! That man ain't stupid! He know 'xactly what he doin'! That mean that he ain't 'sponsible fo' the baby. If y'all was to split up, you won't be able to go af'er 'im fo' no chil' support. He get off scot-free! Have mercy, Jesus!"

"But, Ms. Iris," Delores started. "We ain't gone break up. He love me."

Ms. Iris got up and cleared the table as she said, "Lord, have mercy, Jesus!"

***

"I had heartburn all day at work," Delores told Aletha on their bus ride home. I took something for it, but it ain't go away."

"You sho' you ain't 'bout to have the baby?" Aletha asked.

"Naw, chil'," Delores said. "I would be cramping real, real bad."

"If you say so," Aletha said. "I'm gone stop by Aunt Iris house and tell her to look out for you."

Byron Marshall Wilkerson was born at 1:30 in the morning on May 8, 1954, the Saturday before Mother's Day. Fred drove Delores to the hospital and waited the whole time. Shirley was home with the children.

Pearl-Elizabeth drove Robin, King Solomon, Ms. Iris, Ms. Mabel, and Aletha to the hospital to visit. Ray and Freda came later that day.

The maternity ward consisted of a series of large rooms, called units, that held 12 beds each. The walls were pure white, and the floors were solid marble. Down the hall was a common bathroom that was shared by all patients in a unit.

In the center was the nursery, which was completely surrounded by glass. Down the hall near the elevators was the waiting room where anxious family members waited for news. During that time, men and children weren't allowed to visit with patients in the wards. There were special family rooms just for that occasion.

"Where that no-good Negro at?" Freda asked as she sat by Delores's bedside. "It's 'bout three in the afternoon and I heard he ain't been here all day."

"He ain't been home all night," Ms. Iris said. "We went over there looking fo' him right after Fred drove you up here, Delores. We waited and waited. He ain't never showed up."

"Lizzy here drove me back over there about a hour ago," Aletha said. "I checked the house and they was no sign of 'im. I checked with the neighbors, and ain't none o' 'em seen 'im. I even went by the joint up the street, and ain't nobody seen 'im."

"He probably gone 'bout his bid'ness!" Freda said. "I don't think he gone be back!"

No one else said anything. Deep down in their hearts, they knew that Freda was most likely right. During Delores's four-day hospital stay, Clarence was nowhere to be found.

***

The next week, Delores was back at work. Aletha talked to the supervisor about Delores's condition and made all the arrangements. No one knew about Delores's condition. They were told that she had the flu.

The baby cried a lot at night, and Delores tended to him. She also tended to him in the morning before she took him over to Ms. Iris and in the evening after she picked him up from Ms. Iris. Any extra time was spent helping Robin with her homework, cooking, or cleaning. After that, Delores was so tired that she fell fast asleep after taking her bath for the night.

Clarence started visiting Delores at work. At first, he visited once a day, then the frequency increased to several times a week. The factory was a restricted area, and guests were strictly forbidden. He would not only ask Delores for money in front of her coworkers, but also walked around the building and flirted with other women.

He made himself comfortable in the employees' lounge and watched television for hours at a time. Once, the supervisors called security to ask him to leave. He refused. "I be where I wants to be!" he told the guard. "Don't nobody tell me where I can and can't be!"

Later that day, the supervisor, Mr. Pratt, called Delores into his office. Mr. Pratt was about 45. He was average height and build with light brown hair and blue eyes. "Delores," he said in that Cajun drawl, "I understand that a certain gentleman caller of yours has been causing trouble here at the factory. It be best if you put a stop to it.

"This is a family-run business. My granddaddy started this company 'round the turn o' the century. Then he turned it over to my daddy. Some day, my brothers and me will be running it. We run a clean operation and are proud of it!

"We good Christians. We started hiring women, 'specially colored women, 'round the war. Women folk have a hard enough time being in the work force. They don't need nobody coming off the street and meddling them!

"We provide a nice, clean lounge for our people to relax and enjoy themselves during their breaks and lunch. We're real clean people. We don't want nobody coming in off the street and making a mess of things or causing trouble with our people. Do you understand, Delores?"

"Yes, sir," she said.

"Now go on back to work," he said as he lit a cigar.

The next week, Clarence was back. He roamed about the building and spent about an hour in the employees' lounge before security forced him to leave. Mr. Pratt called Delores into his office again.

"Delores," he started. "You're going to have to tell your gentleman caller not to come around here anymore! I'm sick of him! The ladies are sick of him! The men are sick of him! My daddy and brothers are sick of him, too! Is that clear, Delores?"

"Yes, sir," she answered.

"Good!" Mr. Pratt said. "Does he have a job? If that what he wants, he needs to say so! He should speak up! We got plenty of jobs he can do. Just tell him to come and see me. I'll put 'im to work. He seems like a mighty strong fella."

***

"You gotta tell Clarence to stop coming 'round!" Aletha told Delores on their bus ride home. "They gone fire you fo' sho'! The only reason you still here is 'cause you a good worker and they can depend on you. You been here four years, Delores! Don't throw it away. Just don't!"

"I tried to tell him not to come. I told him that I could lose my job. But he keep coming. I can't stop him," Delores told Aletha.

"Delores, do you want yo' job?"

"Yes."

"Then put yo' foot down and tell that Negro to stop coming!"

"I can't make him. He don't listen to me. Maybe he'll listen to you."

"That's not my place. You gots to stand up fo' yo'self. This is yo' livelihood we talkin' 'bout. Good jobs is hard to come by, 'specially fo' a colored woman. The only other thing coloreds could do is be a maid. You lucky if you can get on wit' a good fam'ly. But if you don't, boy!

"I used to work as a maid befo' the war and ain't never goin' back to that no mo'. That work is demeaning. Them folk treat they dogs and cats bet' 'n they treat they maids. I 'member one time, this family wanted to give me they table scraps. They leftovers! That ol' white heifer said to me, 'We got all this good food. It's a shame to let it go to waste. Why don't you take it instead o' your regular pay?' I walked right outta there and ain't been back since.

"If I was you, Delores, I would put that Negro out. He ain't worth losing yo' job over. You can get any triflin' Negro off o' any street corner in New Orleans. For that fact, you could get a no-good, low-down, good-for-nothin', triflin' man off o' any street corner anywhere in America. They all over the place! From New York to Chicago to Los Angeles to the backwoods o' Miss'ssippi and Al'bama! But ain't so easy finding no good job. I'll talk to Clarence fo' you. I hope he listen to me fo' yo' sake!"

***

The next day, Clarence was in the employees' lounge with his feet on the table and smoking a cigarette. Mr. Pratt walked in.

"I understand that you're Delores's gentleman caller?" Mr. Pratt asked him.

"So what 'bout it?"

"We got some jobs here in the warehouse that could use a strong fella like yourself. It pays real good. And if you'd like, you can work as many overtime hours as you want." Mr. Pratt sat down next to Clarence. "Well? How 'bout it. What do you say?"

Clarence blew a long stream of smoke into the air and looked Mr. Pratt straight in the eyes. "Ain't interested."

"Well," Mr. Pratt was lost for words. "We have other jobs on the shop floor, the assembly line, and... "

Clarence looked him straight in the eyes and said, "Ain't interested!"

"Well, I notice that you come here a lot. If you don't want to work, then what do you want?" Mr. Pratt asked. "You just can't come here harassing our workers and sitting in the lounge all day watching television!"

"I don't want none o' yo' damn jobs! I come here or anywhere else! I do whatever I feels like. Can't nobody tell me what to do!"

"Excuse me for a moment," Mr. Pratt said as he left the room. He returned with three security officers and instructed them to drag Clarence out of the building.

"Let me go!" Clarence yelled as curious workers, including Delores, watched him get thrown out. "Get y'all hands off me! Don't be putting yo' hands on me!"

"Delores," Mr. Pratt said in a short, stern voice. "My office. Now!"

"She shoulda listened," Aletha said to herself. "I tried to talk to Clarence, but that's just like talking to a brick wall!" A few minutes later, she saw Delores clear out her locker as tears flowed from her eyes. Aletha knew that the worst had happened.

Chapter 26.
The Fallen World

About a month later, Delores found a job as a maid for a family on Esplanade Avenue. She had been working there for three months and noticed how the bills started to pile up. She had extra milk and the diaper service to pay for, but made half as much as she used to.

When Delores came home from work, all the food was gone. She and Robin often went to bed hungry. Robin looked forward to going by Ms. Iris's in the morning before school because she was assured of getting a hot meal. Delores couldn't apply for food stamps because a man was living in the house.

Each night, Delores sterilized bottles and filled them with milk that was specially prepared for the baby. Sometimes when she woke up to feed the baby in the middle of the night, empty bottles would be scattered in the sink. The pabulum would be gone, too.

Delores could not afford the nice three-bedroom house they were renting on her maid salary. The rent was three months behind, and the landlord refused to take anymore partial payments. When the eviction notice came, Clarence left. Delores came home from work to find all of his things gone. No one has seen him till this day.

Delores and the children moved to the Ninth Ward projects, which was a few blocks down the street from where she lived at the time. Ms. Iris continued to look after the children. Delores and Aletha weren't on such good terms since the day before she moved.

"I done told you so," Aletha said. "You wouldn't listen. I done washed my hands o' you. Honey, you could do bad all by yourself. You don't need no triflin', no-good Negro to help you starve.

"And besides, Clarence ain't somebody you wanta have 'round yo' chil'ren noway. He a man 'cause he got that dick, but that don't make him no real man. He like having another chil' 'round the house! All he did was sleep, eat, and run the streets! Instead of boo-hooing, you oughta be thanking the Lord that he gone!

"You need to be settin' a 'xample fo' yo' girl, Robin, and yo' new baby boy. You shouldn't be shacking wit' nobody neither. You need to be married. Give yo' chil'ren some good Christian morals.

"That's why some o' these here Negroes don't know how to treat no ladies. That's 'cause when they was coming up, they saw they mommas acting like 'ho's, they grandmammas acting like 'ho's, and all they women folk acting like 'ho's. They don't know what no respectable lady 'sposed to act like."

"I ain't no 'ho'," Delores said. "You always be puttin' me down!"

"I ain't puttin' you down," Aletha started. "You puttin' yo' own self down! I'm just telling you how it is. Delores, I'm telling you like my momma done told me and my sisters. And she done raised three girls and four boys by herself after my daddy passed. We all grown and living good Christian lives. 'Cept fo' me, they all married. I ain't married 'cause all the men was either married or at war. The ones who was left, like Clarence, wasn't worth a shit!

"You alone out here, and I'm just lookin' out fo' you. I'm just doin' what I would want somebody to do fo' me or one o' my kin. You see, the truth hurts. Don't nobody want to hear the truth. Them other folks ain't gone tell you the truth, Delores. They be smiling in yo' face, getting in yo' bid'ness just so they could go talk 'bout you behind yo' back. They mis'ble and want ever'body else mis'ble right there wit' 'em. If you need somethin', they 'void you like the plague. The only two things you can depend on 'em to do is not to be there fo' you in yo' time o' need and to spread yo' bid'ness.

***

Fred, Shirley, and Freda helped them move. Business picked up at the shop, so Ray was busy working and could not help Delores move. He gave Freda 20 dollars to give to Delores. She went to the movies, went out to eat, then kept the rest. So the money didn't make it to Delores as planned.

Fred parked Ray's delivery truck behind the brown brick building. They walked through the courtyard to the front. There were, it seemed, over 100 identical buildings, all with five steps leading to a garret that was enclosed by wrought iron railings. Through the front door was a narrow hallway that led to four separate apartments. Straight ahead was a set of stairs that guided callers to the same sequence of apartments on the second and third levels.

Delores's new home was a first floor flat on Desire Street that overlooked the courtyard. There was one large window dressed in white lace drapes in the living room. Straight ahead was the kitchen, which seemed barely large enough to fit the white refrigerator, stove, and sink. To the right were two bedrooms, across from which was the bathroom. All of the walls were painted a pale green, and the ceilings were white. The floors were done in white vinyl tile with brown specks.

"Time out for Negroes to be cleaning white folks houses," Freda told Delores.

"She gots to do what she gots to do, momma!" Fred interrupted.

"Don't know why you shacked up with that no-good, triflin' black Negro fo' anyway! Look at you with that rag tied around yo' head, raggedy dress, just like a pickaninny. You ain't my daughter. Ain't no daughter of mine gone be living like this!"

"I'm shame to be yo' momma. Getting on gov'ment aid and living in a gov'ment 'partment. You a disgrace is what you is! You a disgrace to me, yo'se'f, and yo' family!"

Freda's loud voice woke the baby. Robin ran to the bathroom to get tissue paper and wiped her mother's tears.

"Look at that," Freda pointed to Byron. "Have naked babies 'round up in here. You ain't even got no money to feed o' put clothes on them chil'ren back. Don't come asking me fo' no money!"

Delores held her head down. Tears fell as she sniffled her nose. They all had sorry looks on their faces.

Fred stepped in. "Let's go. It's getting late." Fred and Shirley started out of the door.

"If you need anything," Fred took her hand, "be sure to call me. You hear?"

"I will, Fred," Delores said.

"Now give your uncle a big hug," Fred told Robin, who hugged his neck so tight it almost choked him.

***

All of Robin's friends talked about going to Lincoln Beach. It broke Delores's heart not to be able to take her little girl. But she had a hard time making ends meet, let alone go out for entertainment.

Fred helped as much as possible. His family was large, but he did what he could. He took Robin when he and Shirley took their children to the beach. Pearl-Elizabeth was a nurse and made a decent salary. But she also was a single parent who didn't get any support.

***

It was six in the evening on Saturday. Delores and Audrey were usually the only two in the laundromat at that time. Most of the other women were housewives and did their laundry during the week.

People knew that they were near the laundromat because they could smell bleach and detergent from three blocks away. The building was white cinder blocks with a black roof. Large glass windows filled the front and sides. Large, white washing machines lined the left and right walls of the entrance door. The large, white dryers lined the back wall. In front of them were two long, wooden tables for folding laundry. Several wooden folding chairs sat to the far left and right corners of the building, right under the windows.

"How ya doin', Delores?" Audrey asked.

"I'm fine. How 'bout yo' self?"

"Oh, baby, I'm doing just wonderfully!"

Audrey Morris was about 40, with gentle brown skin and an hour-glass figure. She wore heavy makeup and had an entourage of hair pieces. Her voice was deep and hoarse from years of heavy smoking and drinking. She had never been married or had children and worked as a manager at a brothel in the French Quarters. Most of her clients were either white or well-to-do colored men.

"How is your job coming, Delores?"

"It's coming okay," she answered in a weak tone, as she held her head down.

Audrey lit another cigarette. "That doesn't sound so good, Delores. Are you sure?" she asked as she exhaled a stream of smoke into the air.

Delores didn't answer.

"You getting any help from Clarence? Money-wise, I mean," Audrey pried further.

"No, ma'am. He ain't. He done skipped town. Don't nobody know where he at."

"You got enough to pay yo' rent and buy food for the baby?"

"I just moved to the Ninth Ward projects. You pay rent based on yo' income. I get food stamps, though."

"Don't they have a laundromat where you live now?"

"Yeah, but they doing work on it, so it's closed."

"You gettin' any help, from anybody?"

"Sometimes, my brother and cousin help. But they got families, too, and it be hard fo' them. They do what they can."

"How 'bout your parents. Why don't you ask them?"

Delores started to sob. "My momma disowned me. She say I shamed the family. My daddy don't help me none."

Audrey hugged Delores with her right arm, and held her cigarette in her left hand, careful not to get smoke into her face.

"That's all right, Delores. That's all right. I'm here for you now."

"What I'm gone do, Ms. Audrey? What I'm gone do?"

Audrey looked Delores straight in the eyes. "As long as you got that there pussy between yo' legs, you should never go hungry."

Delores remembered how Ms. Mabel used to tell people, "You have to use what the Lord done gave you to make it in the world."

But did she mean this too? Delores wondered. "I don't know, Ms. Audrey."

"You got that pear-shaped behind. That's what men like," Audrey informed her.

"What you mean, Ms. Audrey?"

"Stop calling me Ms. Audrey! It's just Audrey. I'm not that old!" she insisted. "Anyway. You got that teeny-weeny waistline, and fruity booty, like I call it. From the back, your ass looks like a pear."

"I don't know Ms. .... . I mean Audrey. What if I get pregnant or some disease?"

"There are ways to protect yourself."

"How?"

"Well, first of all, many of the men are married and are very, very careful."

"Married? I don't know, Audrey."

"Yes, married. Don't act surprised. Delores, you're young and have a lot to learn about life. But that's all right. I'm here to show you the ropes."

"If you say so."

"Yes, I say so," Audrey commented. "Anyway. Getting back to how you can protect yourself. Some men wear rubbers."

"Rubbers? Like rubberbands?"

Audrey laughed. "No, sugar! Rubbers. They protect the man and you from diseases and pregnancy. They look like balloons and men wear them on their penises."

"They who?" Delores asked.

"Their penis. You know, their thing, their dick. Penis is the correct term."

"Oh."

"Girl," Audrey started. "I don't know where you come from or where you've been."

"I ain't been nowhere, Audrey," Delores said.

Audrey looked surprised that Delores answered. She puffed her cigarette and said, "I can tell. But that's all right."

Audrey's two dryers stopped. She secured her cigarette in the corner of her mouth while she emptied the load onto the table. As she folded her laundry, she retrieved an ashtray. She carefully dotted ashes into the tray as she folded her clothes.

"I'm done here," Audrey told Delores. "The laundromat is going to close in about an hour. Let me help you with your clothes," she said between puffs. "Anyway, like I was saying," she continued. "You can mix Vaseline and quinine. That's what many of the girls use and they don't get pregnant. Some of 'em been doing that for years!"

"How 'bout diseases?"

"Well," Audrey started as she took a drag from her cigarette. "You can douche out with a mixture of peroxide and water. Some say that the quinine is supposed to protect you from diseases, too. Or, if you think a man got some disease, you don't have to deal with him."

"How would I know that?"

"Well, you could look at 'em. If they thing is dripping, especially thick, frothy white stuff, then they probably got the claps. If they got bumps or sores or something on 'em, then they got something else much worse. You definitely don't want to deal with them, even if they wear a rubber. Some say that you can take wax from your ears and put it on his pee hole. If they flinch, then they got something. But in time, you'll learn who to mess with and who not to.

"Besides, we got this doctor who check the girls out every month. He make sure they ain't pregnant or got some disease. Ain't none of the girls ever got pregnant or get any diseases. But the doctor did say that men can carry infections."

"What's that?"

"It's not like a disease, but it can cause you to itch, burn, or have a discharge. It can make you infertile, barren. That means that if you want to have a baby in the future, you won't be able to."

"A discharge? What's that?"

"A discharge is something that runs out of your pussy. It could be white, but it smells really nasty, like old, rotten seafood."

"Ooo! That is nasty!"

"The doctor said that the girls should wash all men's dicks with hot soap and water beforehand. Hell, the men like it too, and really look forward to it. Besides, the men deal with us because we're so clean. That's real important to the type of men we deal with." Audrey lit another cigarette. "Well. You interested?"

"I don't know," Delores said. "Can't you go to jail?"

"Sugar, I've been working at the same place for over 22 years. I worked for 10 years. The past 12, I've been the manager. Nobody has ever gone to jail. The owner has connections," Audrey took another drag. "Besides, some of the clients are well known businessmen, government types, and law types. Ain't nobody going to jail!"

"I can't do this. What would people say?"

"Sugar, let me tell you something," Audrey said as she took yet another drag. "You keep worrying about what people say. No matter what you do, somebody is going to say something. Are any of the people you worrying about helping you pay your bills?"

"No," Delores answered.

"Well, they don't have anything to tell you!" Audrey helped Delores fold the last of the clothes. "Look! Either you want to do it or you don't!"

"I don't know."

"What's there to know, Delores?" Audrey asked. "If you want to spend the rest of your life cleaning white folk houses and not having anything, that's fine with me. You see me living in that big white house over there. I have the deed for it, and am proud to say that I did it for myself as a working girl. Nobody helped me. No man, no relatives, no friends, nobody. And that's a good feeling to be able to provide for yourself."

"But, don't you think I'm too black?"

Audrey froze in her tracks. "What! Too black? Where you get that from?"

"What man gone want to pay for a black, black woman anyhow?"

"Delores. Sugar, let me tell you something," Audrey started as she took another drag. "The men don't care. In fact, some of the white ones like their girls the blacker the better."

"For real?"

"For real, Delores," she said as she finished one cigarette, then lit another cigarette. "And with your pear-ass, you will be sure to make a lot of money. And that's the truth."

"You should know."

"That's right, Delores. I know. An old man told me years ago, he said, 'Audrey, the way things being as they is, a colored man have a hard time makin' it. But a colored woman who ain't makin' it must be mighty sorry.' Now I know you're not a sorry young woman, now are you, Delores?"

"No, ma'am. I ain't."

Alone and dejected, Delores knew what she had to do.

Chapter 27.

A New Way, A New Day

Delores was running low on cash and Byron was sick. Pearl-Elizabeth offered to go to Sam's to pay for his prescription. The pharmacist looked familiar. "Now where do I know her from?" she asked herself.

Ernestine Sam was about five-seven with a caramel complexion and jet-black, wavy, shoulder-length hair. From the side, her profile looked like that of an eagle, with that pointed nose and curved eyebrows that seemed to hug her dark brown eyes. Her lips were a light shade of pink and looked as though they had been taken from a 16th century Roman sculpture. She and her brother, Ernest, Jr., studied pharmacology at Xavier and helped their father, Ernest, Sr., run the family business.

As Ernestine handed Pearl-Elizabeth the prescription she said, "I know you. You hang out at the joint over there sometimes."

"I thought you looked familiar," Pearl-Elizabeth said.

"I'm Ernestine Sam," she started. "Everybody calls me Ernie."

"I'm Pearl-Elizabeth Youngblood. Everybody calls me Lizzy."

"Maybe I'll see you there again sometimes," Ernestine said.

"Yeah, maybe I will."

"I'm good friends with Dr. Pickens, the owner," Ernestine said. "I fill prescriptions for a lot of his patients. He's a good doctor. Well, you should know. Looks like you took your baby to see him."

"What?" Pearl-Elizabeth was confused. "Oh, no, no! That's for my cousin's baby."

"So do you have any children?"

"Yes."

"You do?" Ernestine continued. "How many?"

"Only one."

"How old?"

"He's nine."

"What's his name?"

"His name is Solomon."

"You ought to take him to see Dr. Pickens."

"We have a doctor in Algiers where we live."

"I'm telling you, Dr. Pickens is the best. People come from miles around to see him."

"I might just do that. I'll see you later, Ernie," Pearl-Elizabeth said as she left the pharmacy. "I hear so much about this Dr. Pickens. I'm curious as to who he is. He owns the bar, but I have never seen him. He's always surrounded by cronies that I never got a good look at him," she said to herself.

Ernestine followed Pearl-Elizabeth with her eyes all the way out of the store. She paid attention to her large breasts and the full motion of her hips. "Damn, that woman is fine!" she said to herself.

***

Later that week on Friday night, Pearl-Elizabeth was at Pixie's at her usual table sipping Jack Daniels and Coke.

"Is this seat taken?" a voice from behind asked. It was Ernestine.

"Oh, no," Pearl-Elizabeth said.

"May I?" Ernestine asked.

"Sure."

"It's good seeing you here again. I sometimes play pool in the back."

"Me, too," Pearl-Elizabeth started. "Sometimes I play poker with the fellas."

"Hey," Ernestine said. "Me too!"

In the corner of the room, Pearl-Elizabeth caught a glimpse of Delores.

No, Pearl-Elizabeth thought. *That can't be.*

Delores was standing in the corner with three other women. She was wearing a short, clingy, red-sequined dress with matching high-heel pumps. Her hair was curled and heavy makeup covered her face.

"Those are the working girls over there," Ernestine informed her.

Pearl-Elizabeth knew for sure that the young woman she saw was not Delores. Not only did Delores not like bars, but she was definitely not a working girl.

Several men in different parts of the room were pointing at Pearl-Elizabeth. "Men make me sick," she started. "All they do is chase tail."

"Yeah, they do."

"That's why I don't fool with them," Pearl-Elizabeth said.

"Me either."

"You don't?" Pearl-Elizabeth was surprised.

"Uh, uh. No siree, buddy. I leave men folk alone! They're nothing but trouble."

"You're the only woman I've met who feels that way. Everybody else thinks that they can't live without a man no matter how no-good he is."

"Honey," Ernestine started. "I've lived my whole life without touching a man."

"You're a virgin?" Pearl-Elizabeth asked.

"You can say that," Ernestine answered, then gulped her mug of beer.

"I wish I can say that, too," Pearl-Elizabeth started. "But it's too late. I tell any man who tries to get in my drawers that he has to marry me first. That runs them away real fast!"

Several men passed by Pearl-Elizabeth and Ernestine and rolled their eyes. Some of the women did too.

"Let's go someplace else," Ernestine suggested. "It's getting too crowded and too smokey for me. Let's get something to eat. I know this place down the way that stays open late."

"Can't," Pearl-Elizabeth said.

"Why not?"

"I'm running low on money."

"That's all right. Tell you what. How about if I pay this time and next time you pay? We got a deal? That blue car right there is mine."

Pearl-Elizabeth looked out the window and noticed a shiny new Cadillac. "All right. Let's go! Aren't you going to get your purse?" Pearl-Elizabeth asked her.

"I never carry a purse. A wallet will do just fine."

Ernestine always wore slacks and tops that hid her bosom. Most of the time she wore either loafers or sneakers with nylon socks to match her outfit. She bounced from side-to-side as she walked, and sat with her knees slightly apart. Her nails were always cut short, and she wore no makeup, not even lipstick.

The following week, Pearl-Elizabeth and Ernestine went to the Gallo Theater instead of to the Pixie. It was Pearl-Elizabeth's pay week, so she had money to spend. After the movie, they went out to eat. Ernestine let Pearl-Elizabeth pay for the movie and popcorn, but not for dinner. "It's on me," she insisted.

For the next several weeks, they went to the movies, shopped, played pool or poker at the Pixie, or just sat around and talked. Each time that they did something, Ernestine insisted on picking up the tab.

One night Ernestine and Pearl-Elizabeth were sitting at a table and enjoying a few beers. The place was crowded and thick clouds of smoke filled the air. People were dancing to the beat of the live jazz band across the room.

As Pearl-Elizabeth enjoyed the band, Ernestine couldn't take her eyes off of Pearl-Elizabeth's ample cleavage. Ernestine ordered another beer, in hopes that it would quench her lust. It didn't.

Pearl-Elizabeth got up to go to the powder room. Ernestine followed each step she took. That sassy, sensuous gait, the gentle curves of Pearl-Elizabeth's rear end, her long, flowing hair, and her sweet perfume were too much for Ernestine to bear.

After she returned to the table, a man in a tan linen suit staggered over to where Pearl-Elizabeth and Ernestine were sitting. "I see you done went to the other side o' the fence," he said to Pearl-Elizabeth in that slurred dialog of his. "That's why you don't want to give up none o' that there pussy."

Pearl-Elizabeth stood up and slapped him in the face. He raised his hand to strike her back, but she had already thrown him a left hook to the jaw, followed by a quick right to the nose. Fred stepped in and grabbed the man from behind. He literally picked him up and threw him out on the street.

"Moth' fucker!" Pearl-Elizabeth said to herself.

Pearl-Elizabeth was a true lady. But if someone pushed the wrong button, she became the meanest, most brazen vixen. She could whip the crap out of the biggest, most vicious man. That really turned Ernestine on.

"Calm down. Calm down!" Fred told her as he escorted her to the back of the room. "What happened?"

"He said that I don't want to give up my pussy, then I hit him."

"He was wrong," Fred started. "But what do you expect? You always be with Ernie?"

"So," she started. "Ernie is my friend. So what if I be with her? What's wrong with that?"

"People talk, that's all."

"What do you mean, Fred?" she demanded.

"What y'all do is none of my bid'ness."

"What the fuck is that supposed to fuckin' mean, Fred? What the fuck are you getting at?"

"You know," he started. "Y'all been fuckin' each other."

"What!" Pearl-Elizabeth exclaimed. "Where did you get that shit from, Fred?"

"Well, Ernie is a bull-dagger."

"A what? What's a bull-dagger?"

"You don't know?" Fred asked.

"No," she started. "But you sure are going to tell me!"

"A bull-dagger is a woman who fucks other women."

"No," Pearl-Elizabeth started. "Ernie is not like that."

"Look at her. She look real mannish and wear mannish-looking clothes."

"She's just old-fashioned. She's still a virgin. I guess she's waiting for Mr. Right."

"You mean Ms. Right. She prob'ly ain't never had no man, but boy! She get mo' pussy than some o' the fellas!"

"Don't talk about Ernie like that."

"Now, Lizzy," Fred started. "I'm yo' cousin. I wouldn't lie to you. Why don't you ask her yo'self."

"She would be insulted if I asked her something like that!"

"No she won't. I betcha!" Fred looked behind Pearl-Elizabeth and saw Ernestine approach.

"Hey, Lizzy," Ernestine started. "I've gotta go. I gotta get up early to open the store. I'll see you tomorrow, Lizzy." Being in the same room with Pearl-Elizabeth made her so hot that night, she couldn't bear being in her presence any longer. She needed relief, and she needed it really fast.

Fred watched her as she got into her car and drove off into the night.

"See you tomorrow?" Fred asked. "You gone see her tomorrow?"

"So."

"If I was you, I wouldn't be hangin' 'round wit' no Ernie. You talk 'bout the men be tryin' to get in yo' drawers. She prob'bly trying to do the same thing."

"No she's not," Pearl-Elizabeth said. "Well, if she is, she sure do know how to treat a lady," she laughed.

***

Ernestine headed to the French Quarters to Delores's new place of employment. The building was an old Greek Revival mansion. It was a two-story white house with black wrought-iron works around the porch and balcony. Inside, the walls were covered with blue-and-white-striped wallpaper. Beige antique furniture adorned the parlor where clients waited for their tricks.

"Hey, Ernie," Audrey said. "I didn't know you were coming tonight."

"I came on a whim," Ernestine answered.

"Well, Millie ain't here tonight, and Jo is with somebody right now."

"You got anybody else?"

"There are two new girls. Both of them are green, and probably can't do what you want."

"I don't care," Ernestine said. "If they're willing, I'm paying."

"Well all right, then."

Audrey went into the back to speak with Delores and her new coworker. "Now ladies," she started. "When y'all started I told you that you would have to do things you don't like. Well, we have a regular outside who always pay extra because her needs are special."

"Her?" they asked.

"Yes, her," Audrey repeated. "Who is willing to try?"

"At this point, I ain't made no money all day," Delores said. "I'll do anything."

"Good," Audrey said. "It pays double your regular rate. I'll get the bubble bath started."

***

Ernestine walked down the long, narrow hallway. That night, the red carpet seemed more brilliant than usual, and the five clam-shaped sconce fixtures shined brighter than ever. She knew that what awaited her behind that door would quench the fire that burned deep within.

The room was dimly lit, as jazz played softly in the background. Ernestine's favorite blue paisley satin comforter was gently turned down, and revealed those black satin sheets that she loved so much. To the back was the powder room, with its large, antique white tub. The white marble floor accented the deep earth tones of the wallpaper.

Ernestine neatly placed her clothing in the mirror-door closet across from the bed, then joined Delores, who was immersed in a tub full of hot foamy bubbles.

"I know you," Ernestine said as she lathered soap sensually over Delores's soft, delicate body. "You used to come in the drugstore with those children."

"Only the girl is mine," Delores started. "The others is my nephews."

"Oh," Ernestine said as she rubbed the soap between Delores's legs. "You're so fine, I just knew all those children weren't yours. Your nice big ass made me want to run my tongue in your pussy each time I saw you."

Delores lathered soap all over Ernestine. When she reached her large, firm breasts, she could resist playing with them. They were like big, water-filled balloons. "You got some big, soft titties, Ernestine."

"Why don't you go on and suck them," Ernestine told her.

Delores sucked one breast and twirled her tongue about the nipple, as she fondled the other. Ernestine began to pinch Delores's nipples that sent balls of passion straight to her clit.

They got out of the tub, each patted the other dry. Ernestine held her hands around Delores's face and began to slowly lick her lips. They engaged in a deep, hungry kiss as Ernestine eased her hands down Delores's back, then pulled her closer.

Ernestine pulled away for a moment, as lust filled both their eyes. She and Delores rubbed their hard, erect nipples against each other, which stimulated Delores more than ever. They teased and tantalized each other's clit, as their fingers became moister and stickier with each touch.

Ernestine led Delores to the big brass bed in the next room and pulled back the comforter all the way. "Lay on your stomach," she instructed Delores. Ernestine started at the neck, down to her arms, her back, then her legs, and rubbed lotion all over Delores. She paused for a second, and put a heaping handful of lotion on Delores's firm behind. "I always wanted to do this to you," she said as she massaged Delores's behind like she was kneading bread dough, until it started to crackle. Then she turned Delores over on her back.

Ernestine spread Delores's legs and parted her lips below. She twirled her tongue up and down Delores's clit, down to the insides and outsides of every nook and cranny of her femininity, and licked from side-to-side, up and down. Delores swelled like a plum. Her womanhood became hard and erect in anticipation of the next stroke of the tongue.

I ain't know I could feel nothin' there, Delores thought. *Ain't no man ever made me feel this good!*

Ernestine pinched Delores's nipples with one hand, while she thrust her fingers deep inside of her soaking-wet cunt with the other. Delores began to quiver and breathe heavily. Ernestine noticed a white stream of come ooze out of Delores's cunt. She twirled her tongue inside and she licked every drop.

Ernestine then parted Delores's lower lips, then her own lips, and got on top. Their clits rolled around, up and down, and side to side. The sizzling sounds of cracks filled the room.

Delores squeezed Ernestine's ass and ran her fingers between the crack. They engaged in a long, passionate kiss, and their clits remained sealed in sheer lust. It was so natural for Delores. *I woulda 'came a dyke long time ago if I knowed it was this good! Ain't no man could do nothing like this! This feel too good!*

They spent the night embroiled in passion, succumbing to the wicked desires of the other.

Chapter 28.
Tricks or Treats

By the Fall of '55, Delores had become one of Audrey's top girls. She made a lot of money, not just because she took all the outrageous jobs, but she actually enjoyed her work. The clients enjoyed her, too.

She moved out of her apartment and into a house around the corner from Audrey. It had only one level, but it was large, with three bedrooms. The yard was well manicured, with rose bushes planted out front. She bought a nice brown-and-white plaid living room set and coordinating beige draperies. Robin once again had a white bedroom set with pink linen.

Delores started to feel sick, almost to the point where she couldn't work. Audrey suggested that she see a doctor, so Dr. Pickens came by to examine her. Audrey was by her side when the news came.

"Delores," he started. "I don't know how to tell you this."

"Tell me what?" Delores asked anxiously.

"You're pregnant. About three months to be exact."

"Lord, have mercy, Jesus!" Audrey shouted, then lit a cigarette.

"How that happen?" Delores asked. "I been using that quinine and Vaseline like you said. And I been douching with peroxide."

"The peroxide keeps infections away. But the quinine doesn't always work for everybody. How about the diaphragm I fitted you for? Have you been using it on a regular basis? Like I told you before, you have to use it with each contact, and leave it in for several hours."

"Can you take care of it, doctor?" Audrey asked.

"Yes," he assured. "Come by my office around seven at night when the other patients have gone. I'll take care of it for you."

"No!" Delores was disgusted. "Y'all talkin' 'bout killing my baby! Y'all crazy!"

"Delores," Audrey started as she took a drag off of her cigarette. "Honey, you don't even know who the baby's daddy is. It could be anybody. Why do you want to have a trick baby? You don't even have a clue as who the daddy is! Some o' yo' tricks you won't even recognize if you see 'em on the street! You want to go through life wondering if every Tom, Dick, and Harry you see on the street is your baby's daddy?"

"The baby is mine," Delores started. "Like they say, 'Momma's baby, pappa's maybe.' "

"How are you going to make a living being pregnant?" Dr. Pickens asked her. "If you do still work, you can harm the baby. I refuse to have a part in that!" He picked up his bag and left.

"What did he mean by work?" Delores asked Audrey, who lit another cigarette.

"Some women still work when they pregnant," Audrey started. "We ain't never had any of our girls pregnant before, but I hear that they can make boo-coo money. Men say that they pussy feel really, really warm and soft. They be willing to pay extra for that feeling. Maybe two or three times more."

***

Pearl-Elizabeth, Shirley, and Ernestine were playing poker one night at the Pixie. Delores worked nights and could no longer baby-sit. So Ms. Mabel finally agreed to watch the children.

"That looks like Delores," Shirley told Pearl-Elizabeth. "But Delores doesn't like bars, so that can't be her."

"You mean the broad in the red dress? The one with the long hair?" Ernestine asked.

"Yeah," Pearl-Elizabeth said. "Do you know her?"

"Yes. That's Delores Wilkerson. She one of Pickens' girls," Ernestine informed them. "Do you know her?"

"Yes," Pearl-Elizabeth said. "She's my cousin! Don't talk about her that way. You must have mistaken her for someone else."

"No," Ernestine said. "Trust me. She's one of Pickens' girls. If you don't believe me, ask anybody in here."

They noticed her leave with a strange man.

"Now I know that's not Delores," Pearl-Elizabeth said. "She would never go off with some man she doesn't know. Especially have him touch her all over like that!"

"Not Delores!" Shirley said. "Never in a million years!"

They just don't know her like I do, Ernestine thought. *If they only knew.*

***

At three o'clock in the morning on March 30, 1956, Michelle

Annette Wilkerson was born. Because Delores was still legally married to Elgin, his name went on the birth certificate.

Ms. Mabel, Freda, Shirley, and Pearl-Elizabeth were by her side, while Ray, Fred, and the children waited in the visitors' center.

"Who the daddy is this time?" Freda asked.

"Tell her," Shirley urged Delores.

"That's a trick baby," Pearl-Elizabeth said.

"Lord, have mercy, Jesus!" Ms. Mabel exclaimed. "Stop saying that Pearl-Elizabeth! The world don't have to know!"

"Well, it's the truth," Pearl-Elizabeth said.

"What in heck is a trick baby?" Freda asked.

Everyone kept quiet, even Ms. Mabel.

"Well, is somebody gone tell me or do I gotta go get one of them nurses down the hall to tell me?" Freda insisted.

"Sit down," Ms. Mabel told Freda and looked straight into her eyes. "A trick baby mean that she got pregnant while turning tricks."

"What you mean by turning tricks? That gotta do with Halloween or something?" Freda asked.

"It means that she got pregnant working as a prostitute. She has no earthly idea who the daddy could be," Pearl-Elizabeth explained.

"Is that true, Ms. Mabel?" Freda asked.

Ms. Mabel looked her straight in the eyes and said, "Yes, Freda. It's true."

"Delores!" Freda shouted at the top of her lungs. "What you thinkin' 'bout, girl? Bad 'nough you got two babies by two no-good, triflin' Negroes, now you got a baby by some triflin' Tom, Dick, or Harry!"

"Sorry, ladies," the ward nurse said. "Please keep it down. You're disturbing other patients." Then she walked away.

"We're sorry," Ms. Mabel said.

Delores turned away from Ms. Mabel, Freda, Shirley, and Pearl-Elizabeth. Just then, Audrey was on her way in with Dr. Pickens.

Pearl-Elizabeth was seated near the rear wall. She and Dr. Pickens made direct eye contact that sent a tingling sensation to every cell of her body. He was so masculine, so strong. Those thick, black eyebrows and well-maintained moustache complemented his olive complexion. His deep, dark eyes and slicked-back hair gave him a mysterious air. For a moment, she envisioned herself wrapped in the warmth of those big, strong arms, and being caressed by those big, strong hands.

Dr. Pickens noticed a brilliant white aura surrounding Pearl-Elizabeth. She was so beautiful–those full plum lips, that perfect heart-shaped face and flawless complexion, her long, flowing hair. In his eyes, she was an angel sent from heaven to put an end to his loneliness and despair. He was entranced by her strong feminine presence.

"Dr. Pickens," Audrey called as she shook him away from Pearl-Elizabeth's hypnotic spell, "didn't you have some news for Delores?"

Everyone noticed the magnetism between Pearl-Elizabeth and Dr. Pickens and quietly giggled once his trance was broken by Audrey.

"We need to talk in private," Dr. Pickens said.

Everyone started for the door when they noticed Audrey behind.

"Naw," Freda said. "If that gal there can hear what you got to say, then we should, too. We the family. When she in trouble, she come run to us. Her so-called friends turn they back on her. We stayin'! We ain't goin' nowhere!" Freda motioned for the others to come back into the room.

"Well, Delores," Dr. Pickens started. "Like we discussed before. There's an operation that I can perform that will prevent you from getting pregnant again. It's permanent. So, if some day you decide to have more children ... "

"She don't need no mo' chil'ren," Freda interjected. "Go on do what you gotta do, doctor!"

"You're going to need about two or three months to recuperate, though. That may be a problem if you need to work and bring in money," Dr. Pickens continued.

"Let me worry 'bout that," Audrey said. "We got everything covered."

"Who you is?" Freda asked Audrey.

"You don't even want to know," Pearl-Elizabeth told Freda.

"Girl," Freda told Pearl-Elizabeth, "don't go tellin' me what I wanta know. I wants to know." Freda looked Audrey straight in the eyes and asked again, "Now who you is?"

"My name is Audrey. Delores works for me."

"You her pimp, heh?" Freda asked. "I ain't never heard of no pimp who was no woman befo'."

"She what you call a Madame," Ms. Mabel said.

"Madame, pimp, it all the same," Freda said. "You got chil'ren Ms. Audrey?"

"No. I don't," Audrey said. "I'm not married."

"Of course you ain't married," Freda started. "That 'cause you be fooling 'round with other folk husbands. Prob'bly don't nobody wanta marry you no way. You be going 'round with every Tom, Dick, and Harry. A man want somebody fresh, who ain't been used up!"

Audrey rolled her eyes at Freda as she spoke. The only reason she didn't respond was because Delores was there.

"It's gettin' late," Ms. Mabel said. "We bet' be leaving."

When they got in the hall, Ms. Mabel, Shirley, and Pearl-Elizabeth took Freda to a deserted spot.

"Are you crazy, Aunt Freda?" Pearl-Elizabeth asked.

"Do you know who Audrey is?" Shirley asked.

"She have connections with the mob. Don't mess with her," Pearl-Elizabeth warned.

"Yeah," Ms. Mabel started. "They don't play with nobody. You can look at 'em the wrong way and they shoot you or somebody in yo' family just to teach you a lesson."

"Well, how she got mixed up with them anyhow?" Freda asked.

"She was desperate for money. I guess she felt her family let her down. We didn't do what we should have done for her," Pearl-Elizabeth said. "People like Audrey prey on people who are down on their luck. People who they figure don't have anywhere else to turn."

Freda felt a deep sense of remorse. *It's my fault. If I woulda gave her all the money Ray told me to instead of spending it on myself, she wouldn't be living like this. What people gone say if they find out? I won't be able hold my head up no mo' in all o' Algiers.*

Pearl-Elizabeth noticed Dr. Pickens and Audrey come out of the ward. Just standing there, looking at him down the hall sent chills up and down her spine twice over. As he passed by, their eyes locked in an impenetrable trance.

"Let's go get some coffee downstairs," Ms. Mabel suggested. Freda and Shirley agreed. "Meet us downstairs in the coffee shop, Pearl-Elizabeth," Ms. Mabel said as they walked to the elevator.

"Hello," he started. "I'm George Pickens, and you are?" he asked. But he really wanted to finish his sentence, *and you are so incredibly beautiful.*

"I'm Pearl-Elizabeth Youngblood."

"You're Dr. Youngblood's daughter, right?"

"Yes. Yes I am."

"I did my internship under him in Chicago," he said. "How 'bout if we go downstairs and get some coffee?"

"All right," she agreed.

Walking beside George, being on the elevator with him, and across the coffee room were all electrifying experiences for Pearl-Elizabeth. It was like they were in their own microcosm of space, a world charged with a strange energy source.

"It's strange that I've never met you before now," Pearl-Elizabeth said. "I've been by your office, but always see your father. My cousin, Fred, used to be the bouncer at your bar. I've been going there for years too, and still have never met you."

"Maybe it wasn't meant to be until now," he said.

"Maybe," she agreed.

"So, I hear you're a nurse upstairs," he said. "That's strange that we're on staff at the same hospital, but have never run into each other. I see your name all the time."

"This is a big hospital. I usually work with older patients."

"So do I. I work with all patients."

"Like you said," Pearl-Elizabeth started. "Maybe it wasn't meant for us to meet until now."

"Well, I sure am glad that I met you now," he said. "How about if we go out sometimes. To the movies, to dinner, to wherever you'd like."

"All right," Pearl-Elizabeth started. "I would really like that."

"Are you doing anything right now? After you leave here?"

"No," she answered. "Why?"

"How about if we go out to dinner and catch a movie?"

"All right. Let me tell my people."

***

It was hard to believe that all those people fit into Fred's Ford. But they did.

"I'll be glad when they finish the bridge," Fred started. "It would be much faster to get 'cross the river instead of riding on the ferry."

"Amen to that!" Shirley said.

"It's a shame that them people over in Victory Park had to lose they houses so they could make room for the bridge. Them folk worked hard fo' them houses."

"Ain't the gov'ment pay them fo' they houses and land?" Ray asked.

"Well, yes and no," Ms. Mabel started. "Yes, they was paid. No! They ain't got nearly what they property was worth. Some of 'em struggling to make it."

"Me and Shirley started to move to Victory Park. Now we glad we didn't."

"Amen to that!" Shirley agreed.

"What happened to Pearl-Elizabeth? They asked her to stay and work or somethin'?"

"Naw," Freda said. "That there nice fella asked her out."

"What fella?" Fred asked. "She shouldn't be goin' out with nobody she don't know. How y'all know he nice anyhow?"

"He Dr. Pickens," Ms. Mabel started. "Don't you know 'im?"

"Lord have mercy," Fred said. "Y'all let her go out with him?"

"He yo' boss, ain't he, Fred?" Ray asked.

"He seemed like a really nice man to me," Freda said.

"Yeah," Ms. Mabel started. "If somebody seem nice to yo' momma, Fred, then he must really be nice!"

"Y'all just don't know," Fred started. "He damn near 37 years old and ain't married. Y'all ever wondered why?"

"He ain't sweet, is he son?" Ray asked.

"No. He ain't sweet," Fred answered.

"Then what?" Ms. Mabel said. "Don't have us 'round here guessing! Speak yo' mind, Fred!"

"Well, all right," Fred started. "He be messin' 'round wit' a lot of women. He got 'ho's working fo' 'im. He in with the mob. He be selling dope. He into some heavy stuff. If somebody pregnant and don't want the baby, he help 'im get rid of it. No lying! I know 'cause I used to be the bouncer at his barroom on the weekends and saw first-hand what be doing. When I found out Delores was working fo' 'im, I quit. That was some good extra money, too!"

"He a doctor," Freda started. "Doctors don't do what you say he do."

"Momma," Fred started. "You would be surprised. I mean very surprised what they do. Heck, they be the main ones cuttin' up!"

Chapter 29.
The Order of Things

You knew that it was Friday night in the Ninth Ward because sounds of soul and rock 'n roll were heard from several blocks away. The music was almost like a sound-censored trail of breadcrumbs that led partygoers to the Pixie's door. Shirley didn't go anymore since Fred stopped working there two years before. Pearl-Elizabeth went on Friday and Saturday evenings with George, usually on their way out to someplace else.

"I'll be right back," George said as he pecked Pearl-Elizabeth on the cheek. He went to the back office with two of his cronies as she sat at the bar.

The bartender startled Pearl-Elizabeth when he served her usual Jack Daniels and Coke. She had been going to the Pixie for well over eight years, so she was automatically served without even approaching the bartender or one of the waitresses.

"Now don't tell me you done gone dry on me!" Tommy teased.

"What?" she seemed a bit aloof, then noticed the drink beside her. "Oh. Thank you, Tommy."

"You okay?" Tommy asked, as he wiped a white rag over the bar. Tommy was about 30 at the time. He was tall, slim with low-cut hair and always flirted with the ladies.

"Yeah," Pearl-Elizabeth answered and slowly gulped her drink.

"What are you doing here by yourself?" a suave gentleman asked in a deep, mellow voice. His jet-black, wavy hair was slicked back. When he smiled, his pearly-whites lit the room. "May I buy you a drink?"

"Don't mess with her," Tommy warned as he pulled him to the side. "That's Pickens' woman."

"Oh, I'm sorry, Miss!" he apologized. "I didn't mean any disrespect."

Pearl-Elizabeth sensed something peculiar about that night. She wasn't herself and didn't know why. The crowd danced to the beat of the band and went into an uproar as the lead singer slid to the edge of the stage on his knees. Everybody was having a grand old time—dancing, drinking, playing cards, playing pool. But she wasn't excited by any of it. George looked sharp in that tailored suit that accented his big, broad shoulders and strong, masculine chest. But that didn't excite her either.

George was too good to be true, Pearl-Elizabeth often thought. He bought her very expensive jewelry and clothing. He made sure that she went to the salon every week to get her hair done. He even bought her a new car. If King Solomon needed anything, he provided it. If Ms. Mabel needed anything, he provided it.

Ernestine was playing pool in the back room. She lost her concentration when Pearl-Elizabeth approached the powder room to the left. *She looks so, so beautiful tonight!* Ernestine thought as her eyes followed Pearl-Elizabeth until she disappeared behind the door. She stood there in awe, as her hands balanced on the cue stick, and watched in anticipation for Pearl-Elizabeth to emerge.

She's even more beautiful than before! Ernestine thought as she noticed Pearl-Elizabeth's freshly applied glossy lipstick. *I wish I could just hold her in my arms and kiss her all night long.* She imagined her lips surrounding Pearl-Elizabeth's big, voluptuous breasts as her tongue twirled endlessly around her nipples. She yearned to hear Pearl-Elizabeth moan with passion as she licked her ripe, swollen clit and thrust her fingers deep, deep into her hot, moist loins. But George stuck a pin in her fantasy when he walked out of his office and joined Pearl-Elizabeth at their table.

"What's wrong, Ernie?" a man teased as he took over and made a shot. "Yo' woman done left you?"

Completely oblivious to the man's comment, Ernestine watched from a distance as George poured his affections amply onto Pearl-Elizabeth. Seeing her in George's company brought a deep sense of sorrow to Ernestine that wouldn't fade.

"Catch you later," Ernestine told her pool buddies as she put the cue stick next to the table and took one last gulp of beer.

"We ain't finished this game yet, Ernie," one of the men said.

She walked through the crowd along the side of the walls, opposite of where Pearl-Elizabeth and George were seated. Careful not to be seen, Ernestine took one more backward glance at Pearl-Elizabeth before heading out the door.

***

"I need to talk to you about something later on," George said as he caressed Pearl-Elizabeth's hand.

"About what?" she asked.

"Our relationship and where's it's headed," he said, followed by an abrupt, "let's go!"

The drive home was quiet. George flicked through the radio stations of his blue Cadillac to avoid conversation.

He got somebody else, Pearl-Elizabeth feared. But as they crossed the Mississippi River Bridge, she turned her attention to the beautiful dark river below that appeared as black and mysterious as her mood. Brilliant bright lights from several large ships that lined the docks dotted the water with glistening specks of yellow and white. The bright, white moon lit the night sky, like a beacon to guide her safely home.

It was midnight when they made it home. Dogs began to bark as George slammed the car doors. Pearl-Elizabeth headed for the front porch, but George grabbed her hand and looked her in the eyes. "We need to talk."

Pearl-Elizabeth pulled away and went inside just long enough to retrieve the nice picnic basket that she had prepared for the evening. It was complete with white wine, fresh fruit, and finger sandwiches. She always looked forward to their times together, just the two of them, but that night, she wasn't so sure. They walked from Ms. Mabel's to the foot of the levee near Teche Street and spread a nice comforter on the ground near the river. George brought two fragrant, pink candles for the occasion.

It was a steamy, hot summer night, but a gentle breeze from the river provided a bit of comfort. Ship horns echoed in the distance, as an intermittent melody of crickets chirped through the eve.

Pearl-Elizabeth always fed George the sweetest, juiciest, plumpest black grapes, as he sucked her fingers, then gently kissed her hands, up to her elbows. Passion filled his eyes as he pulled her closer and closer, then began to lick her neck, up to her lobes.

"I love you so, so much," he moaned as he nibbled her ears and softly ran his fingers up and down her back. Each gentle stroke of his tongue sent powerful shock waves throughout her body. They lay on the comforter, bodies entwined, electricity on full blast, and kissed the night away, as the stars and moon witnessed from above.

"No," Pearl-Elizabeth always said. "I'm not ready. This isn't right. I need to be married first before I go any further."

But that night, he looked her straight in the eyes, "Pearl-Elizabeth, for the past two years, you've been telling me that you have to be married to go further. You should know by now that I have the highest regard for you." He stroked her face. "I love you and want to marry you. Will you be my wife?"

"What?" Pearl-Elizabeth was shocked. "I love you too, George. I want to marry you, but ..."

He presented her with a large, three-carat diamond ring.

"Oh-my-God!" she shouted. "Oh-my-God! It's so beautiful, George! It's so beautiful," she said as tears ran down her face.

"A beautiful ring for a beautiful lady."

"Oh, George. I love you so, so much. But I can't take this ring."

"Why not? We both love each other. We're both single. What's wrong, baby?"

"All your other women. I can't deal with that. I want to be the one and only or none at all."

"Baby, I gave all that up the moment I laid eyes on you. At that moment, I knew that you were the one I would marry. I want you to bear my children. I want us to raise a family together. To grow old and gray together. I want to adopt King Solomon and raise him as my own. He needs a man around. You need a man around. Baby, it's time for you to leave your grandmother and start a life of your own."

"How about the dope, and the gambling, and the other stuff, George. I'm afraid for you and myself."

"Baby, right before I met you, I found the Lord. I asked his guidance to put me on the right path. Then you showed up in my life, like an angel. I'm trying real, real hard. With you by my side, and the Father above, I know I'll be on the right path. I know it!

"I'm at the point in my life that I want to settle down. I'm tired of living in the fast lane, being surrounded by fast people, and fast situations. I plan to live a long, prosperous life. That fast lane only get you fast to the graveyard! It wears your body down. It wears your spirit down. That's for sure!

"I want a wife and family to come home to. I don't want to be alone anymore. I crave companionship. You don't have to work anymore if you don't want to. Or work part-time. We'll work something out. I need somebody in my corner cheering for me. All the folks I hang around now only want something. They smile in my face all the time, and it's not genuine. It's because of who I am, or what they think would happen to them if they don't act a certain way, or what they can get.

"I want a nice, simple, quiet life. I want to come home to you and our children. I want you and them to ask about my day. I want to spend quiet weekends with all of you in the country, just nature and our family. Maybe you need time to think about it."

"Yes, George," Pearl-Elizabeth started. "I need more time. But I love you so much, George. I want to be with you so much. I want to feel you inside of me. I haven't had a man since ... well you know when. I feel cheated. I wanted to be a virgin for the man I married, and he ruined it! He ruined it!" Tears ran down her cheeks, George held her in his arms and stroked her hair with his strong, masculine hands. "He ruined it!"

"It's all right, Liz," George said. "I'm here for you now. It's okay. I love you and want to take care of all of your needs. Your mind, body, and soul, if you would let me. Only if you let me."

***

"They come to get me," Ms. Mabel told Pearl-Elizabeth one night after King Solomon went to bed. "I ain't long fo' this world."

"Grandma, what are you talking about?" Pearl-Elizabeth asked. "Quit fooling around."

"My momma, my daddy, yo' granddaddy, my sisters, and brothers. They all come fo' me. When you be gone to work, they come visit me."

"Quit fooling, grandma!"

"I ain't foolin'. I'm 85 years old! It's my time, chil'! It's my time. Don't look sad, 'cause I done had a good life. A real, real good life. I owe it all to the Lord.

"I have three good, educated chil'ren, three grandchil'ren, and three great-grandchil'ren.

"I had a good grandmaw and grandpaw, and real good momma and daddy, too. They taught me ever'thing I needed to know to have a good life. They knew that chil'ren is a gift from God, a responsibility from God.

"My momma was a slave. She used to say some people did 'xactly what the master done told them 'cause it was they responsibility. But when it came time to raisin' they chil'ren, a responsibility from God, they ain't do it so good. They wasn't so careful 'bout gettin' it right.

"I had some good friends all through my life. I had a good husband. I made a good living, had a good, decent place to live. I respected other folks and they respected me. I have no regrets.

"I even got to travel to New York, Chicago, and Atlanta. I had a lot of good times. I had a few bad times, bad situations, and bad people in my life. But I put my trust in the Lord and He worked it all out! Yes He did! Life has been real good to me!

"You need to go out on yo' own. Get married. Have a family. King Solomon could use a daddy.

"Since you been in school, I been fixing you and King Solomon breakfast, and have a hot meal waitin' when you get home. You gone have to get used to not havin' me 'round no mo'."

"You sound like George, grandma."

"He a good man and would provide fo' you and King Solomon real, real good. He would do right by you."

"He asked me to marry him." Pearl-Elizabeth showed Ms. Mabel the ring.

"Glory to be!" she shouted. "What you waitin' fo'? Marry him. Like I done said befo', he a real good man. You better take him befo' somebody get they claws in 'im. He ain't gone wait forever!"

"I'm concerned," Pearl-Elizabeth told Ms. Mabel.

"Concerned 'bout what?" she asked. "I done prayed to God that you would have somebody. If he from God, he gotta be good. God know who best fo' you. God know what'll make you happy."

"Look at Delores," Pearl-Elizabeth started. "She's been married and had men in her life. Look what happened. I don't want to be like her."

Ms. Mabel got really close to Pearl-Elizabeth and looked her straight in the eyes. "Let me tell you somethin', Pearl-Elizabeth," she started. "Delores ain't never had the Lord in her life. Her maw and paw, Ray and Freda there, ain't never had the Lord in they life, so what do you 'pect? If she get the Lord in her life, it'll change 'round. But that's Delores. She got to live her own life. Don't hold yo'self back because you think somebody else is mis'ble. The way I see it, ever'body can have the same thing in life. They just got to go fo' it.

"But you, Miss Missy, got the Lord with you. I pray ever'day that the Lord protect you. George is from the Lord. That's been revealed to me. You bet' marry him. He the one fo' you. He gone love you and protect you and provide fo' you. He ain't goin' nowhere. He gone be a real good husband fo' you, and he gone be a real good daddy fo' King Solomon. He gone change 'cause he want to change and he asking the Lord to he'p 'im change. I want to see you happy befo' I leave. Heck, I rather see you with that Ernestine than by yo'self."

"It's not that way with me and Ernie. We're just friends. She never once hit on me. She is not, and has never been, interested in me that way."

"That's what you think," Ms. Mabel started. "She been sweet on you from the beginning. Like them times she came over here for

Sunday dinner. I saw it in her eyes that she hot fo' you. She would take good care o' you, too. But I know you don't know nothin' 'bout being with no woman, but ain't nothin' wrong wit' that!

"I 'member these two old ladies, Ms. Hazel and Ms. Annabelle, who used to live down from me when I was coming up. People used to say they was sisters and kept it hush-hush. But I knew! Ever'body knew! Right befo' me and yo' granddaddy moved to Algiers, Ms. Hazel passed on. Ms. Annabelle was lonely, and passed the next year. They been together fo' over 50 years! They loved each other, respected each other, and was there fo' each other. That's what it's all 'bout!

"King Solomon even like Ernestine! I hate to say it, but she mo' man than some o' these fellas with dicks 'tween they legs. She would provide fo' a family better 'n a lot of them no-good, triflin' Negroes out there.

"You think she ain't hurt that you with George? You broke her heart. She going along 'cause she love you and would do whatever it take to make you happy. But she is hurtin'. And real bad, too. George got the one thing that she can't give you."

***

The next day was a bright, sunny Saturday morning. Ms. Mabel invited all the so-called "grown-folk" for café au lait and beignets, while the children played in the backyard. Fred, Shirley, Ray, Freda, and Delores were all gathered around Ms. Mabel's kitchen table.

"George done asked Pearl-Elizabeth to marry him," Ms. Mabel started. "She turned him down!"

"You what!" Freda exclaimed. "What you want go turn that man down fo'! He a doctor! You better get some sense in yo' head, gal! Ms. Mabel, you better talk to her!"

"I done tried," Ms. Mabel said. "She won't listen to me."

"He seem like a good fella to me," Ray started. "Maybe you bet' think 'bout it some mo'."

"Yeah," Fred started. "He really been turning his life 'round. He don't play the field no mo'. He don't do no dope no mo'. He don't even have no 'ho's no mo'." He looked at Delores. "Sorry," he told her. "His practice is doing real, real good. I heard he don't do no 'botions no mo'. I heard he started goin' to church and got saved."

"He telling the truth," Delores said. "He legit. If I was you I would marry him in a heartbeat."

She'll marry anybody, they all thought.

"For real," Delores continued. "He look good, dress good, talk good, a educated doctor, rich, got his own practice. What mo' do you want?" *He sho' could fuck his balls off with that big, juicy dick. Umm, ummm, Mercy! Pearl-Elizabeth gone get some real good fuckin' fo' sho'!*

"Lizzy, you should marry him," Shirley started. "Delores is right. He's a doctor. He loves you and King Solomon. You and King Solomon both could use a good man in y'all's lives. You deserve that much."

"He wants me to stop working," Pearl-Elizabeth said. "I worked real hard to finish nursing school, and real hard to be the assistant nursing supervisor. I don't want to give that up. I like being a nurse."

"He want you to stop workin'?" Freda exclaimed. "Chil', what is yo' problem? You bet' marry that man!"

"Can you work part-time?" Shirley asked

"Yes," Pearl-Elizabeth answered. "But I won't be the assistant supervisor."

"Honey," Shirley started. "You would have more free time to do what you want to. To me, women have it easy. All we do is cook, clean, and do laundry. Nowadays with the laundromat, doing laundry is not hard. We could get up by six to cook breakfast, then see the family off by eight, do our chores by noon. Heck, we have the rest of the day to ourselves! Then start supper at about three. We got it made! And with you, Mr. Doctor there will probably buy you your own washing machine and clothes dryer, he's so rich. He may even hire a maid to help!" They all laughed.

"Y'all seen his house over there in Gentilly?" Fred asked.

"Yeah, it's real, real big. Like a mansion," Delores said. "He live up in there all by hisself, too. Honey, Lizzy, if you don't want him, I'll be glad to take 'im. Me and a million other ladies. He can have anybody he want. You better grab 'im!"

***

As the others started out the door, Ms. Mabel asked Delores to stay. She asked Fred and Shirley to watch the children for a spell.

"Delores, baby," she started. "You don't spend no time with Ms. Mabel no mo'."

"I been really busy," Delores started. "You know how that is."

"This may be my last chance to tell you this. You been like my own, just like Pearl-Elizabeth. I brought you into this world, and watched you grow up. It pains me to see you living like you do."

"What you mean by that?" Delores asked, insulted.

"You know 'xactly what I mean. You been drinking and smoking.

You ain't never used to do that befo'. You got three babies by three different men. One, Lord knows who her daddy is! You been selling yo' body fo' money. If you know the Lord, he give you all you need. Delores, you need to find the Lord!"

"I don't like going to no church," Delores said. "They like to put people down. And they ain't no better 'n the folk out in the streets!"

"You ain't gotta go to no church to find the Lord. You could pick up yo' Bible and start reading. You could pray in the mornings and befo' you go to bed. Heck, you can pray at any time o' the day, for that fact! Do anything you can to get with God!"

"God ain't never do nothin' fo' me!" she started. "How come God let them no-good Negroes leave me with them chil'ren? How come God let me and my chil'ren starve and go on food stamps? God done let me down too many times."

"God ain't do them things to you," Ms. Mabel started. "You did them to you 'cause you ain't know the Lord. You open to all sorts of things when you ain't connected to the Lord. When you with Him, He protect you."

"I ain't got time fo' this!" Delores grabbed her bag and stormed out of the door. That was the first time in her life that she ever disrespected Ms. Mabel, and the last.

Chapter 30.
Good-Bye Forever

"Momma, momma!" King Solomon yelled as Pearl-Elizabeth came home from work. "Something's wrong with great-grand. She won't wake up! She won't wake up!"

Pearl-Elizabeth ran upstairs to her room. Ms. Mabel appeared to be asleep. She was on her back and was wearing her white nightgown with vertical rows of roses. Her frail hands were by her sides, on top of the floral-print comforter. Her two long, white braids almost stretched the length of the bed. A beam of light from the window shined on her face, like a spotlight that shines on a star on center stage.

"Grandma?" Pearl-Elizabeth said as she approached. "Grandma," she touched her hand and it was ice-cold. She quickly felt her pulse, but there was none. King Solomon had already called for the ambulance about 20 minutes earlier, and it had just arrived.

***

St. Mark's was a white church with a black, gable roof. The belfry welcomed mourners through its doors as the gigantic bell sounded 12 deep, long tones that echoed through the air. Above the entrance in black Roman letters was the name, *St. Mark's Baptist Church*. Through the double pine doors was the foyer, with its white walls and blue Berber floors. To the right was the church office where members lined up to pay their dues. To the left was a gray water fountain for all to quench their thirst.

The top portion of the walls was white, the bottom was adorned with rich, mahogany paneling. The carpet was a deep shade of royal blue. Ten stained glass windows lined each side of the church, tinted with blue, green, red, and gold. The pulpit overlooked its audience and was trimmed in black wrought-iron designs. Behind was the St. Mark's choir that was famous for its rich blending of scales from ultra bass to mezzo-soprano. They brought forth the most uplifting tunes as they praised the Lord. But that day, the blues was all they could sing.

St. Mark's was festive and bustling with activity when Fred and
Shirley were married there. For some reason, funerals elicit deep
emotions from folks. Perhaps because it represents an ending, a final
chapter between the life of the deceased and that of those left behind.

For that day, St. Mark's was transformed into a house for the
mourning, a house of sorrow. Loud cries were heard blocks away.
There was standing room only. People stood in the aisles and along the
side walls. No happy faces or dry eyes were in sight.

Straight ahead were those doors that ushers used to stop patrons
from entering when prayer was in session. But that day, those doors
were wide open. Front and center was the lavender casket, which was
lined with white satin and trimmed in gold. It was surrounded by what
appeared to be thousands of flowers in all varieties and colors. There
lay Mabel Wildhorse-Youngblood, respected mother, devoted friend.
She was always there in time of need, no matter how big or small. Ms.
Mabel always stood by her friends.

She wore a lavender silk dress, her hair was done in braids that
flowed down her sides. Her Choctaw features were more pronounced
than ever, with that broad nose and high cheekbones. She was at rest,
home with the Father.

"Oh grandma, Oh grandma!!" Pearl-Elizabeth cried as she shook
her grandmother. "Wake up, grandma!! Wake up!!"

George and Ernestine tried in vain to console Pearl-Elizabeth, but
she collapsed to the floor at the base of the coffin, and continued to
bawl even louder than before. "Wake up, grandma!! Wake up!!" She
hunched over on her knees, her long hair gently folded on the floor at
her side. Her black, pleated dress inched its way to her thighs and
exposed her black, lace garter belt, stockings, and black, lace panties.
Grief outweighed by far her feminine vanity.

Delores wailed loud and hard as she held the hand of her long-time
friend. She placed her head on Ms. Mabel's chest. "I ain't had a chance
to say I'm sorry, Ms. Mabel!! I'm sorry, Ms. Mabel!! I'm sorry!! I ain't
mean to run out on you like that!! I'm so sorry!!" She repeated over
and over.

King Solomon cried into Freda's bosom, as she rocked him back
and forth at the foot of the casket. Freda lamented the whole time; her
face was red with sadness. She dried her tears with the white, lace
handkerchief that Ms. Mabel gave her so many years ago.

Fred and Shirley wept into each other's arms, their children
cradled between them.

Ray alone sat on the front pew. His masculine ego struggled in vain to fight the tears. He gave in to emotion and hid his feelings in his hands, as he rocked back and forth.

The pastor and choir had a difficult time keeping the tears in line. But they finally managed to make it through the service.

Arthur and Margaret, and Arthur, III and Richard cradled together next to Ray. Martha, Isaac, and their five children sat behind them.

Augustine and Agnes, Ms. Mabel's daughters from Atlanta, cried into each other's arms. They looked like Ms. Mabel did 20 years earlier, only four inches taller. They were slim and wore their long, wavy, salt-and-pepper hair in a bun. The black A-line dresses they wore further hid their slight figures.

Pearl-Elizabeth passed out when it was time to lower the body deeper into the coffin and close the top. George and Ernestine were by her side.

Fred, Ray, Arthur, Jr., Isaac, Arthur, III, and Richard were honorary pallbearers.

* * *

For the next week, Pearl-Elizabeth locked herself in her room. She didn't go to work or accept visitors except George and Ernestine, who stopped by every day. Shirley and Fred watched after King Solomon in the meantime. Arthur, Jr., Margaret, and the boys had already left for Chicago. Isaac and Martha and their family went back to New York. Agnes went back to Atlanta, but Augustine stayed behind to tend to Pearl-Elizabeth.

"I can't stay in this house," Pearl-Elizabeth confided in George. "It reminds me of my grandma."

"When we get married, we'll move into my house."

"I can't stay in here. It's too painful."

"We'll be moving to Gentilly, across the river."

"Everything reminds me of my grandma. I need to leave town."

"Leave town?" George asked. "You don't mean that. You're hurting now. Give it time. You'll heal."

"No. I won't," she sobbed louder. "I don't want to live in New Orleans. It's too painful."

"That means that I will have to sell everything here and start over someplace else. I worked hard to get what I have. I just can't pick up and leave! Besides, my father just retired and needs me to run the practice from now on."

She went into her jewelry chest and retrieved the engagement ring that he gave her.

"Here," she said as she handed George the ring. "I can't marry you."

"Maybe you need more time, Liz. Give it some more thought."

"No," she sobbed. "I've thought about it long and hard. I can't marry you."

"Look, Liz," George started. "I'll be back tomorrow to check on you, okay?"

"All right, George," she said. "But I still won't change my mind." She returned the ring to the jewelry chest.

***

Pearl-Elizabeth and Augustine were just finishing lunch when Ernestine dropped by. Augustine was on her way out to take care of a few legal matters, but decided to stay for a spell.

"I came to say good-bye," Ernestine announced.

"What do you mean, Ernie?" Pearl-Elizabeth asked in a shocked tone.

"My Uncle Edward needs help at his drugstore in Atlanta," Ernestine told Pearl-Elizabeth. "I just came to tell you that I'll be leaving next week for Atlanta. Now that my younger brother and cousin have finished Xavier, my dad has enough help. But Uncle Ed sure could use some!

"I'll miss you, Lizzy," Ernestine said as she gave Pearl-Elizabeth her new address and started for the door. "I'll visit New Orleans when I can, and I'll be sure to write."

Pearl-Elizabeth and Augustine looked at the piece of paper with the address of Ernestine's uncle and the drugstore address.

"This is down the street from our house," Augustine said. "I know your uncle!" she said as she handed the paper to Pearl-Elizabeth. "Excuse me, but I need to go out for awhile. Would either of you like for me to bring you anything back?" she asked, then headed for the side door.

"No, thanks," they said.

Pearl-Elizabeth looked up at Ernestine like never before as she stood behind her. Ernestine stroked her long, lustrous hair as she looked deep into her eyes.

"Everything will be all right, Liz," she said and continued to stroke her hair.

Pearl-Elizabeth closed her eyes and twirled her head as Ernestine ran her fingers through her hair. "That feels good, Ernie," she said, then stood up and turned around to face Ernestine. "Come here," she said with a teasing smirk as she led Ernestine up the stairs to her bedroom.

Ernestine desired to have and to hold Pearl-Elizabeth, and wanted desperately to leave. Being in the same room with her was unbearable.

Pearl-Elizabeth closed the door behind them. She removed her white, lace bathrobe to reveal her large, voluptuous breasts, and soft, delicate body—even more succulent and delicious than Ernestine had imagined it to be. Ernestine looked in awe as the robe quickly fell to the hardwood floor below, and noticed the redness of Pearl-Elizabeth's clit that peeked through her silky, black pubic hairs.

Ernestine swallowed hard and slow as Pearl-Elizabeth slowly walked to her, then unzipped her pants and unbuttoned her white, cotton blouse.

"What. . ." Ernestine started. She was hot and horny, but couldn't believe what was happening. "What are you doing, Liz?" she asked.

Pearl-Elizabeth looked her straight in the eyes, "Take your clothes off, Ernie. I've been waiting for this for a *long* time."

Ernestine carefully hung her clothes in the closet on two white, satin hangers, and folded her lingerie on the mahogany dresser to the right. It seemed that all nerve endings in her body were rerouted to the tip of her clit, as she eagerly awaited Pearl-Elizabeth's gentle touch.

Ernestine sat in the middle of the bed, amidst the soft, white, lace bedspread. The white, lace drapes to the right provided an elegant backdrop to the blistering scene. She spread her legs as she noticed Pearl-Elizabeth part her own lower lips and crawl toward her from the foot of the bed.

Pearl-Elizabeth rolled her clit up, down, and around on Ernestine's tender button as shock waves penetrated both their bodies. Ernestine welcomed Pearl-Elizabeth's tongue against hers, as they both became hotter and wetter.

"Oh, baby," Ernestine repeated over and over as she squeezed her lover's soft behind between kisses. Ernestine slid her hands down farther and penetrated Pearl-Elizabeth's soaking-wet cunt with her fingers.

Pearl-Elizabeth increased her stride as her inner muscles began to tighten.

She's about to come! Ernestine thought as she thrust her fingers deeper and harder. *I'm about to come, too. I'll try to hold back so we can come together.*

Pearl-Elizabeth struggled in vain to hold back, but the ocean that dwelled deep within her could be contained no more. In a snap, her walls began to crackle as they pulsed open and closed.

A warm stream gushed all over Ernestine's fingers, pure evidence that Pearl-Elizabeth had reached the peak of ecstasy. In a violent chain reaction, Ernestine, too, had reached her peak.

***

George stopped by the next day to check on Pearl-Elizabeth. To his dismay, a "For Sale" sign sat on the front lawn. He knocked on the door, but no answer. The front door was unlocked, so he walked inside. He ran upstairs to Pearl-Elizabeth's room, and all her things were gone. All of King Solomon's things were gone, too.

"Hey, Doc!" Fred called from downstairs.

George ran downstairs, with tons of questions for Fred.

"Pearl-Elizabeth left with her Aunt Augustine," Fred started. "They left for Atlanta early this morning. Here," Fred handed George a small, black box. He knew that it was the engagement ring. "Lizzy said to give this to you if you came by."

"What about the house?" George asked.

"Augustine said that it gone be split three ways between her, her sister, and Pearl-Elizabeth's dad. I may want to cut a deal with 'em to buy it," Fred told him. "Augustine said that Pearl-Elizabeth's dad is gone come down for all the antiques."

"Do you know if they're going to sell them? I would like to buy a few pieces."

"I don't know. I have to check with Augustine."

"Do you have Augustine's address by any chance?" George asked.

"Yes," Fred started. "But I have to check with her befo' I let you have it."

George then knew that he would probably never see Pearl-Elizabeth again.

Part IV.
Karmic Debts

When you're with God and things are going bad, they're really going good. When things are going good, they're really good!

When you're with Satan, you think things are going good, but they're really going bad. When things are going bad—watch out!

Chapter 31.
From the Past We Come

Robin looked a lot like her grandfather–tall, dark, with a silky, smooth complexion. She was built like him, too. Just like a big amazon woman. In 1964, Robin became pregnant by Marvin Davis, a 28-year-old schoolteacher.

Marvin was the intellectual type and looked the part. He was tall, slim, and always wore suits. His straight, black hair and pale complexion made him look like a ghostly creature from a horror movie.

His father graduated from Meharry and was the neighborhood doctor. He made sure that his son got a good education and sent him to Howard.

Marvin spoke what they used to call proper. He made a point to stress people's substandard language skills and poor manners. That didn't set too well with Fred.

During the summer of '64, Fred and his two oldest sons, Junior and Stephen, paid a visit to Marvin. He was living in a nice bachelor's pad on Flanders Street in McClennonville at the time, but had no plans to marry Robin.

Robin waited in the car. The week before, Stephen found out that Marvin was about to leave town.

They rang the doorbell, and Marvin came to the door in silk, paisley-print pajamas.

"May I help you gentlemen?" Marvin asked.

"We heard you was 'bout to leave town," Stephen grunted.

"It's 'you are about to leave town,' not that uneducated way you said it."

Fred rolled his eyes. "You be trying to act all sedity and you messin' 'round with a young, innocent girl."

"Well, Mr. Marshall," he started, "I assure you that your niece is hardly the innocent girl you believe her to be, sir."

"That's it!" Fred gave him a blow to the face that knocked him to the floor. "Who the fuck you think we is?"

Fred and his sons took turns punching and kicking Marvin in the stomach. They grabbed him by the collar and dragged him out of his apartment, down two flights of stairs, and into Fred's El Dorado where Robin waited. It was in the middle of the day, so most of the neighbors were at work.

On that day, Robin's seventh month of pregnancy, Marvin and Robin got married by the Justice of the Peace. Later that month, they moved to Baton Rouge, where Marvin was preparing to start a new teaching position in September.

***

Ray was heavily burdened when he found out what had happened. He wondered endlessly about what the neighbors were saying and was deeply concerned about what his customers would think. Nobody knew. Nobody cared.

How could a man let this happen to his granddaughter? Ray often pondered. *I'm supposed to protect her.*

He never forgave himself for the scandalous life Delores lived. So he was relieved when Robin moved to Baton Rouge to be with Marvin.

***

Everybody met at Fred's house on the first Sunday of each month for dinner–Ray, Freda (when she was feeling up to it), and Delores and her children. Fred arranged to buy Ms. Mabel's house from the Youngblood children. He converted the old camelback house where they lived before into two apartments, which they rented out.

Ray was sometimes too busy working to join them. But Shirley usually took a plate to him later. He was getting up in age. Freda's health was failing, and she was in and out of the hospital. Between working in the shop and taking care of Freda, Ray was stretched pretty thin.

Michelle, Byron, and Fred's youngest boy, Kelvin, usually kept their grandpa company in the shed while he worked.

At five o'clock, on September 6, 1964, Marvin called Delores at Fred's to tell her that she had a seven-pound, three-ounce grandson. They decided to name him Raven.

"Momma Delores, we love birds so much that we're going to name all of our children after birds." He sure was a proud pappa. Delores was so excited that she decided to walk down the street to her father's house to share the news.

As she approached the shed, she saw cabinets, chests, and other furniture all about. Ray was working hard to stuff a black leather ottoman when she walked in. Ray put down his tools when he saw Delores coming

"Guess what, daddy?" she asked as she jumped up and down in excitement.

"What?"

"Robin had the baby and his name is ..." Ray started to gasp for air and collapsed to the floor.

"Grandpa, Grandpa!" Michelle yelled.

"Quick," Delores told Byron. "Go call for help!"

***

Except for their wedding, Fred's wedding, and Ms. Mabel's funeral, Ray and Freda never, ever stepped foot inside of a church. So Ray was passed through the funeral parlor. The place was jam-packed with people. Most were neighbors who had come to pay their respects, but many were Ray's customers. In particular, the elder Dr. Pickens and his son, George, and his new family attended. George had hoped that Pearl-Elizabeth would be there, but was disappointed that she wasn't. So he thought.

Freda was weak, but Delores managed to help her to the funeral parlor in a wheelchair. Freda had lost a great deal of weight. She couldn't have weighed more than 100 pounds. Loose folds of skin hung from her bones. That once-lush hair was thin and matted from lack of grooming. Her eyes bulged from their sockets, and her chin shifted up into her jaw. She was clearly weak and ill, but the doctor couldn't find a thing wrong with her.

Delores was dressed in black and hugged her children, one in each arm. Michelle was eight at the time and Byron was ten. Fred and Shirley sat in the back with their six children. Robin and Marvin weren't able to attend because of the baby.

Gloria was there with a young man about 18 years old. He was tall, dark, and looked a lot like Fred's boys.

"I don't believe she has the audacity to come here," Shirley told Fred. "Especially with David. That's disrespecting the family."

"That was his daddy, too, Shirley," Fred told her. "He got every right to pay his last respect to his daddy."

Ray looked as handsome as ever in that gray suit. He was finally at peace.

***

After the services, Fred had a social at his house. The elder Dr. Pickens and his son, George, and his family attended. Delores and the children, and Gloria and David, were there, too. Freda was too weak for any more excitement, so Fred's boy, Stephen, took her home.

"Hey, Fred," George said. "This is my wife, Constance, my son, George, Jr., who is four, and the baby, Craig, who is two."

Constance was tall and dark with long, flowing hair. That sultry walk and full motion of her hips brought attention to her full bosom. Except for her quiet, unassuming demeanor, she was almost a carbon copy of Pearl-Elizabeth.

"So how's your family, Fred?" George asked.

"They're all fine."

"How's your cousin and aunt in Atlanta?" George asked.

"They're fine. Still not married. Still spinsters," Fred told him.

As the crowd began to thin, George saw that Shirley was talking to Pearl-Elizabeth.

"Excuse me, Fred," he said as he walked toward Pearl-Elizabeth. For a split second, he became hopeful that they could go someplace private and discuss the possibility of rekindling the relationship that had ended so abruptly. The magic that he had for her was still with him and was stronger than ever. He remembered the many passionate nights he spent holding her in his arms under the moonlit sky, as they sipped wine and shared a sacred, spiritual level of intimacy. They engaged in an almost hypnotic stare, as George slowly walked toward Pearl-Elizabeth. That bright, white aura that surrounded her when they first met was more illustrious than ever. Time itself began to fade as he neared her strong, feminine presence.

"George!" a familiar voice yelled from behind as a strong hand slapped him across the back. "How ya' been, buddy?"

He turned around and saw Ernestine, who quickly put her arm around an awkward Pearl-Elizabeth.

"I've been in business with my uncle, Ed," Ernestine started. "You remember him, don't you? He's the one who moved to Atlanta."

George was at a loss for words and was relieved when Constance walked over with the children.

"Ernestine, Pearl-Elizabeth, I'd like for you to meet my wife, Constance, and our children."

"It's nice meeting you," Pearl-Elizabeth said as they shook hands. Her feminine ego was crushed when she noticed the ages of his children. *He didn't waste any time, did he?* she thought.

"Good seeing you again, Georgie Boy!" Ernestine laughed as she and Pearl-Elizabeth left through the front door.

"Interesting," was the only word he could think of as he watched Pearl-Elizabeth walk out of his life one last time.

***

"Hey, Ms. Gloria," Delores said. "I ain't seen you since the wedding."

"Yes, I know," she told Delores. "How have you been?"

"Just fine," Delores said as she looked at David. He looked so much like Fred's boys. "Who do we have here?"

"This here is David Marshall," Gloria said, then turned to Delores. "David, this is your sister, Delores."

"Sister?" Delores asked.

Shirley overheard the conversation and quickly ran over.

"I thought you knew," Gloria told Delores. "I thought everyone knew. Fred and Shirley know. Pearl-Elizabeth and Ms. Mabel knew. Freda knows."

"David is Ray's boy. He's 18 now," Shirley interjected.

"I ain't know you know Pearl-Elizabeth. How you know her?" Delores asked Gloria.

"Ms. Mabel brought Pearl-Elizabeth with her when she came to see the baby. Pearl-Elizabeth had her baby with her, too." Gloria began for the door. "Good-bye, everybody."

Delores was speechless, her mouth hung low as she watched Gloria and David get into their blue Thunderbird outside. Everybody knew about David except her. "Somebody shoulda told me somethin'," she told Shirley. "Y'all talk 'bout me havin' babies, and here my daddy havin' babies, too. He ain't got no mo' floatin' out there, heh?"

"If he do," Fred started, "I don't know 'bout it."

"So that's where he used to be all weekend, heh?" Delores asked sarcastically. "Messin' 'round, heh? Who else he been messin' 'round with?"

"It's not what you think, Delores," Fred told her.

"Not what I think?" Delores asked Fred. "What the fuck am I supposed to think then? One o' daddy's 'ho's come strutting herself up in here. That's some tacky! Strutting her stuff 'round the family like that! Bringing that boy up in here! Some women ain't got no shame!"

"Wait a minute!" Shirley stepped in. "Gloria is my aunt you're talking about! Sure, it's wrong what she and Ray did, but she's still my aunt!"

"Gloria was very special to daddy," Fred said. "He really, really cared for her and David. If daddy wasn't already married, he would o' married Gloria."

"So how long he been foolin' 'round wit' her?" Delores asked.

"He knew Gloria a long time. Gloria's late husband and daddy used to be good friends," Fred started. "Daddy and Gloria met up again at the wedding. After that, he used to go over there to Shrewsbury to check on her from time to time. One thing led to another, I guess. And they been together ever since. That was his weekend family. I guess daddy figured we was grown and ain't need him 'round no mo'. He asked her to marry him a few times. But she said that she didn't want to bust up his family. She didn't want to be no home wrecker."

"She ain't want to be no home wrecker?" Delores exclaimed.

"He was planning on divorcing momma to marry Gloria, but she took sick."

"So that make it all right for him to be foolin' 'round like that?" Delores asked Fred.

"I ain't said it was all right, Delores. I'm just tellin' you what happened," Fred started. "I have never, and will never, fool 'round on Shirley. I think it's wrong if people be married and have folk on the side like that."

"Me too," Shirley agreed. "Ms. Mabel told both of 'em to quit it, that the Lord was frowning down on them. They wouldn't listen. He told Ms. Mabel, 'But Ms. Mabel, I love Gloria and loved her ever since I first laid eyes on her. I don't love Freda now or never befo'. It's wrong fo' me to stay married to her and I don't love her. It's wrong fo' me to be away from Gloria and I love her.' "

"Ms. Mabel thought that it was wrong," Fred started. "But you know Ms. Mabel, she just knew things. Things that other people didn't know. She saw what other people couldn't see.

"The day befo' she passed, Ms. Mabel said to daddy, 'It look wrong from the outside. But something inside me, call it a gut feeling, telling me that y'all 'sposed to be together. That Gloria is the one the Lord had fo' you all along. I can't explain it, but that's what was revealed to me.' "

Delores calmed down. She remembered that day clearly. *It was like Ms. Mabel was setting everybody straight befo' she went home to be with her Father,* Delores thought. *If Ms. Mabel said it, then it musta been right.*

Chapter 32.
Family Ties

"Delores," Fred started. "Why don't y'all come on move in the house with momma. Her health is ailing, and she could use the company. Shirley do what she can, but she need somebody with her all the time."

"I don't know, Fred," Delores started.

"You could save some money," Fred started. "You been renting that house all them years. You just throwing yo' money away. You could save that money! You would be he'ping her out, too. She living on the insurance money from the policy daddy had. I got to protect her. Insurance people and other folk be trying to sell her stuff she don't need. They be trying to gyp her out o' her money. "

"How 'bout all my furniture?"

"That furniture in the house is old anyhow," Fred said. "We could just give that other stuff to the Good Will or something and move yo' stuff right on in. They is plenty room in the house fo' yo' stuff, Delores. The chil'ren stuff, too. The house got four bedrooms, so ever'body will have they own room."

"All right, Fred," Delores told him. "I'll think 'bout it."

"Think 'bout it!" Fred exclaimed. "How 'bout that hurricane Betsy in '65. Wasn't you near the place in the Ninth Ward where they got all that flooding? It don't flood in Algiers. This here is high ground. What if they is another hurricane? And what if yo' house get flooded this time? It's almost August. It's that time o' year!"

"All right, all right, Fred," Delores said. "We'll move. Now is you satisfied, Fred?"

"I'm satisfied."

***

Fred and his boys helped to clear out the house and move Delores's stuff right on in.

Freda was excited to have Delores and the children move back in.

"I gone finally have me some comp'ny," she told Fred.

Fred and Shirley were proud of their children, all of whom were spitting images of their father. Fred, Jr. was 23 and had just got married. He and his wife, Veronica, recently bought a new home in Ponchartrain Park, a middle-class, black neighborhood in Gentilly.

Fred, Jr. and his brothers, Stephen, 22, and Reuben, 21, all got jobs working offshore on the oil rigs. Stephen and Reuben moved into their own luxury apartment off of General DeGaulle Drive and drove luxury cars.

Curtis, 20, was studying pharmacology at Xavier. Cyril, 19, was attending Howard University. Kelvin, who was 17...

***

Don't cringe when I say Kelvin's name. The two of you were married for over 18 years before...

Well, anyway. Kelvin was planning to attend Southern University in Baton Rouge in a few weeks and study electrical engineering.

***

Fred was the foreman at the shipyard, so he borrowed one of the trucks that was used to haul equipment to help Delores move. The family worked together and had her moved out of the old place and into the new place in a matter of four hours.

Later that night, Marvin called Fred. Delores, the children, and Fred's clan were sitting in the parlor eating snowballs. They talked and laughed the night away, enjoying each other's company.

"Uncle Fred. Have you seen Momma Delores? I called her house and the line was disconnected!" Anxiety was in Marvin's voice. "You better get up to Baton Rouge right away! I'm at the hospital right now."

"Slow down, son. We just he'ped Delores move. She right here," Fred told him. "Did Robin have the baby?"

Everybody in the room perked up when they heard Fred ask about the baby.

"Please! Please!" Marvin pleaded. "Get up to Baton Rouge right away! There's not much time! Oh, no, here they come!" Someone was talking to Marvin in the background. "Please, get here as soon as you can. I gotta go."

"That was Marvin," Fred told everybody.

"Did she have the baby?" Delores asked.

"I don't know," Fred seemed puzzled. "He said that we need to get up to the hospital in Baton Rouge right away. That we should hurry."

"Then what we waitin' fo', Fred!" Delores said as she grabbed her purse. "Let's go!"

"I'll drive," Fred said. "You two chil'ren stay here with yo' Aunt Shirley."

"Yes, Uncle Fred," Michelle said.

"I'm 15 years old!" Byron started. "I don't need no babysitter!"

"Boy, hush up!" Delores said. "Do what yo' Uncle Fred done told you!"

Fred and Delores began their two-hour drive to Baton Rouge at three o'clock in the afternoon.

***

The entire clan was waiting in the parlor of Fred's house. When Fred and Delores didn't show up or call by the morning, Shirley became worried and called everybody over.

"They probably helping Robin with the baby," Fred, Jr. said. "Everything is probably fine."

"Yeah," Stephen agreed. "Robin probably just want her momma with her, that's all."

"It's nothing, momma," Reuben said. "You worry too much."

"But they left yesterday about this time, Reuben!" Shirley said. "I've been having this real strange feeling for the past two days. Like something is about to happen, but I can't put my finger on it."

"Oh, ma," Stephen said. "You're just being superstitious."

"Y'all remember Ms. Mabel, right?" she asked them. "She used to have these feelings, too. And sure enough, something would happen when she had them."

The boys all laughed.

"She was old, momma," Stephen laughed.

"Y'all laughing. But Ms. Mabel knew what she was talking about! Y'all too educated to believe in feelings. But they exist, whether you choose to believe it or not!"

***

Ten minutes later they heard the car door slam. Shirley peeked out the window and saw Fred getting suitcases out of the trunk. Delores was holding a baby in a pink blanket, and two small boys were with her. "What in the world?" Shirley asked.

"What's wrong, momma?" Stephen asked.

"Y'all come see," Shirley urged, but they had already made their way through the front door.

Fred and Delores had solemn looks on their faces. Everyone in the room looked to them for an explanation. Fred sent the two boys upstairs to sleep and joined the others a few minutes later.

"I'm 'fraid we got some bad news," he said as he put his hands in his pockets, then sat on the corner of the sofa arm.

"Last Monday, Robin went into the hospital and was in labor for 36 hours straight," Delores started. "On Thursday, she started to feel sick, then she started bleeding a lot. Marvin ain't never left the hospital and stayed by her side. One of the neighbors watched the children. Then she started bleeding, and bleeding. They couldn't stop it. They said it was a one in a million chance something like this could happen," Delores started to cry.

"Robin is gone, y'all," Fred said.

"What?" Shirley was shocked.

"Marvin gone too." Fred told them.

"What happened?" Shirley asked.

"When the doctors told him that Robin may not make it, he couldn't take it. So he went home and got a gun and went back to the hospital. When she took her last breath, he took the gun and blew his brains out right there in the hospital room.

"The social worker took us to the people who was babysitting for Robin and Marvin and told 'em what happened. They was shocked, too. Then we went over to Robin apartment and got all the chil'ren things and came back here.

"The social worker made Delores fill out all them papers, so it could be legal. She still have some mo' to fill out to keep the chil'ren. We gone both take off work and go back to Baton Rouge during the week to straighten out some business.

"We got to make fun'ral 'rangements. The social worker done contacted Marvin folks. We gotta decide how to do the fun'ral. They should be buried together."

"They already named the baby," Delores told them. "Her name is Swan Laurel Davis."

"The two boys is too small to understand what happened," Fred told them. "Raven is five and Crane is three."

"It's probably best that way," Shirley said.

Delores admired the beauty of her new granddaughter: her beautiful, brown skin and full head of silky, jet-black hair, her little fingers curled in and out uncontrollably. *She is so sweet and innocent. I wish her life could stay that way,* Delores thought. *You better enjoy it while you can, baby Swan. 'Cause it ain't gone always be that way.*

***

The temperature started to drop, as the gentle summer breeze became more brisk. The sun drowned in a sea of silver-blue clouds.

"It's awful cool fo' this time o' year," Fred told Shirley.

"A storm coming this way." Shirley told him.

Delores and Marvin's family held a private ceremony for their children a few days later. The weather was growing fierce, so they had little time to mourn. Only close relatives were invited. The final resting spot was at Rest Haven, off of Chef Menteur Highway in New Orleans East.

***

The hardware stores were inundated with people buying nails, plywood, and heavy masking tape. Batteries and portable radios were found in every home. Crackers, canned goods, and other non-perishables disappeared quickly from stores. People sterilized every barrel, vat, and tub they could find and filled them with boiled water.

Fred and his boys taped and boarded up every window in his, Freda's, and Fred, Jr.'s houses. They had to work fast as the winds picked up speed. A day before the storm hit land, the Mississippi River Bridge was closed to traffic, and so was the Algiers ferry.

On August 17, 1969, exactly three weeks after Swan was born, hurricane Camille had her way with New Orleans. Freda, Delores, and the children sealed everything and went over to Fred's.

Fred, Jr. and Veronica stayed at their new home. "That's a brick house, Fred, Sr. said. "It ain't going nowhere."

The rest of Fred's boys left their apartments and went to their father's house. Everybody agreed that things would be awkward if Gloria and David came over. So, Fred and his boys made sure that their house was boarded up tight and that they had plenty of supplies, food stock, and water.

All was dark. Two candles in opposite corners served light to the room. Everyone brought blankets and pillows to the parlor and covered the floor. Fred thought that it was best for everyone to stay together in one room. Freda was frail, so Delores brought along two folding cots and strung them together. She arranged extra blankets and pillows for her mother's comfort.

"It sounds like angels singing outside," Stephen said.

"That's the phone wires and street light wires whipping in the winds." Reuben explained.

"No," Shirley said. "I think those are angels. Ms. Mabel and her new family are watching over this house. Protecting us."

The boys laughed.

"No, really," Fred, Sr. started. "Ms. Mabel used to say that things like rain, tornadoes, and hurricanes clean the Earth. The stronger the weather, the more the cleaning."

"Oh, daddy," Reuben said. "You don't believe that, do you?"

"Yes, I do," Fred, Sr. said. "It's like cleaning a house. If it's a small spot, you can just brush it off. If it's big, you may have to use a broom or mop. But if it's really big, then you got to get down on yo' hands and knees and scrub like the dickens. Ms. Mabel used to say that weather is God's way to clean evil out the Earth."

"Well, I heard that Camille is one of the worse ever," Reuben said. "There must be some mighty evil doings going on."

The wind whistled through the night, like a thief, and sneaked off with the family's heartache and grief.

Chapter 33.
Stuff, Stuff, and More Stuff

Camille left Fred, Sr.'s, Freda's, and Fred, Jr.'s houses unscathed. The roof on the shed out back, however, was damaged.

"Heck," Fred said. "Since y'all gotta fix it anyhow, why not turn it into a small house and rent it out?"

"How 'bout Ray tools?" Freda asked as she realized that the tools were the only things left to remember Ray by.

"Ain't nobody usin' 'em," Fred started. "We can sell 'em and make some money."

Fred and Delores sold all of the tools. The insurance company paid for the damage to the roof. Fred and his boys worked hard to add walls and doors to make rooms. Since there was already a kitchen in there, they hired a plumber to add a full bathroom.

Thomas and Gwendolyn Hollis moved into the newly renovated shed out back. Fred's boy, Stephen, and Thomas were good friends and worked closely together offshore. "We're saving to buy a house," Thomas told Delores. "We need someplace nice, but affordable." Gwendolyn worked part-time as a clerk in D. H. Holmes department store in the Oakwood Shopping Center.

They were model tenants and paid at least one week in advance. Gwendolyn kept Freda company when she wasn't working at the store. She even babysat for Delores whenever possible. When it was appointment day, she drove Freda to the doctor and waited with her.

Thomas took turns with Byron cutting the grass. He even helped Delores plant her favorite rose bushes, gladiolas, and elephant ears.

***

That was in June of 1970. By the end of the month, you and your momma moved down the street in the row. Your momma worked as a maid back then. You know now that Michelle's grandparents lived in that same row when they moved from Morgan City. You also know that Fred and Shirley used to live in

the row, too, before they moved to the house they live in now. Now you know how they got what they got.

Priscilla, her husband, Thomas, and the three children moved next door to you a few months later. About the time school started, all five of them, Priscilla, Thomas, Sr., Crystella, Thomas, Jr., and Anastasia, lived in that tiny, one-bedroom apartment.

Thomas worked as a janitor for the Orleans Parish Schools. He took on second and sometimes third jobs. No matter how hard that man worked, he just couldn't get by.

The children went to school dirty, barefoot, and wore raggedy clothes. Their hair was never combed and was knotted with lint all over. Crystella's nose was always congested with thick, green catarrh.

Delores used to drive by in her Cadillac while your mother and Aunt Priscilla waited for the bus to go to work.

***

"I wonder where she work at?" Priscilla asked your mother, Rosemary. "Who she think she is? Trying to act all sedity and stuck up as black as she is."

"She be always goin' 'round wit' her nose up in the air. One o' these days I'm gone slap that nose right on down!" Rosemary told Priscilla.

"She think she too, too much!" Priscilla said. "Just too, too much, with her black self!"

"She got them chil'ren thinkin' they better 'n ever'body else, too," Rosemary said.

"They just too, too black to be tryin' to act all stuck up!"

"She think she rich," Rosemary started. "Tryin' to show off. She got her momma, her grandbabies, and chil'ren livin' wit' her."

"Chil'," Priscilla started. "I heard she done kilt her husband and got his 'surance money. That's how she got that there big house, and that there li'l one in the back."

"How she kill 'im?" Rosemary asked.

"I heard she put some rat poison in his oatmeal."

"That's a damn shame," Rosemary said.

"And look at that car. It's just too big. Why can't she get a regular car like ever'body else?"

***

That was Michelle's first year at L. B. Landry. She was looking forward to the dances, parties, and football games. Delores worked the most on weekends, which was when most school activities were. Thomas and Gwendolyn went out a lot, so did Fred and Shirley. That left Michelle to baby-sit her niece and nephews, which meant that she couldn't go out. Michelle couldn't stay after school because she had to be home in time to watch the children so that Gwendolyn could make it to work.

You told everybody, "She thinks she too good to be with us, with her black self!"

***

About ten years before, in 1961, Audrey finally got married and moved to Los Angeles. Since that time, Delores took her place as the new manager. Delores entertained a lot of gentleman callers, sometimes planned, sometimes unexpected. Michelle was not allowed to bring friends home from school for that reason.

You told people, "She thinks we're not good enough to go to her house!"

***

One day, your momma and Priscilla were sitting on their front stoop smoking cigarettes. They were there all afternoon watching the happenings of the neighborhood. During that time, five cars pulled up to Delores's house. Two Cadillacs, a Continental, and two Thunderbirds.

"How Deborah like the new school, Rosemary?" Priscilla asked your mother. "Especially since she had to leave Carver, this being her senior year and all."

"She like it," Rosemary started. "But she hate it when the teachers see her name and call her Debra. She said she be telling 'em that her name is Dee-boe-rah, not Debra. They is two other girls in school who spell they names like hers, but they pronounce they name Debra."

"Look," Priscilla pointed to a man leaving Delores's house. "There go another one. I wonder if they all know 'bout each other? I heard she got men lined up to marry her."

"She must be working roots on 'im," Priscilla said. " 'Cause I don't know why they want somethin' black like her fo' no way!"

"I look a whole lot better 'n her!" Rosemary started. "If she could get married as black as she is, I know I surely could!"

"You ain't lying," Priscilla agreed.

"Deborah said that that girl o' hers, what's her name?" Rosemary asked.

"Shelly."

"Yeah, that's right. Shelly," Rosemary said. "Shelly told my Deborah that she ain't good 'nough to go to her house. And she ain't good 'nough to be with her."

"Deborah shoulda slapped the shit out o' that Shelly. With her black self and that short, nappy hair," Priscilla said. "That girl wear that short 'fro like a boy. She need to straighten it. Or put one of them new permanents in it."

"Yeah, girl," Rosemary started as she took a drag off of her cigarette. "Delores be going to the beauty parlor damn near every week."

"You think that's her real hair, Rosemary?"

"I don't know. It's hard to tell, Priscilla. Wigs look real these days. It's real long and thick. If it is her real hair, she need to cut that stuff off. That's just too much hair!"

"Yeah, girl! She make that Shelly girl of hers cut all her hair off."

"Yeah, that's right. She be runnin' 'round here with all that there hair and send her baby to the barber to get hern chopped off!"

"What is this world coming to?"

***

Delores didn't do tricks, but picked up a few extra dollars here and there. On Friday and Saturday nights especially, Delores used to sneak men into the house. "Ain't no free pussy up in here," she told men. "If you want some o' my pussy, you gots to pay fo' it! No cash, then out wit' yo' ass!"

Dirk Mélançon was Michelle's only friend. He lived two doors down the street. Dirk was tall and muscular, with smooth, ebony skin and straight, black hair. His teeth were straight and white, with a small gap at the top. It looked as though a skilled artist had sculpted his smile.

Dirk was a junior at the time, and played football, played basketball, ran track, and played tennis. He worked weekends at the grocery store and was able to buy himself the latest fashions. Despite the fact that he was the top all-around athlete at school and top of his class, his choice of lifestyle caused him to have very few friends.

After his games, Michelle and Dirk used to sit at the base of the Teche Street levee and watch the ships go by. They shared their dreams and ambitions for the future. When either of the two had a bad day, the other was there to lend an ear or shoulder to cry on.

"The girls give me a hard time," Michelle started. "They call me stuck up and sedity."

"Don't worry 'bout them," Dirk said as he threw a pebble into the river. "They ain't got nothin' better to do. They just be jealous."

"Jealous of what?" Michelle asked. "I ain't got nothin' fo' them to be jealous of!"

"Sometime people be jealous just to be jealous. It's a waste o' time tryin' to figure 'em out." He threw two more pebbles into the river as he reclined onto the thick Bermuda grass.

"Deborah be the main one," Michelle started. "She a senior, and I'm a freshman."

"That's why she mess with you," Dirk explained as he threw another pebble into the river. " 'Cause she a senior and you a freshman."

"She thinks she's real pretty," Michelle started as she pulled several blades of grass from the levee. "She light-skinneded with long hair and think she too much! She be always calling me black and ugly. I wish she would just go somewhere!"

"Deborah ain't pretty," Dirk said. "Just 'cause she light-skinneded with long hair don't make her pretty."

"And another person I wish would go somewhere is my momma!" Michelle told Dirk.

"She still sneaking folk in the house?"

"Yeah. I hate to hear all that moaning and groaning coming out her room. It's disgusting. It be stinking, too. It smell like musk, a old mangy dog, and old fish mixed together," she said as she frowned and waved her hand over her nose as if to ward off a strange odor. "When she be doing nasty, I call you to come meet me out here."

"Didn't yo' grandmomma talk to her 'bout it?"

"Yeah, but she don't listen." Michelle put her hands on her hips as she moved her neck from side to side like a chicken and said in a mimicked voice, "My grandma told her, 'Delores, you ought not have no men up in here. You be disrespecting me in my own house! You shouldn't be entertaining no men folk no way with them chil'ren in the house!' All my momma say is, 'Shut up, old woman! Mind yo' own damn business! I entertain who the hell I want and when the hell I want!'

"That be embarrassing, too," Michelle started as she reclined back on her elbows. "One day I was passing by the teacher's lounge at lunch. I heard Mr. Holbrook and Mr. Bridgens laugh at my momma."

"Who is Mr. Holbrook?" Dirk asked. "Is he the tall, real-dark one who dress to kill? Or is he the short, skinny, light-skinneded one with the real thick glasses and big, red Afro?"

"Mr. Holbrook is the dark one. Mr. Bridgens is the light-skinneded one," Michelle told him. "Well anyway, Mr. Holbrook said, 'That Delores sho' got some good pussy.' Then Mr. Bridgens said, 'Yeah, she sho' is expensive, too! But worth every dime!' They both started laughing."

"How you know they was talkin' 'bout yo' momma, Michelle? They coulda been talkin' 'bout somebody else."

"I just know, that's all."

"Well, at least yo' momma's men don't be trying to get no booty from you," Dirk told her as he angrily pulled several blades of grass from the root. "And at least yo' momma get paid fo' her pussy. My momma just give her pussy away like a cheap slut!"

"Jimmy still be tryin' to fool with you?" Michelle asked. "Why don't you tell yo' momma?"

"She ain't gone listen. She never listen," Dirk started, then threw two more pebbles into the river. "She think I be jealous."

"Jealous of what, Dirk?"

"Since I'm the youngest, she think I want her all fo' myself. That I don't want to share her with no other man."

"Is that true?"

"No," Dirk started. "The truth is that damn near all her boyfriends wanted to mess wit' me. When I was li'l, I didn't know no better. Some of 'em told me not to tell, or else they would kill me and my momma. Others said that if I tell, they wouldn't buy me no mo' candy or ice cream or snowballs."

"Did they ever mess with yo' two brothers?"

"Naw," Dirk said. "Just me. My brothers don't look like me. They say I used to look like a li'l girl 'cause my skin was so smooth and 'cause o' my good hair. My momma used to brush my hair back into a real long ponytail until I was 'bout seven. Then one of the teachers at school told my momma, 'Ms. Mélançon, the other children make fun of Dirk because you dress him like a girl. They call him a sissy and beat him up every day. You don't want him to grow up to be a sissy, do you?'

"My momma think that 'cause she high-yella with long hair that everybody want her. Sometime I think the men be with her just to get close to me. Soon as she turn her back, her boyfriends be wanting to get some o' my booty."

"How could yo' momma be with men who gone be cheatin' on her like that? Especially tryin' to fool 'round wit' her chil'ren?"

"She don't want to be alone. The way I see it, she be alone most o' the time anyhow. 'Cause all her boyfriends do is run the street all the time. They ain't never home. They just need a place to stay. One time she almost lost her aid 'cause the social worker caught Jimmy up in the house."

"Aid?" Michelle asked. "How yo' momma could afford that house if she on aid?"

"My granddaddy passed 'bout ten years ago. Since she had all o' us chil'ren, my aunts and uncles agreed that my momma should get the house."

"Wasn't yo' granddaddy French?" Michelle asked.

"Yes, he was. That's how we got our last name."

"How do you say yo' last name again?"

"It's May-law-saw," Dirk boasted in a French accent as he smiled, crossed his arms behind his head, and reclined on the levee.

"Oh," Michelle started. "It sho' do have a strange spelling."

"Yeah," Dirk laughed. "I get a kick outta telling people how to pronounce it. People say something like Melon-con."

"How 'bout yo' daddy?" Michelle asked. "How do he feel 'bout yo' momma having all them boyfriends 'round?"

"Daddy! Did you say daddy?" Dirk laughed. "My momma got four children and don't know who any o' our daddies is. We all step ladders and just 'bout a year apart, too!"

"Well," Michelle started. "Don't tell nobody, but I was a trick baby. That's scary. Sometime when I be on Canal Street or out somewhere, every time I see a old man, I think he might be my daddy."

"You and me both," Dirk agreed. "You and me both."

Chapter 34.
To Forgive and Forget

Freda's health deteriorated rapidly with each passing day. She spent weeks at a time in the hospital. When Michelle visited, she read Bible verses to her grandma, who listened like a child who eagerly awaited her parents' bedtime stories.

"Martha, Margaret!" Freda yelled through the day. "I'm sorry. Please forgive me!"

The nurses tried to calm her, but the medications were of little value. Freda's children and grandchildren visited her on the ward every day. Though they were still young, sometimes the doctors let her great-grandchildren in, too.

Delores even sneaked banana pudding in to her mother. But Freda's stomach was too weak to hold food down.

The ward at Charity Hospital smelled of fresh pine. The white walls and white, perfectly polished, marble floors brightened the bleak atmosphere. Five beds separated by a thin white curtain lined each side of the long room.

"Ethel? Is that you, Ethel? I'm sorry. Please forgive me," Freda moaned.

"Who is Ethel?" Michelle asked.

"She was a real nice lady. Not too much older than me and yo' Uncle Fred. She used to tell people that I was her niece, and I used to tell people that she was my aunt." Delores smiled as she reminisced over the good times. "Her husband went off to war. When he came back, they moved to New York. I wonder how she's doing?"

"She the tall, skinny lady standing next to yo' grandma in that picture I got on the mantle," Fred told Michelle. "She was real good peoples."

"She and yo' grandma had a fallin' out. I don't know 'bout what. One day, she and Ms. Mabel started actin' real funny with momma. Tryin' to duck momma. It hurt momma real bad too 'cause Ethel was like her li'l sister. Ms. Mabel was like her momma."

"Who is Ms. Mabel?" Michelle asked.

"She was a real nice old lady who died when you was 'bout two years old. Yo' Uncle Fred and Aunt Shirley bought the house she used to live in from her chil'ren. She was yo' cousin Pearl-Elizabeth's grandma. She was like everybody's momma," Delores explained. "Momma was real sad when she heard Ethel and her husband had done left town without tellin' her. Ms. Mabel and momma finally made up, though. I wonder what caused them to be so mad at each other like that. The three o' them used to go everywhere together. Shopping, to the movies, everywhere. They was real close."

***

Fred got in touch with Margaret and Martha. He urged them to come and visit momma. To his surprise, Martha and Ethel had become good friends over the years.

Fred eagerly awaited Margaret's arrival at the airport. He hadn't seen his aunt in so many years. When he saw her walk toward him, it was like they had never parted.

"Aunt Margaret?" Fred asked.

"Fred?" Margaret exclaimed. "Look at you! Give your auntie a hug."

Margaret's hair was completely gray, but her deep, dark skin was as smooth as silk. That big smile was as bright as ever, and her perfume smelled just as sweet. They walked hand in hand to Fred's Cadillac and savored every moment together.

"How is Uncle Arthur?" Fred asked on the ride to his place.

"He's so-so," Margaret told him. "He's slowing down a bit, but he's fine."

"How 'bout Arthur, III and Richard and they families?"

"They took over their father's medical practice a few years back. Arthur and Mona just got back from Arthur, IV's graduation at Howard. He's starting medical school next term. Donald is still at Morehouse in Atlanta. He is supposed to finish next year. Richard and Adrianne never had any children."

"Have y'all heard from Pearl-Elizabeth? We ain't seen or heard from her in a long time. How's she doin'?"

Margaret frowned, as her entire mood changed from bright to dismal. "She's a disgrace to the family! Living with that Ernestine down in Atlanta! They been together since '60," Margaret shouted. "She lost her mind! I tell you, Fred, she lost her mind! She had the nerve to tell me, 'We love each other, what else matters?' Living in sin!

That's an abomination to God! I don't know where she came from! She doesn't act like any daughter of mine!"

Fred was shocked to hear the news, but his suspicions of Ernestine and Pearl-Elizabeth were finally confirmed. "My boy, Junior, and his wife, Veronica, just had a baby boy, Fred, III. He look just like Junior did when he was a baby!"

Margaret ignored Fred's attempts at conversation. They sat in silence for the remainder of the trip.

***

"Ethel!!" Delores yelled across the airport.

"Delores!!" Ethel yelled back as they hugged and kissed each other.

"Aunt Martha!" Delores cried as she hugged her aunt.

She look the same as she do in the picture, Michelle thought. *Only older.*

"This here my baby, Michelle. We call her Shelly," Delores bragged.

"You look just like your momma did when she was your age, Shelly," Ethel told her as they walked to Delores's Cadillac.

"You know they built the bridge over the river 'round '58," Delores told Ethel. *Ethel sho' do talk different. It must be from livin' up North.*

"I kinda liked the ferry. But I bet it's much more convenient going across that bridge!"

"It sho' is."

"I can't wait to see Fred and Shirley. I hear they have six big, strapping boys," Ethel said. "I didn't hear about Ms. Mabel until much later. I'm so sorry I missed the services. She was like a mother to me."

"She was like a mother to everybody," Martha said. "She loved everybody, and everybody loved her."

"So how you and Irving doing?"

"Irving is a high-school teacher," Ethel bragged. "He teaches math and science."

"Get outta here!" Delores said. *She look and act all sophisticated, like a high-stylin' woman. She musta got herself some ed'cation, too! Well, you go on, Ethel, with yo' bad self!*

"When we moved to New York, Irving worked on the docks. Ms. Mabel gave us Martha's address. We rented one of her houses for awhile. Irving went back to school under the GI Bill. When Irving got his degree, he started teaching in upstate New York. There was another program under the GI Bill that helped veterans get houses. So, around '60 we bought a nice house close to Irving's school and have been there ever since.

"Y'all got any chil'ren?" Delores asked.

"We have two. Irving, Jr. is 22. He just finished his teaching degree. Our girl, Jennifer, is 18. She's starting college in the fall and wants to study teaching also."

"That's so wonderful," Delores said. "Just wonderful."

Delores turned up the volume on the radio in hopes that no one would ask about her life.

***

After they got settled in at Fred's, Delores drove them to the hospital to see Freda.

"For the past two weeks, she been asking fo' all three o' y'all," Delores told them.

When they arrived at the ward, Freda asked to see Margaret and Martha first. She said that she had something to tell Ethel that was important, and asked that Ethel wait outside. Delores went downstairs to the coffee shop.

***

I was waiting outside, too. Ethel looked up and there I was. She was surprised to see that I still looked like I was about 28 years old. I wore some black, hip-hugger, bell-bottoms with a white midruff blouse and a headband around that big Afro. I was looking *good*, I'm telling you!

***

"Mother Ruby?" Ethel asked. "Is that you?"

"Yes, it's me," I told her. Ethel wondered what I was doing there.

***

"Martha," Freda started. "I was always jealous of you."

"Jealous?" Martha asked.

"Yes, Martha," Freda continued. "Jealous. Momma taught you how to cook and clean and wash. You was real good at it, too. All that stuff looked too hard fo' me, so I was too 'fraid to try. Momma didn't make me, so I never learned how to do those things until Ms. Mabel taught me. I wish momma woulda made me do them. I woulda been a better wife and mother.

"Everybody kept saying how pretty I was. Looks fade over time. That ain't 'nough to keep no man no way. My husband didn't want me no mo' 'cause I couldn't cook too good or do other things too good that a wife is supposed to do. You and Margaret learned them things by paying attention in school and paying attention to momma.

"And you was real smart in school, too. I always had trouble in school and couldn't figure things out. Since the teachers didn't make me try, momma didn't make me try, and nobody else made me try, I went through my whole life not knowing how to read, write, or do 'ritmetic. Heck, my grandbaby Shelly got to read the Bible to me. Sometime, my great-grandbaby Raven read his Sunday school stories to me.

"I want to say that I'm sorry fo' how I treated you back then. I hope that you can find it in yo' heart to forgive me."

"Oh, Freda," Martha said, teary-eyed. "I been forgave you," then kissed her forehead.

Freda let out a long sigh of relief, as though a big burden had been lifted.

"Why don't you go downstairs and get some coffee with Delores, Martha," Freda started. "I need to speak to Margaret in private."

***

Freda waited until Martha left the room before she started to speak. I saw her coming and took Ethel into the visitor's lounge down the hall.

***

"Margaret," Freda started. Margaret sat by her side and held her hand. Freda looked her straight in the eyes. "You heard what I told Martha. I was jealous of you, too. You was the best cook in all o' Morgan City, you was real smart in school, you used to go out and have fun without gettin' into trouble, and you could run a house like nobody's bid'ness. Even better 'n momma. Those was the things I always wanted to know how to do myself, but I couldn't. So I just rubbed it in that I was so light-skinneded and I could get all the men I wanted. That was the only thing I had that you ain't had. But in the end, being light-skinneded don't make no difference. I knew deep down that men want somebody who could cook and clean and run the house like you.

"That must be true. I couldn't get Isaac. Martha got him. I wouldna o' got Ray either, but I went to see Bot."

"Bot?" Margaret asked. "You went to see that old man?"

"Yeah, chil'," Freda continued. "I was real desperate 'bout gettin' Ray. I knew that once he tasted yo' cookin', he woulda been hooked."

Bot was really old and lived just outside of town in the woods. He was short, dark, with long, stringy, white hair. Shrunken human skulls, potions, and charms lined the walls of the back room where he saw his customers. If somebody wanted a hex put on somebody or spirits sent to vex somebody, they went to see Bot.

"Bot told me to get at least three things that belong to Ray and bring them back to him. One day when Ray was out on the town, he stopped in the bar down the street. It was real crowded that night, so I had no trouble stealin' the comb outta his back pocket. He went to relieve hisself and left his hat on the bar. I took that, too, then went straight to see Bot.

"Bot took the hair outta the comb and burned it in oil. Then he tied the comb and hat together in twine and sprinkled some stuff on it. He got a pink candle and a white candle. The pink was for love, and a white one was for purity of intent. Bot lit both of 'em. He told me that by the time both candles burned, Ray would want to marry me. The next day, you cooked that dinner fo' him. The spell was starting to work, that's why he ignored you. All this time you thought that it was because you was too black for 'im. Befo' I went to see Bot, Ray wouldn't give me the time o' day.

"The next day, Mother Esther came to see me. She said, 'Girl, you don't know what you messin' wit'. You done open yo'self up fo' anything to come yo' way. You bet' be careful.' When I blinked Mother Esther was gone.

"I ain't know that other town women wanted Ray, too. But the spell Bot put on Ray fo' me musta been mo' powerful 'n somebody else spell. Bot told me to always burn a seven-day pink and a seven-day white candle in a private place. Since I had my own room at momma's, I burned 'em in my bedroom in that black suitcase I used to keep. I kept my room locked so nobody could look inside. Bot also told me that when I married Ray, to keep 'im married to me, I had to keep up burning the candles. To make the spell mo' powerful, he told me to cut out the crouch of his drawers and let the wax melt on it.

"Bot put a protection spell on me. His spell over Ray and the candles I burned was mo' powerful than the other person spell. That person couldn't harm me, but they messed with folk 'round me. The town people started acting real funny, and ain't nobody showed up to the wedding.

"Ray wanted to leave town anyway, so I was glad to leave. I thought the spell woulda been broken. 'Specially since we ain't tell nobody we was leaving.

"But it didn't. When Ray was at sea, somebody started ridin' me. I was real tired all the time and didn't know why. I started to look old, too. When we lived in that row, I didn't burn the candles like I should have.

"I was glad when we moved to the house. I thought it woulda stopped. I bought this big trunk from Dryades Street. It was real light, so I lugged it on the ferry and the bus-ride home. I kept it in the attic and burned the candles in it every seven days. I even threw in a few of Ray's drawers.

"The riding stopped for awhile, but started up again. I went to see Mother Ruby and she said, 'You have to get rid of that trunk in your attic. Somebody has been working you, it's true. But you can't fight evil with evil.' I knew I couldn't get rid o' it, 'cause that meant that Ray would be gone, too. She said, 'It's evil to take control over somebody else. That's just what you're doing by burning candles to make Ray stay with you. I can't do anything for you until you get rid of that trunk! If you're scared, I'll even help you destroy it!'

"I wouldn't listen to her, so she couldn't help me. I needed my Ray! But all the spells in the world didn't keep him true to me. He used to fool around or go hang out with his friends. He never took me nowhere or bought me nothing special like some of the other women's husbands did. Mother Ruby said, 'You burned the candles to get him to marry you. That's all. When you deal with magic, you have to be specific about what you want. When you deal with God, God knows what you need and provides it. You just asked for him to marry you, not to take you out, be faithful to you, and buy you things.'

"One day I found the chest gone. Ray and Fred ain't know what I was talkin' 'bout. But Mother Ruby knew. She said, 'It's been destroyed and the contents were returned to their rightful place.' She always talked in riddles so I didn't think I wanted to know what she was talkin' 'bout.

"They say when the spell is broken, the man get real violent. Real mean and hateful. I started the candles again when Ray started to beat me. But them candles wasn't strong enough to keep Ray around. This woman Gloria just lost her husband. Ray been liking her a real long time. But he was married and she was married, and he just kept his feelings to hisself. They met again at Fred's wedding. His love was so strong that even them candles couldn't keep 'em apart. Mother Ruby said that she was the one God had fo' 'im.' Nothing or nobody could come between two people God put together.

"So I stole Ray from you, then somebody stole him from me. I hope you forgive me. But look like the Lord done blessed you seven-fold. Mother Ruby say that if you try to curse somebody, they get yo' blessin' and mo'.

"You moved to New York, had a good ed'cation, worked as a big-time sec'tary. You traveled the world, married a big-time doctor, you moved to Chicago. Need I say mo'?"

"Freda," Margaret started as she rubbed Freda's frail hand. "I forgave you a long time ago. Don't carry this weight around anymore. You paid for what you did. Just go on! That's the past. Let the past stay where it belongs."

Freda let out another sigh of relief, as though another heavy load had been removed.

"Could you wait outside, Margaret?" Freda started. "I need to talk to Ethel."

***

I came in with Ethel, and we both sat at Freda's bedside.

***

"Ethel," Freda started. "Baby, I missed you all them years. You left without even sayin' a word. What happened, baby? If I did somethin' to 'fend you, I'm sorry. I beg yo' forgiveness.

"I know I was a bit jealous o' you. You was smart, a good cook, and took good, good care of yo' looks. You knew how to be a wife. That's something my momma shoulda taught me. When yo' husband went off to war, you knew how to run the house. I used to think that if something was to happen to Ray, I wouldn't know what to do. I 'member when he went off to war. I watched from my livin' room window when the bus drove by. I lit a orange candle fo' yo' husband. Orange candles is 'posed to be fo' protection and good health. I wasn't so sho' after my Junior was killed during the war. I learned that if you want to be protected, just ask the Father.

"I was hexed. I 'member that night when I came over fo' them sugar rations. That next day was Ray birthday, but we ain't had 'nough sugar to make him his favorite cake. Delores baked him a nice yellow cake with chocolate icing. Boy, it sho' was good, too. It was just Ray, Fred, Delores, and me. I was 'shamed to invite you and Ms. Mabel over. Delores was just learning to bake, and her cake wasn't as good as Ms. Mabel's. But now! I'm telling you, that Delores can cook and bake like nobody's bid'ness! I owe that all to you and Ms. Mabel. Y'all taught her what I shoulda taught her.

"That night I came 'round to the back door. They say that you not 'sposed to let nobody hexed in yo' front do' at night. But I think the hex may have followed me to yo' house. I ain't told nobody this 'til today, but a witch was riding me. I never fount out who it was to this day."

"I know who it was," Ethel started.

"After that night by yo' house, it ain't never vexed me again. I hope it ain't vexed you, 'cause I wouldna o' wish that on nobody. That bothered me. I 'member that morning when I was going to the store. It looked like you was home so I dropped in. I saw Mother Ruby at yo' house and them mustard seeds. I got scared. Them mustard seeds never worked fo' me, since I used to forget to put 'em down. Then I knew I musta brought a hex on you by going by yo' house after dark. I shoulda just waited for the sugar, but I knew you worked all day and I wouldna been able to catch you any other time.

"And I used to find these things called load stones all over the house, like somebody just dropped them in my purse or my clothes. They supposed to make you have troubles. And Lord knows me and my family had our share!

"I was 'fraid to go by anybody house after dark, 'cause if one of them stones fell off me, that person would get real troubles. I used to go by Ms. Mabel house all the time, but I knew she was protected by the Lord. Mother Ruby used to say that if you truly with God, then no candles, magic, hexes, spells, witches or anything evil can even get near you.

"Please forgive me fo' any trouble I caused you. I ain't mean to bring no hex to you. Please! Please find it in yo' heart to forgive me!"

I said, "Ethel has something to tell you, Freda."

"I been forgave you, Freda," Ethel started. "There was nothing to forgive you for! If anything, you should be forgiving me! I missed you all these years. Mother Ruby told me back then that the witch was who I will never see or hear from again.

"When I moved to New York, my sisters and their families wrote and visited. When I asked about my momma, no one said anything. So I kept pressing and pressing. I knew for sure that she was dead, and they were trying to hide it from me.

"I'm the baby, so everybody always tried to protect me. One day, my sister, Bernice, finally told me. She said, 'Ethel, momma done disappeared. It's like she just disappeared off the face of the Earth.'

"I asked her what she meant by that. Then she said, 'Momma was foolin' 'round with things she didn't understand. Dark forces. When you was a li'l girl, momma wanted me to marry Ray Marshall, a man who worked on the boats. I wasn't interested in him, but she kept on. She hexed the girl Ray was 'sposed to marry and ran her outta town. But that wasn't 'nough. She was still tryin' to hex her after that!' "

I told Freda, "Sister Joyce, the reverend's wife, was the one hexing you and your family."

Freda was surprised. "But she was a church-going woman."

"That doesn't mean anything," I told her. "Sometimes they can be the main ones leading people to Satan and away from God."

"Well, what happened to her, Mother Ruby?" Freda asked. "Did she really disappear like Ethel said?"

"In a way, yes," I started. "I got her soul bound in a bottle. She is too wicked to be in the presence of God.

"Satan doesn't want her either. He has no use for her. Satan is interested in conquering kingdoms, fooling large masses of people into doing his will. He punishes those who use his power foolishly, like on petty jealousy, or to make somebody sick, or other frivolous acts. He has demons working overtime to do that. And those demons don't like for mere mortals to help them do their jobs. They get really defensive when people step on their toes.

"Satan loves her husband, though. He hoodwinked the people of Morgan City for a long time by being a false prophet, misinterpreting the word of God. Satan has a place for him."

"So what happened to Sister Joyce?" Freda asked. "Is she going to Hell?"

I said, "I have her soul in that bottle. She didn't ask for it back in time. I saw her walking down the street toward the house. I knew that it would have been too painful for Ethel. Her three days was up at six that morning, so it was too late for her anyway.

"I walked up before she came into the yard. It was just a coincidence that you were there that morning. But maybe it was for good. It would have been too painful for Ethel to know that her mother was evil and causing her pain. Even though it was unintentional.

"As soon as I held the bottle of mustard seeds in my hands, her physical body evaporated, but her soul remained embedded in the mustard seeds."

"Why would she ride her own girl?" Freda asked.

"One of the load stones fell in Ethel's house off of you, Freda,"
I said. "When a witch gets out of its body, it blindly follows the
stone. In that state, it is like a demon and cannot distinguish one
human from another. It rides whoever possesses the stone. That
night, I led Ms. Mabel to the stone, which was hidden well under
the kitchen stove. She rebuked its power.

"You mean all that time you thought I was riding you, Ethel?"
Freda asked.

Ethel put her head down. "Yes, I did," she started. "Please forgive
me, Freda."

"Oh, baby," Freda started. "I forgive you. I always loved you like a
sister. I would never do anything to 'tentionally hurt you!"

Ethel hugged Freda as tears flowed from both of their eyes.

"It's almost time, Freda," I said. "Sister Joyce cursed you so
that you would have heartache and pain for all your days, and all
your female descendants will never receive a man's true affections.
In other words, no man could ever fall in love with your
descendants and truly want any of them as his own. But now, if any
one of them should happen to find and experience true love, then
both your descendant and the man will perish. Your family has had
hardships, it's true, but finding the Lord is the key to breaking the
curse."

"But I found the Lord," Freda said. "Ain't that enough?" she cried.

"No, Freda," I told her. "You turned to the Lord because your
husband was unfaithful and you were heavily burdened, not
because you really loved the Lord. You didn't have anywhere else
to turn, so you turned to Him.

"Your descendants must find the Lord because they truly love
Him and not because they are heavily burdened or want blessings.
A curse can't live in a family that truly loves the Lord and wants to
do His will.

"Delores must turn her life completely over to the Lord in
order to reverse the curse. Delores and Robin have already fallen
victim to the curse. Michelle, Swan, and their daughters will fall
victim, too, unless Delores turns her life over to the Lord, and real
soon."

"I don't want my grandbaby or great-grandbaby to have no hard
life 'cause o' me!"

Freda became worried for Michelle and Swan. She knew that
Delores had strayed too far from the Lord to get her life in order.

"You need to get Delores and Fred in here now." I stepped outside before everyone else came in. Freda and Ethel thought that I had disappeared into thin air.

Delores and Fred were standing outside. Ethel summoned them in. The rest of the clan followed right behind them.

"Fred," Freda started. "You been a good son. You turned out good even though you ain't had the best upbringing. I'm proud of my grandchil'ren and that one great-grandbaby Veronica done gave me. You a real good husband and provider. And you is a real good daddy. I'm proud o' you, son.

"Delores," Freda started. "I'm proud o' you, too. We don't always see eye-to-eye, but you a good daughter. You picked yo'self up by the bootstraps and did what you needed to do to make a good life fo' yo'self and my grandchil'ren.

"Maybe if I woulda been a better mother, you wouldna o' had to live like you did. Yo' daddy used to give me money to give you when you was living on Desire Street, but I used to spend it on myself.

"I shoulda been encouragin' you, not puttin' you down. You real smart and pretty, too. I shoulda told you that mo' often. I did the best I could. I was a piss po' maw, I know, but I didn't know no better. You be better to yo' chil'ren and grandchil'ren than I was to y'all.

"You need to find the Lord, Delores. I know I ain't raised y'all in no church. But like Ms. Mabel used to tell me, you could read the Bible or pray, anything to find the Lord. It sho' helped me, and it brought our fam'ly closer 'cause o' it. If you don't turn yo' life 'round, and fast, I'll be back real soon to come get you!"

Everybody laughed, and thought that she was jiving. But Freda was serious. The whole family was by her side. Margaret, Martha, Ethel, her children, grandchildren, and great-grandchildren. Freda looked around at everybody and made eye contact with each person at her side. She took one deep breath in, then one long exhale. Her body fell limp, but a smile remained frozen on her face.

***

Margaret, Martha, Ethel, Freda's children, grandchildren, and great-grandchildren attended the memorial. After the services, everybody met at Fred's house.

"Momma made arrangements fo' how she wanted things to be handled a few months ago," Delores told Fred. "She just wanted the family. She wanted something short and quick. She used to say, 'I don't want nobody mourning over me. That's too sad. I don't want to put my fam'ly through that.' But I don't think I want the urn. It's too painful to have it 'round the house."

"Okay," Fred started. "I'll keep the urn on the mantle next to her picture."

Chapter 35.
Shattered Dreams

It was graduation night, 1972. Earlier that day, you caught the bus to the Ninth Ward to see Mo. Mo was very old. She was short and dark with long, white hair. Your mother and Aunt Priscilla started seeing her too, didn't they?

***

Mo saw her clients in a shop off of St. Claude Avenue in the Ninth Ward. The place was always dark and smelled of potpourri. Potions, crystals, runes, and tarot lined the walls. She gave you some candles to burn and some chants to say, didn't she?

***

Dirk had a choice of three basketball scholarships, but had trouble deciding which one to accept. But you made it easy for him to decide, didn't you? You saw to it that Michelle didn't have any friends, didn't you? He was her only true friend, and you couldn't stand it, could you?

***

Dirk was on his way to meet Michelle on the levee. Michelle had prepared a nice picnic basket for them. It was one o'clock in the morning and Dirk still hadn't showed up. *I wonder what's keeping him?* Michelle thought. She heard voices behind the levee, but ignored them. She fell asleep in that spot and didn't wake up until the next morning.

Three of his classmates were coming from a party down the street.

"Look at that sissy," Sammy said. Sammy was tall and dark. His poppy eyes and big Afro made him look like a scarecrow.

"Here, sissy, sissy, sissy!" Duck teased. "Here, sissy, sissy, sissy!" His name was Donald, but people called him Duck. He was tall and dark with an Afro out to his shoulders. His long, bushy sideburns and full moustache made it seem like his entire face was covered with hair.

They all laughed. Dirk ignored them as he approached the levee.

"You want to suck my dick, you sissy punk?" Oliver asked. Oliver was tall and dark with low-cut hair. It looked as though he could have gotten by with shaving once every six months.

They surrounded Dirk and started to push him around.

"You want to suck my dick, sissy? Heh?" Sammy asked as he pushed Dirk into Duck.

"You want some o' my booty, sissy?" Duck asked, as he pushed Dirk into a light pole.

Dirk stood there for a second as the others started to charge him. He noticed a tree branch on the ground and picked it up. The gang was right behind him when he shoved the branch into Oliver's stomach. Oliver hunched over in pain.

Sammy and Duck kicked Dirk to the ground. He noticed a pile of red bricks a few feet away. Dirk grabbed one and pounded it into Duck's knees. As Duck fell to the ground, Dirk knocked him over the back with the brick once more.

Dirk and Sammy went toe-to-toe. Dirk gave Sammy a powerful punch to the stomach. As he hunched over, Dirk kicked Sammy's head up with his knee. Dirk then gave Sammy a right to the jaw, followed by a quick left to the chin.

Dirk picked up three more bricks and slammed them into Oliver's and Duck's jaws as they tried to charge him again. Blood oozed to the ground as they struggled to their feet.

Sirens sounded as headlights peeked around the corner. Sammy sneaked up on Dirk from behind. Dirk slammed him to the ground, placed him in a headlock, and issued quick, sharp jabs repeatedly to Sammy's face.

Duck picked up a brick and threw it at Dirk, but missed. The swift movement to dodge the brick caused Dirk to twist Sammy's head in an awkward position. It cracked to the side.

"Freeze!" the officers said as they surrounded the scene, guns drawn. Headlights were shining in Dirk's face as if he were on center stage.

A few seconds later, the ambulance arrived. Sammy lay there as blood oozed from his mouth and nose. His eyes were frozen, his body stiff. He looked like a rag doll with its head twisted down to touch its neck. The paramedics pronounced him dead on the scene.

***

"You heard?" Byron asked as he came to the breakfast table.

"Heard what?" Michelle asked.

"That Dirk is in jail."

"Jail?"

"Yeah," Byron said. "Fo' murder, too. They say he killed Sammy with his bare hands. They gone throw the book at him. He goin' to jail fo' life."

"Stop lying, Byron," Michelle paused when Byron showed her the newspaper article.

***

Thomas got a promotion that required him to move to Galveston, Texas. He and Gwendolyn were expecting their first child. So even if they would have remained in New Orleans, they needed a bigger place and would have moved out of the shed anyway.

Byron had just graduated from L. B. Landry. Before he left, Thomas got him a job working on the rigs offshore. So he decided to rent the shed from his mother.

That made more room in the house. Delores redecorated her mother's old room and moved in. Michelle then moved into her mother's old room, leaving Swan with a room of her own. Raven and Crane still shared a room.

Now that Gwendolyn was gone, Delores needed a babysitter for Swan during the day. It was summer, and Michelle watched her. But when school started, she needed someone during the day.

***

During that time, your mother worked nights as a janitor, cleaning offices downtown on Poydras Street. When she heard about Delores's dilemma, she immediately volunteered for the job.

***

"I heard you lookin' fo' a babysitter," Rosemary told Delores. "You know I work at night. I get home 'bout midnight. I can get some sleep, then get up 'bout seven to watch yo' grandbaby. Just send her on over. But somebody got to come get her by 3:30 so I can get to work."

"All right," Delores said. "I think we can work somethin' out."

***

When the fall came, school got out at 3:15. Michelle had to rush to get Raven and Crane from school, then get Swan from Rosemary's in time. One day, Michelle was running a little late. Rosemary took the liberty to get the mail. She noticed a letter addressed to Michelle from

Angola State Penitentiary. When she noticed Michelle approach the house, she put the letter between the others.

"Here's y'all's mail," Rosemary said. "I thought that's the least I could do since I was waitin'," Rosemary told her.

"I hope you wasn't waiting long," Michelle said.

"Oh, no," Rosemary started. "Just a few minutes, that's all."

***

The three three of you–you, your mother, and Aunt Priscilla–always did your laundry early Saturday morning to beat everybody else to the machines.

***

"Chil'," Rosemary said. "That girl, Shelly, got some man writing her from jail!"

"You lyin'," Priscilla said.

"No, chil'," Rosemary started. "Look like he write her damn near ever'day."

You said, "That's the one who killed Sammy with his bare hands. They did used to see a lot of each other. But now she been seeing this boy Roderick who live down the street. He goes to that magnet school across the river."

"Ain't that somethin'," Rosemary said. "Soon as one go to jail, she can't wait to get another one."

"Just like her momma," Priscilla said.

You said, "Roderick has a lot of girlfriends, too. When I was catching the bus coming from S.U.N.O the other day, I saw him kissing this other girl. Right in the middle of the street, too!"

"Unnnn," Rosemary groaned.

You told them, "He's just trying to get in her pants, that all."

"Y'all seen that new Cadillac Byron got?" Priscilla asked.

"Yeah," Rosemary said. "Delores got one, Fred got one, now Byron got one. That's too many Cadillacs fo' one family."

"They got too much," Priscilla said. "They don't need to be having all that!"

Chapter 36.
In the End

It was June 1974. Michelle had just graduated from L. B. Landry High School. Delores threw her a party in the backyard shed late on graduation night.

Delores and Shirley were up all night cooking. Fred and his younger boys, Cyril and Kelvin, decorated the yard and placed bug candles all about. Michelle's job was to just concentrate on looking pretty for the graduation ceremony.

***

While they were busy preparing for the party, you, Rosemary, and Priscilla paid a visit to Mo.

***

"This potion is powerful," she told Rosemary. "Be careful how you use it. It's really strong and may make you dizzy. Sprinkle it in the path that she takes the most for every day until it works."

"How 'bout other people who take that same path?" Rosemary asked.

"It is intended for her, nobody else," Mo started. "It can't work on nobody else."

Mo handed you a pendant and a load stone in a white sash. Mo said to you, "Here, put this around his neck. Also burn the pink and white candles I gave you. Keep this stone in this pouch. When she holds it up to the light, that will trigger the curse."

***

And that it did. So you thought. You see now, Delores had hardships long before you or your mother even knew her. Because of Freda, Michelle, Swan, and all female descendants were headed down the same path of never experiencing true love. So Mo didn't really do anything for you anyway, did she? Well, except lead you

down a path of destruction. She, and those like her, are demons incarnate whose job is to snare as many souls as possible for their master, Satan, to use as he pleases.

***

That night at the party, you put that charm around Kelvin's neck. The two of you started to date. By that fall, you were engaged. You dropped out of S.U.N.O, but that wasn't going too well, was it? You were on academic probation. They were about to drop you from the rolls, weren't they?

***

"I was starting to worry 'bout that boy," Fred told Shirley after he found out about the engagement. "I thought he was sweet."

"Me too," Shirley agreed. "I'm glad he's getting married. But there's something about that girl that strikes me as odd."

"Well," Fred started, "she may be odd, but she is a she."

***

And between you and your momma, Michelle was heavily burdened. Rosemary sprinkled Delores's path every day with the potion. It gave Rosemary headaches and dizzy spells, but it worked. So you thought.

***

Delores was out drinking with Larry Holbrook, one of Michelle's old teachers. It started off as a trick, but their relationship developed over time. He was planning to leave his wife and be with Delores.

Their favorite bar, the Blue Room, was filled with partygoers. Cigarette smoke clouded the air, as the band played in the background. They had their usual beer and raw oysters on the half-shell with hot sauce.

"You no-good, two-timin', moth' fucker!" a voice came from behind Larry. He looked surprised, so Delores looked up. It was so crowded that he didn't see his wife standing behind him. She was the same young woman who had acted a fool at Michelle's graduation party.

"If I can't be the one and only, then I won't be none at all!" She was holding a revolver behind her back, cocked and ready to go. Before anyone could say anything, she shot them both in the chest at close range, then fired again and again, until the case was empty.

***

Later that summer in August, Michelle found out that she was pregnant. Roderick had already started attending Southern University in Baton Rouge. When Fred found out about it, he went looking for him. That's when Roderick decided to transfer to a school out-of-state after he had completed that term. His mother refused to tell anyone where he was attending school.

***

But you know that Michelle had the Lord watching over her all these years. No matter what you did, it wouldn't work. You tried and tried, too. You know she made it, but never understood how. She trusted in the Lord and that's how she broke the family curse.

***

I've been telling you for the past 25 years to change your path. You wouldn't listen. Now, it's way too late for you to find the Lord, Deborah. It's way too late! You can't go on! When the clock strikes midnight you're mine.

***

Let me tell you something. When you're with God and things are going bad, they're really going good. When things are going good, they're really good!

When you're with Satan, you think things are going good, but they're really going bad. When things are going bad—watch out!

***

You hear that? The good, old, faithful St. Mark's bell has begun the countdown.

***

I'm here to get what's mine. You're too evil for God, so you can't be with the Father. You're not clever enough or ambitious enough for Satan's army. They don't want you. So, that means that... six ... five ... for all of eternity, you belong to me ... two... Karma.

One ...

End

. . . bind the power of darkness in the name of the Father, the Son, and the Holy Spirit. God is the Father, and the power and the glory, forever. Amen.